War of Words

Evelyn Montgomery

Published by Evelyn Montgomery, 2024.

This is a work of fiction. Similarities to real people, places, or events are entirely coincidental.

WAR OF WORDS

First edition. October 9, 2024.

Copyright © 2024 Evelyn Montgomery.

ISBN: 979-8227661388

Written by Evelyn Montgomery.

Chapter 1: A Battle of Wits

The crisp autumn air wraps around me as I step onto the ivy-clad campus of Eastwood University, a place where every brick feels steeped in history and every corner whispers secrets of literary giants. I clutch my well-worn copy of Pride and Prejudice close to my chest, an emblem of my passion as I head to my first lecture of the semester. Just as I enter the lecture hall, I catch sight of Marcus Hale, the notorious book critic, lounging against the wall with an arrogant smirk. Our eyes lock, and I can almost feel the tension crackle between us—his scathing reviews have lit a fire under my scholarly ambitions. I'm ready to take him on.

Marcus is the kind of guy whose presence has a way of making the air feel heavier, charged with unsaid words and unyielding challenges. His tousled hair frames his angular face, and the mischievous glint in his blue eyes suggests he knows something I don't—an advantage I'm determined to wrest from him. He's not just another critic; he's the reason I've poured countless late nights into analyzing prose, deconstructing characters, and cultivating the kind of passion that fuels my dreams. And now, standing mere feet away from him, I feel that familiar mixture of annoyance and intrigue churning in my stomach.

The lecture hall buzzes with murmurs, the air thick with the scent of freshly brewed coffee and the faint whiff of old books. As I take my seat, I can't help but notice the way Marcus casually surveys the room, as if he's deciding which aspiring writer he'll dissect next. My fingers grip the edges of my book, my resolve hardening. This semester is about more than just grades; it's about proving myself, and Marcus will be the first to witness my ascent.

The professor strides in, a whirlwind of energy that brings the hall to a hush. Dr. Elkins is a legend in her own right, with a reputation for pushing students to the brink of their intellectual capacity. I can see Marcus shifting slightly, his smirk fading just enough to reveal a flicker of respect. The woman commands attention with her silver hair cascading like a waterfall over her shoulders, and I can't help but wonder how many times her keen insights have dismantled the pretensions of lesser minds.

"Welcome, my literary warriors," she begins, her voice rich with enthusiasm. "This semester, we'll dive into the world of classic literature, dissecting the layers and nuances that make these texts timeless."

As she launches into a passionate exposition about the societal critiques hidden within the pages of Austen, I find my gaze wandering back to Marcus. He's watching her intently, his lips slightly pursed, as if he's weighing each word against his own opinions. There's something almost magnetic about him—the way he leans back, arms crossed, with that infuriating self-assuredness. He's not just a critic; he's a challenge, and I feel a spark of determination ignite within me.

When class ends, the students file out, but I linger, hoping for an opportunity to confront him. The hallways outside are filled with the vibrant chatter of eager minds exchanging thoughts and theories, but my focus is solely on Marcus. I approach him, my heart pounding with a mix of excitement and apprehension.

"Marcus," I say, striving for nonchalance. "You really should consider a career in public speaking. Your ability to make literature sound dull is truly unparalleled."

He raises an eyebrow, amusement dancing in his eyes. "And you must be the voice of reason, or at least an aspiring one. I appreciate the compliment, though I'm afraid my talents lie elsewhere."

"Right. Like tearing apart aspiring writers in your columns?" I counter, crossing my arms defiantly. "Do you find it fulfilling to crush dreams for a living?"

"Dreams are fragile, just like your enthusiasm," he shoots back, a smirk teasing at the corners of his mouth. "I merely illuminate the truth. If that crushes some egos along the way, so be it."

A surge of indignation rises within me, fueled by the stubbornness I've nurtured throughout my life. "Isn't it better to uplift those who strive to tell stories rather than extinguishing their flames before they've even begun to burn?"

His gaze narrows, assessing me with a seriousness that catches me off guard. "What if I told you that extinguishing the flames now might prevent a forest fire later?"

There's a moment of silence, our heated words hanging in the air like a taut string, ready to snap. I can feel the eyes of the remaining students on us, but this exchange is more than just banter; it's a duel of wills, each of us searching for weaknesses, vulnerabilities.

"Maybe I want to take that risk," I reply, the words tumbling from my lips with unexpected conviction. "Perhaps the world needs more writers willing to push boundaries rather than hide behind the safety of criticism."

He studies me, a glimmer of respect surfacing in those deep blue eyes. "You might just have a point there, though I still maintain that some flames need to be snuffed out before they ignite a whole library."

I can't help but smile, feeling an exhilaration I hadn't anticipated. "Then consider me your firestarter. Who knows? You might enjoy the chaos I bring."

"Chaos can be entertaining," he admits, his tone shifting slightly, the edges of our conflict softening just a touch. "But be prepared; I won't go easy on you."

"Wouldn't expect anything less."

With that, I turn on my heel, striding away with a sense of triumph swelling within me. The battle lines are drawn, and I'm ready to claim my territory in this literary arena. As I walk through the thrumming heart of campus, the leaves crunching beneath my feet, I can't help but feel that this semester is going to be more than just academic. It's a chess game between us—each move calculated, each word a weapon, and I'm determined to outplay him at his own game.

Somewhere in the depths of my mind, a small voice whispers that it's foolish to engage with someone as formidable as Marcus. But I drown it out, focusing instead on the thrill of the challenge. This is my moment, and I intend to seize it.

The energy in the lecture hall buzzes with anticipation, an electric current running through the room as students shuffle in, clutching their notebooks and half-heartedly discussing the assigned readings. I take my seat, my heart racing not just from the thrill of academia but from the awareness of Marcus's piercing gaze lingering on me. He seems to thrive on the chaos of intellectual sparring, and I'm more than willing to indulge him.

Dr. Elkins dives straight into the discussion, her voice a melodic blend of authority and enthusiasm. She challenges us to think critically, to engage with texts in ways that might make even the most seasoned scholars reconsider their perspectives. I find myself scribbling notes fervently, occasionally stealing glances at Marcus, who appears surprisingly engaged. His brow furrows slightly as Dr. Elkins poses a particularly provocative question about character motivations, a hint of vulnerability flickering across his confident facade.

As class ends, I rise, determined not to let this opportunity slip away. I sidle up to Marcus, who is now hunched over his phone, seemingly unaware of the world around him. "So, what's your verdict on today's discussion?" I ask, the playful lilt in my voice belying the intensity of the moment.

He glances up, surprise etched on his features. "I'd say Dr. Elkins could use a lesson in subtlety. Her approach is so heavy-handed, it's a miracle any of us can think straight."

I laugh, genuinely amused. "Right? Because nothing screams literary genius like wrapping the text in a riddle and hoping someone can solve it."

Marcus smirks, a sparkle of admiration flickering in his eyes. "At least you're quick on your feet. Most students just nod along, as if that will earn them brownie points."

"Oh, trust me," I reply, leaning closer, "I'd rather eat the brownies than earn the points. Not much of a fan of being spoon-fed analysis, especially when there's a rich cake of perspective waiting to be devoured."

He raises an eyebrow, an impressed grin breaking through his typical smugness. "You've got a way with words. Maybe you should consider a career in writing."

"Funny you should say that," I retort, feigning innocence. "I've been known to put pen to paper on occasion. Unlike some, I prefer to create rather than critique."

"Touché," he concedes, his tone shifting, a newfound respect creeping into his voice. "But be warned: the world of writing is a beast. It devours the naive."

"Better to be devoured than to sit idly by, don't you think?"

He chuckles, the sound rich and low, sending an unexpected warmth radiating through me. "Fair point. But you'll find that navigating the literary world requires more than just passion. It's about strategy, too."

"Then let the games begin," I declare, a challenge lacing my words as I step back, my heart pounding with the thrill of this intellectual rivalry. "After all, what's life without a little bit of danger?"

Our banter draws the attention of a few nearby students, some exchanging amused glances. Marcus's expression hardens for a moment, as if gauging whether he wants to maintain his reputation as the aloof critic or embrace the challenge of camaraderie. He opts for the latter, a wry smile flickering across his face.

"Let's see if you can keep up. I'll be hosting a book club discussion next week. Consider it an invitation to the lion's den."

"Count me in," I reply, excitement bubbling inside me. "But beware; I might just end up stealing the spotlight."

"Cocky and bold. I admire that," he says, his tone teasing yet genuine.

As I walk away, my thoughts swirl with anticipation. The thought of challenging Marcus in a more intimate setting ignites a thrill that reverberates through me. I spend the rest of the day lost in a flurry of classes and homework, but the impending book club meeting looms large in my mind, an exhilarating promise of potential conflict and connection.

The evening arrives, cloaked in a tapestry of deep indigo and gold as the sun dips below the horizon. I choose my outfit with care—a casual yet polished ensemble that feels like an extension of my personality. As I glance in the mirror, I feel a surge of confidence, my reflection mirroring the resolve that has settled deep within me.

Arriving at the small café where the book club is set to meet, I push the door open and step inside, the comforting aroma of coffee and baked goods wrapping around me like a warm hug. I scan the room, my eyes landing on Marcus, who is already seated at a corner table, an open notebook before him. He looks up, and our eyes connect—an electric moment that sends an unexpected jolt through me.

"Right on time," he remarks, his voice smooth and inviting. "I was starting to think you'd chicken out."

"I'd never back down from a challenge," I reply, slipping into the seat across from him. "Especially one involving literary debates."

"Then let's get started."

WAR OF WORDS

The conversation flows effortlessly as we discuss the intricacies of the book we've chosen, each of us presenting our interpretations with a mix of passion and playful jabs. The café buzzes with the chatter of other patrons, but our little bubble feels as if it's suspended in time.

As the discussion grows heated, I notice a shift in the atmosphere. Other club members arrive, bringing their own opinions and insights, yet the focus seems to continually gravitate back to Marcus and me, drawn like moths to a flame. Our exchanges become a game of wits, a back-and-forth volley where words are the ball, and neither of us is willing to relent.

"Your analysis is commendable, but you miss the essence of the protagonist's struggle," he argues, his blue eyes sparkling with mischief.

"And what exactly is that essence?" I counter, leaning forward. "Perhaps a tad more self-awareness would do you some good."

"Self-awareness doesn't lend itself well to critique," he retorts, his smirk widening. "Besides, I'm merely pointing out the flaws—my job, remember?"

"Ah, yes, the mighty critic," I say, a playful glint in my eyes. "But I think you'll find that my narrative is much more nuanced than your last review of that pretentious memoir."

A ripple of laughter sweeps through the table, and for a moment, the world around us fades away. The tension between us crackles, each quip heightening the stakes of this intellectual duel.

Just as I'm about to make a particularly biting comment, the door swings open, and in walks a group of students I recognize from my classes. One of them, Lisa, is a loud personality who seems to thrive on drama. She strides over, her presence like a whirlwind. "What's this? The intellectual sparring session of the year? Count me in!"

Marcus's expression shifts, and I sense a subtle irritation beneath his charming facade. "Care to join us, Lisa? Or are you just here to distract?"

"Oh, don't be such a grump," she replies, flipping her hair over her shoulder. "I can contribute! I have a very strong opinion about the book's ending."

"Strong opinions don't always equate to insightful commentary," I murmur, a teasing smile playing on my lips.

"Touché!" she quips, plopping down beside me.

Marcus rolls his eyes dramatically but can't suppress a smile. "Welcome to the lion's den, then. Just don't get too comfortable."

As the conversation shifts, I can't shake the feeling that this group dynamic has only amplified the competition between us. With Lisa now in the mix, I have to navigate the waves of discussion carefully, all while trying to maintain my grip on the emerging rivalry that seems to fuel the fire between Marcus and me. The stakes have risen, and I'm more determined than ever to prove that I belong in this literary world, not just as a passive observer, but as a formidable contender.

The night unfolds in a swirl of lively dialogue and laughter, but I can't help but glance at Marcus from time to time, noting the way he responds to my challenges with a mix of respect and amusement. This intellectual tango is exhilarating, but I sense it's just the beginning of a deeper exploration—one that could either lead to an exhilarating partnership or a ferocious battle of wills. Only time will tell which way this story will unfold.

The evening air wraps around me like a shroud as I step into the café, its warm interior buzzing with conversation and the rich aroma of freshly brewed coffee. I'm greeted by the low hum of chatter and laughter, the perfect backdrop for our lively book club discussion. As I approach the table, the flickering candlelight dances across the faces of my fellow club members, creating an atmosphere that feels both intimate and electric.

Marcus sits across from me, his presence commanding as he engages in animated conversation with Lisa, who appears to have taken it upon herself to steer the discussion into uncharted territories. I catch snippets of their dialogue—Lisa's bright, dramatic gestures contrasting sharply with Marcus's cool demeanor. "You can't possibly think the protagonist's choice was justified!" Lisa declares, her voice rising above the chatter. "It was the most ridiculous plot twist I've ever read!"

Marcus, ever the devil's advocate, leans back, his expression one of feigned amusement. "Perhaps it was a twist designed to provoke thought rather than provide comfort. Literature isn't always about tying everything up with a pretty bow, Lisa."

"Oh please, spare me the 'artistic integrity' lecture," she retorts, rolling her eyes dramatically. "Some endings are just bad, and that's a fact."

I watch, intrigued, as the playful tension between them shifts into something more competitive. It seems my earlier banter with Marcus has stirred the pot, and I can't help but relish the idea of diving into this fray.

"What if," I interject, my voice slicing through their back-and-forth, "the ending was meant to reflect the chaos of life itself? Not every choice is about right or wrong, but rather a reflection of the character's journey."

Marcus turns to me, a glimmer of surprise flickering in his eyes. "Look who's channeling their inner philosopher. That's quite a perspective."

"Well, someone has to keep you on your toes," I reply, the corners of my mouth lifting into a smile.

"Careful, you might just become my favorite debate partner," he quips, and I feel a flutter of excitement at his words, a challenge that stirs something deeper within me.

The discussion continues to swirl around us, a cacophony of opinions and spirited disagreements. I find myself slipping into the rhythm of the conversation, bouncing ideas off Marcus while dodging Lisa's more theatrical critiques. There's an undeniable chemistry in our exchanges, a palpable energy that makes the air crackle.

Just as I feel we've reached a crescendo, a sudden silence falls over the group as the café door swings open. A gust of wind sweeps through the room, sending a chill across my skin. My eyes dart toward the entrance, where a tall figure stands silhouetted against the light, face obscured by shadows. The atmosphere shifts, the laughter and chatter ebbing into an uneasy hush.

The figure steps forward, and I catch my breath. It's a familiar face, yet one I hadn't expected to see here—Ryan, a classmate and an aspiring writer whose talent rivals even the most seasoned authors. He's known for his captivating stories, but it's his charisma and infectious enthusiasm that draw people to him. Today, though, his expression is uncharacteristically tense, his eyes scanning the room until they land on me.

"Hey, can I interrupt for a second?" Ryan asks, his voice slightly shaky. The weight of his words hangs in the air, demanding attention.

"Of course," I say, curiosity piqued. "What's up?"

"I just got a call from a friend," he begins, glancing nervously around the table, "and I think you all need to hear this."

Marcus leans in, interest piqued. "Well, don't leave us hanging. Spill it."

"There's been some strange stuff happening on campus," Ryan continues, his tone dropping to a whisper. "A few students have gone missing. Nobody knows where they are or what happened."

The tension in the room thickens, a palpable shift in energy as shocked gasps ripple through the group. Lisa exchanges worried glances with me, her earlier bravado replaced by concern.

"Missing? Like... disappeared?" I ask, trying to wrap my mind around the gravity of his words.

Ryan nods, a grave expression etched on his face. "Yeah. They were last seen at the library late at night. I heard from a friend who works there that the security footage shows they left, but nobody saw them leave the campus."

"Is this a joke?" Lisa interjects, disbelief etched in her features. "You can't be serious."

"I wish I were," Ryan replies, his voice steady despite the tremor in his hands. "It's been going on for a couple of weeks now, but it's being kept under wraps. The administration doesn't want to cause a panic."

"Sounds like they're doing a bang-up job at that," Marcus mutters, his earlier confidence slipping. "What do you suggest we do about it?"

I can't shake the feeling that the missing students are connected to the strange energy that has lingered on campus since the semester began. The very air feels charged, like a storm brewing on the horizon. "We should investigate," I propose, my heart racing at the prospect. "If something's happening, we can't just sit here and wait for someone else to take action."

"You want to play detective now?" Marcus raises an eyebrow, skepticism evident in his tone.

"I'm serious," I reply, frustration bubbling beneath the surface. "If we don't do anything, who will? We have to look out for each other."

"Count me in," Lisa pipes up, her earlier theatrics replaced with resolve. "This isn't something we can ignore."

Ryan nods, a spark of determination igniting in his eyes. "I'll help too. I have some connections that might be useful."

The table erupts into a flurry of ideas and theories, each voice rising above the others, fueled by adrenaline and fear. But amidst the chaos, I find my gaze drawn back to Marcus, whose expression betrays a mixture of intrigue and hesitation.

"Fine," he concedes, arms crossed as he leans back, eyes glinting with challenge. "But I'm leading this operation. You'll need my expertise."

"Expertise in what? Critiquing novels or crafting conspiracy theories?" I shoot back, my voice sharper than intended.

"Let's just say I have my methods," he replies with a smirk, the corners of his lips lifting in that infuriatingly charming way.

"Fine," I huff, a reluctant smile creeping onto my face. "But I'm not letting you take all the credit when we crack this case."

As we begin to outline a plan, my pulse races with a mix of excitement and trepidation. There's something more at play here, something dark and mysterious that pulses beneath the surface of our campus life. I can't shake the feeling that we're stepping into a story far more complex than the ones we've been analyzing in class, and the stakes have never been higher.

Before I can voice my thoughts, a loud crash reverberates from the back of the café, drawing our attention. The door swings open again, and a figure tumbles in, breathless and wide-eyed, their expression a mix of terror and urgency.

"Help!" they gasp, their voice shaking as they clutch the doorframe. "You have to listen—there's something out there!"

A chill races down my spine as I exchange glances with Marcus, uncertainty pooling in my stomach. This is only the beginning of something much larger, and as the figure stumbles toward us, I realize the story we're about to unravel may not just threaten our campus, but our very lives.

Chapter 2: The Spark Ignites

The classroom buzzes with the aftermath of the day's lessons, desks littered with abandoned textbooks and scribbled notes that whisper of half-formed thoughts and unfinished sentences. I stand before Marcus, my palms clammy against the cool veneer of my desk, my heart thrumming a rapid beat that echoes in my ears. "Trivial?" I echo incredulously, the word itself tasting bitter on my tongue. "You dare call my love for Jane Austen trivial?"

He leans back against the wall, arms crossed, an infuriating smirk dancing on his lips. "And you dare to act as if those old novels are anything but a quaint diversion. You should be preparing your students for the real world, not filling their heads with romantic fantasies."

I can feel the heat rising to my cheeks, not from embarrassment but from indignation, a fiery current that compels me to defend not just my passion for literature but also the very essence of storytelling. "Maybe the real world needs more of those 'romantic fantasies.' There's wisdom in Austen's observations about society that resonates even today. Perhaps it's time you opened your eyes beyond your 'elite' pedestal."

The tension crackles like static electricity, and I can sense my students' curiosity piquing as they linger near the door, half-heartedly packing their bags, eyes darting between Marcus and me. I thrive on the spectacle, the thrill of intellectual combat, my words pouring out like an unrestrained river.

"Let's not pretend that we don't know how stories shape us," I continue, my voice rising slightly as I point toward a particularly passionate group of students eavesdropping from the doorway. "Look around! These kids need to see how literature can transform their lives, not just regurgitate what's in their textbooks. Don't you remember the power of a good story?"

His smirk falters, if only for a heartbeat, as I catch a glimpse of surprise in his blue eyes. But then he's back, his expression a well-practiced mask of nonchalance. "Power? Perhaps. But let's not confuse influence with relevance. These texts are artifacts of a bygone era, relics that don't hold weight in today's narrative."

"Is that so?" I challenge, my fingers curling into fists at my sides. "What about the themes of love, sacrifice, and the struggle against societal norms? Tell me they don't resonate in a world obsessed with reality TV and social media. Austen's insights are timeless."

Before I can stop myself, I hurl out an idea, a proposal that catches both him and myself off guard. "Let's collaborate on a project! Analyzing the influence of classic literature on modern storytelling. We can show how Austen's observations of love and society have rippled through time and shaped contemporary narratives."

The room stills, a thick silence settling over us. I can't tell if my heart is racing from exhilaration or fear of his rejection. Marcus regards me with an expression that's almost contemplative, his eyebrows knit in thought as he processes my outburst. "A joint project?" he repeats slowly, a hint of skepticism lacing his tone.

"Yes! You bring your analytical approach, and I'll inject some passion into the mix. I think we'd make quite the dynamic duo." I bat my eyelashes, fighting the urge to giggle, though I manage to keep a straight face, determined to appear both earnest and unshakeable.

He uncrosses his arms, a flicker of intrigue crossing his features, though the smirk remains. "Are you really suggesting that I—Marcus Wright, the modern-day Scrooge of literature—team up with you, the ardent devotee of Austen? Sounds like a recipe for disaster."

"Or an enlightening journey!" I retort, the challenge sparking a fire inside me. "You can't deny that a little chaos might do you good. Think of the students! They'll see literature through a lens they've never considered before."

A reluctant smile tugs at the corners of his mouth, and for a moment, I catch a glimpse of the clever, witty banter that lies beneath his arrogant exterior. "Fine. But don't expect me to sugarcoat my opinions just to make you feel better about your beloved novels."

I can't suppress a grin. "Wouldn't dream of it. Just be ready for a thorough examination of your so-called elitism."

Our argument, once a war of words, transforms into a tentative alliance, igniting a spark neither of us anticipated. As I watch him consider my suggestion, I feel the air around us shift—like the first blush of dawn creeping over the horizon, promising warmth and possibility.

The classroom finally empties, leaving us surrounded by the remnants of our debate. The sun begins to set outside, casting long shadows across the floor. I can't shake the feeling that this project might become something more than just an academic endeavor. The thrill of our intellectual sparring ignites an unexpected excitement within me, a tantalizing prospect of camaraderie mingled with the undeniable tension lingering between us.

"So, when do we start?" I ask, my heart fluttering at the thought of spending more time with him.

Marcus raises an eyebrow, a teasing glint in his eye. "Tomorrow. I expect you to come prepared, Miss Hawthorne. And I will not tolerate any nonsense about the superiority of 'romantic fantasies.'"

"Deal," I reply, unable to hide the triumphant gleam in my eyes. As I gather my belongings, I can't help but feel that this collaboration will challenge not just our perspectives on literature but perhaps even the unspoken barriers we've built around ourselves. In the tangled web of our words and ideas, something beautiful might just blossom—a connection that could change everything.

With a heart full of hope and a mind racing with possibilities, I step out of the classroom, the evening air cool against my flushed cheeks, the spark between us flaring to life as I prepare to embark on this unexpected journey.

The following day dawns, crisp and bright, casting a golden light through the classroom windows. I arrive early, a jumble of anticipation and nerves swirling in my stomach like butterflies on a sugar rush. My desk is adorned with a bouquet of fresh flowers from my garden—sunflowers, bright and cheerful—serving as both a distraction and a reminder of why I love this space. The walls are plastered with motivational quotes and student artwork, a collage of creativity that always fills me with joy.

Today feels different, charged with potential and the heady thrill of collaboration. I set up a whiteboard, scrawling our project title in exuberant letters. "Classic Literature: The Timeless Thread," I write, underlining it with a flourish that makes me giggle at my own enthusiasm.

Marcus walks in a few minutes later, his expression unreadable as he takes in the sight. Dressed in his usual crisp shirt and dark jeans, he looks every bit the scholarly archetype, and for a moment, my resolve wavers. What if he thinks this is ridiculous? But the spark from yesterday ignites once more, pushing me to stand my ground.

He raises an eyebrow, a hint of a smile tugging at the corner of his mouth. "What is this? An art project or a lecture?"

"Both," I say, a playful glint in my eye. "We're merging the best of both worlds. Just think of it as a public service for our students."

He crosses his arms, leaning against the doorframe with an air of mock seriousness. "And here I thought you were merely trying to rescue them from the drudgery of your favorite novels. Perhaps you have higher ambitions."

"Ambition? You're looking at the future queen of literary analysis!" I declare, planting my hands on my hips as if that gives my words more weight. "Now, are you in, or are you going to spend the semester trying to disprove my assertions with your elitist nonsense?"

He chuckles, and for the first time, it feels genuine. "You're impossible, you know that? But I suppose I can't pass up the chance to challenge you."

I can't help but grin, a rush of triumph flooding through me. "Challenge accepted, partner! Let's get to work, shall we?"

The first few days of our collaboration become a whirlwind of energy and laughter. Marcus surprises me with his insights, offering sharp critiques that force me to rethink my approach. He's rigorous in his analysis, diving into themes and motifs with the fervor of a true scholar. I, in turn, weave in my passion for the stories, sharing anecdotes about how Austen's characters navigate love and societal expectations.

"Why can't you just admit that Pride and Prejudice is a textbook case of romantic fantasy?" he teases one afternoon as we sit amid a fortress of books in the library. "Mr. Darcy is a perfect man, and you know it."

"Oh, please," I scoff, rolling my eyes. "You sound like one of those cynical scholars who dismisses true love as a myth. That's rich coming from you."

He leans closer, the space between us narrowing, his voice dropping to a conspiratorial whisper. "True love? Or a well-crafted narrative that exploits our fantasies? It's all just fiction, you know."

"Except when it's not," I counter, my heart racing at the charged moment. "Those stories resonate for a reason. They offer hope."

"Or they lead to unrealistic expectations. You really think anyone can live up to a man like Mr. Darcy?" He shakes his head, a mock-serious look in his eyes.

"Maybe not a Mr. Darcy," I concede, folding my arms dramatically. "But isn't that the beauty of fiction? It allows us to explore those possibilities, even if they seem unattainable."

The back-and-forth becomes our routine, each debate laced with a playful undertone that gradually shifts into something deeper. We challenge each other, pushing boundaries and unraveling layers of our personalities in the process.

As we dig into the project, I learn more about Marcus—his favorite authors, the moments that shaped his views on literature, and his own disappointments in love. In return, I share my dreams, the ambitions that drove me to become a teacher, and my own tangled history with romance.

One afternoon, as we pour over notes and discuss character arcs, I mention my latest escapade—a disastrous blind date my friends insisted I go on, complete with an overly enthusiastic salsa dancer who took his passion far too seriously. Marcus roars with laughter, a genuine sound that sends warmth flooding through me.

"What is it about romance that turns people into complete lunatics?" he asks, still chuckling. "Is there a secret handbook I'm unaware of?"

"Only the one that says to be a hopeless romantic in a world full of cynics," I reply, unable to suppress my smile. "But maybe that's the point—every disaster leads us closer to the right story, or the right person."

"Perhaps," he muses, his expression softening. "But the stories I've seen tend to feature more heartache than happy endings."

The conversation hangs in the air, heavy with unspoken truths. There's a flicker of vulnerability in his gaze, something raw and real that draws me in. I wonder what lies behind his carefully constructed facade, and for a moment, I'm tempted to dig deeper. But then the moment passes, replaced by the easy banter that has become our trademark.

As the weeks unfold, our project gains traction. Students become intrigued, their interest piqued by our passionate debates and unorthodox approach to literature. We organize a panel discussion, drawing in a surprisingly large crowd, the auditorium buzzing with excitement.

The night before the event, I'm a bundle of nerves, pacing my apartment in a whirlwind of anxiety and anticipation. Marcus arrives, his presence grounding me as we finalize our presentation. He looks effortlessly cool, dressed in a simple black shirt and jeans, his hair tousled in that way that makes my heart race.

"Are you ready?" he asks, leaning against the doorframe, arms crossed in that infuriatingly charming way.

"Ready to embarrass myself in front of half the school? Absolutely," I reply, my tone dripping with sarcasm.

He chuckles, shaking his head. "You're going to be great. Just remember to breathe. And don't let me make you doubt your love for Austen. I'll be right there, ready to defend you—well, until I have to argue against you."

"Wonderful. I'm sure that will go over splendidly." I can't help but smile at his reassurance. "If I fall flat on my face, at least I'll have you to laugh at me."

"Trust me, I'll be too busy admiring your passion to laugh," he responds, his tone surprisingly earnest.

And just like that, as the hours tick down to our presentation, I feel the tension between us shift again. There's an electric undercurrent in the air, a mixture of anticipation and something unnameable. It feels like we're standing on the edge of a precipice, where one misstep could send us tumbling into uncharted territory.

The evening unfolds with all the excitement and anxiety of a first date—delightful, nerve-wracking, and impossibly thrilling. As I step onto the stage with Marcus, our eyes lock, and for a brief moment, the world fades away. I can't shake the feeling that this collaboration is about to change everything.

The auditorium buzzes with a mix of excitement and chatter as students find their seats, the anticipation palpable in the air. I stand backstage, peeking through the heavy velvet curtains, my heart doing a wild dance that feels akin to the flutter of a moth caught in a bright light. Marcus, on the other hand, leans casually against the wall, flipping through his notes with an air of practiced nonchalance that belies the gravity of the moment.

"Relax," he says, not looking up. "They're just kids. If you fall flat on your face, they'll only remember it for a week."

"Thanks for the encouragement," I retort, my voice tinged with a mix of sarcasm and nerves. "You know, it's really comforting to know my failure will be the highlight of their school year."

He finally looks at me, a playful glint in his eye. "I'll promise to post it on my blog: 'Local Educator Takes a Dive on Stage—A Cautionary Tale.'"

"Very funny," I mutter, trying to suppress a smile. "Just remember, you're on this sinking ship with me."

"Only if it's going down in flames. Otherwise, I plan to swim."

The playful banter eases my tension, a warm reminder that despite our differences, we've forged a connection that's quickly become indispensable. When we step onto the stage, the bright lights shine down on us, transforming the bustling auditorium into a sea of faces waiting eagerly for our presentation. I catch Marcus's eye, and we share a moment—an unspoken understanding that today, we're in this together.

As I begin speaking, I feel the weight of my passion for literature flooding out. My voice fills the space, the words flowing as I discuss the themes of love and societal norms in Austen's works. I glance at Marcus, who stands beside me, nodding in agreement, his presence reassuring.

"And here we have a character like Elizabeth Bennet," I continue, warming to the topic. "She navigates the minefield of social expectations with wit and intelligence, challenging the status quo at every turn."

Marcus interjects, his tone teasing yet earnest. "Only to fall in love with a man who's the epitome of those same social expectations. Some would argue that Austen is merely reinforcing the very norms she critiques."

I shoot him a playful glare, refusing to let him derail my momentum. "Or perhaps she's illustrating the complexities of human relationships. Love is messy, Marcus. Just like life."

The audience reacts, a mix of laughter and murmurs echoing back. I can feel the energy shift, our dynamic sparking interest. Marcus leans closer, his voice low and conspiratorial. "What do you think, then? Is love just a cleverly crafted narrative device, or is it something more profound?"

"Why can't it be both?" I challenge, leaning in as if we're sharing a secret. "Sometimes the narrative reveals the truth we hide from ourselves."

Our exchange draws laughter from the audience, the rhythm of our debate creating a delightful tension that keeps them engaged. As I speak, I catch glimpses of students whispering to one another, their expressions a mix of amusement and curiosity. It's exhilarating, a rush I haven't felt in years, and I find myself wishing the presentation would never end.

But then, as the discussion unfolds, I notice a flicker of doubt in Marcus's eyes, a subtle shift in his demeanor. For a moment, I wonder if he's truly as confident as he appears. As we move deeper into our analysis of modern storytelling influenced by classic literature, his interruptions become more measured, almost defensive.

"So, how do we reconcile the idealized love stories of Austen with the realities of today?" he asks, his tone serious now. "In a world where relationships often crumble under the weight of social media, can we still find hope in those narratives?"

"Of course we can," I reply, sensing the intensity in his gaze. "Those stories remind us of our capacity for connection and resilience. They teach us what we desire, even if reality doesn't match the ideal."

He nods slowly, but the furrow in his brow deepens. "And yet, those ideals can lead to disappointment. Are we doing a disservice by holding onto these romanticized notions?"

The question hangs in the air, heavy with unspoken implications. I can feel the audience's interest shift, the murmurs quieting as they lean in closer. It's a poignant moment, and I realize we've stepped beyond mere academic discourse into something much more personal.

"Disappointment is part of life, Marcus," I counter, my voice steady. "If we shield ourselves from ideals, what are we left with? Mediocrity? We have to embrace the messiness of love, the possibility of heartbreak alongside the joy."

He searches my eyes, a spark of something unnameable flickering between us. "But what if embracing that messiness means accepting pain?"

"It means accepting that we're human," I reply, my heart pounding in my chest. "Every love story comes with risks. But isn't that what makes them worth telling?"

He stares at me, and I can see the gears turning behind his brilliant blue eyes. In that moment, the air is thick with tension, electric and alive, and I feel as if we've crossed an invisible line—a line that separates colleagues from something more complex.

As the presentation comes to a close, I notice that the audience is silent, a collective breath held as if waiting for an ending that hasn't come yet. Marcus and I exchange a glance, a silent acknowledgment that we've stirred something deeper, both in ourselves and in the students watching.

"Any questions?" I finally ask, breaking the charged silence.

A student in the front row raises their hand, and I can see the spark of curiosity in their eyes. "What do you two think about modern romance novels? Do they still reflect those timeless themes?"

Marcus looks at me, and for a moment, I can't read his expression. "That depends," he replies, a hint of mischief in his tone. "Are we discussing those that glorify unhealthy relationships, or the ones that challenge our perceptions of love?"

"Why not both?" I interject, eager to dive deeper. "It's all part of the tapestry of storytelling."

But before we can continue, the lights flicker momentarily, and a low rumble of discontent reverberates through the room. My heart skips a beat, and I glance toward Marcus, whose expression has shifted from playful to concerned.

"Did you feel that?" he asks, his voice low, almost urgent.

Before I can respond, the lights go out completely, plunging the auditorium into darkness. Gasps ripple through the crowd, a wave of uncertainty washing over us. The emergency lights flicker on, casting an eerie glow that only heightens the tension.

"What's happening?" someone whispers from the back.

As my pulse races, I feel a sense of foreboding settle over me like a heavy blanket. I exchange a glance with Marcus, and in that moment, I see a flicker of concern mirrored in his eyes.

"Stay calm," he calls out, attempting to project authority as he steps forward. "We'll figure this out."

But I can't shake the feeling that something is very wrong. A sudden crash echoes from the back of the auditorium, and the emergency lights flicker wildly.

"Marcus," I whisper, panic rising within me. "What is going on?"

Before he can answer, the doors at the back of the auditorium swing open with a loud bang, revealing a shadowy figure standing in the entrance. The dim light casts a long silhouette, and I feel my heart lurch in my chest.

"Who's there?" I call out, my voice trembling as the figure steps into the light.

The moment our eyes meet, everything shifts. The air thickens with an unspoken challenge, and I realize that whatever is about to unfold will change everything.

Chapter 3: Midnight Discussions

The faint scent of old paper mingled with the rich aroma of freshly brewed coffee as I settled into our favorite corner of the university library. The worn leather chair embraced me like an old friend, its creases a testament to countless late-night conversations and laughter shared in this cozy nook. Flickering fluorescent lights cast a warm glow over the polished wooden table littered with notebooks, highlighters, and a collection of texts that seemed to grow heavier with each passing hour.

"Did you really just compare Lizzie Bennet to Anna Karenina?" Marcus challenged, his dark eyebrows arched in mock disbelief. He leaned back in his chair, arms crossed, the light catching the glint of mischief in his deep-set eyes. A playful smirk danced on his lips, and for a moment, the chaos of our studies faded into the background, leaving only the two of us in our bubble of intellectual rivalry.

"It's not as ludicrous as you make it sound," I countered, suppressing a grin. "Both women grapple with societal expectations, albeit in drastically different ways. Lizzie navigates the shallow waters of early 19th-century England, while Anna is caught in the turbulent currents of Russian high society. It's all about the choices they make in response to the worlds around them." I leaned forward, my excitement bubbling over, my heart racing as his gaze lingered on me longer than necessary.

He let out a soft chuckle, the sound rich and warm, echoing off the library's cavernous walls. "Ah, but Lizzie's wit and resilience shine in a world that tries to box her in, while Anna—well, let's just say she took a more tragic route. How can you compare the two?" His tone was light, teasing, yet something deeper simmered beneath the surface, a current of tension that had been building ever since we began this project together.

"Maybe that's the beauty of literature," I replied, gesturing animatedly, my hand brushing against the pages of a tattered copy of Pride and Prejudice. "We can interpret and twist characters to fit our arguments. Besides," I added, lowering my voice playfully, "everyone loves a good scandal. Besides, you know I'm right."

Marcus shook his head, his grin widening as he leaned in closer, the distance between us diminishing. "You're insufferable, you know that?" he said, his tone teasing but edged with an undeniable warmth. "It's a miracle I haven't gone mad from our late-night debates."

"Madness may be the price of genius," I quipped, unable to resist the urge to flirt. The way he leaned into our discussions, genuinely engaged, sent butterflies swirling in my stomach.

As the night deepened, the library transformed. Shadows stretched across the bookshelves like creeping vines, and the gentle hum of the heating system became a lullaby, lulling the world outside into a soft oblivion. It was just us—two students caught in a passionate whirlwind of ideas and caffeine-fueled banter. My gaze darted to the large windows overlooking the campus, where the moon hung like a silver pendant against the backdrop of indigo skies. I could feel the magnetic pull of the night urging me to embrace the moment.

"Okay, let's settle this once and for all," Marcus declared, reaching for his laptop. "A debate on the merits of romantic ideals in both novels. Winner gets to choose the next book for our reading list."

I feigned contemplation, resting my chin on my hand, but inside, I was bubbling with excitement. "And what will the loser have to do?" I asked, arching an eyebrow.

"Buy the winner coffee for a week," he replied, his grin widening, the challenge igniting a fire in his eyes. "But I think we should make it interesting. Loser also has to share their most embarrassing literary crush."

I gasped, laughter escaping my lips. "Now that's just cruel! You're on."

We dove into the debate, our voices rising and falling like the tide, punctuated by laughter and the clinking of our coffee mugs. The room swirled around us, the outside world fading away. With each argument, each rebuttal, I felt an electric charge in the air—an invisible thread binding us together, tugging at my heart as I navigated the complex landscape of our budding connection.

"Fine, I'll admit," he said, breaking through my thoughts as he swiped through his notes, "Austen's heroes do tend to reflect their societal norms. But think of how Tolstoy transcends time with his raw human emotions. His characters are messy, real. Like life."

"True," I conceded, "but isn't there something to be said for the charm of a well-timed quip or a clever miscommunication? Austen's humor, her romantic tension—it's delicious."

"Delicious?" he echoed, laughter spilling from his lips. "You've been reading too many romance novels."

"Maybe," I replied, allowing my gaze to drift to his lips, the temptation of his laughter wrapping around me like a warm blanket. "But who doesn't love a good love story?"

The challenge hung in the air, a gossamer thread spun from our shared laughter and fierce debate. I could feel my heart thump in rhythm with our banter, the tension between us both exhilarating and terrifying. As our voices softened, I couldn't shake the feeling that the night was a threshold, one that hinted at something deeper—a connection that felt thrillingly inevitable yet terrifyingly uncertain.

With the hour growing late, we reluctantly packed up our things, the warmth of the coffee fading but the energy of our conversation lingering in the air like the final notes of a haunting melody. As we stepped out into the crisp night, the campus sprawled before us, illuminated by the glow of the streetlights and the distant laughter of other students. I inhaled deeply, the cool air crisp against my skin, filled with promise and potential.

"Same time tomorrow?" Marcus asked, his gaze locking onto mine, an unspoken agreement hanging between us.

"Absolutely," I said, my heart fluttering as I watched him walk away, the night wrapping around him like a cloak of mystery. I turned, my pulse racing, anticipation building as I realized this wasn't just a project anymore. It was a journey—one that promised to lead me down paths I had only begun to imagine.

With each late-night session, the library morphed into a sanctuary for our burgeoning friendship, illuminated by the soft glow of desk lamps and punctuated by the rhythmic clatter of keyboards. It was a space where caffeine fueled our thoughts, transforming the sterile air into something charged and alive. The murmurs of our conversations seemed to intertwine with the whispers of the past that clung to the bookshelves, creating a tapestry of ideas that felt almost tangible.

"Tell me," Marcus began one evening, a teasing glint in his eye, "if you had to pick one Austen heroine to be your best friend, who would it be?" He leaned back, hands laced behind his head, the light from the lamp casting shadows across his chiseled features.

"Easy. Elizabeth Bennet," I replied, barely pausing to think. "She's sharp, witty, and never afraid to speak her mind. Plus, I imagine our conversations would be delightfully snarky."

Marcus laughed, the sound bright and genuine. "So you just want a friend who will roast you all the time? Very reassuring." He waggled his eyebrows, and I couldn't help but laugh along.

"Well, what about you? Who would you choose?"

He stroked his chin in mock contemplation, a playful glint in his eye. "I think I'd go for Emma Woodhouse. I mean, she's got connections, a lavish lifestyle, and let's be honest, she's the ultimate matchmaker. Who wouldn't want a friend like that?"

"Ah, yes, but you'd have to endure her misguided attempts at matchmaking," I countered, leaning forward, my coffee cup cradled in my hands. "She'd probably try to pair you with the most insufferable people just for the sport of it."

"True, true. But she does have a way of turning chaos into a happy ending," he mused, his voice softening, and I could see the wheels turning in his mind. "Maybe I could use a bit of that chaos in my life."

A silence settled between us, rich with unspoken words. The playful banter that had defined our discussions took on a new weight, each shared glance feeling charged with meaning. I could feel my pulse quickening, a surge of warmth washing over me as he leaned closer, the scent of his cologne—fresh and woodsy—filling the small space between us.

"What about you?" he asked, breaking the moment, his tone shifting slightly. "What's your chaotic dream?"

I hesitated, the question catching me off guard. In the world of academia and late-night studies, I often kept my aspirations close to my chest, buried beneath layers of intellectual discourse and casual repartee. But there was something about Marcus's earnestness that made my guarded heart want to leap into the open.

"I suppose I've always wanted to write," I admitted, my voice barely above a whisper. "A novel, maybe, that captures the messiness of life—the way love and loss intertwine, the chaos of friendships, the bittersweet moments that define us."

His expression softened, and I could see genuine curiosity flicker in his eyes. "You're a writer?"

"Not officially," I replied with a shy smile. "Just something I do when no one's looking. I keep a journal, jot down thoughts and ideas. It feels safer that way."

"I get that," he said, nodding thoughtfully. "Sometimes, it's easier to hide behind the pages rather than put your work out there for the world to judge."

The weight of his understanding hung in the air, and for a moment, I felt as though we were bound by an invisible thread of shared dreams and fears. It was intoxicating, and I reveled in the connection, letting it wrap around me like a warm blanket.

"Maybe one day, I'll gather the courage to share my words," I mused, trying to lighten the mood. "But for now, I'll settle for sharing late-night coffee and literary debates with you."

"Only if you promise to give me the inside scoop on your writing," he challenged, a playful grin returning to his face. "You know, I could be your biggest fan—or your harshest critic."

"I think I'd prefer the fan," I teased back, feeling lighter than I had in days.

As the conversation drifted toward lighter topics—our favorite books, guilty pleasures in media, and the strangest things we'd ever Googled—an unguarded laugh escaped my lips, echoing through the stillness of the library. I glanced around, half-expecting a stern librarian to shush us, but the library was ours for the night.

"Alright," Marcus said, his voice shifting back to that teasing tone. "Let's settle the score once and for all. What's the most embarrassing book you've ever read?"

My cheeks heated at the question. I was unprepared for this twist, but the challenge sent a thrill through me. "You first!" I replied, crossing my arms defiantly, a grin spreading across my face.

"Okay, fine," he relented, his eyes dancing with mischief. "You're going to love this. In high school, I read this ridiculous vampire romance novel. I mean, complete drivel—full of sparkles and angst. The worst part? I was convinced it was going to be a classic!"

"Wait, you're telling me you fell for the sparkly vampire trend?" I couldn't help but laugh, the sound spilling out uncontrollably. "That's pure gold. What was the title?"

He pretended to think deeply, his brow furrowing dramatically. "I'm not telling you. I have a reputation to uphold."

"Oh, come on! You can't drop that bomb and not expect me to pry!"

"Alright, alright," he said, finally relenting. "It was Midnight Shadows. There, I said it. Your turn."

I feigned a gasp, clutching my heart in mock betrayal. "I'm going to need a moment to recover from that revelation."

"Please do. And while you're at it, share your deepest, darkest literary secret," he encouraged, leaning in, his gaze intent.

"Fine," I relented, my heart racing. "But only if you promise not to judge. I once read a self-help book about finding true love through the power of positive thinking."

He burst into laughter, the sound contagious, and soon I found myself giggling along, the earlier tension dissipating like fog under the morning sun.

"Okay, okay, I can see the appeal," he admitted, wiping tears of laughter from his eyes. "Who wouldn't want to find true love? It's practically a rite of passage."

Our laughter faded into a comfortable silence, both of us lost in thought, the air thick with shared moments and burgeoning feelings. As I glanced up, I found his gaze lingering on me, and the world outside the library faded away. In that intimate space, I felt a warmth blossom within me—a spark that hinted at something more than just friendship.

"Let's get out of here," Marcus suggested, breaking the moment. "I could use some fresh air. Plus, I need to redeem myself for the vampire disaster."

I grinned, my heart racing. "Lead the way, sparkly one."

With a shared chuckle, we gathered our belongings and stepped into the crisp night air, where the stars twinkled overhead like a million tiny secrets waiting to be discovered. The world outside was alive with possibility, and I felt a thrill of anticipation coursing through me. In that moment, I knew our midnight discussions were only just the beginning.

The night air wrapped around us like a cool embrace as we stepped outside the library, a gentle breeze whispering through the trees lining the campus. The stars sparkled overhead, a celestial audience to our midnight escapades. I inhaled deeply, the scent of damp earth and blooming jasmine mingling in the air, invigorating and alive.

"Where to now, my daring vampire-sparkling friend?" I asked, grinning up at him, my pulse still quick from our lively discussions.

"Let's stroll down to the lake," he suggested, pointing toward the dimly lit path that wound its way through the gardens. "I hear the moonlight makes the water look enchanting. Plus, we can avoid getting shushed by the librarian."

I chuckled, recalling the way we'd been caught laughing too loudly just moments before. "You mean the librarian with the piercing gaze and an uncanny ability to appear out of nowhere?"

"Exactly. It's like she has a sixth sense for studying sinners," he replied, shaking his head as we started walking.

As we meandered down the path, the sound of our footsteps mingled with the occasional rustle of leaves and the distant laughter of students lingering outside their dorms. We talked about everything—books, dreams, and the inexplicable compulsion to procrastinate that seemed to plague all students, no matter how ambitious.

"So," Marcus began, glancing sideways at me, "if you could be any character from any book, who would you choose?"

I pondered the question, letting the possibilities wash over me. "Definitely not Emma Woodhouse. She'd be too busy trying to fix my love life, and I'd end up in some disaster," I joked, nudging him playfully. "But maybe someone like Jo March from Little Women—headstrong, passionate, and utterly unafraid to chase her dreams."

He nodded thoughtfully, his gaze fixed ahead, the moonlight casting a silver sheen over his features. "Good choice. Jo is fierce, and she writes what she feels. That kind of honesty is refreshing."

"And you?" I pressed. "Who would you be?"

"Hmm, perhaps Mr. Darcy," he said, a hint of mischief dancing in his eyes. "A brooding man of mystery with a hidden depth."

I shot him a skeptical look. "Brooding? You? Never."

"Hey now, I can brood with the best of them. Just give me a dramatic setting and some passionate internal monologue."

"Are you sure you wouldn't rather be a whimsical character, like Puck from A Midsummer Night's Dream?" I teased, letting the light banter roll between us, the air filled with the kind of warmth that only comes from shared laughter.

"Ah, but Puck is a trickster," he countered, feigning a serious tone. "That might get me in trouble. And I'm still trying to live down my vampire phase."

We both erupted into laughter, and in that moment, the world around us faded away. The playful exchange felt like a bridge, connecting our spirits in a way that was both exhilarating and terrifying. Just as I began to lose myself in the rhythm of our conversation, we arrived at the lake, its surface shimmering under the moonlight like a bed of diamonds.

"Wow," I breathed, taking in the scene before us. The water stretched out, reflecting the moon's glow, creating an almost magical ambiance. "This is stunning."

"Right?" Marcus stepped closer to the edge, peering into the depths. "There's something so serene about it. Makes you want to throw all your worries in and watch them sink."

"Or maybe just dive in and let the water wash everything away," I replied, my voice softer now, as the beauty of the moment wrapped around us.

"Not a bad idea," he said, glancing at me, and for a moment, our gazes locked. The world around us faded into a hushed silence, the night itself holding its breath as if waiting for something to unfold.

"What do you think it would feel like to just let go?" I mused, stepping closer, captivated by the depths of his expression.

"Liberating," he replied, his voice low and husky, sending a shiver down my spine. "But terrifying at the same time. Sometimes, the things we want most are the things that scare us."

The weight of his words hung in the air, the tension shifting as I realized we were teetering on the edge of something deeper—something that could tip us into unknown waters. I could feel my heart racing, a primal instinct urging me to leap, but a voice of caution echoed in my mind, reminding me of the risks.

Before I could respond, the stillness of the night was abruptly shattered by a loud crash nearby. My heart raced as I spun around, eyes wide. "What was that?"

Marcus's expression shifted, the playful light replaced with focus. "I don't know. It came from the direction of the old boathouse."

We exchanged a glance, a silent agreement forming between us. This wasn't the time for hesitation. With a determined nod, we hurried toward the sound, our footsteps quickening as adrenaline pumped through my veins.

As we approached the boathouse, the dim light revealed a scene that sent a chill through my bones. A figure loomed in the shadows, their silhouette almost otherworldly against the backdrop of the night.

"Who's there?" Marcus called out, his voice steady despite the tension crackling in the air.

The figure turned slowly, revealing a face that sent a jolt of recognition through me—a classmate from our literature course, Anna, her eyes wide and panicked. "Help!" she cried, her voice breaking as she stumbled forward. "You need to get away from here. It's not safe!"

My heart raced, confusion swirling in my mind. "What do you mean? What happened?"

She glanced over her shoulder, fear etched across her features. "I saw something... something that shouldn't be here. It was watching me. You have to trust me!"

Marcus stepped closer to Anna, a protective instinct radiating from him. "What did you see?"

But before she could respond, a low growl emanated from the darkness, sending an icy dread washing over me. The air grew thick with tension, and I felt a shiver race down my spine as I turned to see shadows shifting among the trees.

"We need to go," Marcus said, grabbing my hand, his grip firm and reassuring. The warmth of his touch contrasted sharply with the growing fear in the air.

As we started to retreat, a sudden movement in the shadows caught my eye, and the last thing I saw before the world spun into chaos was a pair of glowing eyes staring back at us—unblinking and hungry. The darkness seemed to pulse, alive with untold secrets, and as we turned to run, I couldn't shake the feeling that this was just the beginning of something much larger than the midnight discussions we had grown so fond of.

Chapter 4: Hidden Desires

The sun dipped below the horizon, casting a golden glow that danced through the half-open window, weaving shadows across the room. The soft hum of the nearby café buzzed with laughter and the clinking of cups, but here, in our little corner, time seemed to pause. Books lay strewn across the table, their pages marked by moments we'd shared, each one steeped in our ongoing rivalry that danced a fine line between irritation and exhilaration.

"Honestly, how can you not see the brilliance of Anna Karenina? It's a tragic love story!" I exclaimed, feigning exasperation while leaning closer, drawn to Marcus as if he were the only thing anchoring me in this world of literary debates.

He smirked, the corner of his mouth quirking up in that infuriatingly charming way that made my heart skip a beat. "Tragic, sure, but let's be real. She could have made better choices. A little self-awareness goes a long way, don't you think?"

I rolled my eyes, unable to suppress a smile. "Self-awareness? I think it's hard to be self-aware when you're busy having your heart torn apart by societal expectations." The back-and-forth felt like a well-rehearsed dance, and with every exchange, the tension between us simmered just below the surface.

His gaze locked onto mine, and for a fleeting moment, the world around us faded. It was as if I could hear my heartbeat echoing in the silence, the rhythm pulsating with the weight of all the words unspoken. The air felt thicker, and I was acutely aware of the warmth radiating from him, an electric current that beckoned me closer.

In an impulsive act that surprised even myself, I brushed my fingers against his, a delicate graze that sent a rush of warmth coursing through my veins. It was meant to be a playful gesture, a challenge laced with teasing, but instead, it ignited something deeper. His breath caught, a fraction of a second stretching into eternity as our eyes locked. It was a moment that thrummed with possibility, a glimpse into something beyond rivalry—a flicker of desire I had never anticipated.

Yet, just as swiftly as the connection sparked, Marcus retreated, his fingers slipping away from mine like grains of sand through a sieve. He cleared his throat, and the lightness returned as he quipped, "You know, I think Tolstoy would have written a better ending if he had a thesaurus."

I fought to stifle the disappointment blooming within me, masking it with laughter. "Ah, yes. A thesaurus would have solved all of Anna's problems." The banter felt forced, a defense mechanism against the undeniable chemistry crackling in the air.

"So, what you're saying is that you want me to write your romantic drama?" he replied, arching an eyebrow with a playful grin.

"Only if it ends with a handsome hero sweeping me off my feet," I teased, though the wishful thinking lingered in the back of my mind like a half-formed daydream.

Marcus leaned back in his chair, crossing his arms with an air of mock superiority. "Well, I'm not the kind to swoon. More of a rugged type, you know? Perhaps a brooding poet lost in his thoughts."

"Brooding poet?" I scoffed, waving my hand dismissively. "More like a wannabe Casanova whose best moves are stuck in a classic novel."

"Touché," he laughed, a sound rich with sincerity that somehow cut through the banter's veil. There was something intoxicating about the way his eyes danced, the way he seemed to wrestle with the very same attraction that had me captivated.

Our laughter faded, and the air grew thick with unspoken words. The café around us continued its cheerful hum, a stark contrast to the quiet intensity growing in our little bubble. I could feel it—a pull, a magnetic force that was slowly unraveling the threads of our rivalry, weaving something far more complicated and exhilarating.

It was the kind of tension that felt like standing on the edge of a cliff, teetering between what was known and what could be. I wanted to lean into it, to explore the depths of this uncharted territory, yet part of me hesitated. What if stepping over that line meant losing everything we had built, every playful jab and retort?

I could sense Marcus wrestling with similar thoughts. His gaze flickered away, eyes darting to the bustling crowd, as if searching for an escape from the vulnerability our connection demanded. "You know, I think I left my—"

"Excuse?" I interrupted, desperate to cling to this moment. "You're not going to dodge this, Marcus. We both feel it."

His eyes met mine again, and for a heartbeat, I could see the uncertainty dancing behind his facade. "You really want to talk about feelings? In a coffee shop? Over Tolstoy?"

"Why not?" I countered, emboldened. "It's not like we're writing the next great novel here. We're just two people having a conversation, and I don't mind if it's messy."

"Messy could be fun," he mused, a hint of mischief lurking in his voice.

And in that moment, I realized: the rivalry, the banter, the sharp repartee—it was all a mask, a way to hide our hidden desires. The stakes were higher than ever, and as the air between us crackled with potential, I couldn't help but wonder if we were both ready to face whatever lay ahead.

I held my breath, desperately trying to dispel the lingering warmth from our brief touch. The banter we'd crafted over the weeks was my safety net, yet here I was, standing at the precipice of something far more vulnerable. I couldn't help but wonder if this playful sparring had been a way to hide the truths lurking beneath the surface—like masked dancers in a grand ball, twirling elegantly while hiding their true selves.

"Okay, Mr. Casanova," I said, trying to regain my footing, "if you're going to critique Tolstoy, I'll need you to do it with a little more flair. I want footnotes, wild gestures—perhaps a dramatic reenactment?"

His laughter rang through the café, warm and infectious, pulling me back from my spiraling thoughts. "Ah, so you want me to become the Shakespeare of coffee shop criticism? I can see it now—'To be or not to be... in a love triangle that could end in disaster!'"

"Very Shakespearean indeed," I shot back, crossing my arms as I leaned in, half-amused and half-exasperated. "But I'm still waiting for you to explain how Anna's decisions reflect societal pressures without just rolling your eyes and cracking jokes."

"Touché," he replied, the twinkle in his eye returning as he tilted his head, considering my words. "I guess I'm just trying to lighten the mood. Literature's already heavy enough without piling on the angst."

"Isn't that the point?" I challenged, my heart racing as the playful glimmer shifted into something deeper. "To peel back the layers, to expose the raw truth behind the tragedy?"

Before he could respond, the bell above the café door chimed, interrupting our moment. In walked Claire, a friend of ours who had a penchant for entering at the most opportune—or, perhaps, inconvenient—times. With her bright, fiery hair and a smile that could light up the darkest corner of any room, she swept toward us, oblivious to the charged atmosphere.

"Hey, lovebirds!" she called, grinning like a Cheshire cat. "What are you two plotting in here? A revolution in literary critique?"

Marcus coughed, hastily straightening his posture, while I shot him a sideways glance, desperately trying to keep my expression neutral. "Just your typical discussion about love and tragedy," I replied, forcing a smile that felt far too strained.

"Well, you know what they say—nothing says romance like a little tragedy," Claire quipped, plopping down at our table and swiping a pastry from the plate. She took a bite, her eyes sparkling with mischief. "So, who's playing the tragic hero and who's the villain?"

"Ah, you know me," Marcus said, feigning a melodramatic air. "Always the misunderstood hero, brooding in the shadows."

"Right," I interjected with a laugh, "more like a jester trying too hard to impress the queen."

"Touché again," he admitted, his laughter joining mine, the earlier tension fading into a comfortable camaraderie. Claire's presence, like a sudden breeze on a stifling day, shifted the atmosphere, allowing me to breathe again.

But as we continued our light-hearted banter, I couldn't shake the lingering feelings from earlier, like a shadow following me home. Every glance Marcus threw my way felt charged with unspoken words, and despite Claire's cheerful presence, my mind kept wandering back to that fleeting moment when our fingers had brushed—an electric pulse that had transformed our rivalry into something that felt dangerously intimate.

With Claire in tow, our discussion spiraled into the absurd—topics ranging from the best literary villains to the worst coffee ever brewed. Claire, ever the enthusiastic participant, recounted her disastrous attempt at making espresso, complete with exaggerated gestures and funny faces that had us in stitches. Laughter echoed around us, drowning out the earlier tension, but as the evening wore on, I found myself glancing at Marcus more than I intended.

"Okay, but seriously," Claire said, leaning in conspiratorially, "what's going on between you two? I can practically feel the tension sizzling in the air."

I shot Marcus a look, and he raised an eyebrow, a silent challenge flickering between us. "Tension? Between us? Please. It's just a classic case of literary rivalry."

Claire's eyes sparkled with delight. "Oh, come on! I've seen how you look at each other. If I didn't know better, I'd think you were both trying not to kiss in the middle of a coffee shop."

"Marcus would probably trip over his own feet in that scenario," I joked, desperately trying to deflect the spotlight onto him.

"Only if you were the one leaning in," he retorted, the smirk on his face betraying the underlying tension that still lingered.

Claire clapped her hands, practically bouncing in her seat. "Yes! I knew it! The chemistry is practically palpable! You two are like fire and ice."

"Or like a cat and a dog," Marcus added with a laugh, clearly enjoying the moment. "We just can't seem to decide who's going to chase whom."

I rolled my eyes, a smile playing on my lips. "Please. If anyone's chasing, it's you. I'm merely here, observing from a distance, wondering why I put up with all your nonsense."

"Oh, nonsense?" he echoed, leaning in, his tone mockingly offended. "I thought you enjoyed my brand of charm. It's practically irresistible!"

"Charm? More like an acquired taste," I shot back, but deep down, my heart fluttered at the prospect of what lay beneath our playful exchanges.

As the evening progressed, our conversations meandered, but my thoughts kept drifting back to Marcus, the way he leaned closer when he spoke, the way his laughter lingered like an echo in my mind. Somewhere in the midst of laughter and chatter, I felt a shift—a realization that our rivalry might be a facade for something more profound, more complex.

Then, the unexpected happened. Just as Claire was animatedly explaining her latest escapade, Marcus leaned across the table, his voice lowering to a conspiratorial whisper. "What if we took this literary rivalry to the next level? A real challenge? The next great debate?"

I blinked, intrigued. "And what would that entail?"

His eyes glinted with mischief, the kind that made my heart race. "A date. A night devoted to our favorite novels. You bring yours, I bring mine, and we see who can convince the other to switch allegiances. Winner gets bragging rights for a month."

"Bragging rights?" I laughed, trying to gauge the seriousness in his expression. "That's the best you can come up with? Sounds like a win for me."

"Is that a challenge?" he countered, leaning back in his chair, a confident smirk on his lips.

"Challenge accepted," I replied, unable to suppress the thrill of adventure creeping in.

The stakes had shifted, and as the evening wound down, I realized that in the midst of our playful rivalry, I had unwittingly stepped into a dance of hidden desires, a game that promised to reveal more than just our literary preferences.

The challenge hung in the air like the promise of an impending storm, electrifying and almost tangible. Our banter had taken a daring turn, shifting from mere rivalry to an invitation to explore deeper currents. I could feel my heart racing, propelled by the thrill of what lay ahead, and I was suddenly all too aware of how much I wanted to uncover the layers beneath Marcus's playful exterior.

"Just to clarify," I said, leaning in slightly, "are you suggesting a battle of wits over coffee and classic literature? Because if so, I'll need to prepare." The teasing lilt in my voice was a thin veil over the anticipation bubbling beneath.

"Prepare? Oh, I do hope you bring more than just your well-worn copy of Anna Karenina. I hear a good book can elevate the stakes," he replied, his tone playfully mocking, but his gaze held something serious. "You might want to consider a strategy if you expect to win."

"Strategy?" I scoffed, waving my hand dismissively, yet I felt the thrill of competition welling inside me. "Please, Marcus. I was born ready. You'll need more than clever banter to distract me."

Claire, still nibbling on her pastry, grinned as if she were watching a masterclass in flirtation unfold. "Can I take bets? Because I'm all in on Team You, if only to witness the epic showdown."

"Team You?" Marcus shot back, an eyebrow raised, clearly amused. "And what do I get if I win? A lifetime supply of coffee? A trophy shaped like a book?"

"More like a trophy shaped like your overinflated ego," I countered, laughing.

Marcus threw his head back, a rich, carefree laugh that warmed the entire room. "Touché! But I must say, that trophy sounds appealing. Perhaps I should consider it a fair trade for the inconvenience of sharing coffee with you."

"Oh, please," I said, rolling my eyes. "You're going to need more than coffee to keep up with me."

Our laughter lingered, a gentle reminder of the easy rapport we had cultivated, yet the undercurrents of our unspoken chemistry loomed large. As Claire excused herself to grab another drink, I found myself alone with Marcus, the comfortable noise of the café fading into the background.

"So, when do we do this?" he asked, his voice steady, yet I could sense an edge of seriousness in his tone that cut through the playful banter.

"How about tomorrow evening?" I suggested, surprised at my own eagerness. "I could use a good distraction from the drudgery of studying."

"Tomorrow it is, then," he replied, the corners of his mouth twitching into a knowing smile. "Prepare to be dazzled by my unrivaled charm."

"Dazzled? Oh, I'm sure," I shot back, feeling a rush of adrenaline. "Just don't be too disappointed when you lose."

As the evening wore on, we parted ways, but the air around me felt charged. I couldn't shake the anticipation tinged with nerves as I replayed our conversation. Had we crossed a line? Had we merely given our rivalry a new layer, or was there something more, something that hungered to break free from the constraints of our witty exchanges?

The next evening arrived with a gust of cool wind and a sprinkling of early autumn leaves, the streets dressed in hues of gold and crimson. I stood in front of the café, the familiar sign swinging gently in the breeze. My heart raced with an odd mix of excitement and anxiety as I stepped inside, scanning the room for Marcus.

He appeared moments later, striding in with an air of confidence that made my pulse quicken. He wore a fitted navy sweater that complemented his eyes, the fabric clinging to his frame in a way that made it hard to focus. "Ready to lose?" he asked, a mischievous glint in his eyes.

"Lose?" I scoffed, feigning nonchalance. "I don't plan on doing any losing tonight."

"Ah, the spirit of a champion! I admire it," he replied, pulling out a chair for me. I felt a warmth bloom in my chest at the small gesture, an echo of the chivalry I'd seen only in the pages of novels.

The evening unfolded like a beautifully scripted play. We dove into heated discussions, dissecting characters and themes with a fervor that ignited my mind. Each point made, each rebuttal delivered, only deepened the connection between us, transforming our rivalry into a dance of intellectual intimacy.

Yet, just as I felt we were making progress, Marcus dropped a bombshell that sent my thoughts spiraling. "You know, I almost didn't come tonight. I was about to head home when I received a call from my dad."

"What's that got to do with our debate?" I asked, trying to keep the sudden shift in mood from showing on my face.

"Well," he began, running a hand through his hair, "he wanted to talk about college. And, let's just say, our views don't quite align."

"Ah, parental expectations," I said, leaning back in my chair, my curiosity piqued. "What's the conflict?"

"Let's just say he has this vision of my future that doesn't quite include pursuing a degree in literature." He chuckled, though I could see the tension etched across his features. "He thinks I should be more practical, maybe even take over the family business."

"That sounds... constraining," I said, my heart aching for him. "What do you want?"

Marcus hesitated, a flicker of vulnerability crossing his face before he masked it with humor. "A degree in literature, a quiet life of coffee shops and book discussions? Or maybe a reality show featuring my daring escapades in the literary world?"

The unexpected depth in his response stunned me. "And how does that involve me?" I asked, teasing yet genuinely curious.

His eyes met mine, and in that moment, the world around us faded. "Honestly? I've enjoyed our debates more than I'd care to admit. You challenge me, and that's refreshing."

"Refreshing?" I echoed, the word wrapping around my heart like a warm embrace.

Just then, a sudden commotion erupted at the entrance of the café. A loud crash startled us both, breaking the intimacy of our moment. I turned to see a man stumbling through the door, his clothes disheveled, a wild look in his eyes.

"Help!" he shouted, breathless and panicked, eyes darting around as if searching for a ghost. "They're coming for me!"

Marcus and I exchanged a glance, the warmth of our earlier connection evaporating into an unsettling chill. The man fell to his knees, desperation painted across his face. "You have to help me! They'll find me!"

"Who's coming?" I asked, my heart racing as the tension shifted once again, uncertainty seeping into the air.

The man's eyes landed on Marcus, and something dark flickered in the depths of his gaze. "You don't know what you're involved in," he rasped, his voice trembling.

And in that moment, as dread settled like a stone in my stomach, I realized that our evening of friendly rivalry had just been plunged into something far more sinister than I could have ever imagined.

Chapter 5: The Manipulative Editor

The late afternoon sun cast a golden glow through the expansive windows of Marcus's office, illuminating the stacks of manuscripts and coffee-stained notebooks that surrounded us. It felt like a sanctum, a hidden realm where words floated like fireflies in the evening air. We had been working together for weeks now, sharing ideas and dreams over countless cups of coffee, our laughter mingling with the scent of fresh ink. I could feel a connection blooming between us—something unspoken yet palpable, like the electric charge before a summer storm.

"Maybe if we approach the character arc from a different angle," I suggested, leaning forward, excitement bubbling in my chest. "What if she's not just the victim of her circumstances but actively fights against them? It would add so much depth."

Marcus's dark eyes sparkled with intrigue as he considered my words. "I like that. It gives her agency. It makes her real." He ran a hand through his tousled hair, the action both endearing and maddening. I caught myself smiling, feeling the warmth of his presence wrap around me like a familiar blanket.

But just as the atmosphere in the room shifted into something sweet and hopeful, the door swung open with a suddenness that sliced through the moment. Vera Dawson, Marcus's editor, strode in with the confidence of a general leading a battalion. Her sleek, tailored suit hugged her figure in all the right places, but there was an edge to her demeanor that sent a shiver down my spine. It was as if she thrived on tension, wielding it like a weapon.

"Marcus," she greeted, her voice smooth like honey but laced with a razor's edge. "We need to discuss your progress." Her gaze swept over me, a calculating smile flickering on her lips. "And your... distractions."

I could feel the air grow heavy with her presence. "Vera," Marcus said, his tone clipped as he straightened in his chair. The warmth we had been building was extinguished in an instant, leaving only a cold draft in its wake. "We were just brainstorming some ideas."

She raised an eyebrow, clearly unimpressed. "Brainstorming? I hope you understand that your deadline is looming, Marcus. The world doesn't wait for you to indulge in—" she paused, her gaze cutting sharply towards me, "—what do you call it? Emotional distractions?"

I shifted in my seat, feeling the sting of her words. It was a strange thing, being so quickly reduced to a mere distraction, as if all the late-night discussions and laughter we shared were nothing more than fleeting moments to be swept under the rug. I looked to Marcus, searching for some sign of support, but his expression was locked in a battle between his ambition and our growing bond.

"Vera, I appreciate your concern, but I'm capable of managing my time," Marcus replied, his voice steady, though I could sense the strain behind it.

"Oh, I'm sure you are," she retorted, a sly smile creeping across her lips. "But remember, success doesn't come to those who dally with unimportant matters. I want you focused—nothing less than a bestseller, Marcus. Don't let anyone, especially not... her," she gestured dismissively at me, "derail that goal."

The implication stung, as if her words were barbs thrown with lethal precision. I felt the color drain from my cheeks, and the air between us grew thick with unspoken words. In that moment, I was more than just a mere distraction; I was a pawn on a chessboard, and Vera was determined to win.

"Vera," I interjected, forcing myself to sound more confident than I felt. "I'm not trying to derail anything. I'm here to support Marcus, to help him find his voice again." I held her gaze, challenging her as best as I could.

Marcus's eyes flicked between us, the tension palpable. "That's enough, Vera. I won't have you treating her like this," he said, his voice rising slightly. It was a rare show of defiance, and it sent a flicker of warmth through me. But I also saw the storm brewing in his eyes—a conflict that threatened to tear him apart.

Vera leaned back, her expression shifting to one of amusement as if she relished the drama unfolding before her. "Oh, Marcus. This isn't about her. This is about you. You need to decide what you want. Are you truly prepared to sacrifice your career for a little romance?" Her words dripped with condescension, but it was the truth behind them that cut the deepest.

Silence enveloped us, thick and suffocating. I wanted to scream, to tell her that it wasn't just about romance—that what we shared had the potential to be something more profound, more transformative. Yet, the uncertainty in Marcus's eyes told me that I might just be a fleeting chapter in his life, a pretty footnote in his eventual success.

"Vera, enough," Marcus finally said, his voice low but firm. "I need to think." He turned back to me, his expression softening as he reached for my hand, squeezing it gently. "I'm sorry. I didn't mean for you to get caught in this."

I could feel the warmth of his touch anchoring me, but it was also a reminder of the precariousness of our situation. "It's okay," I murmured, though inside, I was a tempest of emotions—frustration, anger, and an overwhelming desire to protect what we had.

Vera's laughter echoed in the room, sharp and biting. "I'll give you two some space to 'think.' But don't take too long, Marcus. Remember, the clock is ticking." With that, she spun on her heel and strode out, leaving a silence so profound that I could hear the faint ticking of a clock somewhere in the distance.

As the door clicked shut behind her, the atmosphere shifted once more. Marcus let out a breath he didn't know he was holding, his shoulders slumping slightly. "I hate how she does that," he said, running a hand through his hair, a gesture of frustration and defeat.

I took a moment to gather my thoughts, feeling the weight of his career pressing down on him. "You don't have to listen to her, you know. You can choose your path. Your story is yours to tell."

He looked at me, a mixture of gratitude and sorrow etched across his features. "I want to believe that, but it's not that simple. She has a lot of influence, and my success depends on her."

"But what about us?" I whispered, the words slipping out before I could stop them. It felt daring and terrifying, the prospect of laying bare my emotions.

He hesitated, and in that moment, I felt vulnerable, exposed like a tender sprout in the cold. But before he could respond, the door swung open again, and I instinctively pulled my hand away, retreating into myself.

The world outside was once again crashing into our intimate bubble, and I couldn't shake the feeling that no matter how hard I tried, Vera's presence would always loom like a dark cloud overhead, threatening to rain on the fragile connection we had built.

As Vera's heels clicked away, the silence in the office seemed to stretch, the air thick with the residue of her condescension. I took a moment to compose myself, the weight of her presence lingering like a storm cloud overhead. Marcus sat across from me, his expression a mixture of frustration and helplessness, his fingers drumming softly against the polished wood of his desk, a rhythm echoing the turmoil in my heart.

"I'm sorry," he finally said, his voice barely above a whisper. "You shouldn't have to deal with her. She's... she's not like anyone else."

I managed a weak smile, trying to dispel the tension that clung to the room like a fog. "She seems to have a knack for making people feel small," I replied, forcing levity into my tone. "I felt like I was back in high school, waiting for the popular girl to give me the time of day."

Marcus chuckled softly, his eyes sparkling with a hint of mischief. "High school wasn't so bad, was it? At least we had prom, bad music, and questionable dance moves to distract us."

"Ah, yes, the horror of mismatched socks and awkward slow dances," I replied, feeling the warmth of his humor push back against the chill Vera had left in her wake. "But I'd take that over an encounter with her any day."

He leaned back in his chair, the tension in his shoulders easing slightly as we both tried to shake off the remnants of Vera's visit. "I appreciate you standing up for yourself. Most people would just back down. They don't want to risk her wrath." His gaze was sincere, and I could feel the sincerity wrap around me like a comforting blanket.

"Let's be honest," I said, leaning closer, "I'm too stubborn to back down. It's a flaw, really." I raised an eyebrow playfully. "You might want to reconsider your partnership with me."

"Stubborn is good," he replied, a grin breaking across his face. "Stubborn means you're not easily swayed by people like Vera."

I shrugged, feigning indifference, but I could feel a warmth spread across my cheeks. "Let's hope that stubbornness doesn't lead us into more trouble."

"Speaking of trouble," Marcus said, his tone shifting as a glimmer of concern shadowed his features, "I need to figure out how to keep Vera off my back without compromising what we have."

His words lingered in the air, the underlying tension making my heart race. "You're the writer," I teased, trying to lighten the mood despite the seriousness of the situation. "Can't you just write her into a story where she gets eaten by a monster?"

He laughed, the sound rich and infectious. "If only it were that easy. Maybe I should create a villain that embodies everything she represents—a heartless editor who thrives on chaos and drama."

I chuckled, but the truth hung between us, heavy and undeniable. The more time I spent with Marcus, the more I realized just how fragile this moment was. One wrong move, one slip of the tongue, and Vera could crush our budding connection before it had the chance to bloom. "Do you think she'd notice if I slipped a little poison into her coffee?"

Marcus raised an eyebrow, clearly amused by the image. "I don't think that's the kind of plot twist she'd appreciate."

"True," I said, pretending to ponder. "Perhaps I'll stick to a more traditional approach. Maybe I'll show up at the launch party in an evening gown with a stunning tiara, and when she asks about it, I'll just say I'm the queen of distractions."

"Ah, the queen! I like that." His laughter filled the room, and for a moment, the heaviness faded. "In that case, I'll be your loyal court jester."

"Only if you promise to bring the confetti," I replied, reveling in the moment.

Yet, beneath the laughter, an unshakable worry persisted. I watched Marcus's face as he contemplated the challenges ahead, the creases in his forehead deepening as the reality of his situation began to settle back in. "It's just... this is my first big break. I can't afford to mess it up," he admitted, his voice laced with a vulnerability that made my heart ache.

"Then we'll figure it out together," I said firmly, my conviction surprising even myself. "I'm not going anywhere, Marcus. Not now, not ever."

He looked up, a spark igniting in his eyes, but just as quickly as it came, doubt clouded his expression. "You say that now, but you haven't met the full force of Vera's manipulation. It's like she has a sixth sense for exploiting weaknesses."

"Or maybe she just feeds on insecurity," I shot back, feeling a surge of determination. "You're talented, and you know it. Don't let her shadow hang over you."

Marcus's lips curled into a faint smile, but the shadows remained. "Maybe you're right. But I can't help but wonder if she has a point. I mean, can I really balance my work and... whatever this is between us?"

I leaned forward, catching his gaze with unwavering confidence. "We won't know unless we try. We're here now, aren't we? This is our story, and it's just as important as your book."

He opened his mouth to respond, but the tension in the air shifted, and I felt a sudden chill that had nothing to do with the temperature.

The door creaked open again, and in walked Vera, this time with a more ominous energy. The confident facade she wore was replaced by a frigid determination, her eyes gleaming like a predator sizing up its prey. "I hope I'm not interrupting anything," she said, her voice smooth but with a threatening undertone that sent a shiver down my spine.

"No, just discussing strategies for the launch," Marcus replied, his voice steady despite the rising tension.

Vera stepped into the room, her presence swallowing the light and warmth we had just built. "I wanted to remind you, Marcus, that your priorities should be clear. This launch is critical. You need to focus."

"Right," he said, his tone clipped. "But I also need a little time to work on the content, Vera. Quality over quantity, remember?"

"Quality?" She laughed, a sound devoid of warmth. "Let's not get too sentimental. The market demands a hit, not a heartfelt story. Remember, the clock is ticking. People will forget if you don't give them something to talk about."

I watched Marcus's jaw tighten, a flicker of anger sparking in his eyes. "I know that, Vera. But I won't sacrifice my integrity for the sake of a headline."

The tension was electric, and I could feel the chasm widening between them. Vera's smile turned into a predatory grin, and in that moment, I saw the lengths to which she was willing to go. "Just keep in mind, Marcus, that success comes at a price. It's your choice what you're willing to pay."

With those words hanging in the air, she turned on her heel and left as abruptly as she had entered, the door slamming shut behind her. The silence that followed was suffocating, leaving Marcus and me staring at each other, the weight of her manipulation settling heavily between us.

"Don't let her get to you," I urged, sensing the storm brewing within him. "You're more than her chess piece."

"I know, but…" His voice trailed off, the doubt creeping back in.

I reached across the desk, placing my hand over his. "We're in this together. I won't let you down."

He squeezed my hand, and in that moment, a spark of determination ignited within me. I wasn't just a distraction; I was a part of this story. Our story. And as long as we faced Vera's manipulation together, I knew we could forge our own path, one that was uniquely ours.

The air felt charged as I leaned against Marcus's desk, the wood cool beneath my fingertips, grounding me in the moment. His eyes, usually so full of warmth and promise, were clouded with uncertainty. I wished I could somehow erase Vera's venomous words from his mind, but they clung to him like a shadow, making the space between us feel heavier.

"I know she's a piece of work," I said softly, trying to infuse some lightness back into the atmosphere. "But you can't let her dictate your life. Just think of her as a plot twist you didn't see coming."

Marcus let out a short laugh, but it was tinged with frustration. "Yeah, a plot twist that could write me out of my own story. I can't afford to be distracted, not now." He glanced at the half-finished manuscript on his desk, the pages filled with his thoughts and dreams, and for a moment, I could see the battle raging within him.

I stepped closer, my heart pounding as I held his gaze. "What if you let me help you? I mean, really help you? We can turn her words against her. Let's make this launch not just about the book but about you—your vision."

A flicker of something ignited in his eyes, a spark that felt like hope. "You really think we could do that?"

"Of course! Think of it as a creative coup. Vera might be sharp, but she's also predictable. We'll outsmart her, and you'll have the last laugh." My words tumbled out with the enthusiasm I felt, the idea taking root in my mind.

Marcus leaned back, considering the possibilities, and for a moment, the storm clouds parted just enough to let a sliver of sunlight in. "Alright, but it won't be easy. Vera is tenacious."

"Tenacious is her middle name, I'm sure," I quipped. "But so are we. What does she know about passion? About telling a story that matters?"

He regarded me, his expression softening. "I don't know what I'd do without you."

My breath caught for just a moment, the sincerity of his words filling me with warmth. "Well, you won't have to find out."

Before we could sink deeper into this newfound momentum, the phone on Marcus's desk buzzed violently, breaking the fragile intimacy that had begun to weave around us. He picked it up, glancing at the screen, and I could see the color drain from his face.

"It's Vera," he said, his voice suddenly distant.

"Answer it," I urged, my heart racing. "Let's not let her control this moment."

He hesitated, his thumb hovering over the screen as if it were a live wire. Finally, he sighed, his shoulders slumping in resignation. "I have to. I can't ignore her."

With a nod, he swiped to answer, his face shifting into a mask of professionalism. "Vera," he said, his voice steady but strained.

I could only hear her half of the conversation, her voice sharp and cutting, like glass shards in the air. "I need to discuss the details of the launch, and I expect you to be ready. This is your chance to prove you're not just another mediocre writer, Marcus. Don't waste it."

I watched as Marcus clenched his jaw, the muscles in his face tightening. "I understand. I'll have everything ready by then."

"Make sure you do," she snapped before hanging up, leaving a silence that felt as oppressive as a weight on his chest.

"Wow, she really knows how to inspire confidence," I said, trying to inject a hint of levity into the moment.

He ran a hand through his hair again, the familiar gesture returning as a sign of his stress. "It's just—she's right. I have to deliver. If I don't, everything I've worked for could be gone in an instant."

"Then let's make sure that doesn't happen," I insisted, stepping closer, my resolve solidifying. "We'll work together, and you'll show her exactly what you're made of."

He looked at me, the flicker of doubt still present, but something else sparkled in his gaze—gratitude, maybe even affection. "You're really something, you know that?"

"Just a girl with a plan," I replied, flashing a smile that I hoped would encourage him. "Besides, I think your words deserve to be heard. Let's give Vera something to really worry about."

A moment passed, thick with unspoken words, and as he opened his mouth, the phone buzzed again, shattering our bubble once more. Marcus looked down, his expression darkening.

"It's her again," he said, irritation flashing across his features.

"Don't answer," I suggested. "Let her stew for a bit. She needs to learn that you're not her puppet."

But before he could respond, he pressed the button to answer. "Vera?"

Her voice, sharp as a knife, came through the line. "I hope you're ready for tomorrow's meeting, Marcus. I've arranged for some special guests to be there. I expect you to impress them."

"Special guests?" he echoed, confusion flickering across his face.

"Yes, potential investors. They want to meet the mind behind the manuscript," she said, her tone suggesting that this was a privilege he should be grateful for, rather than a threat. "You'll want to have your best foot forward. And make sure your little... friend isn't there to distract you."

My breath caught in my throat, and I felt a surge of anger rise within me. "You can't let her intimidate you like that," I whispered urgently, my heart pounding in my chest.

He looked at me, torn between his loyalty to me and the pressure Vera exerted. "I'll be there," he said finally, the defeat creeping back into his voice.

"Good. We have high expectations, Marcus. Don't disappoint." The line clicked dead, leaving an oppressive silence in its wake.

He dropped the phone onto the desk, his expression a storm of frustration. "I can't believe this. She thinks she can just manipulate me, control everything."

"Then let's turn the tables. We need to be prepared, and we need a plan," I said, feeling a fire ignite within me. "This isn't just about you anymore; it's about us. We're going to show her that we can outsmart her."

"I appreciate you wanting to help," Marcus said, his voice firm but tinged with worry. "But this is my career on the line, and I can't risk—"

"Risk what? Being happy? Being successful? Marcus, you deserve to tell your story without her shadow hanging over you. I refuse to let her dictate our worth."

He hesitated, the weight of my words settling in. "What are you suggesting?"

"We prepare a pitch that makes her wish she hadn't messed with us. I'll help you draft something that's not just good—it'll be spectacular. You have a vision, and we'll make sure it shines through."

He met my gaze, a spark of determination igniting behind the uncertainty. "Alright. Let's do it. Together."

The energy between us shifted, and I felt a rush of adrenaline, the thrill of a challenge ahead. But just as I began to relax, a knock on the door jolted me.

Before we could react, the door swung open, revealing a figure that sent a chill down my spine. It was Vera again, but this time, her expression was colder, her smile more sinister.

"Marcus," she purred, stepping into the room with an air of authority that made my skin crawl. "I have something very important to discuss."

I exchanged a glance with Marcus, an unspoken question hanging in the air.

What now?

Vera's gaze flicked between us, and I could sense the tension tightening around us like a noose. I braced myself for whatever storm was about to hit, knowing that this could change everything.

"Do you really think you're ready to face the industry?" she asked, her voice dripping with condescension. "Or are you just playing at being a writer?"

And just like that, the ground shifted beneath us, the stakes suddenly higher, and my heart raced as I wondered how deep her manipulations ran.

Chapter 6: A Fork in the Road

The air was thick with the scent of old books and ink, a comforting reminder of the countless stories trapped within these hallowed walls. The library had always been my sanctuary, a place where I could lose myself in worlds crafted by others, but today it felt more like a battlefield. I could hear the distant ticking of the clock, each second resonating with the increasing tension between Marcus and me. The project we were working on loomed over us like a storm cloud, and every hour that passed felt like a countdown to an inevitable clash.

Marcus leaned back in his chair, arms crossed, his brow furrowed in concentration as he dissected the literary nuances of our chosen text. His passion for detail was undeniable, but sometimes I wished he could see beyond the margins of the page. "You're missing the essence of it, Marcus," I snapped, my voice sharper than intended. "This isn't just about numbers and statistics. It's about the story—the heartbeat behind the words. Can't you see that?"

He shot me a glance, his emerald eyes narrowing, reflecting both annoyance and disbelief. "This isn't some fluffy book club, Emma. We're aiming for a tangible analysis here. The data has to speak for itself. If you want to write poetry, then maybe you should stick to that. We have a deadline, remember?"

His words stung more than I cared to admit. The way he reduced my passion to mere fluff ignited something fierce within me. I loved literature for its soul, its ability to evoke emotions and weave connections between hearts and minds. But here I was, trying to convince Marcus—a man so ensnared by his spreadsheets and power points—that there was beauty in the chaos of storytelling. Instead, I felt more like an intruder in his carefully constructed world of logic.

"You're so focused on making everything fit into your little boxes that you're missing the magic of it all," I retorted, my frustration bubbling over. "You're so consumed by your career that you don't even realize the beauty of literature can't be quantified."

With every word, I felt the space between us grow larger, the air crackling with unspoken words and unresolved emotions. It was maddening, this push and pull of our differing perspectives, and it left me feeling adrift. Suddenly, without thinking, I stood up, my chair scraping harshly against the floor, the noise echoing in the otherwise silent room. I could feel my heart racing, disappointment and hurt mingling with a sense of betrayal.

"Maybe I should just—" I began, but the words tangled in my throat. Storming out seemed the only way to salvage my dignity.

As I walked out, the door swung shut behind me with a soft thud, sealing off the fraying connection between us. I could still hear his voice, rising in pitch, laced with frustration, but I was too far gone to turn back. The cool air outside hit my face, a refreshing contrast to the heated argument. I inhaled deeply, trying to gather my scattered thoughts as I made my way to the car.

The drive home felt like a suffocating void. The usual radio chatter that filled the space was absent today, leaving me alone with my turbulent thoughts. The silence wrapped around me like a heavy blanket, amplifying the ache in my chest. I drummed my fingers against the steering wheel, feeling each beat resonate with the turmoil within me. Every twist of the road felt like a fork leading me further away from where I wanted to be, both geographically and emotionally.

A flicker of guilt crept in as I replayed our argument. I could picture Marcus sitting in that library, his face a mask of exasperation, perhaps even disappointment. The image pierced my heart, stirring up the memories of our late-night study sessions where laughter flowed as easily as the caffeine we consumed. I remembered the way we used to challenge each other, the thrill of intellectual sparring igniting a fire in both of us. Now, that spark felt like it had dimmed, and the thought left a bitter taste in my mouth.

Pulling into my driveway, I sat in the car for a moment longer, staring at the warm glow of the porch light that spilled onto the pavement like an invitation. My heart ached with the realization that this wasn't just about the project or our differing perspectives; it was about something deeper. I had come to value our connection, our banter, the way we could dive into each other's thoughts and feelings. But today, it felt like a wall had risen between us.

I finally stepped out of the car, the gravel crunching underfoot, a stark reminder of the evening's unresolved tensions. Each step toward the house was heavy, weighed down by the possibility that things might not return to the way they were. Would this argument redefine our relationship? I didn't want it to, but I knew I had to confront it head-on.

Inside, the familiar scents of home enveloped me—freshly baked cookies from earlier, the remnants of a comforting dinner my mother had prepared, and a hint of lavender from the diffuser in the corner. But the warmth felt hollow, a far cry from the companionship I sought. I tossed my bag onto the couch, the fabric crumpling under the weight of my unexpressed emotions.

Sinking into the soft embrace of my favorite chair, I pulled my knees up to my chest, staring out the window at the darkening sky. Each star that twinkled above seemed to mock me, a reminder of all the possibilities I had missed today. I reached for my phone, hesitating as I scrolled through my contacts, my heart racing at the thought of reaching out to him. What would I even say? "Sorry for calling you a career-obsessed robot?"

A soft knock at the door startled me, pulling me from my thoughts. My heart quickened. Could it be? The flicker of hope swelled inside me, battling the uncertainty that threatened to drown it. Taking a deep breath, I stood up, moving toward the door with a mixture of trepidation and eagerness. As I opened it, the cool night air rushed in, carrying with it the scent of impending rain—a sign of renewal, perhaps.

As the door swung open, I found Marcus standing there, drenched from the rain that had begun to fall, his dark hair plastered to his forehead. His green eyes, usually filled with mischief and passion, were clouded with concern. The moment hung between us, charged with the weight of our earlier clash. My breath caught as I took in his presence—the way the raindrops glistened on his jacket, the slight tremor in his hands as he shifted from one foot to the other.

"Emma," he began, his voice softer than I expected, breaking through the tension that had enveloped us. "Can we talk?"

I stood frozen for a moment, my heart racing in anticipation. The way his lips moved around my name sent a rush of warmth through me, battling the chill of the evening air. I finally nodded, stepping aside to let him in, aware that the storm outside mirrored the one brewing inside me.

As he entered, I caught a glimpse of his expression—a mixture of determination and vulnerability that made my heart ache. "I'm sorry," he said, shaking off droplets like a dog emerging from a swim. "I didn't mean to upset you. You were right about needing to capture the essence of the literature. I got so caught up in the details that I forgot what drew me to it in the first place."

I felt my defenses start to waver, the sharp edge of my frustration blurring in the warmth of his sincerity. "I just want us to create something meaningful, Marcus. I thought we were in this together," I replied, my voice quieter now, the weight of my disappointment still heavy on my chest.

He ran a hand through his hair, the gesture revealing a glimpse of the charmingly disheveled side of him I had always adored. "You're right. I've been so focused on making everything perfect that I've lost sight of the bigger picture." His gaze bore into mine, earnest and searching. "I value your perspective. I really do."

I wanted to respond, to tell him how much it meant to hear that, but the words caught in my throat. Instead, I turned and walked into the kitchen, needing space to gather my thoughts. The comforting scent of baked cookies wafted through the air, a reminder of home amidst the chaos of our emotions. I busied myself with pouring two glasses of water, trying to steady the storm within me.

Marcus followed me, his presence filling the room like an uninvited guest. "Can we just... start over?" he suggested, leaning against the kitchen counter, the vulnerability in his stance tugging at my heartstrings. "No more arguing. Just you and me, brainstorming what we really want to say in this project."

I couldn't help but smile slightly at his earnestness. "You make it sound so simple," I teased, turning to face him, my fingers playing with the edge of my shirt. "But you know it's not. We're still two very different people with wildly divergent ideas about literature."

"True," he conceded, his lips twitching into a playful grin. "But I think that's what makes it interesting. I mean, imagine how boring it would be if we just agreed all the time. We'd end up like those bland characters in bad romance novels—unmemorable and utterly forgettable."

"Or like one of those overly logical robots programmed to analyze every emotion out of existence," I countered, chuckling softly. "But seriously, Marcus, I need to feel like we're on the same team. I don't want to compromise the heart of our project for the sake of stats."

He moved closer, the warmth radiating off him like an inviting glow. "Let's find that balance, then. You bring the heart, and I'll bring the structure. We can create something beautiful, something that reflects both of our strengths. But only if we communicate—really communicate."

His earnestness melted away the walls I had built around my heart. Maybe we could find common ground after all. "Fine," I replied, the tension in my shoulders easing. "But we have to promise not to let the stress of the project drive us apart again. I need you in my corner."

"I'm all in, Emma," he said, his voice low and sincere. "No more letting career ambitions overshadow what really matters."

I felt a flicker of hope igniting between us, like the first light of dawn breaking through the darkness. As we settled into a rhythm of brainstorming, the conversation flowed naturally, our ideas intertwining like vines in a garden. We tossed suggestions back and forth, the initial frustration dissipating with every laugh and every shared glance.

The rain pattered gently against the window, a soothing backdrop to our animated discussion. "What if we focus on how the characters evolve through their experiences?" I suggested, my enthusiasm bubbling over. "We could show how their journeys mirror our own struggles with identity and purpose."

"Now you're talking," he replied, leaning in with genuine interest. "And we can layer that with statistics about how those transformations resonate with readers. It's all about connection, right?"

The excitement in his voice sent a thrill through me. It felt like a dance, this back-and-forth, and with every step, I found myself falling a little harder for the passion he brought to our collaboration. The line between friendship and something more blurred tantalizingly, and I wondered if he felt it too.

After a few hours of productive brainstorming, the kitchen counter was littered with notes and empty water glasses, evidence of our shared creativity. I leaned back in my chair, exhausted yet exhilarated. "I think we've actually got something here," I said, glancing at the chaotic spread before us.

"More than something," Marcus corrected, his eyes shining with excitement. "This could be something exceptional. And to think, it all started with a disagreement."

"Who knew that fighting could lead to this?" I replied, feigning seriousness. "Maybe we should argue more often."

He chuckled, his laughter a warm sound that wrapped around me like a soft blanket. "Only if it leads to more late-night brainstorming sessions. I can live with that."

Just then, my phone buzzed on the table, its screen lighting up with a notification. I glanced at it and frowned. "It's my mom. She wants to know how the project is going," I said, my mood dipping slightly. "I haven't updated her since last week."

"Why not tell her you're working with a talented partner?" Marcus quipped, winking. "A little bragging never hurt anyone."

I rolled my eyes but felt a warmth bloom in my chest at his playful challenge. "Okay, I'll send her a message. Just don't expect me to share any details about your questionable spreadsheet skills."

"Hey, my spreadsheets are a work of art!" he protested, feigning indignation. "You just don't appreciate fine art."

With a grin, I picked up my phone and typed a quick response to my mom, letting her know that the project was progressing well. As I hit send, I caught Marcus watching me, a hint of something unspoken in his gaze. It sent a little thrill racing through me, a pulse of potential energy that sparked between us.

"Emma," he said softly, breaking the momentary silence. "I'm really glad we talked. You mean a lot to me, you know?"

My heart raced at his words, and I could feel the flush creeping up my cheeks. "You too, Marcus. I just... I want us to be able to navigate this together."

He stepped closer, and for a heartbeat, I thought he might reach out and take my hand. Instead, he ran a hand through his hair, a habit I found endearing. "I think we're more than capable of handling whatever comes our way. Just promise me we'll keep the lines of communication open."

"I promise," I said, feeling the sincerity in my own voice.

But as I looked into his eyes, I couldn't shake the feeling that this new chapter was just the beginning of something far more complicated than either of us anticipated.

The atmosphere shifted as Marcus and I stood there, unspoken words hanging like the rain that continued to patter against the window. I could feel the weight of the conversation pressing down on us, but the moment held a kind of promise that made my heart race. We were on the brink of something, a new understanding, perhaps even a deeper connection, but the uncertainty loomed as heavy as the clouds outside.

"Let's make a pact," Marcus said suddenly, breaking the spell. "No more letting the pressure of this project make us lose sight of what we enjoy. We need to keep the fun alive, even if we're analyzing the most serious literary themes."

"Agreed," I replied, feeling the tension start to dissipate. "But what does that look like in practice? Because right now, it feels like we're wading through molasses."

Marcus leaned against the counter, a thoughtful look on his face. "How about we set up a reward system? For every milestone we hit, we treat ourselves. Pizza, a movie, maybe even a spontaneous road trip."

"Spontaneous road trip?" I laughed, my skepticism slipping through. "What are we, a pair of college kids looking for adventure?"

"Why not?" He grinned, that signature twinkle lighting up his eyes. "What's life without a little adventure? Besides, I think you could use a break from the seriousness."

"Alright, I'm in," I said, feeling a spark of excitement. "But I want the pizza first. You know how I am with food; I don't do well without sustenance."

"Deal," he said, extending his hand with a grin, and as I took it, I felt an electric jolt that made my pulse quicken. It was just a handshake, but in that moment, it felt like a promise—an unspoken agreement that we were embarking on something more than just a project.

We spent the next hour diving back into our ideas, laughing over our contrasting visions for the analysis. The initial tension gave way to a comfortable rhythm as we bounced thoughts off each other, our creative energy weaving a tapestry of possibilities. It was exhilarating, like discovering a hidden trail that led to a breathtaking view.

"Okay, so how about we take the protagonist's journey and draw parallels to our own lives?" I suggested, leaning forward in my chair, enthusiasm bubbling up. "We could analyze how personal experiences shape character development and explore those themes through our research."

"Now you're talking," he replied, nodding vigorously. "And we can include those interviews you did with the authors last summer. It'll add depth and authenticity to our analysis."

"Perfect! Let's brainstorm some interview quotes that could fit."

We lost ourselves in the conversation, ideas tumbling out faster than I could jot them down. The hours melted away, the only interruptions being the sound of rain drumming against the windows and the occasional pause for a slice of cold pizza.

But just as the creative flow reached a zenith, my phone buzzed, a sharp reminder of the world outside our bubble. I glanced down to see a text from my mother: "Just checking in! How's the project? Let me know when you're free to talk."

"Is that the mom-check-in?" Marcus teased, stealing a slice of my pizza. "How many updates has she demanded today?"

"Just the usual," I replied, rolling my eyes playfully. "You'd think she's waiting for a royal decree. But honestly, I should probably respond before she sends out a search party."

"Tell her you've found your creative muse," he suggested with a mock-serious expression. "She'll love that."

I laughed, shaking my head at his antics. "You've been a huge help, but I don't know if 'muse' is quite the right word. More like 'project partner in crime.'"

"Ah, but crime pays!" he shot back with a wink, and just like that, my heart fluttered. I was beginning to realize how much I enjoyed our banter—how much I enjoyed him.

With a deep breath, I typed a quick message back, assuring my mother that all was well and that I was buried in project work. The moment I hit send, I glanced back at Marcus, whose gaze was fixed on me, a hint of something deeper flickering in his expression.

"Hey, can I ask you something?" he said, his tone shifting slightly.

"Sure," I replied, curiosity piqued.

"What's your favorite book?" he asked, leaning forward, genuine interest shining through his eyes.

"Wow, going for the deep questions, are we?" I replied, my playful tone lingering. "That's like asking me to choose a favorite star in the sky. But if I had to pick, I'd say 'Pride and Prejudice.' It's witty, full of strong characters, and—let's be honest—who doesn't love a good enemies-to-lovers story?"

Marcus raised an eyebrow, a smirk playing on his lips. "So, you're saying you're waiting for a handsome, brooding gentleman to sweep you off your feet?"

"Something like that," I replied, a playful challenge sparking in my eyes. "But I'd prefer he not be an insufferable know-it-all."

"Noted," he said, his voice low, the moment stretching between us. "How about I try to be the anti-insufferable know-it-all?"

We both laughed, but as the laughter faded, I felt the weight of his gaze pressing against me. The playful atmosphere shifted again, charged with something unspoken.

The doorbell rang suddenly, slicing through the moment like a knife. I jumped, surprised, and we exchanged glances, both of us caught off guard. Who could it be at this hour?

"Expecting someone?" Marcus asked, glancing toward the door, uncertainty creeping into his voice.

"No, not at all," I admitted, my heart racing as I moved toward the door. "It's probably just one of my neighbors."

I opened the door cautiously, and my breath hitched at the sight of a familiar figure. Standing there, soaked to the bone and looking both frustrated and apprehensive, was Tyler, the guy from my literature class. He wasn't just a passing acquaintance—he had been a thorn in my side, always challenging my opinions with a smirk and a devil-may-care attitude.

"Hey, Emma," he said, a forced smile plastered on his face. "I need your help with something. Can I come in?"

I hesitated, glancing back at Marcus, who looked equally surprised and intrigued. Tyler's presence felt like a storm cloud had rolled in, darkening the light we had just started to cultivate between us.

"Uh, sure," I finally managed, stepping aside. "What's going on?"

As Tyler stepped in, I caught Marcus's eye, and the moment was heavy with unspoken questions. The tension in the room shifted once more, pulling at the threads of our fragile connection. What was Tyler's sudden urgency about, and how would it affect the momentum we'd built just moments before?

Tyler looked between us, his brow furrowing slightly, as if he could sense the underlying tension. "I just... I really need your insight on something for my paper. It's kind of important."

"Right now?" I asked, glancing at the clock. "It's pretty late."

He nodded, anxiety flickering across his face. "I know. But it's about the upcoming presentation, and I'm in a bit of a bind."

Marcus cleared his throat, crossing his arms. "This is our time, Tyler. Maybe you should have thought of that before showing up unannounced."

Tyler met Marcus's gaze, the tension thickening like fog. "I get that, but it's really crucial. Emma, I wouldn't ask if it wasn't important."

I felt the pull of loyalty to both of them as the weight of their expectations pressed down on me. "Alright, let's hear what you need, but I can't promise anything," I said, my voice steady despite the whirlwind in my mind.

Marcus stepped back slightly, the playful spark between us dimming under the shadow of this unexpected interruption. "Fine," he muttered, leaning against the counter, his expression a mix of frustration and resignation.

As Tyler launched into his problem, the weight of the moment shifted, leaving me suspended between the two—a path diverging beneath my feet, and I couldn't help but wonder which direction I truly wanted to follow.

Chapter 7: The Ripple Effect

Every morning, I enter the faculty lounge like a soldier heading into battle. The aroma of burnt coffee clings to the air, mingling with the hushed voices and the clatter of plastic cutlery on trays. It's a sanctuary for gossip, a place where the walls seem to absorb every secret shared over stale muffins. I position myself at my usual table, a well-worn wooden slab that has seen more than its fair share of caffeinated debates and personal revelations. Today, I busy myself with a stack of papers, my red pen poised for the inevitable.

It's hard to focus when the whispers swirl around me like a pesky fly that refuses to be swatted away. I catch snippets of conversation—a chuckle here, a knowing glance there—as colleagues speculate about my rivalry with Marcus. It's infuriatingly captivating, like watching a train wreck you can't look away from. "Have you seen the way they argue?" one teacher whispers to another, barely masking the excitement in her voice. "You'd think there was more to it than just professional disagreement." I glance up, meeting the inquisitive eyes of my friend Sarah. She raises an eyebrow, and I can feel the unspoken questions hanging between us like the tension before a summer storm.

I suppress a sigh, turning my attention back to the disorganized pile of essays before me. Each paper tells a story, but today, they blur into a sea of words, their messages drowned out by the incessant buzz around Marcus and me. Our disagreements had begun innocently enough—discussions about curriculum changes or grading policies. But somewhere along the way, they morphed into a theatrical performance, with Vera pulling strings from the shadows, stoking the flames of our rivalry. The woman has a talent for drama, which she often channels into her daily interventions, nudging Marcus toward decisions that only widen the chasm between us.

I run my fingers through my hair, feeling the stress weave its way into my scalp. Why does Vera insist on placing herself in the middle of our discussions? It's almost as if she thrives on our discord, savoring the tension like a fine wine. "You know," Sarah says, breaking my reverie, "Vera's trying to make a spectacle of you two. It's like she's got front-row seats to a reality show." I chuckle despite myself, the tension in my chest easing slightly. "If only it were entertaining enough to warrant a viewing," I reply, my tone laced with sarcasm.

As the weeks trudge on, the pressure intensifies. I find myself glancing around the faculty lounge, searching for Marcus. There's a thrill in our battles—a strange electricity that ignites when our opinions clash. It's unsettling yet exhilarating, a dance I can't seem to resist. But as I settle into the routine of avoiding him, I can't help but feel like I'm missing something. The sparks we once ignited seem more like embers now, smothered by a growing distance that neither of us knows how to bridge.

Then comes a day that shifts everything—a professional development workshop. The notice had arrived in our inboxes with the promise of collaboration and innovative strategies, but all I see is an opportunity to further engage with Marcus. My heart races at the thought. I could face him directly, challenge him, and perhaps, just perhaps, reignite the fire that had sparked our rivalry in the first place.

The day of the workshop arrives, and I enter the auditorium filled with a sense of foreboding. It's a cavernous space with bright fluorescent lights buzzing above, the air thick with anticipation. Teachers mill about, clutching lanyards and coffee cups, exchanging small talk. I catch Marcus across the room, his tall frame silhouetted against the bright windows. He looks deep in conversation with Vera, who gestures animatedly, the sparkle in her eye a clear indication of her intentions. I shake my head, a mix of amusement and exasperation coursing through me.

As the workshop begins, I sit at the edge of my seat, my pulse quickening. The facilitator discusses innovative teaching methods, the spotlight bouncing between teachers as they share their experiences. But as the chatter swells, my focus narrows to Marcus. His brow furrows in thought, and I can't help but admire the intensity he brings to every discussion. When he speaks, the room quiets, his voice rich and deep, carrying an authority that draws everyone in. It's infuriating how charming he can be when he isn't on the opposite side of a debate.

Eventually, the facilitator divides us into groups for brainstorming sessions, and I find myself paired with Marcus. My stomach flips—half dread, half excitement. The atmosphere crackles as we exchange pleasantries, the unspoken tension coiling between us like a tightly wound spring. We dive into the topic, and I can feel the familiar spark igniting. Our conversation flows, punctuated by sharp wit and playful banter, a familiar rhythm that feels both exhilarating and maddening.

"You know, for someone who's supposed to be a rival, you're not half bad at this collaboration thing," he teases, a smirk playing on his lips.

I roll my eyes, fighting back a smile. "Don't get too comfortable. I still plan to outshine you in every way possible."

We work tirelessly, tossing ideas back and forth like a game of ping pong, the air thick with creativity. But as the clock ticks down, the discussion shifts. I notice Vera hovering nearby, her gaze sharp, as if assessing whether her machinations are still at play. The realization strikes me; she's been pulling strings, orchestrating our encounters to maintain the façade of a rivalry while also isolating Marcus.

In a moment of clarity, I challenge Marcus directly. "Why do you let her control the narrative? You don't need to hide behind this façade. If anything, it's just making you look weak."

He falters, the edge of his mouth twitching downward. "Maybe I enjoy the chaos," he retorts, a hint of vulnerability creeping into his tone.

"Or maybe you're afraid of what lies beyond this rivalry," I reply, surprised by my own audacity. The moment hangs in the air, thick with tension, a silent acknowledgment of the truth we've both skirted around.

A flicker of something passes through his eyes—surprise, perhaps, mixed with a dash of admiration. "You might be onto something," he finally admits, and I can't help but feel the shift. The dynamic is changing, the water rippling, and for the first time, I sense an opportunity to breach the walls we've both carefully constructed.

The workshop concludes, and the faculty members disperse, but the electric charge between us remains. As I watch him walk away, the weight of our unspoken connection lingers, leaving me breathless and yearning for more.

The weeks slip by like grains of sand through my fingers, each day feeling more monotonous than the last. The faculty lounge, once a sanctuary of camaraderie and laughter, now feels like a cauldron of speculation. I watch the whispers ripple through the room, colleagues leaning in closer, their voices lowered conspiratorially. "It's just a matter of time before they end up together," one teacher whispers, her gaze darting in my direction. I can almost hear the collective sighs of those who relish the idea of a dramatic romance blooming amid the tension.

I hide behind my stack of essays, using the red ink on the papers as both a shield and a distraction. Each scribbled comment feels like an excuse to remain detached from the scrutiny swirling around me. I long for the day when Marcus and I can engage in a battle of wits without the added weight of judgment from our peers. The irony is not lost on me; we started out as mere colleagues with differing opinions, yet somehow we've morphed into this tangled web of fascination and friction.

As I sit there, absorbing the atmosphere of the lounge, my gaze drifts toward Marcus. He's at the coffee station, pouring a cup of that wretched brew that could easily be mistaken for tar. A familiar tension coils in my stomach as I watch him interact with Vera. Her laughter, sharp and too bright, rings out like a bell, cutting through the noise. It annoys me how effortlessly she seems to maneuver around him, like a chess player anticipating every move.

The way Marcus leans into her, engaging with enthusiasm, gnaws at me. I push down the bitterness that rises like bile in my throat. What is it about this dynamic that irritates me so? I want him to succeed, but not at the expense of our rivalry. "I should've thrown a coffee cup at him," I mutter to myself, earning an odd look from Sarah, who's seated across the table, her brow arched in amused disbelief.

"You might want to reserve that for your next heated debate," she replies, stifling a giggle. "But seriously, are you okay? You look like you're about to spontaneously combust."

I force a smile, but inside, I'm unraveling. The lingering feelings I thought I had buried start to rise like a poorly timed wave. The intensity of our exchanges, the way he challenges my intellect, feels like a drug I can't shake. I want to hate him, to fuel the fire of our rivalry until it burns out completely, but instead, I'm drawn to him, grappling with the allure that pulls me into his orbit.

After a particularly exhausting day, I find myself lingering in the empty classroom after the last bell has rung. The silence is almost deafening, punctuated only by the faint echo of students' laughter fading down the hallway. My eyes wander to the bulletin board, covered with flyers for various school events and club meetings.

Among the chaos, a flyer catches my attention—a weekend retreat for faculty members, a chance to engage in team-building exercises and discussions away from the watchful eyes of the students.

With a mix of excitement and dread, I jot down the details. As much as I want to avoid anything that could force me into close quarters with Marcus, the opportunity feels too good to pass up. Maybe it could break the tension, or at least give us a chance to confront our rivalry on neutral ground. Besides, the idea of fresh air and an escape from the rumor mill holds a certain allure.

The day of the retreat arrives, the sun spilling its golden rays across the parking lot as I pull up to the rustic lodge nestled in the woods. The scent of pine and earth fills the air, mingling with the anticipation that hangs like a veil over the gathering of faculty. As we file into the lodge, laughter and chatter ripple through the group, and I can't help but feel a twinge of excitement. This could be a reset, a chance to redefine our dynamic without the prying eyes of the school community.

Once inside, I'm met with an array of cozy seating areas, the smell of coffee brewing in the background. I find a seat near the fireplace, settling into the plush armchair with a cup of steaming coffee in hand. The warmth of the fire seeps into my bones, but I can't shake the sensation of unease as I spot Marcus across the room, engaging with a small group of teachers. His animated gestures and laughter slice through the air, pulling me in despite myself.

Moments later, Vera flits by, her laughter ringing out again, and I roll my eyes so hard I almost lose my balance in the chair. This woman has an uncanny ability to insert herself where she's least wanted, like glitter in a craft project. Just as I'm about to bury my thoughts in my coffee, Marcus saunters over, that cocky grin on his face, a mischievous glint in his eyes.

"Trying to escape the chaos?" he teases, leaning against the mantel with an air of casual confidence. "I hear Vera's been gathering the troops for a game of 'Guess Who's More Important.'"

I can't help but laugh, the tension between us easing slightly. "I'd rather face a horde of angry students than play that game," I reply, a teasing smile forming on my lips.

"True, but there's something entertaining about watching her wield power like a sword," he muses, his tone wry. "It's like watching a toddler with a stick—adorably dangerous."

"Don't underestimate the stick. It's been known to take out a few unsuspecting teachers," I shoot back, and the laughter bubbles up between us, a rare and welcome sound.

For a moment, we share a genuine connection, and the competitive edge that usually colors our conversations takes a backseat. Just as I think we might break through the tension, Vera appears, flitting between us like a dragonfly. "Oh, there you are! I was just telling everyone how you two would be the perfect duo for our team-building activities!" Her eyes sparkle with mischief, and I can feel Marcus stiffen beside me.

"Great," I deadpan, shooting Marcus a sidelong glance. "I was hoping to avoid becoming a team with my number one rival."

"Don't worry, I'll go easy on you," he says with mock seriousness, the corners of his mouth twitching upward. The playful banter rolls off his tongue effortlessly, and I can't help but find myself drawn in again, even as Vera's presence threatens to dampen the moment.

"Now, now, no bickering," she chides, her smile saccharine and sweet. "Let's see what you can do together. We'll start with a little icebreaker, shall we?"

With that, she leads us away from the warmth of the fire into a more open space, leaving behind the flickering light and warmth. I glance at Marcus, his expression a mix of amusement and resignation, and for the first time, I wonder if he might actually be enjoying this as much as I am. The thought sends a thrill through me, one that dances tantalizingly close to hope.

The icebreaker is a flurry of chaos. Vera claps her hands together, her enthusiasm infectious, as she divides us into groups, seemingly oblivious to the fact that I'm clenching my coffee cup like it's the last bastion of sanity in this wild ride. Marcus and I are tossed together, much to my chagrin, and I can feel the weight of the world pressing on my shoulders. It's as if fate has conspired to keep us locked in this dance of tension and unresolved feelings.

"Alright, everyone," Vera announces, her voice brimming with false cheer, "let's play a game of 'Two Truths and a Lie!'"

I can practically hear the collective groan from the gathered faculty. A game designed for trust-building and bonding, but all I see is another chance for Marcus to showcase his charm and wit. The idea of sharing personal truths feels like being thrust into the spotlight, with all my quirks laid bare for him and our colleagues to dissect. I shoot Marcus a look, half pleading and half playful. He smirks in return, the mischievous glint in his eyes hinting at some kind of plot brewing behind that perfectly tousled hair of his.

"Ladies first," he says, leaning in slightly as if to lend me his ear. The playful banter feels almost natural, yet the intensity in his gaze sends a jolt through me.

"Fine," I concede, clearing my throat to suppress the flutter of nerves in my stomach. "I once swam with sharks, I can juggle flaming torches, and I have a pet tarantula named Fred."

"Fred, huh?" Marcus raises an eyebrow, a smirk dancing on his lips. "I'd guess the tarantula is a lie. I mean, who names their pet Fred?"

"Only the bravest of souls," I shoot back, a grin breaking through my facade.

He chuckles, the sound warm and rich, almost like a melody beneath the droning atmosphere of the room. "No, I'm pretty sure the shark thing is your lie. Because who would willingly put themselves in the ocean with those beasts?"

I raise my chin defiantly. "You'd be surprised what lengths I'll go to for adventure, Mr. Rival."

Vera chimes in, her voice slicing through our back-and-forth. "Well, I suppose we'll have to wait and see what the truth is. Marcus, your turn!"

He leans back, crossing his arms with an air of calculated confidence. "Alright, here goes: I've bungee jumped off a cliff, I've met a celebrity, and I once tried to cook a meal and set my kitchen on fire."

I smirk, unable to resist the urge to tease him. "Let me guess, you burned your house down while trying to impress a celebrity?"

His laugh echoes, deep and genuine. "Well, one can hope, but sadly, it was just my poor attempts at pasta that caused the kitchen disaster."

"Pasta can be dangerous," I reply, feigning seriousness. "I once nearly lost a finger trying to peel an onion."

The laughter rolls around the room, creating a small bubble of warmth that almost feels safe, even as I can sense Vera's eyes watching us closely, her interest piqued. But that warmth dissipates quickly as the game moves on, and the reality of our surroundings settles in again. The tension doesn't entirely vanish; it just simmers beneath the surface, waiting for the right moment to erupt.

As the game wraps up, we're asked to gather in a circle for a group discussion. I feel a strange mix of excitement and dread. Vera hovers nearby, a hawk watching her prey, her interest clearly piqued by the chemistry developing between Marcus and me.

"Let's talk about what we've learned," she suggests, clasping her hands. "What insights did you gain about teamwork and collaboration?"

Before I can stop myself, my hand shoots up, spurred by a sudden rush of boldness. "I learned that sometimes, rivals can make the best partners," I declare, my eyes flickering toward Marcus. He meets my gaze, a surprise dancing in his expression, and for a heartbeat, the world around us blurs into insignificance.

Vera's smile tightens, a hint of displeasure creeping into her demeanor. "That's an interesting perspective," she says, her tone dripping with sweetness that feels anything but genuine. "And Marcus, do you have anything to add?"

Marcus leans forward, his expression turning serious. "I've learned that sometimes the most unexpected alliances can lead to the most creative solutions." His gaze sweeps over the group before landing back on me, and the tension crackles like static electricity.

As we continue to share our thoughts, I find myself leaning into the moment, my earlier fears dissipating. This is what I've missed—a connection that feels raw and electric, filled with possibility. Each shared laugh and each exchange of glances ignites something deep within me. Yet, as we settle into a rhythm, I can't shake the feeling that Vera is watching us with an intensity that borders on predatory.

Suddenly, a loud crash echoes from the back of the room, a heavy thud that jolts everyone from our discussion. A large banner that had been hanging loosely on the wall tumbles down, crashing to the ground with an alarming clatter. The laughter and conversation halt abruptly, replaced by gasps and murmurs of surprise.

Marcus stands, instinctively moving toward the noise, and I follow closely behind. As we reach the banner, I spot it—an overturned table, papers strewn everywhere, and at the center of the chaos is one of our newer faculty members, Claire, kneeling on the floor, her face a mask of embarrassment.

"I'm so sorry!" she exclaims, cheeks flushed crimson. "I didn't mean to—"

Vera swoops in like a bird of prey, cutting off Claire mid-sentence. "What were you thinking, Claire? This is a professional retreat, not a playground!" Her voice drips with condescension, her eyes narrowing.

The tension in the room thickens, a heavy weight pressing down on us all. I glance at Marcus, whose expression darkens, a flicker of anger flashing across his features. "It was an accident, Vera," he replies, his tone firm. "No one was hurt, and accidents happen. Let's focus on how we can help Claire instead of tearing her down."

For a moment, there's silence. It feels as though time has frozen, all eyes darting between Marcus and Vera. Then, just as quickly, the atmosphere shifts. Vera's lips curl into a smile that's anything but warm. "How noble of you, Marcus. But don't let your compassion blind you. There's a reason we have rules in place."

I step forward, my heart racing. "Maybe the rules should allow for a little humanity," I add, the fire in my belly igniting.

But Vera turns her gaze toward me, sharp and calculating. "And perhaps you should know your place, dear. After all, not every rivalry ends in a fairy tale."

Her words hang in the air, thick with implication. The laughter that had moments ago warmed the room fades into an uncomfortable silence, and I feel the eyes of my colleagues on me, judgment hanging like fog. I glance at Marcus, and the unspoken connection we had forged moments before feels fragile, almost shattered.

Suddenly, the door to the lodge bursts open, a gust of wind sweeping through, carrying with it a sense of urgency. In strides the principal, breathless and wide-eyed. "There's been an emergency! We need everyone to gather immediately!"

A chill runs down my spine, the tension coiling tighter than ever. I meet Marcus's gaze, both of us sensing that something far beyond our petty rivalry is brewing. As we file out of the room, I can't shake the feeling that our carefully constructed world is on the brink of upheaval, and the ripple effects of our actions are just beginning to surface.

Chapter 8: The Night of Reckoning

The door creaked open, revealing Marcus with his tousled hair and a hint of confusion in his dark eyes, as though I'd just interrupted a deep thought. His flannel shirt hung casually over his lean frame, and the faint scent of coffee wafted through the air, mixing with the warm, lingering aroma of books and old wood that permeated his apartment. In that moment, the world around us faded into a blur, leaving only the charged space between our bodies, filled with unspoken words and an undeniable tension that had been brewing for far too long.

"Hey," he said, the casualness of his greeting not quite matching the weight of the moment. I felt the pull of a thousand unsaid things, each one heavier than the last, as I stepped over the threshold.

"Hey," I echoed, my voice barely a whisper, as if I were afraid that speaking too loudly would shatter the delicate balance between us. The dim light in the room cast shadows that danced across the walls, and I was suddenly acutely aware of every detail—the way his bookshelf sagged slightly under the weight of countless tomes, the scattered papers that hinted at late nights spent cramming for exams, the single, lone plant in the corner that seemed to flourish despite his apparent neglect.

We stood there, the silence stretching between us like an elastic band, taut and ready to snap. I took a breath, feeling the warmth of his presence enveloping me, a mix of comfort and chaos. "We need to talk," I finally managed, my heart racing as I took a step closer, emboldened by the urgency in my chest.

"Yeah, we do," he replied, running a hand through his hair, a familiar gesture that sent a shiver of recognition through me. "I thought we were just going to finish the project."

"Project?" I scoffed lightly, my voice edged with sarcasm. "You mean the facade we've been hiding behind for weeks? Because I'm starting to think that's not all there is between us." My heart thundered in my chest as I met his gaze, and for a fleeting moment, I hoped to see something reflected back that mirrored my own emotions—confusion, frustration, and an underlying current of longing.

Marcus shifted, the tension in his shoulders easing slightly as he stepped further into the room, closing the door behind us. "You're right," he admitted, his voice low and steady, sending a thrill through me. "This project is just a distraction, isn't it? We both know there's more to it."

There it was, the acknowledgment that we'd both been dancing around like two wary wolves circling one another in the moonlight. The rivalry, once a bitter seasoning to our collaboration, had somehow morphed into something far more complicated and tantalizing.

"Why do we keep pretending?" I asked, my voice barely a whisper. "Why do we keep pushing each other away when it feels like..." I hesitated, searching for the right words, "when it feels like we could be so much more?"

He stepped closer, and I could see the gears turning in his mind, the way his eyes sparkled with a mix of surprise and something deeper. "Because I'm terrified," he confessed, his honesty disarming me. "Terrified that if we go down that road, we might ruin everything we've built."

"Or maybe we could build something even better," I challenged, emboldened by the fire in my veins. "We've spent so long fighting each other, pushing buttons, and throwing insults like they were confetti at a parade. What if we just stopped?"

The air between us thickened, each word hanging like a fragile ornament on the tree of our friendship, trembling at the prospect of being plucked. I could feel my pulse quickening, the space between us shrinking with every breath, every heartbeat, drawing me closer to the precipice of something I had only dared to imagine.

"I don't want to lose you," he murmured, his voice softer now, almost vulnerable. "You mean too much to me."

His admission sent a surge of warmth through me, igniting the embers of hope I had buried beneath layers of rivalry and misunderstandings. "You mean a lot to me too, Marcus," I admitted, my words spilling out like a floodgate opening. "You have this way of challenging me, pushing me to be better, even when it drives me crazy. And maybe... maybe I like it more than I should."

He paused, uncertainty flickering across his face, as if my words were a foreign language he was just beginning to comprehend. "So what do we do with that?"

A challenge laced his tone, and I couldn't help but smile—a genuine, unrestrained smile that broke through the tension, lighting up the dark corners of the room. "Well, we could start by being honest," I suggested, feeling a sudden rush of courage. "Maybe we could figure out how to navigate this... whatever it is that's happening between us."

"Honesty? Now that sounds dangerous," he shot back, his lips curving into a playful grin that sent butterflies flitting through my stomach. "But I'm all for danger if it involves you."

I stepped even closer, heart racing, emboldened by the electricity crackling in the air between us. "So, what do you say we embrace the chaos?"

His laughter echoed softly in the room, a beautiful sound that broke through the last remnants of doubt. "I think I could get on board with that."

With that, I felt the walls around us begin to dissolve, replaced by a budding connection that promised to be as tumultuous as it was thrilling. It was terrifying and exhilarating all at once, and as I stood there, looking into his eyes, I knew that whatever happened next would be a reckoning of our own making, one I was finally ready to embrace.

A palpable silence filled the room, wrapping around us like a soft blanket, yet it crackled with an undercurrent of electricity that made my heart race. The moment hung suspended, each second stretching out, charged with the weight of unspoken truths. I could see the conflict in Marcus's eyes, the way he shifted slightly, as if caught between the desire to step closer and the instinct to retreat into the safety of old patterns.

"Are we really going to do this?" he asked, his voice a low murmur, laced with both anticipation and apprehension.

"Why not?" I challenged, tilting my head slightly, a teasing smile dancing on my lips. "We've already mastered the art of tension. How hard can honesty be?"

His lips quirked up at the corners, the tension breaking just a fraction as he regarded me with an intensity that made me feel both exhilarated and utterly vulnerable. "You might regret that statement. Honesty is a slippery slope. One minute you're sharing your favorite pizza topping, and the next, you're exposing your deep-seated fears and feelings."

"Do you think I'm afraid of pizza toppings?" I shot back, my laughter lightening the moment. "No, I'm much more terrified of how you make me feel."

His smile faded slightly as he stepped closer, the distance between us shrinking with each word. "And how do I make you feel?"

I bit my lip, torn between playful banter and the need for something deeper. "Like I'm about to dive into an ice-cold lake in mid-February. Refreshing, shocking, and completely unavoidable."

"Unavoidable, huh?" he mused, his brow arching in mock disbelief. "That's a bit melodramatic, don't you think? I'm just a guy with an unfortunate love for calculus and a really bad flannel shirt collection."

"Don't underestimate the power of a flannel shirt," I countered, gesturing toward his chest. "It can hide a multitude of sins—like lack of fashion sense and those deeply buried romantic feelings."

He chuckled softly, the sound a gentle rumble that sent a thrill through me. "And here I thought I was being subtle."

"Subtle as a freight train," I shot back, emboldened by the growing ease between us. "The moment you called me 'the queen of chaos' during that group presentation, I knew you were hiding something behind that smug smile."

"Okay, fine," he relented, his hands raised in mock surrender. "Guilty as charged. But you know, in the world of competitive projects, one must maintain a level of mystery."

"Mystery?" I echoed, raising an eyebrow. "You're as mysterious as a well-lit bathroom at noon. It's hard to hide anything when you're practically an open book."

He leaned against the wall, arms crossed, his gaze unwavering. "Then let's flip the pages, shall we? What do you want to know?"

In that moment, the air shifted, thickening with the weight of possibility. "Tell me about the last time you were really happy," I prompted, curiosity bubbling to the surface.

Marcus paused, his expression softening as he considered my question. "That's a loaded one," he admitted, his voice dropping to a whisper. "But if I had to pick a moment... it would be the time I went camping with my dad last summer. We spent hours just talking around the campfire, sharing stories and laughing until we cried. It was simple, but it felt perfect."

The sincerity in his voice struck a chord within me, and I couldn't help but smile. "That sounds incredible. Why don't you let that guy out more often? The guy who laughs, who shares his stories."

He shrugged, an endearing sheepishness creeping into his demeanor. "Because it's easier to be the guy with the snappy comebacks than to risk showing any real vulnerability. You know that feeling, right? Being seen... fully?"

"Yeah," I said softly, my own vulnerability creeping to the surface. "But isn't it worth it? To let someone in? To take the risk?"

He nodded slowly, the gravity of our conversation settling between us. "I think it is. But you have to understand that I've built walls for a reason. It's safer on this side."

"Safe is boring," I countered, stepping closer, a spark igniting between us. "And I'm not one for boring."

"Then let's take a leap," he said, suddenly serious, his eyes locking onto mine. "Let's tear down the walls."

The air shifted again, charged with the promise of something deeper, something that felt like the edge of a precipice. "Are you sure?" I asked, my voice trembling slightly with anticipation.

"I've never been more sure of anything," he replied, the intensity in his gaze sending a thrill down my spine. "But it's not just about tearing down walls. It's about building something new together."

I swallowed hard, the weight of his words settling in. "Together?"

"Together," he affirmed, reaching out to brush a strand of hair behind my ear. The simple gesture sent a wave of warmth flooding through me, and I knew in that moment that the path we were stepping onto was uncharted and exhilarating.

But before I could respond, the unmistakable sound of a phone ringing shattered the moment, vibrating on the table beside him. Marcus's face fell, irritation flashing across his features as he glanced at the screen. "It's my brother," he muttered, reaching for the phone. "He never calls unless it's important."

I felt an unwelcome pang of disappointment, the intensity of the moment dissipating like fog in the sunlight. "You should answer it."

"Yeah, but—"

"No 'buts.' Family first," I insisted, forcing a smile, even as I felt the thrill of connection slipping through my fingers. "I can wait."

He hesitated but finally picked up, his tone shifting as he answered, "Hey, what's up?"

While he spoke, I turned my attention to the vibrant cityscape visible through the window, the lights twinkling like stars scattered across an indigo canvas. In that moment, I felt the stirrings of something beautiful, fragile yet bold, slipping just out of reach.

Marcus's voice pulled me back to the present. "Yeah, I can come by. Give me ten minutes."

He ended the call, his expression a mix of frustration and resignation. "Sorry, I need to go. Family emergency."

"Of course," I replied, trying to mask my disappointment. "You should take care of that."

As he gathered his things, I felt the weight of unsaid words lingering in the air between us, an unfinished symphony that hung tantalizingly on the edge of completion. "This isn't over," I promised, my gaze steady on his.

"No," he said, his eyes sparkling with determination. "It's just the beginning."

With one last lingering glance, he slipped out of the door, leaving me in a whirlpool of anticipation and yearning, the flicker of possibility igniting a fire that would not be easily extinguished.

As the door clicked shut behind Marcus, the lingering warmth of his presence slowly evaporated, leaving me alone in the dimly lit apartment. The sudden silence felt heavy, as if the walls were closing in on me, swallowing the vibrant energy that had filled the space just moments before. I stood still for a moment, replaying the intensity of our conversation in my mind, the electric pull between us still humming in the air.

I sank onto the couch, my fingers absently tracing the worn fabric, a remnant of late-night study sessions and lazy afternoons spent daydreaming. It was hard to shake the sense that our moment had been more than just a simple confession; it had been a stepping stone, a promise of something more, and the anticipation of what could be bubbled beneath the surface of my thoughts.

As the clock ticked softly on the wall, I was lost in contemplation when the unmistakable sound of footsteps outside my door broke the stillness. My heart quickened, half-expecting Marcus to reappear, but the footsteps faded away, leaving only the echo of my hopes. A sigh slipped past my lips as I pulled my phone from the coffee table, hoping to distract myself with social media or an email that required my attention.

But my fingers hovered over the screen, and I found myself staring blankly into space. The tension between us had unraveled something deep within me—a thread that tugged insistently, pulling me toward a desire I couldn't quite name. With a frustrated groan, I tossed my phone back onto the table, deciding instead to confront the swirling feelings head-on.

I glanced around my apartment, the chaos of books and half-finished projects seeming to mock my moment of clarity. If I was going to embrace this new chapter, I needed to be proactive. That meant diving headfirst into our project, and not just as a means to an end. I needed to immerse myself in the creative process. I grabbed my laptop and pulled up our shared document, determined to pour my energy into something tangible.

Just as I began typing, my phone buzzed, and I nearly jumped out of my skin. Glancing at the screen, I saw a message from Marcus: "Sorry about earlier. Can we meet tomorrow to talk? I need to see you." The butterflies that had settled uneasily in my stomach sprang back to life, dancing with excitement and apprehension.

With a rapid heart, I typed back: "Definitely. What time?" I hit send, and a rush of adrenaline surged through me. I hadn't realized how much I'd been anticipating this. A few moments later, the response popped up: "How about noon? My treat."

I grinned at the screen, a wave of warmth flooding through me. "How could I say no to a free lunch?" I muttered, my spirits lifting. I didn't know what tomorrow would bring, but the promise of seeing him again lit a spark of hope.

With renewed determination, I returned to the project, pouring my thoughts and ideas into the document with vigor. I lost track of time as I crafted our presentation, interlacing my creative energy with the emotional undercurrents we had begun to navigate. The clock chimed one in the morning before I finally pushed the laptop away, exhaustion creeping in, but a sense of fulfillment washing over me.

I stumbled into bed, thoughts of Marcus swirling in my mind like a kaleidoscope. Would he feel the same when we met again? Would our earlier honesty solidify into something more meaningful? Just as sleep began to claim me, my phone buzzed again. I groggily reached for it, squinting at the light.

Another message from Marcus: "Wait. I just realized something. My brother mentioned he saw you with that guy at the café. Who was he?"

My heart sank, a sudden chill racing down my spine. The "guy at the café" was Jason, a charming fellow who had taken an interest in me a few weeks back. It had been innocent enough—just coffee and conversation, nothing more. But the way Marcus phrased his question sent a ripple of unease through me.

"Just a friend," I typed back quickly, the words feeling inadequate.

A moment passed, and then another message came through: "Are you sure? Because I'd hate to think you're still trying to figure out what you want."

His words struck like a bolt of lightning. My mind raced, caught in a whirlwind of confusion and frustration. Did he really think I was still uncertain? That I might waver between him and someone else? I quickly typed a response: "I know what I want, Marcus."

A tense pause followed, and my anxiety climbed as I wondered how he would interpret my words. The clock ticked on, the darkness of the night wrapping around me like a shroud, and I felt as if I were teetering on the edge of a precipice, about to dive into the unknown.

Finally, my phone buzzed again: "I hope so. Because I'm not sure I can handle another surprise."

I stared at the screen, biting my lip. What did he mean by that? What surprise was he worried about? I set my phone down, my heart racing as the shadows in the room seemed to deepen.

Sleep eluded me, and I tossed and turned, my mind racing through all the possibilities. The underlying current of doubt began to seep in, as I pondered whether my past encounters could jeopardize what Marcus and I were trying to build.

As dawn broke, I finally drifted into a restless sleep, plagued by dreams of what-ifs and uncertainties. The sun streamed through the window, casting a golden hue across my apartment, and I jolted awake, the reality of our impending meeting pressing down on me.

I glanced at my phone; it was already nearing noon. Panic surged through me as I scrambled out of bed and rushed to get ready. My mind whirled with thoughts of what Marcus might say, how he might react to my earlier messages, and the question that lingered in the air: Was I ready to take the leap?

When I finally arrived at the café, my heart raced, anticipation buzzing through my veins. The familiar scent of coffee greeted me, and I took a moment to gather my thoughts. But as I pushed through the door, my breath caught in my throat.

Marcus sat at our usual table, his expression unreadable as he looked up, and beside him—Jason, that same charming smile plastered across his face. The sight of them together sent a wave of confusion crashing over me. Had Marcus brought him here to confront me?

"Hey, you made it!" Marcus greeted me with a warm smile, but the tension in the air was thick enough to cut with a knife. I stood frozen for a moment, my mind racing as I processed the unexpected twist unfolding before me.

"Uh...hi," I managed, my voice barely above a whisper, as my heart pounded in my chest, a whirlwind of emotions threatening to spill over.

Chapter 9: A Choice to Make

With the project finally wrapped up and the deadline creeping closer, the air in the studio crackled with a tension that felt almost electric. My mind raced, flitting between the triumph of completing the work and the nagging anxiety that clung to me like a heavy fog. It was the kind of tightrope walk where every decision could send us plummeting into chaos. I could sense Vera's presence even before she entered the room, her sharp heels clicking against the polished floor like a metronome counting down the seconds until our world tilted on its axis.

"Marcus," she began, her voice smooth as silk, yet laced with an undercurrent of ambition that was impossible to ignore. "You need to think about your future. There's an opportunity on the table—one that could catapult you into the literary stratosphere." She leaned closer, her words dripping with honeyed persuasion, as if she were offering him a taste of paradise just out of reach.

I glanced at Marcus, whose brow furrowed with uncertainty. The flicker in his eyes suggested he was torn, trapped between the tantalizing lure of success and the connection we had forged over late-night brainstorming sessions and stolen glances that lingered just a heartbeat too long. We had navigated through storms of ideas and sleepless nights, and now, just as we were starting to find our rhythm, the ground beneath us began to shake.

"I don't know, Vera," Marcus replied, his voice a mix of hesitance and intrigue. He stood there, tall and strong, his handsome features illuminated by the warm light streaming through the studio windows. I admired the way his hands moved as he spoke, punctuating his thoughts with an energy that drew me in. But today, that spark felt dimmed, like a candle flickering in the wind.

Vera leaned back, arms crossed, the corners of her lips curving into a smile that didn't quite reach her eyes. "This isn't just a book tour. It's exposure, Marcus. It's what you've been dreaming of since you first put pen to paper. Don't let your collaboration with... her," she gestured toward me dismissively, "hold you back. You could be a household name."

The sting of her words shot through me like ice water, chilling the warmth of our camaraderie. I knew she saw me as a mere stepping stone, a means to an end. My heart sank as I recognized the truth: our partnership could easily become a casualty of ambition. But that didn't diminish the bond Marcus and I had built. I refused to be the anchor that dragged him down.

"Is that what you really want?" I asked, my voice steady despite the turmoil within. "To chase after fame and recognition at the cost of our work together?" The question hung between us, a fragile thread threatening to snap under the weight of our emotions.

Marcus hesitated, his eyes darting between Vera and me, searching for the right words to express the storm brewing inside him. "I've worked so hard for this opportunity," he finally said, a hint of desperation creeping into his voice. "But I don't want to throw away what we've built, either."

The sincerity in his tone wrapped around my heart, squeezing it tightly. I couldn't bear the thought of being the reason he missed out on his dreams, yet the idea of losing what we shared felt like an unbearable weight.

"Then don't," I urged, stepping closer to him. "You don't have to choose between us. We can make this work." The warmth radiating from his body was intoxicating, a magnetic pull that made the chaos of the moment fade into the background. I could feel the pulse of possibility thrumming in the air around us, and it was exhilarating and terrifying all at once.

Vera rolled her eyes, clearly unimpressed. "This isn't some fairy tale where you can have your cake and eat it too. You need to make a choice, Marcus." Her voice cut through the tension like a knife, sharpening the moment into something razor-edged and urgent.

He turned to face me, his expression a mixture of determination and fear. "What if I can do both?" he asked, his gaze searching mine for a glimmer of hope. "What if I can go on this tour, and we can still collaborate? I don't want to abandon you or our project."

The sincerity in his eyes made my heart swell, but I knew the reality was far more complicated. I could see the path diverging before us, two roads stretching out into the unknown, each leading to its own set of consequences.

"I want you to succeed, Marcus," I said, my voice a whisper as I stepped even closer, allowing the space between us to dissolve. "But success without integrity isn't worth much. You have to decide what matters more to you—your dreams or our connection."

For a moment, silence enveloped us, a thick blanket of contemplation that pressed down on the air. The world outside the studio faded away, leaving just the three of us suspended in this moment of reckoning.

As Marcus stood there, caught between the conflicting forces of ambition and emotion, I realized we were at a crossroads. A choice lay before him—one that could shape the course of our lives forever. The gravity of the moment wrapped around us, and I couldn't help but wonder if our bond would weather the storm or become another casualty in the relentless pursuit of success.

As the silence enveloped us, a wave of uncertainty surged through the air, thick and palpable. Marcus shifted on his feet, an uncharacteristic nervousness dancing in his eyes. I watched, my heart pounding, as he wrestled with the weight of the decision ahead. The lines of his jaw tightened, and for a fleeting moment, I could almost see the gears turning in his mind, caught between the intoxicating allure of the world Vera was offering and the comforting familiarity of what we had built together.

"Can I just say, I hate it when people make me choose?" he finally blurted out, a half-hearted chuckle escaping his lips. The sound was light, but the underlying tension was undeniable. "It feels like choosing between chocolate cake and pie." He paused, furrowing his brow in mock concentration. "And you know how much I love dessert."

I couldn't help but laugh, the absurdity of the metaphor cutting through the tension. "So you'd prefer a buffet instead?" I quipped, hoping to lighten the moment. But beneath my humor lay a dread I couldn't shake. The reality was that, in this scenario, dessert wasn't the only thing at stake.

"Exactly! Who wouldn't want all the options?" His smile faded slightly, a flicker of seriousness crossing his features. "But, I mean, if I go on this tour, I'd be away for weeks, maybe even months. What does that mean for our project? For us?"

The questions hung between us, and I felt the urge to reach out, to reassure him that everything would be okay. Yet the words felt heavy, laden with a truth I wasn't sure I was ready to share. "It could mean everything, Marcus. Or nothing at all," I replied carefully, weighing my words. "We've built something special here, but you have to follow your dreams."

He raked a hand through his tousled hair, a gesture that was both familiar and heart-wrenching. "I never intended to lose what we have. You're not just a collaborator to me. You're...you're more than that."

His admission lingered in the air like a delicate promise. I held my breath, the warmth of his words washing over me, but even as my heart fluttered, the reality of the situation weighed down like an anchor. I wanted to scream at the universe for putting us in this position. It was cruel, forcing us to balance ambition against affection.

"I want you to have your cake, Marcus, but I'm terrified of being the one to push you away," I finally said, my voice barely above a whisper. The words slipped out, raw and unfiltered, as I clutched the edge of the table, grounding myself in the moment. "I don't want to be the reason you miss out on your dreams."

He took a step closer, the distance closing as he reached out to take my hand, his warmth enveloping me in an instant. "You're not. This is my choice to make. I just... I wish it didn't have to be this way." The sincerity in his gaze made my heart ache, yet the weight of our situation felt insurmountable.

Vera, watching our exchange with a smirk that was more condescending than congratulatory, cleared her throat. "Well, gentlemen, while you two play emotional tug-of-war, I have a book tour to finalize." She flicked her gaze toward Marcus, the sparkle of her ambition hardly dimmed. "Think of it as a once-in-a-lifetime chance. You don't want to miss it, do you?"

I could almost see her calculated approach, the way she wielded her influence like a weapon. The battle lines were drawn, and she was determined to win, regardless of the collateral damage.

"I don't know, Vera. Maybe..." Marcus hesitated, glancing between the two of us as if seeking a sign that might tip the scales one way or the other.

"Oh come on," she said, rolling her eyes dramatically. "What's life without a little risk? You're going to look back at this moment and either regret not taking the chance or thank yourself for seizing it." Her words were slick, polished to perfection, each one designed to echo in his mind long after she left the room.

"What if this is the only chance I get?" Marcus finally asked, a hint of desperation creeping into his voice. The fear was palpable, the uncertainty looming like a thundercloud ready to burst. "What if I turn down this opportunity and it never comes around again?"

I felt a pang in my chest as I recognized the truth of his words. This was a defining moment for him, and while I wanted to support him, I also couldn't shake the feeling that something deeper was at play. "You have to do what's best for you, Marcus," I said softly, squeezing his hand for reassurance. "Just promise me that whatever you choose, you'll think about us too. Our connection is real. I don't want to lose that."

"Yeah, I'm definitely not looking to lose anything," he said, a ghost of a smile flickering across his lips. "But... what if I could have both?"

I let out a breath I didn't know I was holding, the notion lighting a spark of hope within me. "Is that even possible?"

"Why not?" He turned toward Vera, his demeanor shifting as he squared his shoulders. "What if I took the tour but stayed connected with you? We could work together remotely—collaborate over video calls, share ideas. I don't want to abandon this project or you."

Vera's expression darkened slightly, the glint of ambition overshadowed by annoyance. "Marcus, you can't split your focus like that. You need to be fully committed to either the tour or the project. You can't have it both ways."

"Watch me," he replied, determination seeping into his tone. The fire in his eyes reignited, and I couldn't help but admire his resolve.

Vera's frustration was palpable, the tension in the room thickening like fog. "You're making a mistake," she warned, her voice low and almost threatening.

"I think I'm making the right choice," Marcus shot back, his gaze unwavering.

I felt a swell of pride as he stood his ground, a renewed sense of agency blooming between us. Perhaps this was the moment we had both needed—a chance to reclaim our narrative amidst the chaos. As we stood there, the world outside faded away, leaving just the three of us suspended in this fragile dance of ambition, love, and the pursuit of dreams. The choices lay before us, uncharted territory filled with the promise of possibility, each step forward shrouded in uncertainty but brimming with potential.

The atmosphere crackled with intensity, a taut string waiting to snap, as Marcus and I stood in the eye of the storm that was Vera. Her ambition was palpable, almost suffocating, as she held her ground with an assertiveness that bordered on the ruthless. I could see it in the set of her jaw and the narrowing of her eyes—the kind of determination that steamrolled over anyone who dared to stand in her way.

"I really think you should reconsider, Marcus. A book tour can change everything for you," she pressed, her voice smooth as glass but cold as steel. "You could be signing copies in New York, getting featured in interviews. You wouldn't just be another name in the credits; you'd be a literary sensation."

He looked back at me, uncertainty shadowing his features. "What if I could do both?" he countered, voice steady but laced with doubt.

I wanted to lean into that idea, to wrap it around us like a warm blanket. "That's the thing, Marcus. We have something unique here. But the reality of it is, your name might be out there in the world, but will it be worth it if we lose what we've built?"

"Please," Vera interjected with an exaggerated sigh, "are we really going to act like this is just about feelings? This is business, and Marcus has a golden ticket in his hands."

He shifted again, the tension of the moment igniting a fire in my stomach. "But it's not just business for me, Vera. It's personal too," he said, turning back to me, the warmth of his gaze igniting something within me. I couldn't help but feel a little thrill at his words, even if they left me with a lingering uncertainty.

"Personal?" Vera scoffed, clearly unimpressed. "This is a career we're discussing, not a high school dance. You need to decide if you want to be a star or a sidekick."

Marcus shot her a frustrated glance, then turned back to me, the resolve hardening in his posture. "I want to be a partner. I don't want to walk away from us or this project."

A flicker of hope sparked between us. We were standing on the edge of a precipice, balancing dreams against reality, with Vera pushing us toward an uncertain fate. I took a step closer, our hands brushing together, and for a brief moment, it felt like we were the only two people in the universe.

"Then let's figure this out," I suggested, my heart racing. "We can come up with a plan. We'll collaborate remotely while you're on tour. You could still be part of this; I won't let it slip away."

Vera's laugh was sharp and dismissive, cutting through the intimacy of the moment like a knife. "You're dreaming. He'd be lucky to get any work done on the road. It's all glamour and no grind out there. Don't let her sweet words fool you, Marcus. You'll regret this if you choose her over your career."

"I'm not choosing yet," he retorted, clearly fed up with her meddling. "I want to hear your thoughts first."

"Why don't we just ditch this little tête-à-tête?" she said, waving her hand dismissively, a plastic smile plastered on her face. "Let me take you to meet the publisher. They're eager to get you signed up for the tour, and the sooner you're on board, the better."

I could see the gears in Marcus's mind turning. The idea of signing with a publisher, of going on a tour, glimmered in his eyes like a firefly, alluring and bright. But behind that excitement lay a shadow of doubt. "How soon?" he asked, his tone cautious.

"Tomorrow. The sooner we get you in the spotlight, the faster your career takes off." Vera's smile widened, a predator stalking her prey.

I felt a surge of panic, the idea of him leaving tomorrow sending my thoughts spiraling. "Marcus, wait. You don't have to rush into anything," I interjected, my voice slightly trembling. "This is a huge decision. You should think it over."

He turned back to me, the conflict visible on his face, and I could see the weight of the world resting on his shoulders. "What if this is my chance?" His voice was steady but carried the unmistakable tremor of someone standing at a crossroads, heart pounding with indecision. "What if I don't get another opportunity like this?"

I took a deep breath, my heart a war drum in my chest. "And what if you lose this connection we've created? What if you become just another name lost in the shuffle?"

For a moment, everything hung suspended in the air, a fragile thread of possibility that could snap with a single word. The atmosphere thickened, as if the very walls were closing in, and I could feel my pulse quickening.

"Enough!" Vera snapped, the force of her words echoing off the walls. "You're wasting time. I can't believe you're even considering this. You're a talented writer, Marcus. You owe it to yourself to seize this opportunity."

"Maybe I don't want to owe anything to anyone," he shot back, his voice a blend of frustration and clarity, as if he was finally finding his footing amid the chaos. "Maybe I want to do things my way."

"Marcus," I started, but my words were swallowed by the tension spiraling between us, thick and electric. "I..."

Suddenly, the studio door swung open, crashing against the wall with a force that startled us all. A figure burst in, disheveled and breathless, eyes wide with urgency. "Marcus! You have to come quickly! There's—"

The intruder paused, catching sight of Vera, and the tension in the room shifted, thickening like fog rolling in off the ocean. The urgency in the stranger's expression was palpable, a jolt of reality shattering the carefully constructed bubble of our discussion.

"What is it?" Marcus demanded, his heart clearly racing at the sudden shift in atmosphere.

"There's been a situation—something you need to see. It's about your manuscript." The words hung heavy in the air, dripping with implication, pulling us all into an unexpected twist.

My heart sank. "What about it?"

The figure took a deep breath, hesitating as they glanced at Vera, then back at Marcus. "It's gone. The digital files have been deleted, and all backups have been wiped. We need you now."

A silence engulfed the room, a crushing weight of dread settling over us. The very foundation of our work threatened to crumble, a nightmare pulling us under as the stakes soared. Marcus's expression shifted from determination to disbelief, and as I watched the color drain from his face, I realized that the choice before him had just become infinitely more complicated. The road ahead twisted like a labyrinth, each turn fraught with unforeseen dangers, and I couldn't shake the feeling that we were about to plunge into uncharted territory.

Chapter 10: Unraveling Threads

The sunlight streamed through the tall windows of the café, casting intricate patterns of light and shadow across the polished wooden tables. The scent of freshly brewed coffee mingled with the sweet aroma of pastries, wrapping around me like a warm embrace. I sat at my usual spot, fingers poised above the keyboard, but my thoughts were tangled in the chaotic web of feelings that had taken root in my heart. The weight of anticipation hung in the air as I glanced at Marcus, who stood just a few feet away, his brow furrowed with determination.

"Are you really going to take the tour without me?" I asked, attempting to inject levity into the heavy moment. The truth was, I could hardly bear the thought of him leaving, of being separated from the whirlwind of creativity we had ignited together.

He turned, his hazel eyes meeting mine, a flicker of surprise flashing across his face. "I wasn't going to. I mean, I thought it would be...better this way." He hesitated, his fingers brushing through his tousled hair, a familiar gesture that set my heart racing. "But now, standing here, I'm not so sure."

His admission sent a rush of warmth through me, igniting the tiniest spark of hope that maybe, just maybe, he felt the same way I did about our partnership—and perhaps about each other. Yet before I could grasp this fragile possibility, the atmosphere shifted, as if a cloud had rolled in to snuff out the sunlight.

Vera burst through the café door, her presence an immediate storm front. She was a force of nature, the kind of woman whose confidence seemed to suck the air from the room. "Marcus!" she called, her voice sharp enough to slice through the tension. He turned, and I felt an instinctual pang of protectiveness rise within me. Vera wielded her authority like a finely honed sword, and I had little doubt she'd use it without hesitation.

"I need to speak with you," she said, her gaze flicking to me with a barely concealed smirk, as if she relished the control she held over the situation. My stomach twisted at the sight of her, an all-too-familiar feeling creeping back in—one of inadequacy and doubt.

"Uh, sure. Just give me a second," Marcus replied, his voice hesitant. He took a step toward her, and I could feel the connection we had begun to build slipping away like grains of sand through my fingers.

I pretended to type, but my focus was solely on them. Vera leaned in, her tone low and conspiratorial. I couldn't hear the words, but the gestures were clear—her body language dripped with a kind of manipulation that made my skin crawl. I hated that I was forced to play the role of the outsider in this scene, the third wheel in a dance I thought we were all leading together.

With every flick of Vera's hair or arch of her eyebrow, I felt my confidence waver. Was I really prepared to dive headfirst into this partnership, knowing someone like her was looming in the background? The very thought made my heart sink. I could feel the heat of jealousy rise, hot and prickly against my skin. What could she possibly say to him that would make him reconsider what we had?

As they continued their hushed conversation, my mind began to spin a thousand scenarios. What if Marcus decided he wanted to take a different path? What if he bought into whatever doubt Vera was planting? The uncertainty wrapped around me, squeezing tight until I could barely breathe.

Finally, the tension became unbearable. I stood abruptly, the chair scraping against the floor, a sound sharp enough to slice through their conversation. "Excuse me," I said, forcing my voice to sound steady as I approached them. Vera's smile widened, a predatory glint in her eyes that sent chills racing down my spine.

"Is everything alright?" I asked, though my voice wavered, betraying the confidence I desperately wanted to project.

"Just a little business talk," Marcus replied, though the hesitation in his tone sent alarm bells ringing in my head. "Vera's got some insights about the tour."

"Insights?" I echoed, the word tasting bitter on my tongue. "What kind of insights?"

"Just the usual things we need to consider before hitting the road," Vera interjected smoothly, as if she were a seasoned magician performing sleight of hand. "You know how it is, always planning for the worst."

"Right," I said, my voice tight as I fought to keep the jealousy from seeping through. "And what's that supposed to mean?"

Vera's smile faltered just a fraction, but it was enough to give me hope. "It means we need to be strategic about this. Not everyone gets to join the spotlight right away, darling," she purred, her tone sickly sweet.

"Actually, I think we're stronger together," I shot back, surprised by the fire in my own voice. "This is a team effort. Isn't that right, Marcus?"

The look on his face told me everything I needed to know. I saw a flicker of panic, as if he was caught between two worlds—the safe, familiar realm of Vera's carefully constructed plans and the vibrant chaos that had become our shared dream.

"Maybe we should just take some time to think things through," he suggested, a vague uncertainty threading through his words. "Vera's point has merit."

The disappointment crashed over me like a wave, pulling me under. I felt exposed, raw. "I see," I replied, keeping my voice steady. "Well, I guess I'll let you two figure out what you want."

As I turned to leave, my heart racing and my mind spiraling, I overheard the quiet murmur of their conversation slipping into the background, fading with every step I took away from them. It felt like betrayal, a bitter aftertaste that lingered long after I left the café.

The soft ding of the café's bell as I exited felt like a distant chime, signaling the end of something I wasn't quite ready to acknowledge. Outside, the world was a cacophony of sound—the chatter of passersby, the laughter of children, and the distant rumble of traffic. I inhaled deeply, letting the fresh air seep into my lungs, hoping it would wash away the bitter taste of betrayal that clung to my tongue. I needed to regroup, to find my footing again in this swirling storm of emotions that seemed determined to sweep me off course.

Walking along the tree-lined street, I felt the sun's warmth envelop me, the golden light weaving through the branches and casting playful shadows on the sidewalk. It was beautiful, the kind of day that begged for optimism, yet my heart was a weight, dragging me down. Marcus had been my anchor, my creative partner, and seeing him with Vera had rattled the very foundation of what I believed we were building together.

I paused in front of a shop, its windows adorned with colorful glass and local artwork, my reflection blending with the vibrant hues. I caught a glimpse of myself—hair tousled, eyes shadowed with doubt—and it struck me just how vulnerable I felt.

"Hey, you alright?" The voice broke through my thoughts like a welcome breeze. I turned to find Ava, my closest friend and a self-proclaimed caffeine aficionado, approaching with a cup of steaming coffee in hand.

"I am now," I replied, forcing a smile, though it felt like lifting a boulder. "Just had a bit of a moment back there."

"Vera again?" she asked, arching an eyebrow. She knew me well enough to see through my façade.

I sighed, rubbing my temples as if to massage away the tension. "She's got him twisted around her little finger. I'm starting to think I'm just...in the way."

"Sweetheart, you're not just in the way. You're the main event," Ava said, her voice firm yet gentle. "You and Marcus have something special. Don't let her scare you off."

"Easier said than done," I muttered, eyeing the café's entrance. "What if he decides that she has better insights than I do?"

Ava took a step closer, her presence a comfort. "Then he's a fool. You've poured your heart and soul into this project. You deserve to be at the forefront, not in her shadow."

Her words sparked something within me, a flicker of defiance that was hard to ignore. Maybe I wasn't ready to back down just yet. "You're right. I need to talk to him again, clear the air."

"That's the spirit! But first, let's grab a bite. You can't solve the world's problems on an empty stomach."

We made our way to a quaint little bistro down the street, its outdoor seating bathed in sunlight. The clinking of dishes and the soft murmur of conversation created a welcoming atmosphere. I ordered a savory quiche, and as we settled into our seats, I found myself more at ease.

"Tell me about this tour," Ava said, leaning forward, her curiosity genuine. "Is it really that big of a deal?"

"It's a chance for us to connect with our audience, to really share what we've created together," I explained, the passion in my voice bubbling to the surface. "But now I can't help but feel it's become a power play. I mean, Vera's been in the industry longer, and Marcus seems so eager to please her."

"Forget Vera. Focus on what you bring to the table. Besides, maybe a little competition will spice things up." She grinned, a wicked glint in her eye. "I mean, who doesn't love a good rivalry?"

I chuckled despite myself. "A rivalry is one thing, but she's not playing fair. It's like she's using everything she can to drive a wedge between us."

Ava raised her glass in mock salute. "Then show her what you're made of. You're not just some sidekick in this story. You're the co-author of your own fate."

Our food arrived, the quiche beautifully golden and fragrant. I took a bite, letting the rich flavors dance on my tongue, trying to savor the moment. Each forkful felt like a reminder that amidst the chaos, there was still joy to be found, still life to be lived.

After lunch, emboldened by Ava's words, I headed back to the café, determination propelling me forward. I needed to find Marcus and lay everything on the table. The sun hung high in the sky, casting everything in a warm glow, but I was about to step into the storm again.

The café door swung open, and as soon as I crossed the threshold, the familiar aroma hit me like a wave of nostalgia. Marcus was seated at our usual table, his fingers dancing across the keyboard, the screen illuminating his focused expression.

"Hey," I said, trying to keep my voice steady. "Can we talk?"

He looked up, surprise flickering in his eyes. "Of course. I thought you were leaving?"

"I almost did. But I realized I couldn't walk away without saying what I needed to say." I took a seat across from him, the distance between us feeling vast, charged with unspoken words.

"I've been thinking about everything. About Vera, about the tour...and us," I started, meeting his gaze directly. "I don't want to be sidelined. We've created something together that means a lot to me, and I need you to see that."

"I know, and I appreciate that, but—"

"But nothing," I interrupted, frustration bubbling to the surface. "I understand Vera has experience, but that doesn't mean we can't find our own way. I believe in our vision, Marcus."

His brow furrowed, and I could see the gears turning in his mind. "I want to, but there's so much pressure. Vera has connections, and I can't afford to mess this up."

"You won't mess it up," I insisted, leaning in closer. "You have me by your side, and together, we can handle anything. I promise."

Just as the words left my mouth, the café door swung open again, and Vera strode in, her heels clicking against the floor like a metronome counting down to a dramatic climax. The tension in the air thickened as she spotted us, her lips curling into a smile that didn't quite reach her eyes.

"Good, you're both here," she announced, her voice smooth as silk. "I just wanted to discuss our plans moving forward. There's a lot to cover."

"Actually," I began, ready to assert my place in this conversation, but Marcus's hand raised, a gesture that stilled the words on my lips.

"We were just talking about that, Vera," he said, his tone cautious. "I think we should consider all options."

A chill ran down my spine at his words, as if I was witnessing a shift, a subtle change in the dynamic. I couldn't help but feel a flicker of doubt rising again, weaving its way back into my heart like an unwelcome guest.

Vera took a seat, her eyes glinting with a calculated sharpness. "Wonderful. I have some ideas that I think will benefit us all. Let's make sure we're on the same page."

I swallowed hard, the weight of the moment crashing down on me. This was not the partnership I had envisioned. It felt more like a chess match, with each of us playing for stakes that were higher than I had anticipated. I had come here to fight for what I believed in, but instead, I found myself on the precipice of an unexpected battle.

As Vera settled in with an air of triumphant authority, I felt an icy knot form in my stomach. The way she commanded the room, leaning slightly toward Marcus, as if she were sharing a state secret, made my heart race with a mix of annoyance and insecurity. I had come here determined to fight for what I believed in, yet I suddenly felt like a shadow flitting at the edges of their conversation.

"Let's talk strategy," she said, her voice silky, laced with an undertone that suggested she was already two steps ahead. "Our audience needs to see us as a cohesive unit, not a mismatched trio."

"Trio?" I echoed, my tone sharp as I shot a glance between them. "I'm not in your plans, Vera. I'm part of this project."

Marcus hesitated, looking between us as if trying to gauge the air's temperature. "What I mean is, we need to present a united front. I think we should consider Vera's ideas."

There it was, that pang of insecurity tightening around my chest. How easily the words slipped from his mouth, as if he had just accepted defeat without a fight. "What ideas?" I asked, forcing the words through clenched teeth, my hands curling into fists on the table.

Vera flashed a smile that looked too much like a cat that had just cornered a mouse. "I was thinking we could leverage our social media presence to create a buzz—maybe even a live Q&A session to engage with our readers before the tour."

"Sounds like an excellent plan," Marcus said, enthusiasm creeping into his voice. "I could reach out to my contacts—"

"Excuse me, but why does it have to be just your contacts?" I interrupted, heat flooding my cheeks. "What about our followers? We've built this together. I can help manage our online engagement, too."

Vera's smile faltered for a split second, but she recovered with practiced ease. "Of course, darling. But let's not forget the power of experience. I have contacts who know how to elevate us. You wouldn't want to miss out on that."

The word "darling" dripped with condescension, and the way she said it sent a shiver down my spine. I needed to regain my footing before I let her push me into a corner. "Elevate us? Or elevate you?"

Marcus sighed, a hint of frustration creeping into his voice. "This isn't a competition, you two. We're all on the same team here, right?"

I shot him a look that said, Are we? "Right, but it's hard to feel like a part of the team when you both seem to be making decisions without me."

Vera leaned back, crossing her arms as if preparing for a debate. "It's not my fault you're not aware of the stakes, sweetheart. This is a chance to gain visibility in a competitive market."

I grit my teeth, feeling as if I was being pushed into a chess game where I wasn't even allowed to move. "I get it. But I refuse to sit on the sidelines while you two play puppet master. I'm not just a bystander."

Marcus glanced at me, his expression softening, and for a moment, I caught a glimmer of the connection we shared, but it was quickly extinguished as he turned his attention back to Vera. "Let's at least hear what else you have in mind, Vera."

Great. I could feel my resolve crumbling, a sandcastle under a rising tide. I wanted to scream, to shake him out of this trance, but instead, I settled for silence, my heart thudding painfully in my chest.

Vera dove into her pitch, outlining ideas that sounded polished and flashy, yet felt utterly devoid of the soul that I believed our project held. I nodded along, but inside, frustration bubbled. She wasn't just trying to win him over; she was trying to erase me.

As they continued to converse, I slipped into the background, battling the waves of doubt crashing over me. I knew what I had to do. I couldn't allow this to slide any longer. I needed to assert myself, to remind them of the passion and the vision we'd built together, not just the polished façade Vera was trying to present.

Suddenly, my phone buzzed in my pocket, jolting me from my spiraling thoughts. I glanced at the screen, the name flashing before me—Renee, my editor. She rarely called unless it was important. I quickly excused myself, the café fading behind me as I stepped outside to take the call.

"Hey! I hope I'm not interrupting," she chirped, her voice a mix of warmth and urgency. "I've been wanting to talk to you about the tour and some exciting opportunities."

"Uh, hey, Renee! No interruption at all. Just...working through some things," I said, feeling the weight of the earlier conversation still pressing down on me.

"Good! I wanted to let you know that I've received some fantastic feedback about your work, and it looks like you might get an opportunity to pitch for a feature in one of the larger magazines."

My heart raced, the idea swelling within me. "Really? That's incredible!"

"Yes! But it's a time-sensitive opportunity, and I think it would really elevate your presence before the tour."

"Elevate..." The word echoed in my mind, tying back to the earlier conversation with Marcus and Vera. "What's the catch?"

"No catch! Just a chance for you to shine, darling," she said, a teasing lilt in her voice. "You'd need to prepare a compelling pitch and some sample pieces. It could lead to more readers—and maybe more power when you're out there on tour."

Power. The word felt like a jolt, igniting a spark of rebellion within me. "Okay, I'm in. Just tell me what I need to do."

"Great! Let's meet up tomorrow to brainstorm. I'll send over some guidelines."

As we ended the call, a newfound sense of clarity washed over me. I wouldn't just be a participant in this project; I could take control.

When I returned to the café, I found Marcus and Vera deep in discussion. Their heads were close together, voices low, and the camaraderie between them was palpable, igniting a fire of jealousy in me. But this time, I felt different—empowered, ready to reclaim my voice.

"Marcus," I interrupted, my tone resolute. "I just got off the phone with Renee. I'm pitching for a feature, and I need your support."

Vera's eyebrows shot up, and a flicker of annoyance crossed her features. "A feature? That's ambitious."

"Why not? You have your connections, and I have mine," I replied, refusing to let her diminish my excitement.

Marcus looked torn, glancing between Vera and me. "That's great! But—"

"There's no but. I'm taking this opportunity," I asserted, my heart pounding. "I want us to go out there and show everyone what we can do, not just what you think we can do, Vera."

"Fine. If you think you can juggle that and the tour," Vera replied, the words like ice shards.

"I can and I will," I shot back, the defiance settling like armor around me.

Just then, the café door swung open with a dramatic flourish, and a tall figure stepped inside. My heart dropped. It was Daniel, Marcus's ex, the last person I wanted to see at that moment.

"Hey, is this a party?" he announced, a smirk dancing on his lips as he caught sight of our table. The tension thickened as he approached, his eyes darting between Marcus, Vera, and me.

"What a lovely surprise," Vera said, her tone dripping with mock sweetness.

"Daniel," Marcus greeted, a hint of wariness in his voice.

As the conversation shifted toward Daniel, my heart raced. What was he doing here? I couldn't shake the feeling that this was the catalyst for something even more unpredictable.

"Did I miss something?" Daniel asked, his gaze lingering on me, a glimmer of intrigue in his eyes.

"Just discussing our exciting plans for the upcoming book tour," Vera said, her voice smooth.

"Oh? I'd love to hear more," he replied, taking a seat at our table as if he belonged.

I felt a knot twist in my stomach, the air thickening with the weight of unspoken words and buried tension. Daniel had always had a way of inserting himself into conversations, and as he leaned in closer, I could almost sense the impending chaos swirling in the air.

Suddenly, I realized that I wasn't the only one fighting for my place at the table anymore. As the stakes climbed higher, the unexpected twist of Daniel's arrival sent a tremor of uncertainty through me, leaving me wondering just how far we'd all go to claim our spot in this tangled web of ambition and desire.

Chapter 11: The Unexpected Invitation

Days unfold like a book whose pages I can't seem to turn fast enough, each moment steeped in a cocktail of anticipation and dread. Ever since Marcus slipped that invitation into my hand, the world outside my window has taken on an ethereal quality. Amethyst Falls, usually a backdrop to my mundane existence, has transformed into a vibrant canvas painted with the hues of my nervous excitement. The golden leaves swirl in the crisp breeze, dancing like they know something I don't, as if the very air is charged with unspoken possibilities.

When I first saw the invitation, my fingers trembled with the weight of it. The elegant script promised an evening celebrating local authors, a gathering where words flowed like the wine that would surely be poured. Marcus wants to attend together. Me! With him! The thought sent my heart skittering around in my chest. It's not just the event itself, but the intimacy of sharing such an experience with him that sends flutters through me.

Preparing for the gala becomes a ritual of sorts, an adventure steeped in anticipation. I sift through my closet, tossing aside clothes like forgotten chapters, each discarded garment a reminder of how often I've settled for ordinary. Finally, I pull out a deep green dress, the kind that makes me feel like the heroine of my own story. The fabric hugs my curves in all the right places, the color echoing the rich greens of the trees outside my window. I can almost hear them whispering encouragement as I admire my reflection, hair cascading in soft waves around my shoulders, a stark contrast to the practicality that usually defines my look.

"Are you sure you want to wear that?" Jess asks, peering over my shoulder with a mischievous grin, her own outfit already selected—a stunning black dress with a daring neckline that screams sophistication. She's always had an eye for fashion, a flair I sometimes envy. "You might just outshine the authors."

I roll my eyes, but a smile tugs at my lips. "Outshine? Please, it's about making a good impression, not stealing the spotlight."

"Oh, sweetheart, when it comes to Marcus, you're bound to steal the spotlight without even trying," she teases, her eyes sparkling with mischief.

With a final spritz of perfume—an indulgent floral scent that reminds me of a garden in full bloom—I grab my clutch and head out. The streets of Amethyst Falls feel alive, each corner pulsing with energy, the lights reflecting the golden autumn light in a kaleidoscope of warmth. The gala is being held in an old theater, a place steeped in history, its facade adorned with intricate designs that whisper tales of the past.

As I step inside, the air thickens with the mingled scents of polished wood, fresh flowers, and the soft hum of chatter that swells around me. I spot Marcus across the room, his tall frame outlined by the warm glow of chandeliers overhead. He looks so dapper in a fitted navy suit, the deep color bringing out the warmth in his hazel eyes. My breath catches, the world blurring momentarily as our eyes lock.

"Wow, you look incredible," he says when I finally reach him, a genuine smile breaking across his face. I can feel my cheeks flush under his gaze, the weight of his compliment wrapping around me like a favorite blanket.

"Thanks! You're not too shabby yourself," I reply, trying to sound more composed than I feel. His laughter fills the space between us, rich and inviting.

As the evening unfolds, we weave through the crowd, the laughter and conversation forming a tapestry of voices that envelop us. I meet local authors, each one more intriguing than the last, their passion igniting a fire within me. I engage in spirited discussions about their works, my confidence growing with every exchanged word. Marcus stands by my side, a quiet pillar of support, occasionally chiming in with thoughtful insights that make the authors nod in appreciation.

"Tell me, what's the most unusual thing you've ever done for inspiration?" I ask a poet who describes his habit of wandering through graveyards, seeking inspiration in the silence of the departed.

He leans closer, eyes sparkling with mischief. "I once spent a week living in a treehouse. Nature has a way of whispering stories to those willing to listen."

"Maybe I should start climbing trees, then," I muse, earning a chuckle from Marcus.

As the night deepens, the atmosphere becomes electric, a blend of laughter, clinking glasses, and the faint strains of a string quartet filling the air. Yet, beneath the surface of the joviality, I sense a current of tension. The moment is punctuated by the arrival of a controversial author, a man whose name echoes through the literary world for all the wrong reasons. He's known for his scathing reviews and cutting critiques, a polarizing figure whose presence sends a ripple through the crowd.

I watch as he holds court, his voice a booming declaration that cuts through the gentle buzz. "Literature is dying! It's being watered down by mediocrity and niceties. We need to return to the rawness of storytelling!"

His words hang in the air, causing a palpable shift in the room. Marcus and I exchange glances, a shared understanding passing between us. The night's enchantment flickers, replaced by an undercurrent of unease.

"You know, there's something to be said for niceties," I remark softly, glancing at Marcus. "Sometimes it's the gentleness that resonates the most."

"Absolutely," he replies, a hint of warmth in his gaze. "Literature should evoke emotion, not just shock value."

Just as the conversation deepens, I notice a figure lingering at the edge of the crowd. A woman, her presence magnetic yet oddly unsettling, seems to be watching Marcus and me with a keen intensity. Her eyes are sharp, assessing, as if she knows more about us than we do about ourselves. I shiver slightly, a sense of foreboding creeping in as I wonder what kind of twist this night has yet to reveal.

The unexpected invitation had opened doors, yet something about this evening hinted at deeper mysteries, waiting to unfurl like the pages of an unwritten story.

The room hums with a warm energy that seems to embrace us, but I can't shake the feeling that the arrival of the controversial author has cast a shadow over the evening. As he continues his diatribe about the death of genuine storytelling, I find myself unconsciously inching closer to Marcus, as if his presence could shield me from the negativity permeating the air. He notices, a slight smile playing at the corners of his mouth, and I can't help but return it, grateful for the grounding sensation he brings amidst the swirling tension.

"Is he always this... dramatic?" I whisper, tilting my head toward the author, who is now gesticulating wildly as he makes his point.

"Only when he wants to be," Marcus replies, his voice low and smooth. "He thrives on the chaos of controversy. It's like a moth to a flame."

"I wonder how many flames he's burned," I quip, earning a soft laugh from Marcus. The laughter feels like a lifeline, pulling me back into the moment, a reminder that despite the noise, we can still find joy in each other's company.

The gala continues around us, the sound of clinking glasses and laughter creating a symphony of camaraderie. As the evening unfolds, we navigate through the sea of faces, each one more familiar and intriguing than the last. I'm introduced to authors whose names I've read in the local papers, their works like footprints in the literary landscape of Amethyst Falls. I ask questions, soaking up their stories like a sponge, each one richer than the last, until I'm left breathless and yearning for more.

At one point, I find myself in conversation with a woman who has penned a collection of short stories about lost loves. She has the kind of presence that commands attention, her voice smooth as silk, wrapping around each word. "Love is like a river," she says, leaning in slightly as if sharing a secret. "It flows, bends, and sometimes overflows its banks. The trick is to ride the current, not fight against it."

"I like that," I respond, imagining the metaphor weaving through my own experiences, the relationships I've navigated like shifting tides. "But what if you end up caught in a whirlpool?"

"Ah, but that's where the adventure begins!" she replies, her eyes sparkling with mischief. "It's those moments of chaos that shape us."

Just as I'm about to delve deeper into her philosophy, a sudden commotion draws my attention. The controversial author, emboldened by a few glasses of wine, has taken it upon himself to challenge a well-respected local novelist. The tension thickens, palpable like the aroma of rich coffee that fills the air.

"Your writing is nothing but fluff!" he bellows, his voice echoing across the room. "We need honesty, not sugarcoated tales!"

The room stills, every conversation halting in its tracks as eyes turn toward the unfolding drama. The novelist, a dignified man with silver hair and a kind smile, takes a moment, clearly weighing his response. "And yet, sometimes sugar is exactly what we need to balance the bitterness of reality," he counters, his tone calm but firm.

The author huffs in indignation, but I'm amazed at how gracefully the novelist handles the exchange, a reminder of the strength that often lies in gentleness. I glance at Marcus, who watches the scene with an amused expression, clearly enjoying the banter as a spectator rather than a participant.

"What do you think?" I ask him, curious about his take on the fray.

"I think it's delightful," he grins. "It's a reminder that passion often fuels art. And, of course, it's a distraction from my own nerves."

"Yours? I thought you were born for this," I tease, nudging him playfully.

"Only if you promise to keep me grounded," he retorts with a mock-seriousness that makes me laugh.

As the night progresses, the discussion surrounding the author's controversial stance morphs into a spirited debate among the guests. Voices rise and fall like the ebb and flow of the ocean, a delightful chaos I hadn't expected. I watch, entranced, as people pour out their opinions, their love for literature spilling from their lips like fine wine. It's exhilarating and intoxicating in its own right, the shared passion igniting the air around us.

Then, just as I'm feeling swept away in this whirlwind of camaraderie, I catch sight of the woman from earlier—the one whose piercing gaze has been following me since I arrived. She stands apart from the group, her expression inscrutable as she surveys the room. Something about her presence sends a shiver down my spine, a sense of foreboding that makes my heart race.

"Do you know her?" I ask Marcus, nodding discreetly in her direction.

He squints in her direction, brows furrowing. "I've seen her around, but I don't know much about her. Just... keep an eye on her. There's something unsettling about her."

I can't shake the feeling as the evening progresses. Her eyes are like shards of ice, cutting through the jovial atmosphere with a precision that leaves me breathless. Yet I can't help but wonder what secrets lie behind that cool exterior.

Eventually, the literary debate begins to fade, and the evening drifts toward its natural conclusion. As the clock approaches ten, a soft announcement echoes through the theater, inviting everyone to gather for the evening's final act—a reading from the esteemed novelist.

Marcus and I find a cozy spot near the front, the ambiance shifting into something more intimate as the lights dim. The novelist steps onto the stage, his demeanor exuding warmth and wisdom. He begins to read from his latest work, his voice wrapping around the words, pulling us into a world filled with heartache and hope.

Every word he speaks feels like a balm to my soul, the tales weaving through my mind like delicate threads. As he narrates a story about love lost and found, I can't help but glance at Marcus, who watches with rapt attention, his expression softening as he gets lost in the rhythm of the prose. In that moment, I feel an unspoken connection between us, as if our hearts are syncing to the cadence of the story.

But just as the final lines leave the novelist's lips, a sudden commotion erupts at the back of the room. I turn to see the icy woman standing, her voice cutting through the soft afterglow of the reading. "This is a farce!" she declares, her tone sharp as glass. "What is the point of this sentimental drivel?"

Gasps ripple through the audience as she continues, her voice rising, fueled by some unseen fire. "We need raw truth, not this pandering to emotion!"

A hush falls over the crowd, tension thickening like fog. The novelist pauses, clearly taken aback, and I watch as Marcus's face hardens, a flicker of anger igniting in his eyes.

"Is this really the time?" I whisper, feeling the weight of the moment pressing down on us.

He shakes his head, a mix of disbelief and irritation. "Some people thrive on chaos. Let's hope this doesn't turn into a full-blown spectacle."

As the woman continues her tirade, I can't help but feel a sense of dread creeping in. This night, which began with such promise, seems to be teetering on the brink of disaster. I want to reach out, to calm the brewing storm, but all I can do is sit in stunned silence, feeling the atmosphere shift once more as the unexpected turns yet again, like the winding streets of Amethyst Falls outside.

The tension hangs in the air, thick enough to cut with a knife. The woman's interruption sends ripples of discomfort through the audience, like a pebble dropped into a serene pond, the calm surface shattered. As she stands there, defiantly challenging the gathered crowd, I can feel Marcus tense beside me, his eyes narrowing slightly as he assesses the situation.

"What is she hoping to accomplish?" I murmur, the question barely escaping my lips, though I know he can hear the worry laced in my tone.

"Attention, it seems," Marcus replies, his voice edged with irritation. "Some people live for the spotlight, even if it means burning a few bridges."

The novelist, taken aback but regaining his composure, clears his throat. "Art evokes emotion, and perhaps that's the most important truth of all," he responds, a calmness in his voice that contrasts sharply with the woman's outburst. "Whether it's raw or sentimental, the beauty of literature is its ability to connect us, to reflect our shared experiences."

"Spare us the sentimentality!" she shoots back, her voice resonating with an almost theatrical flair. "I didn't come here to listen to a bedtime story. I came for the truth—the unvarnished reality that your precious words hide behind."

Gasps ripple through the audience again, and I feel the heat of embarrassment wash over me. It's like watching a play go horribly wrong, the actors forgetting their lines while the audience shifts uneasily in their seats. Marcus's hand finds mine, squeezing gently, grounding me amidst the rising storm.

"She really knows how to kill a vibe," I whisper, trying to inject some humor into the tense moment.

"Should we throw her a lifebuoy?" he quips back, a glimmer of mischief dancing in his eyes despite the chaos.

While others begin to murmur amongst themselves, the novelist holds his ground, his demeanor unfazed. "If you're looking for something raw, perhaps you should write it yourself," he counters, his voice steady. "Every story has its place, even those wrapped in layers of sweetness. Isn't it our responsibility to share the many shades of our humanity?"

The woman's expression falters for a brief moment, but she quickly recovers, her gaze sweeping the crowd like a hawk surveying its territory. "Humanity is messy, and your stories don't reflect that. You want to present a polished version of life, but let's face it: most of us are struggling to stay afloat."

The crowd shifts again, a wave of discontent washing over the assembled authors and patrons. I feel my heart pounding as I glance around, trying to gauge the reactions of those who had earlier been charmed by the novelist's reading. Some look uncomfortable, while others appear intrigued, caught in the pull of the debate.

"Should we get out of here?" I suggest to Marcus, suddenly feeling trapped in this unfolding drama. "I'd rather not witness the apocalypse of literary debates."

He chuckles softly, but his eyes remain focused on the stage. "Let's see how this unfolds first. Who knows? It could turn into a riveting spectacle."

As if on cue, the tension escalates. The novelist stands tall, ready to respond, but before he can utter another word, the door swings open with a loud creak, drawing everyone's attention. A tall figure steps into the room, silhouetted against the light. The newcomer is striking, with an air of confidence that seems to demand attention without even trying.

He strides forward, cutting through the murmurs like a hot knife through butter. "Apologies for my tardiness," he announces, his voice smooth and resonant, effortlessly captivating the crowd. "I couldn't resist the urge to witness the birth of a literary catfight."

Laughter erupts, breaking the tension and redirecting the crowd's focus toward the newcomer. I can't help but smile at the distraction. His arrival feels almost serendipitous, like a plot twist in a novel that breathes new life into the story.

"What a way to enter!" Marcus whispers to me, and I can't help but agree.

The man stands confidently at the front of the room, glancing between the novelist and the woman with an amused smile. "I see we have differing opinions on the state of literature. Care to enlighten us?"

The woman narrows her eyes, sizing him up as if he were another opponent in this literary bout. "What do you know about it?" she snaps, but there's a flicker of curiosity behind her steely gaze.

"I know that every voice deserves to be heard," he replies smoothly. "But let's not pretend that every opinion carries equal weight. Some stories resonate more profoundly than others."

"Ah, the elitism of literature rears its ugly head," she retorts, but I sense a shift in her stance. She seems intrigued, perhaps even challenged by the newcomer's presence.

As the two engage in a rapid exchange of banter, I turn to Marcus, whispering, "Do you think he'll take her down a peg or two?"

"Seems like it could go either way," he says, clearly entertained by the unfolding drama. "But it's best to sit back and enjoy the show. The evening just turned from dull to entertaining."

But my amusement is short-lived. Just as the tension begins to ebb, a faint commotion arises at the back of the room. I glance over my shoulder, spotting a group of late arrivals who are making their way to the front. Their hushed voices and furtive glances suggest something is amiss, and an unsettling feeling starts to bubble in my stomach.

Marcus notices my unease. "What is it?" he asks, his brow furrowing.

"Those people..." I point subtly, keeping my voice low. "They look... shifty. Like they're here for more than just the gala."

Before Marcus can respond, the atmosphere shifts again. The tall man, who has been captivating the crowd, suddenly narrows his eyes at the newcomers. "And who might you be?" he calls out, his tone shifting from playful to stern.

"Just some friends," one of them replies too casually, but I can see the tension radiating off them. There's something off in their demeanor—an edge that prickles at my instincts.

The crowd falls silent once more, the earlier debate forgotten as all eyes turn to the new arrivals. I watch in disbelief as one of them steps forward, a sly smile spreading across his face.

"We're here for the literary scene, of course," he smirks, his gaze sweeping the room with a sense of entitlement. "But it seems like we've stumbled into a bit of drama."

As whispers of confusion ripple through the audience, the woman who had been the source of earlier tension squares her shoulders. "And who gave you the right to crash this event?"

The newcomers exchange glances, the sly smile morphing into something darker. "We're here to make our own mark," the leader of the group retorts. "After all, every good story needs a twist, don't you think?"

My heart races, a sense of foreboding settling in. The festive atmosphere has evaporated, replaced by an undercurrent of uncertainty. I look to Marcus, my anxiety rising, but before I can speak, the leader leans closer to the front of the room, his voice dropping to a conspiratorial whisper.

"You think you're all safe here, playing your little games?" he taunts, glancing between the novelist and the woman. "But let me assure you, the real story is just beginning, and you're all part of it."

The weight of his words hangs in the air like a thundercloud, and I can feel the tension coiling around us, tightening like a noose.

"What does he mean?" I whisper urgently to Marcus, but he doesn't have an answer, his eyes locked on the unfolding drama.

The novelist takes a step forward, a flicker of defiance in his gaze. "We don't have time for threats. We're here to celebrate literature, not be intimidated by wannabe disruptors."

But the leader only laughs, a low, menacing sound that sends chills down my spine. "Let's just say, the gala has only just begun. And the best stories often come from unexpected places."

In that moment, I realize we're teetering on the edge of something much darker than I had anticipated. My instincts scream that this night is about to spiral out of control. I squeeze Marcus's hand tighter, trying to ground myself as the atmosphere shifts again, the threat looming closer with every breath.

Before I can process what's happening, the lights flicker, plunging the room into darkness. Gasps erupt as confusion reigns. My heart pounds wildly in my chest, and I can barely hear myself think over the cacophony of voices raised in surprise and alarm.

"Marcus!" I shout, panic gripping me as I feel the press of bodies around me, the once-celebratory atmosphere now heavy with dread. The realization crashes over me: we're not just participants in a literary gala anymore; we've unwittingly stepped into the plot of a story where the stakes are suddenly much higher than we ever expected.

Chapter 12: The Gala Dilemma

The gala unfolds before me like a scene from a dream, bright and vibrant, each detail designed to dazzle. I step inside, momentarily blinded by the glittering lights that cascade from the chandeliers above, their glow mingling with the soft laughter of guests weaving through the elegantly draped tables. A kaleidoscope of colors bursts forth from the lavish arrangements of sunflowers and wildflowers, their cheerful yellows and gentle blues a stark contrast to the slightly more subdued tones of the evening attire surrounding me.

As I adjust the delicate silk of my dress—an ethereal shade of cream that brushes against my skin with each movement—I can't help but feel a rush of exhilaration. Yet, beneath the surface of my excitement lies a current of unease. The thrill of being here is inevitably tethered to the weight of expectations that Marcus and I now share. Our budding romance dances precariously on the precipice of public scrutiny, caught in the crosshairs of Vera's manipulative games.

I search for Marcus through the throng of elegantly clad bodies, my heart racing. When our eyes finally meet, a spark ignites in the pit of my stomach, and I can't suppress a smile. He stands across the room, a vision in his tailored suit that hugs his shoulders just right, exuding an effortless charm that draws in everyone around him. Yet, even from a distance, I can see the glimmer of worry in his eyes, and it sends a shiver down my spine.

As I make my way through the crowd, laughter and clinking glasses fill the air, creating a symphony of celebration. But the further I get from him, the more palpable the tension becomes, like a taut string ready to snap. I know that beneath the surface of our laughter lies the undeniable truth: I am terrified that the precarious balance we've struck might shatter under the weight of ambition and ambition's ruthless allies.

"Marcus," I say softly, finally reaching him. The warmth of his presence envelops me like a blanket, chasing away the chill of my unease.

"Hey there, beautiful," he replies, his voice smooth and reassuring, though I can hear the hint of a tremor beneath. He takes my hand, the warmth of his skin against mine sending a wave of comfort through me. Yet, the comfort is fleeting, for the memory of Vera's warning dances like a shadow at the edge of my mind.

We stand in a bubble, the music swirling around us, but I can't shake the feeling that we're about to plunge into murky waters. "Can we talk?" I murmur, glancing around to ensure no one is close enough to eavesdrop on the storm brewing between us.

He nods, and with a quick glance toward the nearest exit, he leads me to a quieter corner of the hall, away from the laughter and the prying eyes. My heart pounds as we settle into the alcove, the dim lighting wrapping around us like a curtain. "What's going on?" he asks, concern etching lines across his handsome face.

I take a deep breath, grappling with the knot of emotions swirling inside me. "I just... I don't want to lose you. With everything happening—the gala, Vera's meddling... It's all so much." My voice wavers slightly, and I see his expression soften as he processes my words.

"Losing me?" he echoes, incredulous. "You're not going to lose me. I promise." The sincerity in his eyes gives me a flicker of hope, but the worry won't dissipate that easily.

"But what if you have to choose? Between your success and—" I hesitate, the words tasting bitter on my tongue. "And us?"

He steps closer, the air between us thickening with unspoken thoughts. "That's not fair," he counters gently. "You know I want both. You think I'd let some manipulative woman come between what we have?"

His eyes blaze with determination, and for a fleeting moment, I feel a rush of relief. Yet, the weight of our situation settles heavily on my chest. "It's not just her. It's everything. The pressure, the expectations..." My voice trails off, and I look down at the polished floor, the tiles reflecting the glittering lights above.

He reaches for my chin, lifting my gaze to meet his. "We can figure this out," he insists, his tone firm yet gentle. "You're not just some distraction for me, you know that, right?"

I nod, though the doubt lingers like a shadow. "I know, but—"

"Vera wants to create a rift between us. That's her game, not ours. Don't let her win," he interrupts, his voice low but fierce. The intensity in his gaze sends shivers down my spine, igniting something deep within me.

"I just want you to see that I'm not just here for the ride. I'm here because I care about you," I say, my voice barely above a whisper. The truth spills from me like an uncontained flood, raw and real.

He hesitates for a moment, absorbing my words, before taking a deep breath and letting it out slowly. "Then let's enjoy this night. Let's not allow anyone to ruin it."

A glimmer of hope ignites in my chest, but I can't shake the feeling that we're teetering on the edge of a precipice, caught between the present's warmth and the uncertainty of what lies ahead. As we turn back toward the festivities, I feel a shift in the atmosphere, a swell of something unnameable lurking just beneath the surface of our conversation. The excitement of the evening pulses around us, but I sense that the real test of our connection is yet to come.

The night unfolds in a whirl of swirling colors and laughter that feels both enchanting and surreal. As we step away from the quiet alcove and rejoin the celebration, I'm greeted by the sight of swirling gowns and impeccably tailored suits gliding across the polished marble floor. The music, a gentle waltz, beckons couples to the dance floor, where the air vibrates with the mingled sounds of joy and anticipation. I clutch Marcus's hand, anchoring myself to him as we weave through the crowd.

Just beyond the thrumming heart of the gala, I spot a table piled high with extravagant desserts. A tiered cake, layered with rich chocolate and adorned with delicate sugar flowers, stands as the centerpiece, enticing enough to steal anyone's attention. My stomach rumbles in response, reminding me that beneath the glamour and glitter of the evening, I am still human, driven by basic needs and desires.

"Shall we?" I nod toward the table, an eager grin breaking through the tension still clinging to my heart.

"Absolutely, but only if you promise to share," Marcus quips, raising an eyebrow playfully.

"Only if you promise not to steal the entire cake," I retort, matching his teasing tone. Our playful banter distracts me, if only for a moment, from the weight of the expectations that shadow us. As I approach the table, I can't help but admire the artistry of the dessert displays. Each confection seems to beckon me closer, whispering sweet nothings that promise blissful indulgence.

Just as I reach for a chocolate-covered strawberry, a voice cuts through our light-hearted exchange. "Well, if it isn't the lovebirds!" Vera's silky tone drips with insincerity, and my heart sinks. She glides into our space, her eyes glimmering with mischief like a cat toying with a mouse. The smile she offers is as sweet as the desserts before me, but it carries the weight of something far more sinister.

Marcus tenses beside me, his grip on my hand tightening imperceptibly. "Vera," he says, his voice steady yet edged with caution.

"Still together, I see," she purrs, her gaze flitting between us. "How lovely. I'd hate for anything to come between such... passionate affection."

"Everything is fine," I interject, trying to dismiss her presence with a forced smile. "Thanks for checking in."

Vera tilts her head slightly, her smile widening. "Oh, I'm just a concerned friend." She takes a step closer, her tone lowering to a conspiratorial whisper, "I just hope you two aren't too distracted by each other. You know how high the stakes are tonight."

I can feel the tension in Marcus's jaw, the way his posture shifts subtly as he leans slightly toward me, as if to shield me from her venom. "We can handle ourselves, Vera. We're here to enjoy the evening, not to worry about your games," he replies, his voice low but resolute.

"Games?" she feigns innocence, batting her lashes like a mischievous fairy. "Oh, dear Marcus, you wound me. I would never dream of playing games with such serious matters. But you know, people do love a good story. A tale of triumph, romance, and, of course, betrayal."

Her words hang in the air like smoke, and I can feel the chill seep into my bones. It's not just the heat of her gaze but the implications behind them. I want to scream that I won't let her manipulate us, but the words falter on my tongue. Marcus glances down at me, his expression flickering between anger and concern.

"Let's go," I say, tugging him away from Vera's suffocating presence, desperate for the fresh air and freedom of the outside balcony.

We step outside, the cool night air washing over us like a balm. The soft glow of string lights overhead mingles with the distant sound of laughter from within, creating a serene backdrop against the swirling tempest of emotions roiling inside me. I lean against the railing, drawing in a shaky breath, trying to shake off the weight of Vera's words.

"Are you okay?" Marcus asks, his voice gentle yet probing as he stands beside me, his presence solid and reassuring.

"I will be," I reply, but the tremor in my voice betrays my uncertainty. "It's just... I thought we could enjoy a normal evening. But she has a way of showing up at the worst possible moments."

"She thrives on chaos," he mutters, running a hand through his hair in frustration. "But we can't let her spoil what we have."

"What if she succeeds?" I ask, my heart pounding in my chest. "What if she finds a way to come between us?"

His gaze darkens, and he turns to face me, his expression earnest. "I won't let her. You mean too much to me."

The sincerity in his words sends warmth flooding through me, wrapping around my heart like a protective shield. Still, doubt lingers, gnawing at the edges of my confidence. "But she has connections, Marcus. She's not just a spoiled girl looking to cause trouble. She's dangerous."

"I'm aware," he replies, his voice steady. "But I've dealt with her before, and I'm not afraid to do it again. What we have is worth fighting for."

His declaration sends a thrill through me, yet it's quickly eclipsed by an overwhelming sense of dread. Just then, the faint sound of a raised voice drifts through the open doors, pulling my attention back toward the gala. I glance at Marcus, and he's already looking back at me, his brow furrowed in concern.

"Do you hear that?" I whisper, straining to make out the words.

As we lean closer to the entrance, the voice sharpens, and I realize it belongs to Vera, her tone laced with anger. "I won't let you throw everything away! You need to focus on what truly matters!"

Curiosity piqued, we inch closer, hiding behind a column as we try to catch a glimpse of what's unfolding. Vera stands with another woman, her posture rigid, her expression a tempest of frustration and indignation. The other woman's features are obscured in the dim light, but she appears to be in the midst of a heated discussion with Vera.

"Your priorities are skewed, and you know it," the woman replies, her voice equally sharp. "You're letting your emotions cloud your judgment. You need to think strategically if you want to maintain control."

I exchange a glance with Marcus, and the tension in the air thickens, curling around us like a fog. The stakes are clearly rising, and the dynamic at play is shifting with each passing moment.

"Control?" Vera scoffs, waving her hand dismissively. "You think I care about control? I'm trying to protect what's mine, and that means getting rid of distractions. I won't allow anyone to jeopardize everything I've worked for."

A chill runs down my spine as the implications of her words settle in. The shadows of manipulation are darker than I had anticipated, and the consequences of her schemes ripple outward like a stone thrown into a still pond. My mind races, caught between the desire to confront her and the instinct to retreat.

"Let's go," I murmur to Marcus, the urgency of the moment pushing me forward. "We need to get out of here."

With one last glance at the unfolding drama, we slip away from the gala's brightly lit façade and into the embrace of the night, leaving behind the clamor of voices and the weight of unspoken truths. In that moment, I realize the evening's events are only just beginning, and we've only scratched the surface of the challenges awaiting us.

As the cool night air envelops us, I can feel the tension from the gala fade into the background, replaced by the soft rustle of leaves in the gentle breeze. The stars overhead twinkle like diamonds scattered across a velvet sky, casting a serene glow over the garden adjacent to the grand hall. I let out a breath I didn't realize I was holding, my heart still racing from our earlier confrontation with Vera.

"What's next? Should we climb a tree and look for escape routes?" Marcus jokes, attempting to lighten the mood as he leans against the railing beside me. His playful tone pulls a smile from my lips, and I can't help but appreciate the warmth of his presence beside me.

"Only if you promise not to drop me," I shoot back, nudging him with my shoulder, enjoying the way his laughter mingles with the sounds of the gala.

"Trust me, I've got you. I'm all about safe landings," he replies, his eyes sparkling with mischief. But beneath his teasing, I sense an undercurrent of concern, a weight that presses heavily on both of us.

We stand in comfortable silence for a moment, soaking in the night, the sounds of distant laughter and clinking glasses creating a symphony of celebration behind us. But the weight of what we overheard lingers in my thoughts, gnawing at my resolve.

"What do you think she meant?" I finally ask, breaking the stillness. The words tumble from my lips before I can stop them. "About distractions and priorities?"

Marcus's smile fades, replaced by a thoughtful frown. "I think she's trying to manipulate me. She's always been good at playing mind games, especially when it comes to power plays."

I shiver slightly, the night air suddenly feeling colder. "But what if she's right? What if your success really does come at the cost of us?"

He turns to face me fully, a determined look etched on his features. "Listen, I'm not going to let anyone come between us. Not Vera, not anyone."

"Easy for you to say," I mutter, a twinge of frustration creeping into my voice. "You're not the one with your entire future on the line."

"Neither are you," he insists, his gaze intense. "You're more than just a distraction to me. You're part of my plans, whether I'm at a gala or not."

His words wrap around my heart, making it swell with something akin to hope. But I can't shake the feeling that we're standing on shaky ground, and the ground beneath us could shift at any moment.

Just then, the doors to the gala swing open again, and I see a flurry of movement. A tall figure steps out, a silhouette backlit by the golden glow from inside. My heart drops when I recognize Vera striding toward us, her heels clicking on the pavement with an authority that feels like an impending storm.

"Marcus!" she calls, her voice cutting through the air.

"Seriously?" I hiss, my stomach sinking. "Can't she take a hint?"

Marcus's jaw tightens, and he takes a step forward, shielding me slightly as if to create a barrier against her advances. "What do you want, Vera?"

She stops a few feet away, her expression cool and calculated. "I want to talk about what you just overheard," she says, her voice silky smooth. "But I think it's better if we do it in private."

I can feel the tension coiling in the air, thick enough to slice through. "You think I'd let you pull him away?" I shoot back, my voice steady but my heart racing.

She smirks, a glimmer of amusement flickering in her eyes. "Oh, sweetheart, I don't need to pull him anywhere. You see, I have a way of making people listen. Especially when there's something to gain."

"What do you mean by that?" Marcus interjects, his brow furrowing with concern.

"Oh, just a little insight into how the world really works," she replies, leaning closer, her voice dropping to a conspiratorial whisper. "You think you're safe, but the truth is, success has its price. And if you want to thrive in this environment, you'll need to make some… sacrifices."

I glance at Marcus, uncertainty flickering in my chest. "What kind of sacrifices?"

"Let's just say," Vera continues, "that the higher you climb, the more your choices matter. People will do anything to keep their positions. Even if it means letting go of what they hold dear."

"Is that a threat?" Marcus asks, his voice low, barely concealing his anger.

"Not a threat, dear Marcus. Just a reality check." She straightens, taking a step back, her expression suddenly all business. "And if you're not careful, you could lose more than just your future. You could lose her."

The weight of her words settles between us like a heavy fog, chilling my bones. I want to protest, to argue that our connection is unbreakable, but doubt begins to creep in like an insidious vine.

"Let's go," Marcus says, his voice steely as he grips my hand tightly. He leads me away from Vera, the air thick with tension, but I can't help glancing back at her. She stands there, watching us with a satisfied smirk, as if she's just played a masterstroke in a game I didn't even know we were playing.

As we make our way back inside, the laughter and music seem to fade into the background, replaced by the pounding of my heart. I can feel the weight of the night pressing down on us, each step echoing with uncertainty.

"Marcus," I begin, but he holds up a hand, silencing me.

"I don't want to talk about her anymore. I want to focus on us," he says, his voice firm but with a hint of vulnerability that softens the edges of his determination.

"Easy for you to say," I retort, my frustration bubbling up again. "You don't have to worry about losing everything. I do."

He stops, turning to face me fully. "You're not going to lose me," he insists, his eyes locking onto mine with fierce intensity. "But we need to be cautious. I won't let her sabotage us."

I nod, but the unease remains, gnawing at my thoughts like a persistent itch. "What do we do now?"

Before he can respond, the lights flicker, and the music cuts out, plunging the hall into an unsettling silence. The sudden stillness sends a ripple of anxiety through the crowd, and I can feel my heart racing once more. Whispers ripple through the guests, confusion mingling with apprehension.

And then the lights flash back on, but the atmosphere has shifted dramatically. A group of men in dark suits has appeared at the entrance, their expressions grim and determined. The murmurs grow louder, a swell of concern echoing through the room as they scan the crowd.

Marcus grips my hand tighter, his eyes narrowing as he studies the newcomers. "What's going on?"

I don't have time to respond before one of the men steps forward, a commanding presence that silences the crowd with a mere wave of his hand. "We need to speak with Marcus Blackwood immediately."

The room goes still as all eyes turn toward us, the weight of scrutiny palpable. My heart races as Marcus's gaze flickers between the man and me, uncertainty etched in every line of his face.

"What the hell is this about?" Marcus demands, his voice steady despite the tension crackling in the air.

I hold my breath, my pulse thrumming in my ears, as the man takes another step forward, his gaze unyielding. "It's about your future, Marcus. And what you're willing to do to secure it."

The air grows heavy with the promise of something dark and uncertain, and I realize in that moment that the stakes have just risen higher than I ever imagined. The evening's glitter and glamour feel like a distant memory, overshadowed by the impending storm.

Chapter 13: Literary Revelations

The gala shimmered like a mirage in the heart of the city, a spectacle of lights and laughter that threatened to overwhelm my senses. Crystal chandeliers hung from the ceiling, refracting a kaleidoscope of colors onto the polished floor, where elegantly dressed couples twirled in time to the lilting strains of a string quartet. Each note seemed to pulse with a life of its own, wrapping around us like a silken ribbon. I adjusted my grip on the glass of sparkling water, the effervescence tickling my nose as I searched the room for a familiar face.

That's when I saw her—Vera. She stood across the vast ballroom, her presence cutting through the merriment like a knife through soft butter. Clad in a dress the color of midnight, she commanded attention with an effortless grace that seemed almost otherworldly. A wave of unease washed over me, memories of our last encounter flooding back, heavy as the velvet drapes that framed the windows. She was a storm on the horizon, and I felt the electricity in the air, a reminder of the obstacles lurking just beyond the glimmering façade of this gala.

"Are you alright?" Marcus's voice pulled me back to the moment, his brow furrowed with concern. He stood beside me, his handsome features illuminated by the soft glow of the chandelier above. The sharp cut of his jaw contrasted with the warmth in his eyes, and in that instant, I felt a connection between us that was both startling and undeniable.

"Just... taking it all in," I replied, forcing a smile as I tried to shake off the chill that Vera's gaze had instilled in me. The way she scrutinized the crowd was disquieting, as though she could see the threads that wove our lives together—and was plotting how to unravel them.

Marcus motioned for us to continue our exploration of the gala, and I followed, determined to focus on the moment. As we wove through the throngs of people, the atmosphere enveloped us, a blend of laughter and the rich scent of gourmet hors d'oeuvres wafting through the air. I let myself relax, immersing in the electric energy that crackled around us.

"Do you have a favorite author?" Marcus asked, his eyes bright with curiosity as we navigated the crowd.

I pondered his question for a heartbeat, my thoughts flitting through a library of characters and stories. "It's hard to choose just one. I think I'd have to say Jane Austen. There's something about her wit and keen observations on society that I find utterly enchanting."

"Ah, a classicist," he teased, a smirk tugging at the corners of his lips. "I suppose that makes me the rebellious type, then. I've always been drawn to the raw, unfiltered chaos of contemporary fiction—especially authors like Haruki Murakami. There's a dreamlike quality to his stories that pulls me in, like I'm stepping into another reality."

"Murakami? That's a bold choice," I replied, my heart fluttering at the way his passion ignited his features. "What is it about his work that resonates with you?"

As he shared stories of how Murakami's characters often mirrored his own childhood struggles, the world around us faded, and I hung on every word. He spoke of long nights spent reading under the covers, using the glow of a flashlight to escape into far-off worlds when his home felt too turbulent. "Books were my sanctuary," he said, the sincerity in his voice washing over me like a balm.

"Me too," I confessed, my voice barely above a whisper. "When my parents fought, I would hide in my room with my books. They were my escape, a way to live a thousand different lives."

We stood still for a moment, the buzz of the gala fading into a distant hum as the intimacy of our exchange drew us closer. I saw a flicker of understanding in his eyes, a shared recognition of our vulnerabilities, and it electrified the air between us. It was as if we were cocooned in our own bubble, insulated from the chaos around us.

Suddenly, laughter erupted nearby, jarring me from my reverie. A group of elegantly dressed women swept past, their laughter ringing like wind chimes in a summer breeze, and I caught a glimpse of Vera again. She was watching us now, her eyes narrowing slightly as though she could sense the shift in my focus.

"Hey," Marcus said, breaking my concentration. "You okay? You seem a little distracted."

I forced myself to shake off the tension creeping back in. "I'm fine. Just... the crowd, I guess. It's a bit overwhelming."

"Let's find somewhere quieter then," he suggested, his hand gently guiding me through the sea of bodies. We slipped away from the main hall, finding ourselves on a balcony adorned with twinkling fairy lights, the night sky stretching above us like a velvet canopy sprinkled with diamonds.

"Wow," I breathed, leaning against the railing. The city skyline glimmered in the distance, and for a moment, I allowed the beauty of it all to wash over me. "This is perfect."

Marcus stepped beside me, his presence warm and comforting. "It's nice to escape the noise for a bit, isn't it?"

"It really is," I replied, meeting his gaze. The chemistry between us felt palpable, an invisible thread weaving our fates closer together. But as I stood there, the weight of Vera's lingering presence gnawed at the edges of my mind. The gala had promised enchantment, yet I couldn't shake the feeling that shadows lurked just out of sight, ready to disrupt the delicate magic of this moment.

"Tell me about your dream," Marcus said suddenly, his voice low and earnest. "What do you want to do with your life?"

Caught off guard, I hesitated. Dreams felt fragile, easily broken under the scrutiny of reality. But in that intimate space, something inside me stirred, urging me to share. "I want to write," I admitted, the words spilling out before I could second-guess myself. "I've always wanted to create worlds and characters that resonate, that make people feel less alone."

"Then you should," he said, his eyes brightening with encouragement. "You have the passion for it. Don't let anything or anyone hold you back."

A smile tugged at my lips, buoyed by his belief in me. Yet, even as we stood there, a part of me remained tethered to the looming specter of Vera. Her sharp gaze felt like an uninvited guest, ready to crash the party, and I couldn't shake the sense that this night was far from over.

The night air was thick with the scent of blooming jasmine, wrapping around us like a warm embrace as Marcus leaned against the balcony railing, his posture casual yet undeniably inviting. I watched him, captivated by the way the soft glow of the fairy lights caught the angles of his face, illuminating the boyish charm that had begun to work its way into my thoughts with an unsettling regularity. We stood on that balcony, an oasis amid the gala's fervor, and for a moment, the outside world felt inconsequential.

"So, what kind of stories do you want to write?" he asked, breaking the comfortable silence that had settled between us. The question lingered in the air, charged with possibilities, and I felt a surge of excitement rush through me.

"I think I want to write about the messy parts of life—the love, the heartbreak, the laughter in the chaos," I said, my voice gaining strength. "Something that feels real, you know? I want people to pick up my book and think, 'This is my story.'"

"Ah, so you're aiming for the heartstrings, then?" His teasing tone coaxed a laugh from me, a lightness that sent butterflies flitting through my stomach.

"Definitely," I shot back, my smile widening. "Just call me the literary heartbreaker."

He raised an eyebrow, his interest piqued. "And here I thought you were a romantic at heart."

I shrugged, feigning nonchalance. "Can't I be both? Besides, there's a certain thrill in breaking hearts with a pen instead of, you know, actual heartbreak."

He chuckled, the sound rich and warm against the cool night air. "Fair point. It's much safer to shatter emotions on paper rather than in real life. Who knows how many hearts you'd crush if you tried the latter?"

"Hey, I'd need to have a heart to break one, so it's all theoretical." I glanced away, my bravado faltering as I caught sight of Vera once more. She was deep in conversation, but her eyes darted around the room, and I could feel her gaze settling in our direction. I swallowed hard, forcing myself to shake off the unease.

"Your heart is definitely there, hiding behind that humor," Marcus said, his voice softer now, as though he could sense the shift in my mood. "It's a brave thing, to expose yourself through writing. The world can be a brutal place for those who dare to feel deeply."

His words struck a chord within me, resonating with the complexities I often kept buried. "It's true," I admitted. "But it's also where the magic happens. I think we all carry around these stories, waiting for someone to listen. Or maybe even to tell them in a way that someone else can feel less alone."

"God, I love that. You're going to make me cry, and then I won't be able to attend another gala without looking like a soggy mess," he teased, and the playful glimmer in his eyes brightened the weight of my earlier apprehensions.

As we continued to exchange thoughts on the literary world, I couldn't shake the feeling that our connection was more than a passing fancy. The kindred spirit I sensed in him felt rare and precious, like stumbling upon a long-lost friend in an unexpected place.

"Are you familiar with Virginia Woolf?" he asked suddenly, the glint of mischief returning to his eyes.

"Of course," I said, my curiosity piqued. "She's a brilliant mind. Why?"

"Well, I think she would've appreciated the setting of this gala. So many different narratives blending together, yet each person here has their own inner turmoil. Everyone wearing their best masks—quite literally." He gestured to the crowd, where laughter echoed, mingling with the clinking of glasses.

"True," I said, contemplating his words. "This event feels like a dance of facades. Each person, including us, putting on a show while something deeper simmers beneath the surface."

"Exactly!" His enthusiasm was infectious, and I couldn't help but smile as he continued, "And maybe if we're lucky, we'll catch a glimpse of the real stories hidden behind those polished exteriors."

Just as I opened my mouth to respond, the glass doors swung open with a flourish, and in stepped Vera, her presence like a thundercloud darkening an otherwise clear sky. My heart dropped, and I fought the urge to look away. The crowd parted for her, and she glided toward us, her smile bright but icy, a façade perfected through years of practice.

"Marcus," she purred, her voice smooth as silk, laced with something I couldn't quite place. "Fancy meeting you here, of all places."

He straightened, his expression morphing into one of polite indifference. "Vera, what a surprise."

I could feel the tension crackle in the air like static electricity, a palpable force that threatened to ignite. My earlier elation began to wane, replaced by a tightness in my chest. Vera's gaze flicked between Marcus and me, her smile narrowing, as if she were sizing me up like a connoisseur inspecting a rare artifact.

"Still playing with words, I see. It must be exhausting," she remarked, her tone light yet edged with something sharper. "Careful, darling. Sometimes, words can be treacherous."

"Unlike your intentions, I presume?" I shot back before I could stop myself, the words spilling out like water from a broken dam. The boldness surprised even me, but Marcus's faint grin encouraged me to lean into the moment.

Vera raised an eyebrow, the surprise fleeting before she regained her composure. "I admire your spirit, but don't mistake it for bravery." Her eyes narrowed, a flash of something dark and predatory flickering behind the veneer of sophistication.

"I'm not mistaking anything," I countered, holding her gaze. "Just observing the truths hidden behind your well-crafted words. Bravery takes many forms, and I'd wager that clinging to a facade takes far more than being vulnerable."

The tension between us hung like a storm cloud, electric and thick, and for a fleeting moment, I saw something shift in her expression—was it surprise or anger? I couldn't tell.

"Enough of this," Marcus interjected, his voice steady yet firm. "We're just having a conversation. No need to turn it into a competition."

"Perhaps you should learn to choose your companions wisely, Marcus," Vera replied, her voice dripping with a saccharine sweetness that made my skin crawl. "After all, the company one keeps says a great deal about their character."

Before I could respond, a server approached, breaking the palpable tension. He offered us a tray of delicate pastries, and I seized the moment to step back, grabbing a tartlet and using it as a shield against the confrontation that had escalated so quickly.

"Thank you," I murmured, and the server nodded, blissfully unaware of the verbal duel unfolding just moments before.

"Nothing like a little sugar to sweeten the conversation, right?" Marcus said, flashing a lopsided grin as he grabbed one of the pastries for himself.

"Is that your strategy? When in doubt, feed the beast?" I replied, laughing despite the lingering discomfort.

"Hey, it works for me," he retorted playfully, his charm cutting through the tension like a knife.

As we exchanged banter, I could feel Vera's icy glare bore into my back. With every light-hearted exchange I shared with Marcus, the weight of her presence lingered, a dark shadow threatening to engulf the vibrant atmosphere we had built. I wanted to focus on the budding connection with him, but her watchful eyes felt like a hawk circling its prey, reminding me that the evening was far from finished.

The sound of laughter and clinking glasses filled the air around us, but it felt distant, as though we were sealed in a bubble away from the chaos of the gala. I found myself leaning closer to Marcus, drawn in by his captivating stories. The way he spoke about the worlds he had explored within the pages of books was infectious, his passion igniting a spark of excitement within me.

"Books are like portals," he mused, a glint of mischief in his eyes. "One moment, you're in a mundane existence, and the next, you're dodging dragons or solving crimes with your favorite detective. It's a much better alternative than confronting family dinners with my relatives. Trust me."

I chuckled, imagining the dramatic scenes he must have navigated through his life. "I can relate. My family dinners resemble a circus, complete with unexpected performances and emotional high-wire acts."

He raised an eyebrow. "Oh, do tell. I need to know if your life is more entertaining than mine."

I hesitated, but the warmth of his gaze encouraged me to share. "Well, there was the Thanksgiving where my uncle mistook the cranberry sauce for gravy and poured it all over the turkey. The look on my grandmother's face was priceless. It was like watching a horror movie unfold in slow motion."

Marcus laughed, the sound rich and genuine. "Now that's the kind of story that could be a bestseller! 'Cranberry Catastrophes: A Family's Culinary Nightmare.' I'd read that."

As the banter flowed effortlessly between us, I felt a shift in the air, a subtle change that made my heart race. I turned slightly, half-expecting to see Vera lurking nearby, but instead, I caught sight of something even more surprising. A woman, elegant and poised, had approached us. Her dress shimmered under the lights like the surface of a lake at dawn, and her eyes held a piercing intensity.

"Marcus," she greeted, her voice smooth but laced with an edge. "I see you've found yourself an interesting companion."

I felt the tension seep back into the moment as Marcus's demeanor shifted. "Samantha, this is—"

"—someone who enjoys literature and prefers not to engage in pointless games," I interjected, finding my voice more resolute than I felt.

Samantha smiled, but it didn't reach her eyes. "How refreshing. I'd wager you know all about the importance of appearances, then." Her gaze flicked between Marcus and me, assessing, as if trying to gauge the strength of our bond.

"What is it with people today? It's as if my presence is a bad omen," I quipped, attempting to lighten the mood.

"Perhaps it's just the thrill of new relationships," Marcus added, his tone light, but I could see the flicker of annoyance beneath the surface.

Samantha leaned in slightly, her expression curious. "Relationships can be precarious, especially in a world where everyone is hiding something. You never know who might be playing a role in your story."

I felt a shiver run down my spine. "That's the beauty of stories, isn't it? They give us an opportunity to rewrite our narratives, even when reality feels too constricting."

"Such optimism," she said, tilting her head slightly. "But it's often those who wear their hearts on their sleeves who end up getting hurt the most."

With that, she excused herself, leaving a wake of tension in her departure. The air felt charged, as if someone had just switched on a high-voltage wire, and I turned to Marcus, who wore an expression of bemusement. "What was that all about?" I asked, a hint of worry creeping into my voice.

"Ah, Samantha likes to stir the pot," he said, his smile returning but with a touch of weariness. "She's an old friend, but her advice comes wrapped in riddles. Don't take her too seriously."

"Easier said than done," I muttered, still feeling the weight of her words hanging between us. I was starting to sense that the night was shifting in ways I hadn't anticipated.

"Let's get back to more pleasant topics," he suggested, steering the conversation back to safer ground. "What's a story you'd love to tell if you could write anything without boundaries?"

I considered his question, the wheels of my imagination turning. "I think I'd want to write a tale about a young girl who discovers a hidden talent for painting, only to find that her art can alter reality. Every brushstroke could change something significant, but there's a cost."

"Now that's intriguing! But how would she manage the consequences?" Marcus's eyes sparkled with enthusiasm.

I launched into an explanation, my excitement bubbling over as I wove the narrative, but then the gala erupted into chaos. A loud crash echoed from within the ballroom, and the music screeched to a halt.

"What was that?" I exclaimed, my heart racing as I exchanged a panicked glance with Marcus.

We moved back toward the crowd, curiosity and dread mixing in my gut. The laughter had vanished, replaced by murmurs of confusion and fear. A group of people was gathered near the entrance, their faces pale and mouths moving in hushed tones.

"Something must've happened," I whispered, anxiety flooding my voice.

As we approached the cluster of onlookers, I saw a figure crumpled on the floor, surrounded by concerned attendees. My stomach dropped as I recognized the person—someone I knew, a familiar face from my past, and they were in distress.

"Is that...?" I started, but Marcus grabbed my arm, his expression grim.

"It can't be," he said, his eyes widening. "We should stay back."

But I couldn't move. My legs felt rooted to the spot, the pull of recognition anchoring me. I pushed through the crowd, desperately trying to see what was happening. As I drew closer, I caught snippets of conversation that made my heart race.

"She collapsed without warning. Someone call an ambulance!"

"What happened? Is she okay?"

I squeezed past a few more people, finally breaking through to the front. My breath hitched as I laid eyes on her—the woman who had once been my mentor, a figure I had admired from a distance. She lay unconscious, a stark reminder of how fragile life could be, even amid the glittering facade of a gala.

Marcus was at my side, his presence a grounding force, but I could feel the urgency rising like a tide around us. "We need to do something," I insisted, my heart pounding.

Just then, Vera emerged from the throng, her face a mask of shock. "What happened?" she asked, but there was an undertone of something else in her voice—was it concern or something more calculating?

As I glanced between the crowd and her, I sensed an unspoken tension in the air, as if we were all holding our breaths, waiting for the next wave to crash down.

"Don't move her," a voice called out, slicing through the chaos. A paramedic rushed forward, pushing through the throng.

The atmosphere shifted again, this time heavier with dread. I felt the prickle of fear creeping up my spine as I realized this event, meant to be a celebration, had morphed into something far more sinister. The night was unraveling, and with it, the threads of my understanding began to fray.

What had happened to my mentor? Was this truly just an accident, or was there something lurking in the shadows of this seemingly perfect evening? The tension was palpable, the air thick with uncertainty, and as I turned to Marcus, I could see the questions mirrored in his eyes.

Suddenly, Vera's voice cut through the noise, an eerie calmness settling over her words. "Sometimes, in the pursuit of truth, we uncover more than we bargained for."

The words hung in the air like a dark omen, and in that moment, I realized this night held more secrets than I had ever anticipated. I felt the ground beneath me shift as the tension coiled tighter, leaving me suspended in a web of uncertainty, the answers just out of reach, but the stakes growing higher with each passing moment.

Chapter 14: A Dance with Destiny

The music envelops us, an intoxicating blend of violins and soft piano notes that dances through the air like gossamer threads. With Marcus's hand firmly clasping mine, we glide onto the floor, where swirling gowns and tailored suits create a kaleidoscope of color and energy. I can feel the heat radiating from him, a steady pulse that seems to sync with the cadence of our movements. It's exhilarating, as though every worry, every doubt, is melting away with each step we take.

His gaze is intense, those deep brown eyes reflecting the myriad lights from the chandeliers above, making them shimmer like molten chocolate. I can't help but smile, feeling the corners of my lips lift with a mix of excitement and trepidation. There's something magnetic about him, a draw that pulls me closer, igniting a warmth that spreads through my veins. With each turn, the world around us fades into a blur—our troubles, the expectations, the unspoken tensions—everything dissolves into the rhythm of the music.

But as the melody swells, I can't shake the sensation of being watched. My heart races, not only from the heady thrill of dancing with Marcus but also from the unsettling feeling creeping up my spine. I turn slightly, my gaze sweeping over the throng of elegantly dressed guests. And there she is—Vera, standing against the far wall, her expression one of cold calculation. Her eyes narrow, glinting like shards of ice, and I feel as if she's dissecting the scene before her with a surgeon's precision.

What is she plotting?

The joyous atmosphere around me feels suddenly fragile, as if a shadow has been cast over the vibrant colors of the gala. I attempt to shake off the feeling, forcing myself to focus on Marcus, whose laughter spills over, rich and warm like honey. He twirls me, spinning me out and pulling me back in with a flourish that makes my heart flutter. "You're an incredible dancer," he says, his voice low and smooth, pulling me back from the edge of my anxious thoughts.

"Is that your way of saying I don't look like a complete fool?" I tease, raising an eyebrow, and he chuckles, the sound resonating in my chest like a promise.

"Only a little," he quips back, his smile dazzling. "But you wear it well."

Our playful banter weaves through the music, lightening the air between us, but each twirl reminds me of the precariousness of our situation. I had hoped that this gala, this chance to escape reality even for a moment, would bring clarity. Instead, it feels like I'm caught in a storm, and Vera is the eye of it, watching, waiting.

The crowd around us shifts, a wave of laughter and chatter rising and falling like the tide. But as the song transitions into something slower, the atmosphere changes, too. Couples melt into one another, lost in the romance of the moment, while the world beyond our little bubble blurs even further. I lean into Marcus, my cheek resting against the warmth of his shoulder, and I breathe him in—spicy cologne mingling with the scent of woodsy notes, an intoxicating combination that makes me feel both safe and exhilarated.

"Do you think we're crazy?" I ask suddenly, pulling back just enough to look into his eyes, gauging his reaction. "I mean, after everything we've been through?"

He raises an eyebrow, the corner of his mouth quirking up. "Crazy? Maybe a little. But isn't that what makes life interesting?"

A shiver runs through me—not from fear, but from the thrill of our connection. His words sink deep, igniting a spark of rebellion within me. Perhaps embracing the chaos was our only option, a way to defy the tangled web we found ourselves caught in.

Yet, as if summoned by my thoughts, Vera steps forward, her presence slicing through the intimacy we've created on the dance floor. She approaches with an elegance that feels more predatory than graceful. "Marcus, darling," she purrs, her voice dripping with false sweetness. "I couldn't help but notice how well you two are getting along."

"Vera," Marcus replies, his tone cool, yet I can sense the tension coiling between them like a taut wire. "We were just enjoying the evening."

"Oh, I can see that," she retorts, glancing at me with an inscrutable smile that sends another chill down my spine. "But I do wonder how long this little fantasy can last."

Her words hang in the air, heavy and loaded, and I feel Marcus stiffen beside me. I can see the gears turning in his mind as he contemplates how to respond to her thinly veiled threat.

I straighten, emboldened by our moment. "It's a dance, Vera," I say, trying to inject a lightness into my voice that I don't quite feel. "Perhaps you should join us instead of lurking in the shadows."

The surprise flickers across her face before it settles into something akin to annoyance. "I wouldn't want to interrupt your little fairy tale," she replies, her smile tight. "But fairy tales, dear, often come with a price."

I can feel the weight of her words sink in, and the dance floor around us suddenly feels constricting, like the walls are closing in. Marcus tightens his grip on my waist, his energy shifting as if he's preparing for a confrontation.

"Why don't you leave her out of this, Vera?" he says, his voice steady but laced with tension. "This isn't your show."

Her laughter rings out, sharp and cutting through the ambiance, and for a moment, I fear it may shatter the fragile peace we've created. "Oh, Marcus," she coos, "you always were so naive. This is all part of the game. You should know by now that every move has consequences."

Just then, the lights dim slightly, and the music shifts again, but the air feels charged, a tempest brewing beneath the surface. I glance at Marcus, searching his eyes for reassurance, but the warmth I found earlier is overshadowed by an impending storm of uncertainty.

He takes a step forward, a protective instinct flaring within him. "I'm done playing your games, Vera." His words are firm, a declaration that makes my heart race with a mix of fear and admiration. "I will not let you manipulate the people I care about."

The tension hangs thick, a taut line ready to snap, and I can't help but hold my breath, waiting for the inevitable clash.

The atmosphere grows tense as Vera's laughter fades, replaced by an almost suffocating silence that envelops us like fog. My heart pounds, an erratic rhythm that matches the cadence of our previous dance, but now it feels as though I'm teetering on the edge of a precipice. Marcus stands protectively close, his demeanor shifting from carefree to resolute, and I can't help but admire the fierce determination in his eyes.

Vera's smile remains plastered on her face, but the glimmer of amusement has turned cold, sharp like a blade. "Oh, Marcus," she says, her voice silky but dripping with malice. "How romantic, this little show of defiance. But you're forgetting something crucial: this is not just a dance; it's a game. And I always play to win."

"Good thing I'm not in the market for second place," Marcus shoots back, his tone laced with defiance that sends a thrill coursing through me. It's that momentary rush, the exhilarating mixture of danger and courage, and I find myself wanting to lean into it rather than retreat.

"Isn't it charming?" Vera continues, her eyes darting between us, a predator savoring her prey. "Two star-crossed lovers, trapped in a tangled web of deception. How fitting." She leans in slightly, her voice dropping to a conspiratorial whisper. "But what happens when the curtain falls, darling? What happens when the fairy tale unravels?"

"Then we'll rewrite the ending," I retort, feeling a surge of confidence as I meet her gaze. "After all, I have a knack for plot twists."

Her eyebrows shoot up, genuine surprise flickering across her face for just a heartbeat before her expression morphs back into that cool mask of disdain. "I admire your spirit," she says slowly, as if weighing her words carefully. "But spirit alone won't save you from the consequences of your choices."

The music swells again, a melodious backdrop to this tense exchange, but it feels as if the whole world has narrowed down to just the three of us. I can feel the eyes of the crowd shifting, sensing the charged air around us, but I refuse to let fear dictate my actions. This is my moment, not just for Marcus and me, but for everyone who has ever felt trapped by someone else's ambitions.

"You've underestimated me, Vera," Marcus replies, his voice steady, unwavering. "And it's going to be your downfall."

I can almost see the wheels turning in Vera's mind, her lips twitching as she contemplates her next move. The moment stretches, taut and electric, and I hold my breath, waiting for the inevitable fallout. But before she can respond, a figure slips into our orbit, cutting through the tension like a hot knife through butter.

"Ah, there you are! I was searching everywhere for you!" A voice bursts forth, exuberant and unexpectedly cheerful. It's Rachel, one of my closest friends, her smile wide and her energy infectious. She twirls into the space between us, oblivious to the storm brewing. "Marcus, darling! You simply must come see the dessert table—it's a work of art!"

I can't help but let out a laugh, tension easing slightly at Rachel's entrance. Her enthusiasm is like a burst of sunlight breaking through the clouds. She grabs my hand, pulling me along with her. "Come on! I need you to see this. I'm convinced there's a life-sized chocolate fountain, and if there is, we have to take a picture!"

Marcus hesitates, glancing between me and Vera. "Are you sure you want to leave?"

"I'll be fine," I assure him, giving Vera a look that dares her to follow. "Besides, I'm dying for some chocolate."

Rachel drags me toward the back of the grand ballroom, her chatter bright and buoyant as she recounts the various displays she's seen. "The floral arrangements are stunning! And you wouldn't believe how extravagant the centerpieces are," she gushes, and I can't help but soak up her energy, grateful for the diversion.

As we round the corner, the noise of the gala fades, replaced by the sound of gentle laughter and clinking glasses. We step into a lavishly decorated lounge area, filled with rich velvet couches and an array of delectable treats. The air is sweet and inviting, a stark contrast to the tension we just escaped.

"Look!" Rachel points to a lavish display of desserts, a true feast for the eyes. A magnificent chocolate fountain stands at the center, cascading streams of velvety chocolate, surrounded by strawberries, marshmallows, and various confections. "Isn't it magnificent?"

I can't help but grin, stepping closer to inspect the setup. "This is definitely Instagram-worthy," I agree, picking up a skewer of strawberries and dipping it into the flowing chocolate.

Just as I'm about to take a bite, the door swings open, and a rush of guests spills into the lounge, laughter and chatter blending into a cheerful cacophony. Among them is Ethan, a mutual friend, his presence a welcome distraction. His bright blue suit makes him stand out, a beacon of good humor in the dimly lit room.

"Did someone say chocolate?" Ethan announces with mock seriousness, his eyes sparkling with mischief. "I knew I felt the call of the cocoa!"

Rachel laughs, and soon we're all gathered around the fountain, indulging in the sweets as if they're a panacea for the night's earlier tension. "What did I miss?" Ethan asks, his brow furrowing slightly as he notices my flushed cheeks.

"Just a little tête-à-tête with our favorite ice queen," I say, motioning back toward the ballroom. "But nothing I couldn't handle with a swift escape."

"Ah, the sweet taste of freedom," he muses, dipping a marshmallow into the chocolate with exaggerated relish. "It's the best flavor. Better than any of Vera's schemes, that's for sure."

The laughter flows easily now, and I find solace in the camaraderie, the warmth of friendship banishing the shadows Vera had cast. But as the moment unfolds, a part of me remains acutely aware of the storm brewing just beyond the door.

Even with the laughter and the sweet taste of chocolate dancing on my tongue, the evening isn't done with me yet. The world feels precarious, like the edges of a cliff where the fall could either be exhilarating or disastrous. I can't shake the sense that the night holds more secrets, more revelations that will soon come to light.

As we finish our treats and share stories, I glance back toward the ballroom, where Vera remains a figure of intrigue, no doubt plotting her next move. My heart races with a mix of excitement and apprehension; I'm drawn to the uncertainty that lies ahead, aware that every choice we make weaves us deeper into this intricate tapestry of ambition, desire, and danger.

As the laughter and chatter swirl around us, I let the chocolate's sweetness linger on my tongue, trying to forget the prickling sense of danger that still clings to the air. The lounge fills with familiar faces, a tapestry of friendships that interweave to create a comforting haven amidst the chaos of the gala. Ethan makes a grand show of piling marshmallows onto his skewer, oblivious to the tension that had just moments before gripped the dance floor.

"Careful there, Ethan," I joke, eyeing his precarious confection. "You might have to start a support group for chocolate addicts if you keep this up."

"Support group? I was thinking of a chocolate fan club," he replies, a playful glint in his eye as he takes a generous bite. "Chocolate enthusiasts unite! I'll be president, and you can be my VP. We'll hold meetings every Friday night and taste-test until we're too full to move."

Rachel laughs, leaning in to snatch a marshmallow from his skewer. "Count me in! We can even have themed meetings: 'Dark Chocolate Night' or 'Gourmet Truffles and You.'"

I can't help but grin at their antics, the ease of their camaraderie making me feel more at home. I take a moment to appreciate the way the warm lights reflect off the gold and silver decorations, creating a shimmering effect that dances across the walls. It's all so lovely, and for a heartbeat, I can forget the lurking shadows.

But as the excitement ebbs and flows, I can't quite shake the awareness of Vera's watchful gaze. I glance back toward the ballroom, half-expecting to see her lurking at the edge, a specter against the vibrant backdrop of laughter and music. Instead, she seems to have disappeared into the throng, but the unease lingers like a storm cloud on the horizon.

"Hey, you alright?" Ethan's voice cuts through my thoughts, a flicker of concern in his eyes. "You look like you've just seen a ghost."

I shake my head, brushing away the feeling of dread. "I'm fine. Just... absorbing the ambiance. And maybe a little too much chocolate."

"Your aura screams 'sugar high,'" he quips, grinning. "Just don't let it turn into a full-blown sugar meltdown. Those are harder to recover from than any hangover."

I laugh, thankful for the distraction. "You have no idea how many times I've faced the perils of a sugar meltdown. The trauma runs deep."

As we share more banter, I feel the tension easing, but the sense of impending doom gnaws at me. The gala is a beautiful illusion, but beneath its glossy surface lies a brewing storm, one that threatens to disrupt our fragile peace. I take a deep breath, mentally shaking off the dread as I focus on the laughter surrounding me.

Rachel nudges me, glancing toward the entrance. "Looks like the crowd is getting rowdier. Let's head back to the dance floor! I need a break from sweets before I turn into a chocolate fountain myself."

I follow her lead, glancing back at Ethan, who nods encouragingly, and we push through the throng of guests. The music calls to us, a siren song urging us to lose ourselves in its embrace once more. As we return to the floor, the energy feels different; it's electric, charged with anticipation.

Suddenly, the lights flicker, momentarily plunging the room into shadow before the chandeliers burst back into brilliance, illuminating the faces of the guests in hues of gold and white. My heart quickens, the flicker feeling ominous, like a prelude to something unexpected.

Then, amidst the swirling lights and laughter, Vera reappears. She strides onto the dance floor with an air of purpose, her expression a mask of calculated charm. My stomach tightens, the familiar dread creeping back. It's as if she's magnetized, drawing everyone's attention, her presence darkening the festive atmosphere.

"Marcus!" she calls, her voice slicing through the music like glass. "Do join me for a dance, won't you?"

I feel a surge of anger, a primal instinct to protect what we have built, to shield the fragile happiness that had just begun to blossom. Rachel's hand grips my arm, sensing the shift in the air. "What's her deal?" she whispers, her eyes narrowing.

"No idea, but I'm not about to let her ruin this moment," I reply, my voice low but firm.

Marcus hesitates, glancing between Vera and me. "I—"

"Don't even think about it!" I interrupt, my voice rising slightly, surprising even myself. "You just finished dancing with her. Why would you want to?"

"Because it's a gala, and I'm being polite," he replies, his frustration evident.

"Polite? Or simply a pawn in her game?" The words tumble out before I can catch them, fueled by an emotion I can't quite contain.

"Enough!" Vera interjects, cutting through the tension like a knife. "Marcus, you're far too talented to waste time on trivial disputes. Dance with me. Let's show them what true chemistry looks like."

The way she leans toward him, the inviting lilt in her voice, sends a flash of anger through me. The crowd's eyes are shifting, drawn to the spectacle unfolding, and I can't let this play out like some scripted drama. "You know what she's trying to do, Marcus!"

"I know what I want," he replies, a hard edge creeping into his voice. "And right now, it's to enjoy this night without the theatrics."

Vera's smile widens, a glimmer of victory flickering in her eyes. "Come now, darling. Don't let her jealousy spoil your fun. You wouldn't want to deny a lady a dance, would you?"

He opens his mouth to respond, but the words falter. I can see the struggle in his expression, the flickering flame of desire caught between loyalty and attraction. It's maddening, and I feel as if the very air around us is thickening, suffocating.

"Why don't you both just dance?" I spit out, anger flashing in my eyes. "After all, it seems you've already rehearsed your lines."

The crowd buzzes with anticipation, eyes darting back and forth, and my heart races as I feel the weight of their scrutiny. Just then, Rachel steps forward, her expression determined. "Listen, Vera. If you think you can just waltz in here and claim what isn't yours, you've got another thing coming."

"Who are you to challenge me?" Vera counters, her composure slipping slightly as she sizes Rachel up.

"Someone who knows that kindness doesn't mean weakness. And someone who knows how to stand up for her friends," Rachel replies, her voice steady, unwavering.

For a heartbeat, it feels like time stops, the air crackling with the weight of our confrontation. I can sense that this moment is tipping toward something pivotal, a point of no return. But just as I brace myself for whatever might unfold, an unexpected voice cuts through the tension.

"Ladies, ladies! What's all this fuss about?" A smooth, authoritative voice fills the room. My heart sinks as I turn to see the figure approaching: Mr. Lawson, the gala's organizer, a man known for his strict adherence to decorum and order.

His eyes sweep over the scene, assessing the escalating tension. "This is a celebration, not a battleground. I expect a certain level of civility."

I feel a surge of frustration. "We're just trying to—"

"Let's keep it light, shall we?" he interrupts, his smile strained, yet charming. "I suggest we return to the dance floor and leave the bickering for another time."

Vera smirks, clearly enjoying the intervention. "See? Even the adults agree. Now, Marcus, how about that dance?"

Before I can utter another word, Marcus steps back, a conflicted look on his face, caught in the undertow of Vera's influence. My heart pounds in my chest as the world tilts, the looming storm finally bursting forth, unraveling everything we've fought for.

And just as I think I might lose him, a sudden commotion erupts from the entrance. The door flies open, and a group of people rushes in, faces flushed with urgency. "We need to speak to Marcus!" one of them shouts, breathless and wild-eyed.

My breath catches, the revelation slicing through the air like a bolt of lightning. I can feel the weight of destiny shifting, and as I look at Marcus, I know—this night is far from over, and everything is about to change.

Chapter 15: Cracks in the Facade

The grand library of the Hawthorne estate envelops us in a warm embrace of polished wood and soft, golden light. Sunbeams filter through the tall, arched windows, illuminating dust motes that dance in the air, creating a magical atmosphere that feels both inviting and suffocating. I love this room—the way it smells of old books and the whispers of stories waiting to be discovered—but today it feels like a cage. I sit across from Marcus at the long mahogany table, the distance between us charged with unspoken words and unresolved feelings.

His fingers trace the spine of a book absentmindedly, and I can't help but notice how he seems to retreat into himself, a familiar habit when the weight of his thoughts becomes too much to bear. "We should focus on the project," he says, his voice low and almost defeated. It's a gentle reminder that cuts deeper than I want to admit, hinting that our connection may be less important to him than the task at hand.

"You can't keep pushing me away like this," I respond, my heart racing as I lean forward, desperate for him to hear me. The words spill out, laced with frustration and vulnerability. "I know you feel something. We both do."

He looks up, his blue eyes swirling with confusion and something else I can't quite place—fear, perhaps. "It's not that simple," he replies, his brow furrowing as if he's wrestling with the complexities of our situation. "Vera is...she's always there, looming. You know how she is, always watching, always judging."

"Then let her watch," I snap, my voice rising. "Why do we have to let her dictate what we can feel?"

The tension in the air thickens, crackling like electricity, and for a moment, it feels as though the entire estate might shatter under the weight of our unacknowledged desires. He shifts in his chair, and I can see the battle raging inside him. I want to reach out, to bridge the chasm that's suddenly widened between us, but I'm rooted in my seat, a statue made of heartache and hope.

"Because she's not just some shadow, Avery," he replies, his tone now a mix of pleading and frustration. "She's my mother. And her expectations...they're not just words. They're a legacy. If I step out of line, everything could collapse."

I take a breath, trying to temper the fire of my emotions. "And what about us? Are we just collateral damage in her world? I refuse to be a secret, Marcus. I refuse to let her dictate who I am, or who I can love."

For a moment, the silence stretches, taut as a drawn bowstring, and I can see the conflict etched on his face. It's a strange and exquisite torment to watch him wrestle with his feelings—torn between loyalty and desire, family duty and personal happiness. "You don't understand," he says, his voice barely above a whisper. "She'll never accept us."

"Then maybe it's time for you to stop seeking her approval," I fire back, the words tasting bitter on my tongue. "You're not a puppet, Marcus. You can break free."

His gaze drops, and I feel the shift in the atmosphere, a subtle shift that hints at a fracture in the foundation we've built. "What if I don't know how?" he murmurs, and in that moment, my heart breaks for him, for us.

The flicker of uncertainty in his voice strikes me like a bolt of lightning, illuminating the depths of his struggle. I know that beneath his confident exterior lies a man wrestling with shadows that threaten to consume him. My anger dissipates, leaving behind an ache of empathy. "You're stronger than you think," I say softly, my heart swelling with the need to reassure him. "You've faced so much already. You can face her."

"I don't know if I can lose her," he admits, vulnerability leaking into his voice. "She's all I have left."

"But what about me?" I whisper, the question hanging in the air like a delicate thread, fragile and trembling. "I want to be part of your life, Marcus. I want to be the one you fight for."

His eyes meet mine, and in that shared moment, the distance between us seems to shrink. Yet the tension still simmers, unyielding. "You don't understand the stakes," he says, almost pleadingly. "If I stand up to her, it could ruin everything—my family, my future."

"Or it could set you free," I counter, my heart pounding in my chest. "You can't live in fear of what might happen. What kind of life is that? I want you to fight for us."

The air thickens with the weight of our words, and for the first time, I see a flicker of hope in his expression, like the first rays of dawn breaking through a stormy night. But the moment is fleeting, overshadowed by the reality of our situation. He turns away, gazing out the window at the sprawling gardens beyond, his expression unreadable.

"Maybe I'm not ready," he finally admits, the vulnerability in his voice slicing through the silence. "Maybe I need more time to figure this out."

Time. The one thing we seem to be running out of, the very essence that slips through our fingers like sand. My heart sinks at his words, but I refuse to let despair take root. "Then let's take that time together," I suggest, my voice steady. "Let's not lose what we have while we figure it out. I can't walk away from you, Marcus. Not now."

He turns back to me, a glimmer of something hopeful flickering in his eyes. "You're...you're not going to give up, are you?"

"Never," I reply, my voice firm, grounding us both. "We're in this together, whether you're ready or not."

As we sit there, surrounded by the stories trapped in the books around us, I can't help but wonder how many other tales are written on the edges of love and fear, triumph and heartache. Perhaps ours is just one of many, but I'm determined to write it in bold strokes, refusing to let anyone dictate the narrative.

The late afternoon sun pours into the library, casting elongated shadows that stretch like fingers across the polished wood. It feels like a sanctuary, yet today it has become a battleground for emotions I didn't know could surge so violently. Marcus leans back in his chair, his brow furrowed, and I can see the wheels turning in his mind, a silent storm brewing behind those striking blue eyes. My heart races as I try to bridge the widening gap between us.

"What's it going to take for you to believe we can have something real?" I ask, my voice softer now, attempting to peel away the layers of frustration. "This project, this—whatever this is between us—it deserves a chance."

He takes a moment, glancing around the room as if searching for answers in the dusty tomes that surround us. "I just don't want to be reckless," he finally replies, his tone heavy with hesitation. "With Vera hovering over everything, it's hard to breathe, let alone act. She has her expectations—my future mapped out like a damn treasure map, and I'm afraid to stray from the path."

"Your future? Or her future?" I challenge, a spark igniting in my chest. "It's your life, Marcus. You're the one who has to live it. Don't let her dictate your happiness."

He shifts in his seat, his posture a mixture of defensiveness and weariness. "You make it sound so easy," he retorts, a hint of bitterness lacing his words. "But what if I fail? What if stepping out of line means I lose everything?"

The air between us grows thick, as if the books themselves are leaning in, eager to witness this moment. "Everything?" I echo, incredulous. "You mean your mom's approval? You've already said that's not worth your happiness. So why cling to it?"

"Because it's all I've got!" His voice rises, a rush of emotion escaping like a floodgate finally yielding. The intensity of his frustration catches me off guard, and for a moment, the truth of his situation crashes over me like a wave.

"Marcus," I whisper, trying to pull the pieces back together, "what do you want? Really want?"

His gaze softens, and in that fleeting moment, I catch a glimpse of the boy beneath the layers of expectation and obligation. "I want to feel free," he admits, the weight of his honesty settling between us. "But that freedom feels so far away when I'm surrounded by people who only see what they want to see."

"I see you," I say firmly, the words tumbling out with urgency. "The real you. Not just a reflection of someone else's dreams."

He leans forward, and I can feel the shift in the energy between us, the tension morphing into something more profound, more intimate. "And what if that's not enough?" he whispers, his voice a breathless confession.

"It's enough for me," I reply, daring to take a risk as my heart pounds in my chest. "You're enough. But you have to believe that too."

The silence stretches, wrapping around us like a warm embrace, but it is punctuated by an uncomfortable truth. We're dancing around the precipice, teetering on the edge of something both terrifying and exhilarating. Just as I think we might find solid ground, the door swings open, and Vera strides in, her presence like a sudden gust of cold wind.

"Marcus," she calls, her tone clipped and authoritative. "There you are. I've been looking for you."

My stomach sinks, the moment shattered like fragile glass. The warmth evaporates, replaced by an icy tension that hangs heavy in the air. I exchange a glance with Marcus, and in that instant, I can see the walls he had begun to lower spring back up, fortified against the intrusion.

"Mother," he replies, a note of irritation creeping into his voice. "I was just—"

"Working on your project?" she interjects, glancing at me with an unreadable expression. "I trust you're making progress. The gala was a wonderful opportunity for you to network, after all."

"Right," I murmur, trying to sound casual, but her sharp gaze makes it clear I'm anything but welcome in this moment.

"Let's talk about the plans for next week's charity event," Vera continues, her voice unwavering. "It's time to solidify our strategy. We can't afford any slip-ups, especially with those high-profile donors coming."

"Can't we talk about this later?" Marcus asks, frustration leaking into his tone. "I'm busy."

Vera's eyes narrow, and for a moment, I see a flash of something fierce—a protectiveness that feels less maternal and more like ownership. "This isn't just about you, Marcus. You have a role to play, and you need to fulfill your obligations."

The coldness in her voice sends a shiver down my spine, and I can see Marcus struggling against her words, a silent war waging behind his clenched jaw. "I understand, but—"

"There are no 'buts,'" she snaps, her authority brooking no argument. "You're better than this indecision. Don't let anyone lead you astray."

Her words hang in the air like a weight, pressing down on both of us. I watch as Marcus's expression hardens, the moment we'd shared evaporating like mist in the morning sun. I feel a surge of anger on his behalf, but also a strange sadness for him. He's caught in a storm that I can't shield him from, no matter how desperately I want to.

"Vera, I—" he begins, but she interrupts again.

"We'll discuss this later," she says, her tone final. "I expect you to be ready for the meeting tomorrow."

With that, she sweeps out of the room, leaving behind a suffocating silence. I turn to Marcus, who sits back in his chair, shoulders slumped, the fight drained from him. "I'm sorry," I whisper, feeling the weight of her presence linger like a shadow in the room.

He runs a hand through his hair, frustration etched into his features. "It's not your fault. She always does this—always knows how to crush any sense of freedom I think I might have."

"You don't have to let her," I insist, leaning forward once more. "You can fight back. We can fight back."

"I wish it were that easy," he mutters, his voice heavy with defeat. "I feel like I'm in a chess game where every move is calculated for me."

"Then change the game," I urge, the determination bubbling inside me. "You're the player. You control the board, Marcus. You just need to realize it."

He meets my gaze, and for a fleeting moment, I see a spark of something resembling hope. "Maybe," he concedes, the word hanging in the air, filled with possibility. "But it feels so daunting."

"Great things often are," I respond, offering a wry smile. "But remember, every great achievement starts with one brave step. You don't have to take it alone."

As the shadows of doubt start to creep back in, I resolve to stand by him, even when the world around us feels like a cage. The weight of uncertainty remains, but I refuse to let it crush the fragile bond we've begun to forge. Together, we will navigate the tumultuous waters ahead, seeking a way to break free and embrace the lives we deserve.

The weight of silence settles over us, thickening the air in the library like an unwanted fog. I can feel the remnants of our earlier confrontation lingering, an electric tension that refuses to dissipate. As Marcus stares out the window, his expression distant, I wonder if he's caught in a whirlwind of thoughts too complex for me to comprehend. The golden rays of the setting sun pour in, highlighting the dust motes that float lazily in the air, but the beauty of the moment is lost on us.

"Maybe I should just go," I suggest tentatively, the words tasting bitter as they escape my lips. It feels like a betrayal, but the thought of staying here, locked in this emotional limbo, is unbearable. I can't be the reason he feels trapped, can I?

He turns to me, surprise flashing in his eyes. "You don't mean that."

"I don't know," I reply, frustration edging my voice. "I just feel like I'm fighting a losing battle. You're not ready to stand up to your mother, and I can't keep waiting for you to decide if I'm worth it."

Marcus steps closer, and I can see the determination harden in his features. "You are worth it. Don't you ever doubt that. It's just... complicated."

"Complicated doesn't have to mean impossible," I counter, trying to reignite the spark that had flickered between us. "We're already tangled up in each other's lives. Maybe it's time we embrace the chaos rather than run from it."

He runs a hand through his hair, a gesture that's becoming all too familiar. "You make it sound so simple, like we can just wave a magic wand and everything will be fine."

"Maybe we don't need a magic wand," I reply, leaning into the moment, desperate to pull him closer. "Maybe we just need to take a leap of faith together."

For a heartbeat, his eyes soften, and I see a glimmer of hope before it dims again, overshadowed by the burdens of expectation and duty. "You don't know what you're asking, Avery. You don't know what she's capable of."

"Then tell me," I urge, my voice earnest. "Help me understand. I can't fight a battle I don't know exists."

He hesitates, his gaze drifting to the shelves lined with leather-bound books. "My mother...she has a way of manipulating people. She won't hesitate to turn those around me against me. I can't risk losing you."

"Then let me in," I plead, feeling the urgency of the moment. "Let's face her together."

Just as he seems to weigh my words, the library door swings open again, and the last person I want to see steps in: Vera. Her presence floods the room with an aura of command, her tailored suit accentuating her perfectly poised figure. She looks us over, her sharp eyes scanning for signs of rebellion.

"Marcus," she says coolly, her tone devoid of warmth. "There you are. I was hoping to catch you before dinner."

"Mother," he replies, his voice flat, the fight we'd just ignited dissipating like smoke.

"Is everything all right?" she inquires, tilting her head as if she can read the tension in the air. I can see Marcus swallow hard, the weight of her gaze pressing down on him like a physical force.

"Of course," he lies, and my heart sinks at the sound of his forced smile.

"Good," she replies, her smile sharp and calculating. "I need you to help me with the charity gala arrangements. It's crucial that we present a united front. I expect nothing less."

As she speaks, I feel a cold pit forming in my stomach. The charity gala. The very event that had loomed over our conversations, now barreling toward us like an inevitable storm. "Can't it wait?" I ask, my voice cutting through the air, filled with a boldness I don't quite feel.

Vera's gaze snaps to me, and a flicker of surprise crosses her face, quickly replaced by the calculated poise I've come to associate with her. "Excuse me?"

"It's just that Marcus and I were discussing our project," I continue, forcing a steady tone. "I think it's important that we focus on it, especially with all the uncertainties right now."

Her smile fades, revealing a flash of irritation. "Your project is secondary to the legacy we are building, dear. Family comes first."

"Family, huh?" I retort, the words escaping before I can reign them in. "I didn't realize that meant sacrificing your son's happiness."

Marcus shoots me a warning glance, but it's too late. The words hang in the air, bold and defiant, a challenge thrown into the fray. Vera's expression hardens, her eyes narrowing, and I can practically feel the temperature in the room drop.

"Be careful, Avery," she says, her voice low and dangerous. "You might find yourself in over your head."

"Over my head?" I scoff, my heart racing. "Or are you just afraid of losing control?"

Marcus takes a step forward, concern etched across his face. "Avery, please—"

"No," I interrupt, shaking my head as adrenaline pulses through my veins. "I won't back down. Not now."

"Is that so?" Vera challenges, her voice smooth yet menacing. "You think you can just barge into our lives and play the heroine? You're in way over your head."

"I'm not playing anything," I fire back, my anger igniting like a flame. "I'm standing up for what's right."

The tension becomes palpable, a crackling energy that threatens to erupt. "You're brave," Vera says, her tone dripping with condescension, "but bravery without wisdom is foolishness. I suggest you tread carefully."

Before I can respond, she turns on her heel, gliding out of the library with the grace of a predator stalking its prey. The door swings shut behind her, and I can feel the weight of the encounter pressing down on us.

"What did you just do?" Marcus asks, disbelief etched into his features.

"I stood my ground," I reply, feeling both exhilarated and terrified. "We can't let her dictate everything. You deserve to be happy, Marcus."

"I can't believe you talked to her like that," he murmurs, a mix of admiration and trepidation in his eyes. "You have no idea what she'll do next."

"Maybe it's time we find out," I say, my voice steadier than I feel. "I'm not backing down, Marcus. Not for her or anyone."

He watches me, uncertainty flickering across his face. "I want to believe that," he admits, "but it's not just me at stake here."

"Then let's change the game," I challenge, feeling the weight of our shared resolve. "Together."

Just then, the heavy silence in the library is shattered by the sudden blaring of Marcus's phone. He glances down at the screen, his expression shifting from curiosity to dread. "It's my dad," he says, his voice dropping to a whisper. "I have to take this."

As he steps away to answer, I can feel the ground beneath me shifting. The stakes are rising, and the threat of Vera hangs like a storm cloud overhead. I move to the window, staring out into the sprawling grounds of the estate, lost in thought.

Then I hear Marcus's voice, rising sharply on the other end of the call. "What do you mean you're pulling out?"

Panic knots in my stomach. What could this mean for us?

As I strain to catch every word, I realize the calm facade he's been wearing is slipping. "No, you can't do this!"

His voice rises again, and I turn, anxiety flooding my senses. I know something has changed, and as he hangs up, his face is pale, as though the very foundation of his world is crumbling beneath him.

"I need you to listen to me," he says, urgency in his voice.

"Marcus, what's wrong?" I ask, my heart racing.

"They're threatening to back out of the gala altogether," he says, his voice taut with tension. "If that happens, it could ruin everything—my mother's plans, my future. We need to find a way to stop it."

And in that moment, I realize that our battle against Vera is just beginning. The stakes have escalated, and with every passing second, it feels like we're racing against a clock that's ticking down to an uncertain future.

"Then let's figure it out," I reply, steeling myself for the challenge ahead. "Together."

But just as I step toward him, a chilling voice cuts through the air, freezing us both in place. "What a touching moment."

I turn slowly to see Vera standing in the doorway once more, a triumphant smile playing on her lips, and dread floods my veins.

"You won't be figuring out anything without me."

Chapter 16: A Turning Point

The door creaked slightly as I entered my apartment, the familiar scent of aged paper and lavender air freshener wrapping around me like a soft blanket. Stacks of books towered in various corners, a chaotic testament to my insatiable need for escape. I weaved between them, my fingers brushing over the worn spines, seeking solace from the characters and plots that had become more than just stories—they were my lifeline. A twinge of sadness washed over me, a reflection of my current turmoil that clung to the air like a summer storm threatening to break.

I sank into my well-worn armchair, its upholstery faded to a soft ochre, a relic from my grandmother's living room. Nestled among my beloved tomes, I found refuge, losing myself in the world of Heathcliff and Catherine. Their tumultuous love story mirrored my own chaos, the jagged edges of passion and despair echoing in my heart. I read the words over and over until they began to swirl and blend, the ink bleeding into my consciousness. "Whatever our souls are made of, his and mine are the same."

The quote struck a chord within me, reverberating through the very fibers of my being. In those fleeting moments, my doubts began to wane. If I were to be true to myself, I needed to confront the storm brewing inside me and outside my door. My relationship with Marcus, electric and raw, had flickered beneath the weight of my insecurities. Now, with the echoes of Wuthering Heights whispering in my mind, I felt the stirring of courage. I could not allow fear to dictate my choices; I needed to fight for what we had, to bring that passion back to life.

I reached for my phone, my heart racing as my fingers hovered above the screen. It was a simple act, yet it felt monumental. What would I say? Would my words come out jumbled, a reflection of my inner turmoil, or would they carry the weight of my resolve? Taking a deep breath, I typed out a message: "Can we talk? I need to see you." My thumb hovered over the send button, hesitation creeping in, but I pressed it before I could think too hard. I closed my eyes, letting the warmth of my decision wash over me.

Moments later, the screen lit up with a response. "Sure, I'll be there in a few." His promptness sent a thrill through me, a mix of excitement and dread. I jumped to my feet, pacing the room, my heart drumming a frantic beat in my chest. The walls seemed to close in, urging me to steady myself. I felt like a warrior preparing for battle, determined to reclaim the part of my life that had begun to slip through my fingers.

As I waited, my mind drifted back to our last encounter, the way his laughter echoed in my ears long after he'd left, and how his gaze had made me feel both cherished and terrified. Marcus had a way of peeling back the layers I had so carefully constructed, revealing the vulnerable parts I had kept hidden. It was intoxicating, yet it frightened me to my core. What if he saw too much? What if I was not enough?

The sound of my doorbell sliced through the thick atmosphere of anticipation, and my heart leaped. I opened the door to find him standing there, his presence filling the space with an electric energy. Marcus's dark hair tousled in a way that seemed to defy gravity, and those deep-set eyes held a tempest of emotions—curiosity, concern, and perhaps a hint of longing. "Hey," he said softly, stepping inside, his voice a smooth melody that washed over me, calming the storm brewing within.

"Hey," I replied, closing the door behind him. The moment stretched between us, heavy with unspoken words and lingering doubts. The silence felt palpable, the kind that vibrated with the potential for both connection and conflict.

He leaned against the wall, arms crossed, his posture casual but his eyes sharp, dissecting my expression. "What's going on? You seemed... different in your message."

"I was being dramatic," I admitted, forcing a lightness I didn't quite feel. "You know how I can get. I thought it was a good idea to summon you for an emergency meeting."

Marcus arched an eyebrow, a smirk tugging at the corner of his mouth. "An emergency meeting? Is that like a book club but with more existential crises?"

I couldn't help but chuckle, the sound surprising me. "Exactly. Only with fewer snacks and more angst."

His laughter rang through the room, a warm balm that eased the tension slightly, but the weight of my feelings remained. "Alright, let's hear it," he prompted, his tone shifting to one of sincerity.

Taking a deep breath, I gathered my thoughts. "I've been... scared, Marcus. Scared of what we have and what it means. I've let that fear control me, and I realize now that I can't do that anymore."

His expression softened, understanding flickering in those intense eyes. "Fear can be paralyzing. I get that."

"I want to fight for us," I said, the words tumbling out in a rush, each syllable laced with urgency. "I've been running away from my feelings, but I don't want to lose you. You mean too much to me."

His gaze bore into mine, and for a moment, I thought he might say something to defuse the gravity of the moment. Instead, he stepped closer, the space between us crackling with unspoken tension. "I thought I was the only one feeling that way," he murmured, his voice barely above a whisper.

"What do you mean?"

"Like, I didn't know how to bridge the gap between us. I was afraid I'd push you too hard or not enough. It's hard to gauge someone's feelings when they're wrapped up in layers of walls."

"Exactly," I replied, the realization dawning upon me that we were both fighting the same battle, albeit from different fronts.

"Let's stop dancing around it then," he said, his expression shifting to one of determination. "I want to fight, too."

As his words settled in the air, a rush of relief swept through me. In that moment, it felt as if the world outside had fallen away, leaving just the two of us, suspended in a fragile yet potent connection.

"What do we do now?" I asked, my heart racing with anticipation.

Marcus reached out, his hand brushing against mine—a gentle, electrifying contact that sent a shiver coursing through me. "We figure it out together," he replied, the sincerity in his tone both grounding and exhilarating.

In that instant, I knew we were embarking on a journey that would redefine everything, a dance that would either lead us closer together or spiral into chaos. But as I looked into his eyes, I felt the promise of what was to come—the thrill of the unknown and the undeniable pull of our shared souls.

The warmth of Marcus's hand against mine lingered, an echo of his promise to fight for us, a pledge that felt both terrifying and exhilarating. It was a spark igniting a long-dormant fire within me, and I wanted to stoke it into a blazing flame. In that moment, our shared vulnerability morphed into something potent and fierce, a charge that sent my thoughts tumbling in chaotic directions.

"Alright, so what's the battle plan?" I said, trying to infuse levity into the weight of our conversation. "Do we need to draft a manifesto or something?"

Marcus chuckled, the sound reverberating like a melody through the air. "I was thinking more along the lines of open communication. But if you want to get all dramatic with a manifesto, I'm game."

"Dramatic is my middle name," I quipped, leaning into the lighthearted banter to mask the tension still knotting in my stomach.

"But let's keep the political pamphlets for another day. For now, I just want to know what you're thinking."

He ran a hand through his hair, a gesture that never failed to distract me. "Honestly? I think we should take it one step at a time. Let's get to know each other on a deeper level, without all the... external noise."

"External noise?" I asked, my curiosity piqued. "You mean the looming specter of my fear and insecurity?"

He smirked. "Exactly. I mean, don't get me wrong, I appreciate a good haunting, but maybe we can try for a quieter ghost story."

"Touché," I conceded, a smile creeping onto my face. "But how do we even begin? What's the first step in a deeply unscientific relationship experiment?"

"How about a dinner?" he suggested, his eyes lighting up with a hint of mischief. "Just the two of us. No books, no distractions—just food and whatever you're willing to share about that beautiful mind of yours."

"A dinner? You mean like a real date?" I raised an eyebrow, feigning surprise even though my heart raced at the thought.

"Is there any other kind?" He leaned closer, his gaze steady and earnest. "Let's keep it simple. Just two people trying to figure each other out without the added pressure of all the expectations we've placed on ourselves."

"Okay, but only if I get to pick the restaurant," I countered, the playful challenge reigniting my confidence.

"Deal," he replied, a grin spreading across his face that melted away any residual tension. "Just let me know when and where."

The night flowed seamlessly from that moment, the conversation blossoming like the blooming tulips outside my window. We exchanged stories—his penchant for adventure, mine for the extraordinary in the mundane. I learned about his knack for cooking, how he'd once burned a pot of spaghetti and thought it a personal failure, while I regaled him with tales of my disastrous baking attempts that turned into unintentional fire alarms.

Laughter danced between us, easing the heaviness that had plagued our earlier encounters. Each chuckle, every shared smile, created an intricate tapestry of connection. I felt the walls around my heart begin to crack as I allowed myself to enjoy this moment, this newfound possibility.

After a while, the conversation drifted toward our aspirations, the dreams that fueled our lives. "You know, I've always wanted to write a novel," I confessed, twirling a stray lock of hair around my finger. "But I've convinced myself that no one would want to read what I have to say."

"Why not?" Marcus asked, his tone earnest. "I'd read it. You have a way with words, even when you're unsure."

"I appreciate the vote of confidence, but really, what do I even have to offer?" I shrugged, the uncertainty creeping back in. "I'm just another twenty-something trying to figure it all out."

"Yeah, but you're also you," he said, leaning back, his gaze unwavering. "That's more than enough. You have stories, experiences, and perspectives that are uniquely yours. Why not share them?"

I pondered his words, the seed of encouragement taking root in my mind. "Maybe you're right," I replied slowly, considering the thrill of putting my thoughts to paper. "But it's terrifying to think of exposing my soul to the world."

"Nothing worth having comes without a little fear," he said, his voice steady and reassuring. "If you're passionate about it, you owe it to yourself to try."

Just then, the phone on the coffee table buzzed, cutting through our moment like a sudden rain shower on a sunny day. I glanced down, the brightness of the screen momentarily blinding, revealing a text from my best friend, Clara. "Need to talk. Urgent. Can't wait."

Marcus noticed the shift in my expression. "Everything okay?"

"Yeah, just Clara being dramatic," I replied, rolling my eyes, but my stomach knotted with uncertainty. "I should probably respond."

"Go ahead," he encouraged, his tone supportive. "We can always pick this up later."

With a reluctant sigh, I texted Clara back, agreeing to meet her at a nearby coffee shop in half an hour. As I gathered my things, I felt a twinge of regret. I didn't want to leave this connection we had reignited, the warmth of our conversation still swirling in the air like the rich aroma of fresh coffee.

"Are you sure you have to go?" Marcus asked, his voice low, laced with the same reluctance I felt.

"Clara is like a caffeine-fueled tornado. If I don't respond, she'll start sending out search parties," I explained, my tone light.

He chuckled, his eyes sparkling with mischief. "You have to save the world from the drama then. But I want to see you again soon."

I smiled, the fluttering in my chest intensifying. "Definitely. Just let me know what works for you."

As I made my way to the door, he reached for my hand once more, that warm touch igniting a rush of courage. "And remember," he said softly, "no more fear. Just possibilities."

With that lingering promise hanging between us, I stepped out into the cool evening air, the soft sounds of the city wrapping around me like a gentle embrace. The streetlights flickered to life, casting a warm glow against the fading light, and I felt a renewed sense of hope stirring within me.

The coffee shop was buzzing with activity when I arrived, the chatter of patrons blending with the rich scent of roasted beans. Clara was already seated, her face a mix of excitement and urgency, like a kid who had just stumbled upon a hidden treasure.

"There you are!" she exclaimed, her voice rising above the din. "You won't believe what just happened!"

I slid into the seat across from her, my heart still racing from my earlier conversation with Marcus. "What's going on?"

"Okay, so you know that guy I told you about—the one from the bookstore?" Clara leaned in closer, her eyes wide with enthusiasm. "He asked me out!"

My heart swelled for her, but then a pang of jealousy flickered through me. "That's amazing, Clara! When?"

"Tomorrow! I'm freaking out! What if I mess it up?"

I reached across the table, squeezing her hands. "You won't. Just be yourself. That's all anyone can ask."

She sighed dramatically, her excitement battling with nerves. "You're right. But I need your help! I want to look perfect."

Before I could respond, her phone buzzed, and she glanced down, her expression shifting. "Oh no. I need to take this."

As she stepped away to take her call, I felt a flicker of unease creep back in, like a shadow lingering at the edge of my thoughts. For every step I took toward something good with Marcus, it felt like the world was countering it with complications. I couldn't shake the feeling that my resolve was about to be tested again, and this time, I wouldn't be able to rely solely on Marcus's warm gaze or reassuring words.

When Clara returned, her enthusiasm was barely contained. "Okay, back to me! You're going to help me choose the perfect outfit!"

"Of course!" I smiled, though my thoughts danced between my own desires and the complications Clara's excitement brought into the mix. We spent the next few minutes sifting through options, but my mind kept drifting back to Marcus, to the promise we had forged amidst uncertainty. I couldn't shake the sense that I was on the precipice of something monumental, where choices would shape not just my destiny, but the destinies of those around me.

As we left the coffee shop, the night air felt electric, charged with possibility. But in the back of my mind, I couldn't help but wonder how this new chapter would unfold. Would I have the strength to navigate my own fears while supporting Clara? Would my blossoming relationship with Marcus withstand the trials that lay ahead? Only time would tell, and with each step into the uncertain night, I felt ready to face whatever came next.

The streets buzzed with life as I made my way home, Clara's excitement trailing behind me like the lingering scent of fresh coffee. My thoughts flickered between her plans for the date and my own hopes for Marcus, creating a mosaic of possibilities that was both thrilling and terrifying. I couldn't shake the feeling that everything was about to change, but whether it would be for better or worse remained shrouded in uncertainty.

Once I stepped into my apartment, the familiar scent of lavender welcomed me like an old friend. I closed the door, leaning against it for a moment, trying to absorb the energy that buzzed in the air around me. My phone buzzed again, startling me out of my reverie. It was a message from Marcus: "Can't stop thinking about our conversation. Let's make tomorrow night our official first date. What do you think?"

My heart did a small flip. Official. There was something about that word that made it all feel so real. I quickly replied, "I'd love that! How about that Italian place we talked about?"

Within moments, his reply appeared. "Perfect. Can't wait to see you."

I placed my phone down, a smile creeping onto my face. There was something undeniably thrilling about the anticipation of a date, especially with someone who made my heart race and my mind swirl with curiosity. But beneath that excitement lay an undercurrent of anxiety, a nagging whisper reminding me of the complications yet to surface.

With a determined huff, I stepped into the kitchen and began rummaging through my refrigerator. I was practically starving, having been so consumed by thoughts of Marcus and Clara that I'd skipped dinner. After a brief wrestling match with a bag of wilted spinach, I settled on a quick stir-fry. The bright colors of bell peppers and broccoli filled the pan, sizzling under the heat. The aroma wafted through my apartment, a comforting reminder of the simple pleasures that made life sweeter.

As I stirred, I found my thoughts drifting back to Marcus. What if this date didn't go as planned? What if I stumbled over my words or spilled marinara sauce down the front of my favorite dress? A smirk played on my lips as I imagined his reaction if I did manage to create a culinary disaster. "Well, this is a unique way to experience Italian cuisine," he would quip, that trademark smirk of his lighting up his face.

Just as I was about to dish out my meal, a sharp knock on the door jolted me. I paused, the wooden spoon hovering mid-air. Who could that be at this hour? My pulse quickened slightly as I wiped my hands on a dish towel and approached the door, the tension in my chest tightening.

I peered through the peephole and saw a figure standing there, illuminated by the soft glow of the hallway light. It was a familiar silhouette, but the feeling of unease remained. I opened the door to find Clara, her face flushed with excitement and a hint of distress.

"Clara, what's wrong?"

She burst in, her energy filling the space like a whirlwind. "You won't believe it! I just got a message from Ryan. He's coming back into town, and he wants to see me. Like, right now!"

"Wait, the Ryan? The one you said you were over?" I raised an eyebrow, intrigued.

"I know, I know! But he just texted, and he sounded... I don't know, sincere? I need your help. I don't know what to do!"

I stepped back, letting her pace the room, her agitation palpable. "Clara, take a breath. What do you want? Do you want to see him?"

"I think so? But what if it's a mistake? What if I fall back into the same old patterns?" She rubbed her temples as if trying to massage away her doubts.

"You won't know unless you try," I replied, my mind racing with my own uncertainty. "But you have to be honest with yourself. Are you ready for that?"

Her eyes darted around the room, finally landing on me. "You're right. I just... I want to make sure I'm not doing this for the wrong reasons."

Before I could respond, the tension in the room shifted, the air thickening with an unspoken weight. Just then, the phone rang, slicing through our conversation like a hot knife. My heart dropped as I recognized the name on the screen—Marcus.

"Hey, I should take this," I said, glancing at Clara, who nodded encouragingly.

"Hey," I greeted, trying to keep my voice steady despite the anxiety fluttering in my stomach.

"Hi! I was just thinking about tomorrow. I really want it to be special," he said, his tone light but tinged with seriousness. "What do you think about starting with a walk by the river before dinner?"

"Sounds perfect," I replied, feeling the tension from earlier dissipate. "I love that area."

"Great! I'll pick you up at six?"

"Perfect," I said, but as we spoke, I caught Clara's gaze darting toward my phone, her expression shifting to one of concern.

"Are you alright?" Marcus asked, his voice laced with an undercurrent of worry.

"Yeah, just my friend is here. She's... having a moment." I glanced at Clara, who seemed to be on the edge of a decision, her fingers tapping nervously against the table.

"Tell her I said hi," he said, the warmth in his voice evident even through the phone.

"Will do. See you tomorrow!"

After ending the call, I turned to Clara, who looked at me as if she were piecing together a puzzle. "You're really into him, huh?"

"Is it that obvious?" I sighed, running a hand through my hair.

"Only a little. But you deserve this. Just don't lose yourself in it."

"I won't," I promised, but the weight of uncertainty still settled heavily in the air.

"Okay, okay, back to me!" Clara said, shaking off her earlier tension. "I need your input! Do I text Ryan back or let it simmer?"

"Go for it. But don't overthink it. You know how he gets; you have to set the tone from the start."

"Yeah, you're right," she said, her eyes brightening with determination. "I'm going to do it!"

She whipped out her phone, fingers flying over the screen as she composed a message. I watched her, both in admiration and envy, wondering if I had the same courage to leap into the unknown.

A moment later, Clara's phone buzzed again. She glanced down, her expression shifting from excitement to bewilderment. "What the—"

"What is it?" I asked, my heart racing in tandem with her rising anxiety.

"It's Ryan. He wants to meet now! Like, right this second!"

"Are you serious?" I asked, feeling the weight of the unexpected shift.

"I can't just leave you here!" she exclaimed, her expression torn. "But I really want to see him."

"Go!" I urged, a mix of excitement and fear bubbling up within me. "I'll be fine! This is your chance, Clara. Don't let it slip away."

"Are you sure?" she asked, her eyes wide.

"Positive! You'll regret it if you don't."

With one last glance, Clara dashed for the door, her energy reinvigorated. "Thanks! You're the best!" she called back, already disappearing into the hallway.

As the door closed behind her, I sank back onto the couch, feeling a strange mix of exhilaration and loneliness. The evening had been a whirlwind, and now I was left with my own thoughts swirling around like autumn leaves caught in a gust.

Just as I began to collect my thoughts, a shadow passed by my window. My heart jumped as I looked out, seeing a figure standing beneath the streetlamp—a familiar face I hadn't expected to see.

My heart raced as I squinted, a mixture of confusion and dread settling in my stomach. What was he doing here? As the figure stepped closer, I recognized him instantly. Ryan.

I felt a knot tighten in my chest, the air thickening with a rush of emotion. Was Clara ready for this? Did she even know he was back in town? And why was he here, hovering just outside my apartment?

Before I could react, he glanced up, his eyes locking onto mine through the glass. A shiver of uncertainty coursed through me as I took a step back, unsure of what this unexpected encounter would lead to.

But then, with a deliberate action, Ryan raised his hand and knocked. The sound reverberated in the silence of the room, echoing my tumultuous thoughts. I hesitated, heart pounding, as the weight of the moment pressed down on me.

With a sudden burst of courage, I opened the door, stepping into the unknown. And just like that, I found myself at the crossroads of chaos, with decisions that could change everything hanging in the balance.

Chapter 17: The Confrontation

The café buzzes with the gentle hum of conversation and the clinking of cups, a warm cocoon of normalcy enveloping me as I settle into the plush corner booth, my heart racing in rhythm with the barista's frothy creations. Sunlight spills through the large bay windows, illuminating the delicate patterns of steam that curl lazily from my coffee cup, creating an ethereal dance that only I seem to notice. The smell of roasted beans mixes with the sweet scent of pastries, making my stomach flutter with both hunger and anticipation. I can't shake the feeling that today could shift everything between Marcus and me, but a thick fog of uncertainty wraps around my mind like an unwanted scarf.

As I wait, my fingers trace the rim of my cup, lost in thought. I imagine Marcus walking in, his confident stride cutting through the crowd, his smile lighting up the dim corners of my heart. We've been tiptoeing around our feelings for what feels like an eternity, each moment charged with unspoken words, but today feels different. Today, I want to challenge him, to peel back the layers of his fears and insecurities, to make him confront the truth of what lies between us.

When the door swings open, a soft jingle announcing his arrival, my breath catches in my throat. There he is, looking effortlessly handsome in a fitted navy shirt that accentuates the strong line of his shoulders. He scans the room, his gaze finally landing on me. I can't help but smile, the warmth spreading through me like sunshine on a chilly morning. He approaches, a hesitant grin playing at the corners of his mouth, and I'm struck by the mixture of hope and fear that darkens his eyes.

"Hey," he says, sliding into the booth opposite me. "Sorry I'm late. Traffic was a nightmare."

I wave away his apology, my heart racing. "No worries. I'm just glad you made it. I've been looking forward to this."

The moment feels electric, the air between us crackling with unspoken tension. We exchange pleasantries, but the small talk feels like a flimsy façade. I can sense the weight of everything we've been avoiding, lingering just beneath the surface.

"Listen, Marcus," I start, my voice steady despite the fluttering in my stomach, "we need to talk about where we stand. I can't keep pretending everything is fine while we're both stuck in this limbo."

He leans back, his brows knitting together, the playful banter slipping away like sand through fingers. "I know. I've been thinking about it too, but—"

"Then let's not dance around it," I interrupt, leaning forward. "What do you want? What are you afraid of?"

He exhales slowly, a pained expression crossing his features. "It's complicated. I like you, but there's so much going on in my life right now. I don't want to drag you into my mess."

My heart sinks, but I refuse to let despair take root. "Marcus, I want to be in your life. I want to help you through this. But I can't do that if you won't let me in."

He studies me, and I can see the conflict waging a war behind his eyes. Just as I feel a glimmer of hope, the bell above the door jingles again, and a familiar figure walks in. Vera. My stomach twists as she strides across the café with an air of confidence that can only be described as suffocating. Her perfectly styled hair and tailored dress scream power, and I can almost hear the fabric whispering promises of success as she approaches our table.

"Marcus!" she exclaims, her voice dripping with sweetness that feels like honey laced with poison. "Fancy seeing you here."

My breath hitches, and I brace myself for the storm I can already feel brewing. She leans in closer to Marcus, her fingers brushing against his arm, a gesture that feels far too intimate. I can almost see the gears in her mind turning as she looks at him, her gaze filled with ambition and unrelenting determination.

"I was just telling the team how much you could bring to our project," she continues, her voice a sultry purr that threatens to drown out everything we've been discussing. "Your insights would be invaluable, don't you think?"

I can feel the tension in Marcus's posture shift, his expression caught between confusion and the weight of obligation. "Uh, I—"

Before he can finish, I clear my throat, the need to reclaim my space palpable. "Actually, Marcus and I were just having a private conversation."

Vera's eyes narrow slightly, but her smile remains intact, a mask of disarming charm. "Oh, I didn't mean to interrupt. But you know how work can be," she says, waving a dismissive hand as if my presence is an inconvenience. "It's important to prioritize the future."

I can feel my heart pounding in my chest, a war between my rising anger and the calm facade I struggle to maintain. "I think we're both aware of what's important here," I shoot back, my voice sharper than intended. "And right now, it's about Marcus making a decision that isn't just about work."

She arches an eyebrow, a bemused expression twisting her features. "Decision? You mean about joining the project? Because I think we both know where his true talents lie."

The words hang in the air like a tension-filled balloon, ready to burst. I watch as Marcus's eyes flicker between us, caught in a whirlwind of emotions that I can't decipher. Just when I think I've gained the upper hand, Vera's presence looms larger than life, casting shadows over our budding connection.

"Look, Vera, I appreciate your enthusiasm, but I need some time to think," Marcus finally says, his voice firm, though I can hear the hesitance beneath.

"Time is money, darling," she replies, the sweetness in her tone tinged with steel. "But if you're not ready to seize the opportunity, someone else will."

With that, she turns, casting a lingering glance at me before she strides away, the sound of her heels echoing in the café as she leaves a trail of tension in her wake. I meet Marcus's eyes, a storm of emotions swirling within us both, each of us grappling with the implications of what just transpired. The weight of her presence still lingers, and I know we're far from finished.

The moment Vera departs, the air shifts, crackling with unresolved tension. Marcus's gaze drops to the tabletop, fingers tracing the rim of his coffee cup as if searching for answers within the patterns of the wood. I watch him, a mix of frustration and empathy churning in my chest. He looks so lost, caught between two worlds—the exhilarating possibility of us and the suffocating demands of his career.

"Marcus," I say softly, hoping to break through the thick layer of uncertainty enveloping him. "What did she mean by seizing the opportunity?"

His head jerks up, and there's a flash of something—anger, confusion, maybe even fear—in his eyes. "She's just... trying to pull me into a project that I'm not sure I want to be part of. It feels like a trap sometimes."

"Sounds like you already know what you want," I reply, my voice laced with encouragement. "So why let her get into your head?"

He chuckles, but it's devoid of humor. "If only it were that easy. It's not just about what I want; it's about what everyone expects from me."

"Who cares about expectations? You're the one living this life." I lean forward, elbows resting on the table, my heart racing as I urge him to see the light. "You deserve to pursue what makes you happy. If Vera's not part of that, then why entertain her?"

For a moment, the flicker of hope ignites in his eyes, but it quickly dims. "It's complicated, you know? There's pressure from my family, from the office. I feel like I'm supposed to be someone I'm not."

"Marcus," I say, my tone firm yet gentle, "the only person you need to be is yourself. And if being yourself means stepping away from whatever pressure Vera is putting on you, then do it. Life is too short to get caught up in someone else's agenda."

He opens his mouth to respond, but a shadow passes over his face, a look of guilt mixed with longing. "You make it sound so simple. I wish I could just walk away."

"Then start small," I suggest, warmth flooding my voice. "Take a step. Tell her you need to focus on your own projects. You're talented; she can't define your worth."

His lips curve into a hesitant smile, and for a heartbeat, I believe we're on the precipice of something beautiful. But just as quickly, the storm clouds return.

"I appreciate that, really. But what if she uses it against me? She's got a way of twisting things."

"Then let her twist all she wants," I reply, feeling a spark of my own defiance. "You can't live your life in fear of what someone might do. You have to choose your path. And if that means standing up to Vera, then do it."

He leans back, contemplating my words, and I can see the gears turning in his mind. But the moment hangs heavy, and I can't help but feel that familiar ache of helplessness creeping in.

Just as I'm about to encourage him further, the door swings open again, a sharp gust of wind sweeping through the café. I glance over, and my heart sinks as I recognize the silhouette entering—a man dressed impeccably, an air of confidence radiating off him. It's Ethan, Marcus's childhood friend and Vera's secret weapon.

Ethan saunters toward us, his smile as polished as his designer shoes. "Well, well, if it isn't the dynamic duo," he says, his voice dripping with charm. "What's the meeting about? Plotting world domination?"

Marcus straightens up, a flash of irritation crossing his features, while I suppress a groan. "Ethan," he acknowledges, though the tone suggests he's not in the mood for pleasantries.

"I hope I'm not interrupting anything too serious," Ethan continues, sliding into the booth beside Marcus without waiting for an invitation. He leans in closer, as if drawing Marcus into his magnetic orbit. "You know Vera's been looking for you. She wants to discuss some big plans."

"What plans?" Marcus replies, his irritation bubbling to the surface.

"Ah, just some strategic moves that could make or break your career. You know how it is," Ethan shrugs, his casual demeanor a stark contrast to the tension thickening the air. "You wouldn't want to disappoint her, would you?"

"Disappointing Vera isn't my top concern right now," Marcus snaps, a spark igniting in his eyes.

Ethan raises an eyebrow, clearly enjoying the back-and-forth. "Come on, you know she has connections that can help you. Think of your future."

"Maybe I don't want a future dictated by someone else's whims," Marcus shoots back, his voice rising slightly, the intensity in his gaze sparking.

The playful banter fades, replaced by an awkward silence that settles like fog over the table. I can feel the atmosphere shift, my heart pounding as I sense the battle lines drawn. Marcus's frustration is palpable, and Ethan seems intent on pushing his buttons, the glint in his eye betraying an almost predatory instinct.

I take a deep breath, my resolve hardening. "You know, Ethan," I interject, keeping my tone steady, "Marcus is more than capable of deciding his own path without your unsolicited advice."

Ethan turns to me, surprise flashing across his face. "Oh? And who might you be?"

"Someone who actually cares about what Marcus wants," I reply, my voice unwavering. "Not everyone needs to rely on your playbook."

He chuckles, but there's a hint of annoyance beneath the surface. "Cute. But I'm just looking out for him. You can't blame a guy for trying to steer his friend in the right direction."

Marcus shifts uncomfortably, caught between us like a deer in headlights. "I don't need steering, Ethan. I need to make my own decisions."

"Really?" Ethan retorts, leaning back with a smirk. "You've got someone like Vera eager to help you climb the ladder, and you want to throw that away? Sounds like a bad idea."

"No," Marcus counters, his voice low but steady, "it sounds like I'm tired of feeling like a pawn in someone else's game."

The words hang between us, charged with a mix of defiance and hope. I can see Marcus standing his ground, the barriers of uncertainty beginning to crumble. In that moment, I realize that our budding connection isn't just about romance; it's about finding the courage to choose our own paths, even in the face of manipulation and expectation.

"Maybe it's time to consider what you truly want, Marcus," I say softly, meeting his gaze. "And if it means taking a stand against those who would use you, then I'm here to support you."

The moment stretches, a fragile tension hanging in the air, but it feels different now. With each heartbeat, the foundations of our unspoken connection strengthen, and for the first time, I see a glimpse of the man I know Marcus can be—the one unafraid to chase his own dreams, free from the shadow of others.

The air thickens with unspoken words as Ethan's presence looms large over our table, but I refuse to let him steal this moment from

WAR OF WORDS

Marcus. His challenge ripples through the café, drawing curious glances from nearby patrons, their interest piqued by the charged atmosphere. I sense the tension wrapping around us, a fragile bubble threatening to burst at any moment.

"Ethan, you may think you're helping," I begin, my tone steady, "but all you're doing is complicating things. Marcus needs to focus on what he wants, not what you think he should want."

Ethan narrows his eyes, the easy charm slipping slightly. "And what is it that you think he wants, hmm? A career built on dreams and fairy tales?"

"No, Ethan, he wants a career built on his own terms," I retort, crossing my arms defiantly. "Something fulfilling, not just a series of stepping stones that someone else has laid out for him."

Marcus shifts in his seat, caught between the two of us like a spectator in a tennis match. "Guys," he interjects, his voice strained, "can we not do this here?"

Ethan leans closer, an almost predatory glint in his eye. "What's the matter, Marcus? Afraid of what you might find out? Maybe it's time to wake up and realize that life isn't about chasing rainbows. It's about making hard choices and sacrifices."

The words hang heavy in the air, but I can't let him have the last word. "Hard choices, yes, but they should be yours, Marcus. Not dictated by someone else's expectations or ambitions. You have the right to choose your own path."

Silence stretches, a taut line connecting the three of us, and I can feel Marcus's internal battle playing out in real time. His eyes flicker between Ethan and me, the weight of his decision pressing down on him like a thousand-pound anchor.

"Maybe I do need to make some choices," he finally says, his voice a mere whisper yet tinged with newfound resolve. "But I won't be pushed into something I don't want. Not by you, not by Vera, and certainly not by you, Ethan."

Ethan straightens, the surprise evident on his face, but instead of retreating, he leans in closer, his expression shifting to something more intense, more calculating. "Be careful, Marcus. You might just end up with nothing if you don't play the game right."

Marcus's eyes flare with defiance. "I'd rather have nothing than be a pawn in someone else's game."

The words settle like stones on my heart, and I can almost feel the crackling energy between us shifting. I reach for Marcus's hand across the table, my fingers brushing against his, a simple gesture of support that says everything I want to communicate. His gaze softens as our fingers intertwine, and the warmth of his touch sends a jolt of determination coursing through me.

"You're not alone in this," I assure him, my voice low but firm. "Whatever happens next, we face it together."

Before he can respond, the café door swings open again, the jingle of the bell marking another arrival. This time, it's Vera, her sharp gaze scanning the room like a hawk hunting for prey. My stomach twists at the sight of her, all too aware of the turbulence she brings with her.

"Marcus," she calls out, striding toward us with an air of authority. "I was just speaking to Ethan about our meeting. I thought I might find you here."

I tighten my grip on Marcus's hand, trying to ground him as Vera approaches, her presence enveloping us like a cold draft. "I see you've been busy," she continues, her gaze sliding over to me with thinly veiled disdain. "Making friends, I see?"

"Actually, we were just discussing some important decisions," Marcus says, his voice steady, but I can hear the tension simmering beneath the surface.

Vera's lips curl into a condescending smile. "How lovely. I'm sure whatever plans you've hatched here can wait. We have much to discuss, Marcus—opportunities that don't come around often."

I can sense the undertone of manipulation in her words, a carefully crafted attempt to reel Marcus back into her orbit. "You don't need to go with her, Marcus," I say, feeling the urgency swell within me. "You've made your feelings clear. Don't let her sway you."

His gaze flickers to me, uncertainty written all over his face, and in that instant, I realize how deeply this moment matters. This isn't just about him choosing a career; it's about asserting his autonomy and defining what he wants from life—both professionally and personally.

Vera steps closer, her voice dropping to a conspiratorial whisper. "You know, Marcus, every moment you waste with distractions could cost you. Are you willing to throw away your future for—" she gestures dismissively towards me, "—this?"

I can feel the heat rising in my cheeks, but I refuse to back down. "This isn't a distraction; this is real. You just can't handle the fact that he might choose something outside your plans."

"Ah, I see," Vera retorts, a mocking lilt to her voice. "You think you're special, don't you? Just because you've made a little connection here. But I've seen so many people come and go, all claiming to know what's best for him."

The challenge in her eyes is unmistakable, and I can feel the stakes escalating. "But they weren't real, were they?" I counter, my heart racing. "They were just passing through. You, on the other hand, want to keep him trapped in your world."

Vera's expression darkens, her smile fading as she turns her full attention back to Marcus. "So, what's it going to be, Marcus? Are you going to waste your time here with... her?"

There's a long pause, thick with anticipation. Marcus's expression wavers, uncertainty dancing in his eyes as he weighs the options laid before him. In that moment, I realize how critical this decision is—not just for him, but for both of us.

"I think I need to—" he starts, but before he can finish, the café door swings open once more, the sudden rush of wind causing a collective gasp from the patrons.

In walks a figure shrouded in shadows, the atmosphere instantly shifting with the unannounced arrival. The moment the person steps into the light, I freeze. It's Clara, Marcus's estranged sister, her features pale and eyes wide with urgency, as if she's just stepped out of a whirlwind.

"Marcus!" she cries, desperation etched on her face. "You need to come with me. It's about Mom."

A cold shiver runs down my spine, and everything around me blurs into the background. The stakes have just risen higher, and the weight of impending chaos hangs in the air, wrapping around us like a noose.

"Clara, wait!" Marcus shouts, rising from his seat, his hand slipping from mine. But it's too late. The door swings shut behind her, sealing off whatever life-altering revelation she brings with her.

As the world outside the café carries on, I can only stand there, heart racing, knowing that everything is about to change in ways none of us could have anticipated.

Chapter 18: Bonds Strengthened

The sun dipped low in the sky, casting a warm, golden glow over the workshop. Dust motes danced lazily in the slanted rays of light filtering through the tall windows, and the scent of freshly cut wood mingled with the faint trace of paint and varnish, creating an intoxicating blend that buzzed in my senses. This was our sanctuary—a space filled with the promise of transformation, where raw materials could be shaped into something beautiful.

As Marcus grasped my hand, the warmth of his palm enveloped me, sending a ripple of electricity through my fingertips. The simple gesture felt monumental, grounding me in a way I had long yearned for. The chaotic noise of the world outside faded, leaving only the soft hum of our shared aspirations. "Let's make this happen," he said, his voice low and steady, a beacon of reassurance amidst the swirling uncertainty.

I looked up, catching the glint of determination in his eyes, and felt a swell of gratitude for his presence. It wasn't just that he understood my dreams; he shared them. Together, we could turn this dream of ours into a reality—a venture that would showcase not just our talents but the bond that had been quietly forming between us.

Marcus had always been the type to throw himself wholeheartedly into whatever challenge lay ahead. I admired that about him, the way he faced obstacles with a mix of pragmatism and raw enthusiasm that made everything seem possible. But as we began to sketch out our plans for the community project, I could sense the shadow of Vera lurking in the back of my mind. Her words echoed like a haunting melody, reminding me of the hurdles we would face not just from the community, but from within ourselves.

"Do you think we can pull this off?" I asked, trying to mask the trepidation threading through my voice. It was a question I knew I had to confront, even if the answer felt daunting.

"Of course we can," he replied, confidence radiating from him like sunlight breaking through a cloudy sky. "We just need to stay focused and keep our lines of communication open."

His grip tightened around my fingers, and I felt the steady pulse of his heartbeat sync with my own. In that moment, the fears that had clung to me like an unwanted cloak began to unravel. The very essence of partnership began to take shape—not just in our project, but in the quiet understanding that we were choosing to be vulnerable together.

We spent hours in that workshop, bouncing ideas off one another, sketching designs, and laughing at our shared mess-ups. I loved the way his brow furrowed in concentration, the way his laughter could light up the dim corners of the room. With every stroke of the brush and every piece of wood we fashioned, the air grew thick with possibility.

Yet, just as I began to revel in the blossoming potential of our endeavor, the door creaked open, a sharp sound that sliced through our bubble of creativity. Vera stood there, framed by the doorway, her presence instantly shifting the energy in the room. Dressed impeccably in a fitted blazer that accentuated her poised demeanor, she had a way of making the mundane feel... well, lesser.

"Working hard or hardly working?" she quipped, a sardonic smile curling at the corners of her lips as her gaze flicked between Marcus and me.

I could feel my heart rate spike as I instinctively stepped closer to Marcus, his body radiating warmth and protection. It was infuriating how she could invade our moment, like a storm cloud threatening a sunny day. "Just trying to bring a little light to the community," I replied, injecting a dose of defiance into my tone.

Her laughter was sharp, cutting through the air. "Ah, yes, the community. How noble. But remember, it's not just about passion; it's about execution."

With a practiced ease, she sauntered into the workshop, her heels clicking on the wooden floor. I glanced at Marcus, who narrowed his eyes slightly, clearly irritated by her intrusion. I could sense the tension building, the air thickening with unspoken words and veiled intentions.

"What do you want, Vera?" he asked, the edge of his voice betraying his annoyance.

She waved a hand dismissively, as if we were merely pawns in her game. "Oh, I just wanted to remind you both of the bigger picture. It would be a shame to get lost in your little bubble of creativity and forget that there are others invested in this project too."

Her words dripped with condescension, but I refused to be intimidated. "We're well aware of the stakes, Vera. We're committed to making this work," I shot back, my heart pounding with the thrill of confrontation.

For a moment, her facade flickered, and I saw a glimmer of something vulnerable beneath her polished exterior. But just as quickly, it was gone, replaced by the steely determination I had come to recognize. "Just keep your priorities straight," she replied, her tone cool and dismissive.

As she turned to leave, I felt the tension seep from the room, replaced by an exhilaration that surged through me. "You know," I said, smirking slightly, "if she spent half as much time working on this project as she does trying to undermine us, we might actually be successful."

Marcus chuckled, the sound easing the tension that had lingered like a shadow. "True. But we're not here to compete with her. We're here to build something together, and I think we can make it work, no matter what."

In that moment, I realized that Vera's presence, though formidable, would not deter us. If anything, it would only strengthen our resolve. With our hands still intertwined, we dove back into our plans, buoyed by a newfound determination that felt like a gust of wind beneath our wings. The workshop became our universe, filled with laughter, creativity, and the undeniable promise of something beautiful unfolding.

Marcus and I fell into a rhythm, our days consumed by the hum of creativity and the thrill of building something meaningful. The workshop transformed into our private realm, each corner filled with the remnants of our labor—paint-splattered canvases, half-finished sculptures, and the aroma of sawdust that clung to our clothes like a second skin. It was intoxicating, invigorating, and in those moments, I could hardly remember the weight of Vera's words or the challenge they posed.

One afternoon, as we worked on a mural that would grace the community center, I caught Marcus stealing glances at me, a smile teasing at the corners of his lips. "What?" I asked, wiping my hands on my apron, my curiosity piqued.

"You just look... happy," he said, his gaze warm and sincere. "It's nice to see you like this."

A blush crept up my cheeks, and I brushed it off with a wave of my hand. "Well, can you blame me? We're creating a masterpiece here!" I gestured dramatically at the chaotic splashes of color on the wall, where abstract shapes began to take form. "I mean, who wouldn't feel like Picasso?"

"More like a very enthusiastic finger painter," he teased, laughter dancing in his eyes.

I tossed a brush at him playfully, which he dodged with a laugh that echoed through the workshop. It was moments like these, filled with lightness and laughter, that made the outside world fade away. But just as quickly as the joy filled the air, a shadow crept in—a reminder that we were on borrowed time.

As we leaned closer to the mural, our elbows brushing against each other, the door swung open with a creak that sent a shiver through the moment. Vera re-entered, her presence immediately suffocating the laughter.

"I thought you two might be lost in your little daydream," she said, her tone oozing sarcasm. "But I see you're just a few brush strokes away from your masterpiece. How delightful."

I shot Marcus a glance, his jaw tightening slightly. "What do you want, Vera?" I asked, my voice steeling itself against her barbs.

"Just wanted to check in on the project," she replied, feigning innocence. "After all, I wouldn't want to see it go up in flames due to lack of oversight."

"Or lack of support," Marcus interjected, his tone sharp and pointed.

Vera's expression turned calculating. "Ah, but that's the thing, isn't it? Support is only as good as the plan. Have you two thought about how you're going to fund this little venture of yours?"

"Plenty of ideas," I said, a surge of defiance coursing through me. "We're still in the brainstorming phase."

"Of course," she replied, her smile a tight line. "But brainstorming doesn't pay the bills, darling."

"Neither does your constant negativity," Marcus shot back, and I felt a rush of pride at his defense.

With a flick of her wrist, Vera dismissed us, striding across the workshop like she owned the place. "Just remember, the community doesn't have patience for amateur hour," she called over her shoulder, her voice trailing as she left.

As soon as the door clicked shut behind her, I let out a breath I didn't realize I'd been holding. "She's relentless," I murmured, running a hand through my hair.

"She's also wrong," Marcus replied, his tone fierce. "We can figure this out without her."

I felt a warmth blossom in my chest. "You really believe that, don't you?"

"Absolutely," he said, meeting my gaze with an intensity that sent a flutter through me. "We just need to keep pushing forward, no matter what. We have each other, and we can make this work."

With renewed determination, we refocused on the mural, each brushstroke a testament to our resolve. The colors began to swirl together, telling a story of hope and resilience, reflecting our journey and the dreams we held.

But as the days passed, the burden of Vera's words clung to the edges of my mind like a shadow. We needed funding, and the thought gnawed at me during quiet moments. How could we move forward without financial backing? The reality of our situation sank in, heavy and unrelenting.

One evening, as the workshop hummed with the sounds of our labor, I turned to Marcus, an idea bubbling up inside me. "What if we held a fundraising event? We could invite the community to come see our work and contribute."

He paused, tilting his head as if weighing my suggestion. "You mean, like a showcase? That could work. We could turn it into a celebration."

"Exactly! We could have local musicians, food stalls, maybe even a silent auction for our pieces," I said, my excitement mounting. "It could draw attention to the project and help us raise the funds we need."

A grin spread across his face, and I felt a surge of energy radiate between us. "That's brilliant. Let's start planning it."

And so, our focus shifted once more, the project expanding beyond the walls of the workshop and into the heart of the community. We spent countless evenings brainstorming ideas, gathering supplies, and putting together a plan. With every decision we made, our bond tightened, intertwining our hopes and dreams as we navigated the logistics of our budding event.

As the day of the showcase drew near, I felt a thrill of anticipation mingled with trepidation. I wanted this to succeed, not just for the project but for us. Each flyer we posted around town was a piece of our heart sent out into the world, and I couldn't shake the feeling that it could either elevate us or crumble under the weight of expectation.

The night before the event, I found myself pacing the workshop, the soft glow of string lights casting playful shadows across the walls. Marcus leaned against the doorframe, watching me with a bemused expression. "You know, for someone who planned a fundraiser, you're acting like you're about to jump out of a plane."

I stopped mid-pace, crossing my arms. "What if no one shows up? What if we fail?"

"Then we'll pick ourselves up and try again," he said, stepping forward, his voice steady and calm. "But I doubt that's going to happen. You've poured your heart into this, and so have I. People will see that."

His words wrapped around me like a warm blanket, easing the knots in my stomach. "You're right. I guess I just want it to be perfect."

"Perfection is overrated. Let's just make it genuine. If we show up as ourselves, that's more than enough."

As the words hung in the air, I felt a warmth bloom within me—a reminder that we were in this together, ready to face whatever lay ahead. And as we prepared for the showcase, I realized that no matter the outcome, the journey was already worth it.

The day of the showcase arrived, cloaked in an electric energy that buzzed through the air like a summer storm. I woke up to the sun filtering through my bedroom window, casting playful patterns on the floor. The light danced across the walls, illuminating the sketches I'd pinned up as reminders of the vision I had for the community project. I felt a flutter of anticipation in my chest, a mixture of excitement and nerves that was impossible to ignore.

After a quick breakfast that I barely tasted, I donned the outfit I had carefully chosen—a vibrant blue dress that hugged my waist and swayed like a breeze with every step. Marcus had assured me it brought out the color of my eyes, and today, I needed every bit of encouragement I could muster. I spent a few minutes in front of the mirror, attempting to tame the wild curls that refused to cooperate, but ultimately, I decided to embrace the chaos. A few spritzes of perfume later, I was ready to face the day.

Arriving at the workshop felt like stepping into a different world. The space was transformed; colorful banners fluttered from the ceiling, and fairy lights twinkled like stars above our heads. The mural we had painted loomed large, vibrant and inviting, a testament to our hard work and shared dreams. My heart swelled with pride as I took in the sight, and I knew that no matter what happened today, we had created something beautiful together.

Marcus was already there, fussing over the final touches, adjusting the placement of a few art pieces with the focus of a seasoned curator. "You look amazing," he said without looking up, but the genuine warmth in his voice made my cheeks flush.

"Thanks! You don't look too shabby yourself," I replied, admiring his casual ensemble—a simple white shirt paired with jeans that fit just right, making him look effortlessly handsome.

As guests began to trickle in, the atmosphere shifted from anticipation to excitement. The hum of chatter filled the air, punctuated by laughter and the clinking of glasses. Friends and neighbors wandered around, taking in our work while local musicians strummed their instruments in a cozy corner. It felt like the community was enveloping us, wrapping us in a cocoon of support that was both exhilarating and terrifying.

I caught sight of Vera across the room, her presence a stark contrast to the warmth enveloping us. She stood with a small group of people, her smile polished but lacking any real warmth, as if she were putting on a show. I couldn't help but wonder how she would perceive this moment, whether it would provoke jealousy or inspire her to rally behind us. Either way, it didn't matter. This was our moment, and I was determined to soak it all in.

"Ready?" Marcus asked, his voice a low murmur as he leaned closer, his breath tickling my ear.

"Ready as I'll ever be," I replied, my heart racing as we prepared to address the crowd.

With a deep breath, we stepped onto a makeshift stage, a small platform draped in white fabric that gleamed in the soft light. As I looked out at the sea of familiar faces, my nerves began to dissipate, replaced by a sense of purpose.

"Thank you all for being here today," I began, my voice steady despite the pounding in my chest. "This project has been a labor of love, and it's because of all of you that we're able to bring our vision to life."

As I spoke, I could see Marcus's encouraging smile, a beacon of support that anchored me. I introduced our project, detailing the ideas and aspirations that had fueled our journey, and as I spoke, I felt the audience leaning in, captivated by our passion.

When it was Marcus's turn to speak, he captivated the crowd with his charm and charisma, weaving tales of creativity and community that made my heart swell. He talked about the importance of art in bringing people together, how our project could serve as a catalyst for change in the community.

The applause that erupted at the end of our speeches filled the room with an exhilarating energy. The sense of accomplishment surged through me, a delightful rush that momentarily drowned out the specter of doubt that had lingered in the back of my mind.

But as the evening progressed, I noticed Vera moving among the guests, her sharp gaze assessing every interaction. I could see her whispering to a few people, her laughter ringing out like a distant storm cloud, casting a shadow over our sunny gathering.

"Are you okay?" Marcus asked, concern knitting his brow as he caught the direction of my gaze.

"Yeah, just... keeping an eye on the competition," I replied, attempting to maintain a lighthearted demeanor.

"Let her think she's in charge," he said, a smirk playing on his lips. "We're the ones with the heart of the project. She can't take that away."

As the showcase continued, I moved through the crowd, engaging with attendees and soaking up their positive feedback. The energy in the room was contagious, and I felt buoyed by the support surrounding us. But even as I smiled and laughed, the unease about Vera's presence persisted, lurking just beneath the surface.

Later in the evening, as the sun dipped below the horizon and the lights twinkled like stars, I caught a glimpse of Vera near the refreshments table, deep in conversation with one of the local business owners. My gut twisted as I saw her slide a stack of papers across the table, her demeanor conspiratorial. Something about it set off alarm bells in my mind.

"Marcus!" I called, waving him over. "I think Vera's up to something."

He followed my gaze, brow furrowing as he spotted Vera. "What do you mean?"

"I don't know yet, but we need to find out."

Just then, the crowd fell silent, and all eyes turned to the stage. A woman stood up, her expression grave as she cleared her throat. "I'm sorry to interrupt, but there's something important we need to discuss regarding the project."

A chill swept through the room as the atmosphere shifted. I could sense Marcus tense beside me, the joyous celebration suddenly feeling like it was on the brink of collapse.

"What's going on?" he whispered, concern threading through his voice.

I could only shake my head, uncertainty swirling in my chest. As the woman began to speak, her words weaving a tale that threatened to unravel everything we had worked for, I felt the ground beneath me shift, and I braced myself for the storm that was about to break.

Chapter 19: The Power of Words

Our late-night brainstorming sessions had become an intoxicating blend of caffeine and creativity, the air thick with ideas and the flickering glow of our laptop screens illuminating the contours of each other's faces. The soft hum of the campus was a distant backdrop, a reminder that while the world outside continued to spin, we had created our own sanctuary in the cluttered confines of the library's study room. Stacks of books surrounded us like old friends, their pages whispering secrets we were determined to unearth.

Marcus leaned back in his chair, the fabric straining slightly against his shoulders as he swept a hand through his tousled hair, frustration etched across his brow. "What if we approached it from the angle of how language shapes identity?" he suggested, his eyes brightening as he leaned forward, suddenly animated. "You know, like how every character in a novel reveals something profound about themselves through the choices they make in dialogue?"

I couldn't help but smile at his passion. He had a way of turning even the most mundane concepts into a vibrant tapestry of ideas, and I found myself drawn to him—not just as a partner for this project, but as someone who ignited a spark deep within me. "That's brilliant," I replied, my voice playful yet earnest. "And it's also a little scary. You're asking us to dissect the very essence of what makes us human. Who are we without our words?"

He smirked, a crooked grin that sent my heart racing. "Well, that's the challenge, isn't it? To strip away the layers and see what lies beneath. Kind of like peeling an onion, except this one might make us cry."

"Or laugh," I shot back, teasingly. "And we both know I'd rather not wear onion-scented tears to class."

The tension between us danced like fireflies on a warm summer night, flickering with the promise of something more. I leaned in closer, the scent of his aftershave—a blend of cedar and something uniquely him—swirling around me like an embrace. "So, we need to include personal stories. How about we each share a defining moment from our lives that relates to the power of words?"

Marcus's expression softened, and for a moment, he looked almost vulnerable. "I've never really thought about that," he admitted, a hint of hesitation creeping into his tone. "Most of my stories involve me reading someone else's words and pretending they were mine."

"Everyone has their moment," I reassured him, my curiosity piqued. "What about the first time you read something that really resonated with you? Something that made you feel less alone?"

He paused, his fingers drumming against the wooden table as he seemed to retreat into his thoughts. I held my breath, waiting, sensing that whatever he was about to share would reveal a part of him he kept carefully hidden. "I think it was in high school," he finally said, a wistful smile creeping onto his lips. "I stumbled upon 'Catcher in the Rye' in my English class. Holden Caulfield's struggle to find his place in the world was like looking into a mirror. I remember thinking, 'This guy gets it.' I felt so out of place back then, you know?"

I nodded, captivated by the way his eyes lit up as he spoke. "I get that. It's incredible how words can create a lifeline when everything feels overwhelming." I took a deep breath, steeling myself to share my own story, hoping it would encourage him to open up even more. "For me, it was when I read Maya Angelou's 'I Know Why the Caged Bird Sings.' Her journey of overcoming adversity resonated with me. I was struggling with my own voice, feeling trapped in the expectations of others, and her words were like a key that unlocked my heart."

Marcus's gaze intensified, and I felt as if we were suspended in a moment that was uniquely ours—a cocoon of understanding and shared vulnerability. "You have a way with words, Sophie," he said softly, the sincerity in his voice making my cheeks flush. "Maybe we're both just trying to find our wings."

The metaphor lingered between us, as delicate and significant as the gossamer strands of a spider's web glistening in the morning light. As we continued to brainstorm, our conversation began to weave in and out of literature and our lives. With each shared story, we built bridges between our souls, and the barriers I had carefully constructed started to dissolve.

Suddenly, a burst of laughter echoed from the corridor, jolting me back to reality. I glanced at the clock—midnight. The library would be closing soon, and I wasn't ready to leave this bubble we had created. "Let's take a break," I suggested, my voice laced with a hint of reluctance. "We can grab some coffee and see if that sparks any more ideas."

"Only if you promise not to spill it on me," he replied, his eyes sparkling with mischief. "Last time I checked, I'm not a fan of caffeine burns."

"Fine," I said, rolling my eyes playfully. "I'll do my best to keep it contained, but no promises if you keep making me laugh."

As we made our way to the café, the air crackled with anticipation. The walk felt less like a chore and more like an adventure, each step echoing the rhythm of our unspoken connection. The dim lights illuminated Marcus's features, casting a warm glow that softened the sharp angles of his face, making him look almost ethereal.

"Have you ever thought about how words can be weapons?" he mused as we navigated the quiet hallway. "People can cut you down with just a few syllables."

I considered his words, my heart suddenly heavy with the weight of past experiences. "Yeah, I've felt that sting. But words can heal, too. It's all about how we choose to use them."

"Wise words, Sophie," he replied, his tone teasing but tinged with sincerity. "You should write a book."

"Only if you promise to read it," I shot back, feeling bold. "And not critique it to shreds like you do with everyone else's work."

With that, we stepped into the café, the rich aroma of freshly brewed coffee enveloping us like a warm hug. The clatter of mugs and soft murmurs provided a comforting backdrop as we placed our orders. While we waited, I glanced around, taking in the cozy ambiance, the vibrant chatter around us, and the thought that maybe, just maybe, I was beginning to find my place in this swirling world of words and connections.

The clinking of ceramic mugs punctuated the air as we settled into a cozy corner of the café, our respective drinks steaming between us like a bridge linking our thoughts. The faint chatter of late-night patrons surrounded us, a comforting hum that felt almost intimate. As I wrapped my hands around my mug, its warmth seeped into my skin, grounding me in the moment. Marcus leaned back in his chair, a playful smirk dancing on his lips, and I couldn't shake the feeling that the connection we were building was as rich and layered as the coffee we were savoring.

"Alright, Sophie, what's our next move?" he asked, his brow arched with mock seriousness. "You've dazzled me with your words of wisdom; now it's time for me to dazzle you with my...well, whatever it is I do." He waved his hand in an exaggerated gesture that made me laugh, dispelling any lingering tension from our earlier conversations.

"Your dazzling abilities are on par with the best of them, Marcus," I teased back, feigning a thoughtful expression. "I mean, who else can turn a simple coffee run into an epic journey of self-discovery? But seriously, we need to focus on our analysis. How about we brainstorm some key themes to dissect?"

"Fine, but only if we can include the theme of caffeine addiction," he shot back, raising his mug in mock salute. "I think it speaks to a universal struggle."

"Now that's profound," I replied, shaking my head, unable to suppress a grin. "But let's save the existential crises for later. We can incorporate how addiction to literature often mirrors our addiction to caffeine—how both fuel us but can lead us to questionable choices."

He chuckled, clearly enjoying the banter. "I can already see the headline: 'Sipping and Scribbling: The Dark Side of Literary Obsession.'"

Our laughter wove through the café like a familiar song, comforting and filled with the promise of more. Each quip and playful jab deepened the bond that was blossoming between us. I realized how much I had come to cherish these moments—these exchanges filled with laughter, vulnerability, and the gentle exploration of who we were.

"Okay, but on a serious note," Marcus began, his expression shifting slightly, a glimmer of sincerity flashing in his eyes. "What about exploring how words can create barriers just as much as they can build bridges? Like how people often hide behind their language—using it as a shield?"

The change in tone caught me off guard. I leaned forward, intrigued. "That's an excellent point. I've seen it firsthand. Sometimes people mask their feelings, using words to deflect rather than connect."

He nodded, his gaze intense. "Exactly. Like, how often do we really say what we mean? I mean, I've spent most of my life analyzing everyone else's words, but I've never really stopped to think about my own."

"What's stopping you?" I asked, unable to contain my curiosity. The vulnerability in his voice sparked something inside me, a need to delve deeper into this unexpected revelation.

He hesitated, the weight of his thoughts seemingly tangible in the air between us. "I think I'm afraid of what might come out. There are layers to me that I've kept buried, you know? It's easier to critique a book than to lay your own soul bare."

"Believe me, I get that," I replied, my voice softening. "Sometimes it feels safer to hide behind clever quips and sharp retorts rather than expose what truly matters. But I think you'd be surprised at how much strength it takes to be vulnerable."

His expression shifted, and for a fleeting moment, I saw the storm of emotions swirling behind his eyes. It was both exhilarating and terrifying. "Maybe that's the real power of words," he said finally, his voice barely above a whisper. "The courage to let them be a reflection of who we are, the good and the bad."

In that moment, the café faded away. The laughter and chatter around us melted into a dull murmur as we locked eyes, an electric tension coursing through the space. I felt the weight of our shared truths hanging between us, and I knew we were crossing a threshold—one that would irrevocably change everything.

Just as the silence thickened, an enthusiastic group of students burst through the door, laughter ringing out as they commandeered the counter. The moment shattered, drawing me back into the reality of our surroundings, but the air still crackled with unspoken possibilities.

"Seems like we're not alone in our caffeine-fueled epiphanies," I said, attempting to lighten the mood as I watched the group exchange animated stories about their latest escapades.

Marcus grinned, his usual demeanor returning. "Just our luck. We should probably head back soon. We don't want to get caught in a caffeine-fueled free-for-all."

We both rose to leave, but as I turned to walk out, I felt a gentle tug on my sleeve. I looked back, surprised to see Marcus still standing there, his gaze serious. "Hey, before we head out, I just want to say... I appreciate you, Sophie. More than you know."

His words struck a chord deep within me, resonating like a tuning fork. The weight of his appreciation filled the air between us, and I felt something shift—something profound. "I appreciate you too, Marcus. I never expected to find someone who could challenge me while also making me feel so... understood."

He smiled, a genuine smile that lit up his face and made my heart flutter. "Well, that's what we're here for, right? To challenge and support each other?"

"Exactly," I replied, emboldened by the warmth of our shared moment. "Let's keep pushing each other to be better—on this project and in life."

As we stepped outside into the cool night air, I couldn't help but feel invigorated, a sense of purpose swelling within me. The moon hung high above, casting a silver glow over the campus as if illuminating the path ahead. I glanced at Marcus, who walked beside me, and I knew that this partnership had evolved into something richer, more intricate, like a beautifully woven tapestry of our lives.

The night continued to unfold with the potential of endless possibilities, and for the first time, I felt ready to embrace whatever came next. The power of words had ignited a fire in me, and I could see the outline of a future that shimmered with promise—one where vulnerability and courage intertwined, creating something uniquely ours.

As we wandered back toward campus, the cool air wrapped around us like a cozy blanket, the scent of freshly brewed coffee lingering in my mind as a reminder of our exhilarating conversations. The night sky sprawled above, a canvas sprinkled with stars, and for the first time in what felt like ages, I was filled with a sense of possibility. Marcus walked beside me, his presence both grounding and electrifying.

"Do you think we're ready for this presentation?" I asked, glancing sideways at him. The way the moonlight danced in his eyes made my heart skip a beat.

"Ready? I've been ready since you convinced me that our caffeine-infused insights would revolutionize the way the faculty views literary analysis." He shot me a playful grin, and I couldn't help but laugh.

"Great, now I feel the pressure. If we revolutionize literary analysis, I might as well start charging admission for our sessions."

"Only if you promise to wear a beret and speak dramatically," he replied, mimicking a French accent that sent us both into fits of laughter.

Our playful banter melted into a comfortable silence, punctuated by the distant sounds of laughter from students gathering for late-night study sessions. Yet, beneath that lightheartedness, an undercurrent of tension simmered—a tension I could feel coiling tighter between us with every shared glance and lingering touch.

As we reached the steps of the humanities building, I paused, my heart racing. "Marcus, about what we talked about earlier—"

"Are you sure you want to go there?" His expression turned serious, the playful glimmer replaced by something deeper, more intense.

"I think we should," I replied, my voice steady despite the flutter in my chest. "I mean, we're exploring all these layers in our project, and it feels... right to explore the layers in us, too."

He took a deep breath, his eyes searching mine as if weighing the weight of our words. "What if I told you I've never really let anyone in? Not like this."

"Then I'd say it's about time," I said, feeling a surge of bravery wash over me. "You're a brilliant guy, Marcus. You deserve to be known for all of who you are—not just the critic or the guy who makes everyone laugh."

His gaze softened, and for a brief moment, the world around us faded into the background, leaving just the two of us standing on that step, hearts racing and words unspoken hanging in the air. "You really think so?"

"Absolutely," I affirmed. "But it has to go both ways. I want to share my layers, too."

"Deal," he said, a tentative smile creeping back onto his lips. "So, what's the first layer?"

I hesitated, feeling a rush of vulnerability that made my stomach churn. "I suppose the first layer is that I often feel like I'm playing a role. In school, at home, everywhere. I'm the reliable one, the straight-A student. But underneath that, I'm terrified of not measuring up—of being found out."

"Playing a role is exhausting," he said, his tone grave yet comforting. "I get that. I feel like I'm wearing a mask half the time. There's this pressure to be the smart one, the one with all the answers."

"Maybe we can start taking off those masks," I suggested, my heart pounding. "One layer at a time."

Marcus looked at me, his expression shifting from uncertainty to determination. "Okay. I'm in."

As we stood there, the soft glow of the building lights casting long shadows behind us, I felt an undeniable pull, an urge to step closer, to bridge the gap between us. But before I could move, a sharp voice broke through the moment like glass shattering.

"There you are!" Jess's voice rang out, piercing through our bubble. She approached, her expression a mix of relief and annoyance. "I've been looking everywhere for you! We have to go over the plans for the party this weekend. You're coming, right?"

"Uh, yeah," I stammered, the moment slipping away as I stepped back, the warmth between Marcus and me dissipating like morning mist. "Of course, I'll be there."

Jess's gaze darted between Marcus and me, her eyebrows knitting together in confusion. "Are you two, like, bonding? Because I can wait, but we really need to finalize everything."

"It's fine, really," Marcus said, his voice steady as he slipped back into his usual charm. "We were just brainstorming."

"Right, brainstorming," I echoed, feeling the ache of what could have been slip further from my grasp. "Let's go."

As we walked back toward the main campus, Jess launched into a detailed rundown of the party plans, her excitement infectious. But I could feel Marcus's presence lingering beside me, the unspoken words hanging in the air, waiting for another chance. I could see the flicker of unresolved tension in his eyes as he cast sideways glances at me, and it only deepened the weight in my chest.

Just as we neared the quad, a sudden shout erupted from the direction of the dorms, slicing through Jess's enthusiastic chatter. "Help! Somebody help!"

Instinctively, we all turned toward the sound. A crowd had gathered near the entrance to the dorms, voices rising in panic. I exchanged a worried glance with Marcus, my heart racing as I pushed through the throng.

As we reached the front of the crowd, my breath caught in my throat. A student lay sprawled on the ground, his face pale and his eyes unfocused. "What happened?" I asked, my voice trembling.

"He just collapsed!" someone shouted. "Call 911!"

I knelt beside the fallen student, scanning his features and searching for signs of life. "Stay with me," I urged, my heart pounding in my ears. "Can you hear me?"

His eyes fluttered open for a brief moment, a flicker of awareness that vanished just as quickly. A chill swept through me, and I felt Marcus's hand grip my shoulder, anchoring me to the moment.

"Someone get a medic!" he shouted, the tension in his voice sharp and urgent.

The crowd buzzed around us, a cacophony of gasps and murmurs blending into a backdrop of fear. In that chaos, I felt a sense of foreboding wash over me. This was no ordinary collapse. Something dark loomed in the shadows of our carefree college life, and in that instant, I realized our world was about to change irrevocably.

With the adrenaline coursing through my veins, I leaned closer to the student, trying to keep him conscious, but deep down, I knew that this was only the beginning of a storm that was about to break.

Chapter 20: The Presentation

The lecture hall is a vibrant hive of energy, a kaleidoscope of hushed whispers and the rustling of papers. Rows of students lean forward in their seats, their expressions a blend of curiosity and judgment, eager to dissect our every word. Sunlight streams through tall windows, casting a warm glow on the polished wood of the lectern, where we stand poised at the forefront of a sea of expectant faces. My heart races, thudding like a bass drum in my chest, as I take a deep breath, inhaling the scent of fresh paper and slightly stale coffee that permeates the air.

Marcus stands beside me, his presence a sturdy anchor amidst my swirling thoughts. I catch a glimpse of him, his dark hair falling just above his eyebrows, framing a face that is both boyishly charming and profoundly earnest. Today, he wears a crisp white shirt that complements his lean build, and as he adjusts his glasses, I can't help but feel a thrill of pride at the sight of him. We've come so far from those early awkward exchanges in the library, when we were just two students lost in our own worlds. Now, we are partners—not just in this presentation, but in a shared journey of discovery and camaraderie that has blossomed unexpectedly.

The room quiets as we begin, my voice ringing clear and confident. I launch into our topic, a carefully crafted exploration of the interplay between technology and human connection, a theme that resonates deeply in our increasingly digital lives. As I speak, I notice the way Marcus's eyes light up with every point I make, his nods of encouragement fueling my determination. We dance through the material, our voices harmonizing like a well-rehearsed duet, each idea building upon the last, creating a narrative that feels alive and pulsing with potential.

"Isn't it fascinating," I say, glancing toward Marcus, "how the very tools that bring us closer together can sometimes create a chasm of isolation?" He leans in, his gaze steady and unwavering. "Exactly. It's like we're all interconnected yet more alone than ever," he replies, his voice rich with conviction. I can't help but smile at his enthusiasm, the way he brings depth to every conversation, transforming simple exchanges into intellectual banter that makes me feel seen and valued.

The audience is captivated, their eyes fixed on us, and I can almost feel the collective breath being held as we navigate the nuances of our research. The click of a pen or the rustle of fabric seems amplified, each sound echoing the gravity of the moment. My nerves begin to ease, replaced by a flow of adrenaline that invigorates me. It's as if the atmosphere crackles with an electric charge, feeding our performance.

As we delve deeper, I share anecdotes and insights that breathe life into our findings. "Imagine scrolling through social media," I propose, "where every post is a carefully curated glimpse into someone's life, yet often masks the reality behind the façade." The audience shifts, a wave of understanding rippling through them. I catch a couple of students exchanging knowing glances, and it fills me with a sense of triumph. This is what we aimed for—engagement, connection, a call to reflect on our habits.

When it's Marcus's turn to speak, he steps forward, an effortless confidence radiating from him. He gestures animatedly as he lays out our conclusions, the intricate connections we've drawn between our research and its implications for future interactions. His words flow like a stream, captivating and fluid, pulling the audience into his narrative. "We have a choice," he asserts, looking out at the sea of faces. "To harness these technologies to foster genuine connections rather than let them suffocate our humanity."

The applause that follows feels like a warm embrace, a validation of our hard work and shared vision. We exchange a glance, a silent acknowledgment of our achievement, the camaraderie we've built sparking a deeper connection between us. My heart flutters, caught between pride and something more intoxicating.

As we finish, a sense of accomplishment washes over me, but the real surprise comes next. Our professor, Dr. Hayes, stands up, his imposing figure casting a long shadow over the room as he strides toward us. "Remarkable work," he begins, his voice booming with authority, "but I have a question that might challenge your conclusions." The room buzzes with curiosity as he poses a thought-provoking query, turning the very foundation of our arguments on its head.

I brace myself, heart racing anew. This is the moment I've dreaded—what if we've overlooked a crucial point? But as Marcus responds, his brow furrowing in concentration, I realize that his thoughtful approach is exactly what we need. His mind races as he engages with Dr. Hayes, weaving in counterarguments and building upon our previous points with finesse. I watch him, entranced, as he navigates the questions with a skill I never expected to witness.

"While it's true that technology can create barriers," Marcus articulates, "it also provides a platform for voices that might otherwise remain unheard. It's about finding balance, rather than vilifying the very tools we have at our disposal." His passion shines through, illuminating the discussion with a vibrant energy that resonates in the room.

The exchange unfolds with a rhythm that feels both challenging and exhilarating, igniting a fire within me. I leap into the conversation, adding my perspective to bolster Marcus's point, and soon, we're engaged in a lively debate that has the entire audience on the edge of their seats.

This moment isn't just about our presentation; it's about the synergy we've developed, the way our minds mesh to create something far more profound than either of us could have achieved alone. And as we exchange ideas, I realize that the tension—this exhilarating challenge—has woven an invisible thread that pulls us closer together.

A subtle shift in the atmosphere pulls my attention back to the present moment, a crackle of tension that dances just below the surface of our discussion. Marcus and I stand before the crowd, invigorated but acutely aware that our every word is under scrutiny. As the debate with Dr. Hayes continues, I can see the students around me leaning forward, intrigued, their faces flickering between admiration and confusion. We've turned the stage into a battleground of ideas, where each point made is met with applause or contemplation.

"Of course, technology has its pitfalls," I interject, adrenaline surging through me. "But think about how it allows people to connect across miles, share experiences, and even find communities that resonate with their struggles. Isn't that a form of liberation?" I look out into the audience, catching sight of a girl in the front row who nods vigorously, her eyes bright with understanding. It's this connection I crave—to know that my thoughts, our thoughts, are echoing beyond the walls of the hall.

"Exactly! It's a double-edged sword," Marcus adds, his voice steady and warm. "We can't ignore that. The challenge lies in our ability to wield it wisely." He glances at me, and for a fleeting second, the room disappears. There's a flicker of something unspoken in his gaze, a shared understanding that transcends mere academic discourse.

Dr. Hayes, sensing our momentum, leans in with a slight smile, his eyes gleaming with the thrill of intellectual sparring. "Then tell me this: with every new platform that emerges, do we not find ourselves facing new forms of alienation? Isn't it possible that, in our quest for connection, we lose sight of what genuine intimacy looks like?"

The audience murmurs, considering his challenge. I can feel the weight of expectation pressing down on us, a palpable pressure that makes my pulse quicken. My mind races as I grasp for a compelling response. Just as I prepare to speak, Marcus jumps in again, his enthusiasm sparking a fire within me.

"Human beings have an incredible capacity to adapt," he says, his voice filled with conviction. "We've seen it throughout history! With each innovation, we find ways to reconnect on deeper levels. Take, for instance, the rise of social media. It has given a voice to the voiceless and created movements that challenge the status quo." He pauses, looking around the room as if trying to gauge how well his message is landing. "Sure, it's messy, and sure, it can breed toxicity, but isn't that just a reflection of human nature itself? We are complex beings with the ability to learn and grow."

A soft applause rises from the audience, and I feel a swell of pride for Marcus. He's commanding the room, and with each word, I'm reminded of why I enjoy collaborating with him so much. I want to leap up and cheer him on, but instead, I focus on the task at hand, knowing that I have my own insights to contribute.

"Moreover," I add, eager to contribute to the dialogue, "the isolation we often feel isn't solely the result of technology. It's also about our choices. We can use these platforms to build relationships, or we can hide behind screens. That choice is ours."

The professor nods appreciatively, and I bask in the moment, feeling emboldened. "If we want meaningful connections, we have to be willing to put ourselves out there—risk vulnerability. Isn't that what it really comes down to?" The room falls silent as my words settle, the audience considering the weight of my statement.

Just then, a hand shoots up in the back of the room, and I blink, startled. It's Clara, a classmate known for her sharp wit and occasional snark. "What about those who become addicted to the illusion of connection? Isn't it dangerous to promote something that can so easily spiral into obsession?"

Marcus and I exchange a quick glance, but before I can respond, he leans forward, a grin creeping across his face. "Ah, but Clara, aren't you the same one who said you couldn't put down your phone during that binge-worthy show last week? And yet, here we are, having a real conversation."

Laughter bubbles up around the room, and I can feel the tension dissipating. Clara blushes, unable to suppress her smile. "Okay, point taken! But I still think moderation is key."

"Absolutely," I chime in, buoyed by the atmosphere of camaraderie. "It's about balance. If we focus solely on our devices and ignore the people right in front of us, then we're the ones responsible for that disconnection."

The conversation flows like a well-tuned orchestra, each participant adding their unique instrument to the symphony. Ideas bounce back and forth, and the audience becomes a collective organism, breathing and pulsating with the exchange. In the midst of the lively dialogue, I feel a strong sense of unity and excitement for what we're all discovering together.

As the discussion winds down, Dr. Hayes takes the opportunity to commend us. "Impressive insights from both of you. This kind of engagement is what I love to see." His praise wraps around me like a warm blanket, filling me with gratitude and disbelief.

"Thank you," I say, a little breathless. "It's been an incredible opportunity to share and discuss these ideas."

"Indeed," Marcus adds, his eyes sparkling. "And I believe the conversation shouldn't end here. It's just the beginning of exploring how we navigate our interconnected lives."

With that, the applause grows, echoing off the high ceilings, and I can't help but let out a soft laugh of relief mixed with elation. It's over. We did it. And more than that, we thrived in the challenge.

As the audience begins to disperse, I feel a wave of exhilaration wash over me. The two of us step off the stage, and the chatter of our classmates surrounds us, but all I can focus on is Marcus's smile. It's the kind of smile that lights up his entire face, a glimmer of joy that draws me in like a moth to a flame.

"Did you see Clara's face?" I laugh, unable to contain the rush of adrenaline still coursing through me. "I think you might have officially turned her into a fan."

He chuckles, running a hand through his hair, the gesture somehow both endearing and slightly chaotic. "What can I say? I have a talent for persuasion."

"I think you have a talent for captivating an entire room," I tease, my heart fluttering in a way that feels both thrilling and unsettling. The atmosphere crackles with a shared energy, an unspoken promise of more discussions, more moments like this.

"Maybe we should take this on the road," Marcus suggests, the sparkle in his eye growing. "Our next stop? A lecture series on the art of charming a room full of skeptics."

"Only if I get to wear a fabulous outfit," I reply, laughter spilling from my lips.

"Consider it a deal," he grins, and for a brief moment, I wonder if this is just friendly banter or something more. The air between us feels charged, electric, and I can't help but hope that this isn't the end of our collaboration, but rather the beginning of something deeper.

As the crowd disperses, I sense a change in the air, an impending shift that leaves me teetering on the edge of something exhilarating yet frightening. What lies ahead? I can't help but think that this moment, this connection, might just be the spark igniting a flame I never knew I needed.

The buzz of conversation fades as Marcus and I step off the stage, adrenaline still coursing through my veins. The applause echoes in my ears like a sweet melody, and the lingering warmth of the audience's appreciation wraps around us. For a fleeting moment, the lecture hall feels like our own private universe, a realm where we have created something beautiful together. The realization washes over me: we've not just presented ideas; we've forged a connection that defies the ordinary.

"Can you believe we pulled that off?" Marcus grins, a spark of excitement lighting his eyes. His infectious enthusiasm draws me in, and I feel a rush of exhilaration.

"Not only did we pull it off, but we practically set the place on fire!" I reply, teasing him. "At least metaphorically, of course. I think Clara might have to rethink her entire life after our deep dive into social media dynamics."

His laughter bubbles up, a rich sound that dances through the remnants of the crowd. "I should send her a thank-you note for being the perfect audience member."

Our banter flows effortlessly, and as we make our way through the dispersing crowd, I feel a magnetic pull between us, a tension that hangs in the air like static electricity. We weave through clusters of students, each exchanging high-fives and excited chatter, but my attention remains solely on Marcus. He's animated, gesturing wildly as he recounts the moment when Dr. Hayes challenged our ideas, a sparkle of mischief in his eyes.

"Did you see the look on his face when you tossed that zinger back at him?" he says, eyes wide with laughter. "I thought he was going to choke on his coffee!"

"I was just trying to keep the energy alive," I respond, unable to hide my smile. "Besides, it was your charm that got us this far."

He pauses, the playful glint in his eye shifting to something deeper, something that makes my heart flutter. "Well, I couldn't have done it without my trusty sidekick. You really brought your A-game today."

His words hang in the air, rich with unspoken meaning. For a brief moment, the world around us fades, leaving only the two of us in a bubble of possibility. But just as I contemplate what that might mean for us, the moment shatters as Clara approaches, her expression a curious blend of admiration and mischief.

"Nice job, you two! You practically had the whole room hanging on your every word. I didn't know you had it in you, [insert my name]." Her teasing tone cuts through the moment, and I laugh, grateful for the interruption that snaps me back to reality.

"Thanks, Clara. I just channeled my inner rock star," I reply, trying to sound nonchalant.

"More like your inner overachiever," she quips, a playful glint in her eye. "Seriously, though. Are you two planning to take your show on the road?"

Marcus grins, but I can see a flicker of uncertainty cross his face. "Not without the proper costumes," he jokes, lightening the mood as he leans closer to me. "I'm thinking sequins and maybe a cape."

"Oh, definitely. Nothing screams intellectual authority like sequins," I laugh, the tension melting away once more.

As our conversation continues, I can't help but notice the glances exchanged between Marcus and Clara. A sense of camaraderie exists, but beneath the surface lies an unspoken undercurrent that I can't quite decipher. It leaves me feeling unsettled, but I brush it aside, determined to enjoy this victory with my friends.

After a few more lighthearted exchanges, Clara heads off to catch up with some classmates. Marcus turns to me, his expression shifting as if he's weighing his words. "So, what's next for you? Have you thought about the final project? It's coming up fast."

"I was thinking of exploring more about our topic, maybe delving into how online communities can transform lives," I say, my excitement building again. "It feels like there's so much potential to unpack."

He nods, a thoughtful look crossing his face. "That sounds amazing. I'd love to collaborate again if you're open to it."

"Definitely! I can't imagine tackling it with anyone else." My heart races at the prospect of spending more time with him, of diving deeper into this journey together.

Just as the moment settles, Marcus's phone buzzes in his pocket, pulling him from our conversation. He glances down, his brow furrowing slightly. "Sorry, I need to take this," he says, his voice apologetic but distant.

I nod, feeling a sudden sense of loss as he steps away to answer the call. I watch him, heart racing with anticipation and curiosity, trying to catch snippets of his conversation. He speaks in low tones, his body language shifting from relaxed to tense as he runs a hand through his hair, a nervous habit that I've come to recognize.

"Everything okay?" I ask when he returns, the worry creeping into my voice despite my best efforts to sound casual.

"Yeah, just a... family matter," he replies, his smile returning but not quite reaching his eyes. The shift in his demeanor doesn't go unnoticed. "But enough about that! I'm just glad we got to present together. Seriously, it felt electric."

I smile back, though a thread of concern lingers. "It really did. I've never felt more alive than I did up there."

As we head toward the exit, the hallway buzzes with the chatter of students eager to escape the confines of academia for the day. But something feels off, like the calm before a storm. Just as we step outside, I catch sight of a figure leaning against the brick wall, shrouded in shadow, watching us with an intensity that sends a chill down my spine.

"Do you see that?" I murmur, my voice barely above a whisper.

Marcus turns to follow my gaze, his expression morphing from relaxed to alert. "Who is that?"

"I have no idea," I reply, my heart pounding as the figure shifts, stepping into the light. My breath catches in my throat as recognition dawns—someone from our past, someone I thought was long gone.

Before I can process the implications of this unexpected encounter, the figure raises a hand, an enigmatic smile playing on their lips. "Well, well, well. If it isn't the dynamic duo. We need to talk."

A sense of foreboding envelops me, the promise of unresolved questions looming as the air thickens with tension. I glance at Marcus, who wears a look of confusion mixed with concern, and I know, deep down, that nothing will ever be the same again.

Chapter 21: A Bitter Revelation

The celebration buzzes around me, a whirlwind of laughter and compliments swirling through the air like confetti. The room glows with the soft light of chandeliers, casting warm hues over the elegant attire of my colleagues. I lean against the polished mahogany conference table, basking in the afterglow of our successful presentation. My heart dances to a rhythm of pride and exhilaration, each clap of approval igniting a spark within me. Marcus stands beside me, his grin wide, his eyes sparkling with shared triumph. Together, we've woven our ideas into something vibrant and compelling, a tapestry of innovation that has captivated the audience.

But the moment is shattered like glass striking a tile floor. The heavy wooden door swings open, and in storms Vera, her fury slicing through the air like a knife. I feel the room tense, the laughter dying in an instant, replaced by a heavy silence that drapes over us like a damp cloak. Vera's face is a storm cloud, dark and ominous, her eyes flashing with disdain as she zeroes in on Marcus, her lips curling in a sneer. "You're ruining your reputation by working with her," she hisses, her voice a venomous whisper that echoes in the stillness.

I can almost feel the air being sucked out of the room, the collective breath held in disbelief. My heart plummets, a weight pressing down as her words hang heavily between us. I glance at Marcus, searching for a flicker of reassurance in his expression, but instead, I find conflict etched deep in his brow, his jaw tightening as he processes the accusation. He opens his mouth, but no sound emerges, leaving a chasm of uncertainty.

"Vera, that's not—" he begins, but she cuts him off, a whirlwind of indignation.

"Don't you dare defend her!" she spits, her eyes locking onto mine with a fierce intensity. "You think this collaboration is going to elevate you? It's dragging you down, Marcus. You're too good for this... this amateur hour." Each word drips with scorn, and I feel the heat of embarrassment creep up my neck, a flush of shame igniting my cheeks.

The tension in the room thickens, wrapping around me like a vise. I can't breathe. It's as if all the light has been snuffed out, leaving only the shadows of doubt lurking in the corners of my mind. I remind myself that I am here, that I deserve this moment, yet her contempt reverberates through me, a cruel echo of insecurity.

"I thought we agreed to keep this professional," Vera continues, her voice rising, sharp as glass. "You're allowing personal feelings to cloud your judgment." She turns, sweeping her arm toward the gathered team, her disdain radiating from her like a palpable force. "Look at them! They're all laughing, thinking you're some sort of star because you decided to play house with the newcomer."

"Vera, stop," Marcus says firmly, a crack of authority in his voice that pulls me back to reality. I can see him standing tall, but I know he feels the pressure of her words as acutely as I do. "This isn't just about the project; it's about the team. Emma has contributed valuable insights—"

"Valuable?" she interjects, incredulity spilling from her lips. "You think that makes up for the embarrassment she's bringing on you? This isn't a game. You're building a career, and you're risking it for what? A few glances? A friendship that's nothing but a façade?"

Her words slice through my heart, sharp and unforgiving. I've spent countless hours pouring my heart into this project, my late nights fueled by coffee and hope. I wanted to prove myself, not just to Marcus but to the world. The bitter taste of her accusations lingers, leaving a sour residue of doubt on my tongue.

"Is this how you want to be remembered, Marcus?" she presses on, her tone dripping with calculated malice. "As the man who threw it all away for a fleeting connection? Think about your future."

Marcus shifts uncomfortably, glancing at me, and in that fleeting moment, I see his hesitation, the cracks forming in his previously unwavering confidence. It feels like a betrayal, an unspoken admission that maybe Vera's right. The weight of her disdain bears down heavily on us, and I feel my stomach twist painfully.

"Vera," I manage to say, my voice barely above a whisper, laced with vulnerability. "I'm not trying to undermine anyone. I've worked hard—"

"Hard?" she sneers, stepping closer, her eyes narrowing. "You think hard work entitles you to a spot at this table? You're playing in a league far above your head. I'd hate to see how quickly it all crumbles when you can't keep up."

My heart races, and I take a step back, the world around me blurring into a haze. I wanted to stand my ground, to show her that I belonged here, but the weight of her words feels insurmountable. The tension is palpable, a raw current crackling in the air as everyone waits for Marcus to respond.

He opens his mouth again, determination flooding his features. "Emma is my partner in this," he says, a spark of defiance lighting his gaze. "We're a team, and I won't let your bitterness affect our work. It's not about what you think—"

But Vera isn't done; her voice rises, tinged with desperation. "This is not just about you, Marcus! You're letting her drag you down into her mediocrity. You're better than this!"

And just like that, the energy shifts again, a tension spiraling beyond our control. The room watches, breathless, as Marcus squares his shoulders, the fire in his eyes igniting a flicker of hope within me. I had thought we were strong enough to withstand this storm, but now, doubts swirl like a tempest, threatening to pull us apart.

Vera's voice rings out again, relentless and cutting. "I won't stand by and watch you ruin everything you've worked for."

The stakes rise higher, and my heart pounds in my chest. I can't let her shatter what we've built. I refuse to be the reason Marcus falters, the reason his dreams collapse into dust. In this moment, a resolve solidifies within me, a fierce determination to prove not just to Vera, but to myself, that I am worthy of this chance.

"Then let me show you," I say, my voice firm, the words escaping my lips like a challenge.

As we bask in the glow of our successful presentation, the energy shifts when Vera storms in, her face a mask of fury. She accuses Marcus of compromising his reputation by collaborating with me, her voice dripping with contempt. The room falls silent, and I can see the conflict in Marcus's eyes as he grapples with her accusations. I stand there, heart racing, knowing that Vera's words threaten to unravel everything we've built together. My confidence wavers, and I feel the weight of her disdain crashing down on us.

"Really, Marcus?" Vera sneers, her hands clenched into fists at her sides. "Is this what you've come to? Tying your career to—what? An intern who wouldn't know a good idea if it bit her?"

I can almost hear the collective intake of breath from our colleagues, their eyes darting between us as if waiting for a spectacle. A circus act they didn't ask to see. Marcus straightens his shoulders, a flicker of determination sparking in his gaze. I can tell he wants to defend me, to brush aside Vera's venom like an annoying fly, but he hesitates, his loyalty caught in a tug-of-war between the formidable woman who has been his mentor and the budding partnership he's forged with me.

"Vera, that's unfair," he says, his voice steady but softening at the edges. "Lily's ideas are innovative, and our collaboration produced results. This isn't about her; it's about what we can achieve together."

"Together?" Vera scoffs, the derision pouring from her lips like hot lava. "You mean you playing house with your little project while the rest of us take this seriously? You've always been too soft, Marcus. It's going to cost you."

I can feel the heat rising in my cheeks, a cocktail of embarrassment and indignation bubbling just below the surface. "I didn't ask for any favors," I manage to say, my voice firm enough to cut through her tirade. "I earned my place here, and if you can't see that, then maybe it's you who needs to reconsider your perspective."

For a heartbeat, the room is frozen, all eyes locked on me as if I've just performed a high-wire act without a net. Vera blinks, momentarily taken aback by my unexpected boldness, and in that pause, I see a crack in her armor. But the moment passes, and her eyes narrow, brimming with the intensity of a storm.

"Watch your tone, Lily," she warns, her voice low and dangerous. "You might be riding high on this little victory, but remember who has the power to make or break your career here."

With that, she turns sharply on her heel and storms out of the conference room, leaving a palpable tension hanging in the air like a thick fog. The silence that follows is deafening, a cacophony of unspoken words swirling around us. Marcus runs a hand through his hair, frustration evident in his demeanor.

"Are you okay?" he asks, his voice a gentle murmur, tinged with concern as he shifts closer to me, the heat of his presence a comforting balm against the storm Vera has unleashed.

"I will be," I reply, my heart still racing but my resolve hardening. "I'm tired of people trying to dictate my worth based on their insecurities. I didn't come this far to be intimidated."

Marcus nods, his expression shifting from worry to admiration. "That's the spirit. Don't let her get to you. You've got talent, and it's clear the presentation was a success."

"Only because we worked as a team," I remind him, the camaraderie we've forged suddenly feeling fragile, as if it might shatter under the weight of external pressures. "I just hope she doesn't poison the well for you."

"I can handle her," he says, a fire igniting in his eyes. "But you're right; we need to be careful. She'll twist this to her advantage if we let her."

In that moment, I feel a spark of hope igniting within me, a flicker of what our partnership could be—a defiant force against the looming shadows of doubt. As we gather our things, I can't shake the feeling that this is just the beginning of something bigger than either of us anticipated.

Later that evening, the office buzzes with a mix of excitement and apprehension. The aftermath of the presentation is palpable, colleagues discussing the impact of our work while casting wary glances toward Marcus and me. I can't blame them; Vera's influence runs deep, and she has a knack for turning whispers into roars.

"Hey, did you see the way she was after you?" a fellow intern, Claire, says as she slides up next to me at the coffee machine. "That was intense. But honestly? You held your ground. I wouldn't have had the guts."

"Thanks, I think?" I chuckle nervously, pouring myself a cup of lukewarm coffee. "It was either that or let her steamroll me. I'd prefer to remain upright, thanks."

Claire grins, her admiration evident. "Well, you've got a fan in me. Just don't let it get to your head. You don't want Vera targeting you like she's some kind of predator."

"Too late for that," I reply, glancing over to where Marcus stands talking to a group of senior executives, his posture confident despite the lingering tension. "But I'll take my chances. Besides, I'm starting to think she's more afraid than we are."

The shift in atmosphere is subtle, but it's there—a new determination rippling through the office as we collectively decide not to be cowed by the looming presence of Vera. I can see the whispers starting to fade, replaced by camaraderie and support, like an undercurrent carrying us forward.

The next few days unfold with a renewed sense of purpose. I dive headfirst into my work, inspired to push the boundaries of what Marcus and I can achieve. Each brainstorm session, every late-night coffee run, feels charged with possibility, the spark of our shared ambition igniting a fire beneath us. As our ideas flow and evolve, I find myself growing more confident, shedding the layers of doubt that once held me back.

Then, just as we reach a pivotal point in our project, a message arrives that changes everything—a cryptic email from an anonymous sender, hinting at a secret lurking within the company's foundation. The words dangle before me like a tantalizing thread, promising revelations that could shake the very core of our work.

I glance at Marcus, who is engrossed in a spreadsheet, and my heart races at the thought of sharing this with him. The thrill of a potential breakthrough mingles with a tinge of anxiety. What if this leads to trouble? What if Vera is behind it all, playing her game once more? But something in my gut tells me that this is too important to ignore.

Taking a deep breath, I lean over and whisper, "Marcus, I just received something strange. An email about—well, I'm not entirely sure what, but it feels important. We need to check it out."

His eyes lift from the screen, curiosity piqued, and for a moment, I can see the wheels turning in his mind. "Let's do it," he says, determination flashing across his face. "No one's going to dictate our narrative."

As we bask in the glow of our successful presentation, the energy shifts when Vera storms in, her face a mask of fury. She accuses Marcus of compromising his reputation by collaborating with me, her voice dripping with contempt. The room falls silent, and I can see the conflict in Marcus's eyes as he grapples with her accusations.

I stand there, heart racing, knowing that Vera's words threaten to unravel everything we've built together. My confidence wavers, and I feel the weight of her disdain crashing down on us.

"Really, Marcus?" Vera sneers, her hands clenched into fists at her sides. "Is this what you've come to? Tying your career to—what? An intern who wouldn't know a good idea if it bit her?"

I can almost hear the collective intake of breath from our colleagues, their eyes darting between us as if waiting for a spectacle. A circus act they didn't ask to see. Marcus straightens his shoulders, a flicker of determination sparking in his gaze. I can tell he wants to defend me, to brush aside Vera's venom like an annoying fly, but he hesitates, his loyalty caught in a tug-of-war between the formidable woman who has been his mentor and the budding partnership he's forged with me.

"Vera, that's unfair," he says, his voice steady but softening at the edges. "Lily's ideas are innovative, and our collaboration produced results. This isn't about her; it's about what we can achieve together."

"Together?" Vera scoffs, the derision pouring from her lips like hot lava. "You mean you playing house with your little project while the rest of us take this seriously? You've always been too soft, Marcus. It's going to cost you."

I can feel the heat rising in my cheeks, a cocktail of embarrassment and indignation bubbling just below the surface. "I didn't ask for any favors," I manage to say, my voice firm enough to cut through her tirade. "I earned my place here, and if you can't see that, then maybe it's you who needs to reconsider your perspective."

For a heartbeat, the room is frozen, all eyes locked on me as if I've just performed a high-wire act without a net. Vera blinks, momentarily taken aback by my unexpected boldness, and in that pause, I see a crack in her armor. But the moment passes, and her eyes narrow, brimming with the intensity of a storm.

"Watch your tone, Lily," she warns, her voice low and dangerous. "You might be riding high on this little victory, but remember who has the power to make or break your career here."

With that, she turns sharply on her heel and storms out of the conference room, leaving a palpable tension hanging in the air like a thick fog. The silence that follows is deafening, a cacophony of unspoken words swirling around us. Marcus runs a hand through his hair, frustration evident in his demeanor.

"Are you okay?" he asks, his voice a gentle murmur, tinged with concern as he shifts closer to me, the heat of his presence a comforting balm against the storm Vera has unleashed.

"I will be," I reply, my heart still racing but my resolve hardening. "I'm tired of people trying to dictate my worth based on their insecurities. I didn't come this far to be intimidated."

Marcus nods, his expression shifting from worry to admiration. "That's the spirit. Don't let her get to you. You've got talent, and it's clear the presentation was a success."

"Only because we worked as a team," I remind him, the camaraderie we've forged suddenly feeling fragile, as if it might shatter under the weight of external pressures. "I just hope she doesn't poison the well for you."

"I can handle her," he says, a fire igniting in his eyes. "But you're right; we need to be careful. She'll twist this to her advantage if we let her."

In that moment, I feel a spark of hope igniting within me, a flicker of what our partnership could be—a defiant force against the looming shadows of doubt. As we gather our things, I can't shake the feeling that this is just the beginning of something bigger than either of us anticipated.

Later that evening, the office buzzes with a mix of excitement and apprehension. The aftermath of the presentation is palpable, colleagues discussing the impact of our work while casting wary glances toward Marcus and me. I can't blame them; Vera's influence runs deep, and she has a knack for turning whispers into roars.

"Hey, did you see the way she was after you?" a fellow intern, Claire, says as she slides up next to me at the coffee machine. "That was intense. But honestly? You held your ground. I wouldn't have had the guts."

"Thanks, I think?" I chuckle nervously, pouring myself a cup of lukewarm coffee. "It was either that or let her steamroll me. I'd prefer to remain upright, thanks."

Claire grins, her admiration evident. "Well, you've got a fan in me. Just don't let it get to your head. You don't want Vera targeting you like she's some kind of predator."

"Too late for that," I reply, glancing over to where Marcus stands talking to a group of senior executives, his posture confident despite the lingering tension. "But I'll take my chances. Besides, I'm starting to think she's more afraid than we are."

The shift in atmosphere is subtle, but it's there—a new determination rippling through the office as we collectively decide not to be cowed by the looming presence of Vera. I can see the whispers starting to fade, replaced by camaraderie and support, like an undercurrent carrying us forward.

The next few days unfold with a renewed sense of purpose. I dive headfirst into my work, inspired to push the boundaries of what Marcus and I can achieve. Each brainstorm session, every late-night coffee run, feels charged with possibility, the spark of our shared ambition igniting a fire beneath us. As our ideas flow and evolve, I find myself growing more confident, shedding the layers of doubt that once held me back.

Then, just as we reach a pivotal point in our project, a message arrives that changes everything—a cryptic email from an anonymous sender, hinting at a secret lurking within the company's foundation.

The words dangle before me like a tantalizing thread, promising revelations that could shake the very core of our work.

I glance at Marcus, who is engrossed in a spreadsheet, and my heart races at the thought of sharing this with him. The thrill of a potential breakthrough mingles with a tinge of anxiety. What if this leads to trouble? What if Vera is behind it all, playing her game once more? But something in my gut tells me that this is too important to ignore.

Taking a deep breath, I lean over and whisper, "Marcus, I just received something strange. An email about—well, I'm not entirely sure what, but it feels important. We need to check it out."

His eyes lift from the screen, curiosity piqued, and for a moment, I can see the wheels turning in his mind. "Let's do it," he says, determination flashing across his face. "No one's going to dictate our narrative."

We huddle over my laptop, the glow of the screen illuminating our faces in the dim office. The email is untraceable, with no sender information, just a series of lines that tug at my instincts. "It talks about discrepancies in the funding reports," I say, frowning as I read. "They hint at something big being covered up. It mentions Vera."

"Of course it does," Marcus replies, his voice a mixture of disbelief and frustration. "She's always been shifty with the numbers. It wouldn't surprise me if she's involved in something illegal. But why send this to you? That's what doesn't make sense."

I shrug, the uncertainty gnawing at me. "Maybe they want to expose her? Or maybe they think I'm a pawn in her game? Either way, we can't ignore it."

A plan begins to form in my mind, each step falling into place with a clarity I hadn't expected. "What if we dig deeper? See if we can find out more about the funding reports? If this is true, it could change everything."

"Right," Marcus agrees, his eyes shining with the thrill of the chase. "But we need to be careful. If Vera catches wind of this, it could backfire spectacularly. We should gather evidence before making any moves."

As we pore over the files on my laptop, the atmosphere crackles with tension. The hours slip by unnoticed, our focus unyielding as we sift through documents, piecing together a puzzle that feels both exhilarating and dangerous. Just as I start to feel a sense of momentum, a shadow falls across my desk.

I look up, and my stomach drops. It's Vera, her expression a mask of cold fury. "What are you two doing?" she asks, her voice low and threatening, laced with the sharp edge of authority.

Caught in the act, I freeze, a thousand thoughts racing through my mind. There's no way to backtrack now; the dam has burst. But as I look at Marcus, his jaw set with determination, I know we won't be easily intimidated. This is the moment of truth, and there's no turning back.

With a feigned calmness, I respond, "Just working on some figures for the project, Vera. You know how it is—always striving for perfection."

But in my heart, I know that the facade won't hold, and the storm is only beginning.

Chapter 22: The Fallout

The aftermath of the presentation hangs heavy in the air, like the lingering aroma of burnt coffee. Each passing day feels like a tightrope walk over a chasm of uncertainty, the rickety boards beneath my feet threatening to splinter at any moment. The spotlight that once burned so brightly now feels more like a spotlight on my flaws, illuminating every crack in my carefully crafted façade. Marcus retreats into his world, a shadow of the charming man I once knew, consumed by the pressure to appease Vera and reclaim his standing in the literary community. His obsession with success gnaws at him, and I watch helplessly as he becomes a mere echo of himself.

It's as if a layer of fog has rolled in, obscuring not just our connection but the vibrant landscape of our shared lives. The coffee shop where we used to linger over steaming mugs and playful banter now feels like a mausoleum of our laughter, each table a tombstone marking the loss of what we once had. I find myself sitting alone in the corner, nursing a lukewarm cup, the chatter of patrons blurring into a dull roar that barely registers. My heart sinks as I see him walk in, his face set in a mask of determination, eyes glazed with ambition, a stark contrast to the spark that used to ignite our conversations.

"You're looking sharp," I remark, forcing a lightness into my tone, but it feels like shouting into a void. He glances my way, and for a fleeting moment, I catch a glimpse of the warmth I miss so desperately, but it's quickly extinguished.

"Thanks," he replies, his voice lacking the familiar lilt that used to dance between us. "I have a meeting with Vera. Important stuff." He avoids my gaze, focusing instead on the barista preparing his drink. The distance between us seems to widen, and I wonder if it's too late to bridge it.

"Want to talk about it?" I venture, my heart racing at the prospect of pulling him back from the precipice.

"No, it's just... work." The finality in his tone makes my stomach twist. It feels like I'm grasping at sand, each word slipping through my fingers, leaving me feeling more isolated than before. I want to reach out, to shake him awake from whatever trance has ensnared him, but I'm left staring at the remnants of our shared moments, relics of a bond that feels more fragile than a butterfly's wing.

Desperate to mend the rift, I throw myself into my work, pouring every ounce of energy into my students. Their bright eyes and eager questions provide a temporary balm for my aching heart. Each lecture becomes an escape, a cocoon where I can forget my troubles, if only for an hour. I relish the sound of their laughter and the excitement that crackles in the air when a particularly challenging concept clicks. They're a reminder that passion exists outside the confines of my relationship with Marcus, yet the moment I leave the classroom, that bubble of warmth bursts, leaving me shivering in the cold reality of our estrangement.

One afternoon, while organizing my notes, I find myself reflecting on my last conversation with Marcus. He had been so alive, so passionate about his work, and it feels like a betrayal to remember him that way when he's become a shadow of that person. I replay the moment in my mind like a film on repeat, searching for clues that might help me understand the shift between us. The weight of unspoken words hangs heavy in the air, thickening my throat with uncried tears.

"Ms. Harrington?" A soft voice pulls me from my reverie. It's Sophie, one of my quieter students. She stands at my desk, clutching her backpack tightly, her brows furrowed with concern. "Are you okay?"

"Of course, dear. Just... thinking." I smile, but it feels forced, like a mask I'm trying to wear but can't quite manage.

"You don't seem okay. You're... different." Her honesty stings, a sharp reminder of the mask I've tried to keep intact. I nod, grateful for her concern, but the walls I've built around my heart are too thick to breach with just one earnest inquiry.

"I'm fine, really. Just a bit tired." I can see her eyes searching mine, hoping for more. "How about you? How's your project coming along?"

Her face brightens, and for a moment, I'm reminded of the joy I used to feel teaching. As she launches into an enthusiastic explanation, I let her words wash over me, soaking in the delight she exudes. The brief reprieve allows me to breathe, but the moment she leaves, the silence returns, enveloping me in its cold embrace.

That evening, I decide to take a different route home. Instead of my usual path through the park, I wander through the bustling streets, hoping the energy of the city might infuse some life into my weary spirit. The sunset casts a golden hue over the buildings, and the air is thick with the smell of street food, a mixture of spices that tickles my senses. I stop at a food cart, the sizzle of marinated chicken making my mouth water. I order a skewer, the vendor's warm smile a balm for my bruised heart.

As I walk, the night unfolds around me, each sound and light becoming a symphony of life. Yet, despite the vibrancy of the world, a dull ache remains within me, a gnawing reminder of what's missing. I can't help but wonder if Marcus will ever break free from the chains he's forged with his own ambition. As I bite into the tender chicken, a warmth spreads through me—not the comforting warmth of love, but the fleeting pleasure of a moment savored, a reminder that life continues, even when my heart feels heavy.

The streets begin to hum with the sounds of laughter and conversation, and for a brief instant, I allow myself to be swept away in the tide of human connection. I take a deep breath, inhaling the rich aromas of street food and the sounds of people living their lives unabashedly. I can't help but smile as a couple passes by, their laughter ringing in the air like a melody I wish I could carry with me.

I momentarily forget the solitude that has become my unwelcome companion and lose myself in the beauty of the moment.

But as I near home, a familiar figure catches my eye—a silhouette leaning against a lamppost, head bowed, lost in thought. My heart leaps, and for a moment, hope flickers like the streetlights around us, casting a warm glow on the cold pavement. Is it Marcus?

He stands there, a figure both familiar and achingly distant, the lamplight casting a golden halo around him. The way the light catches the unruly curls of his hair makes my heart skip a beat, a remnant of the boy who once made the mundane sparkle with promise. But beneath the surface of this brief enchantment lies a tension so palpable it feels like a taut string ready to snap at the slightest touch.

"Hey," I call, my voice tentative, as if I'm afraid to disturb the fragile peace that surrounds him. He looks up, and for a moment, I see the spark I've been missing—the flicker of recognition that ignites in his eyes. It's fleeting, almost like a secret shared between us before the weight of reality pulls it back into the shadows.

"Fancy running into you here," he replies, his tone light but edged with an underlying seriousness that makes my stomach flutter uneasily. "I thought you were buried under a pile of student essays."

"Only the usual amount of existential dread," I quip, trying to mask the heaviness of my heart with humor. "What about you? Hiding from your literary responsibilities?"

He snorts, a sound that feels oddly comforting amidst the tension. "No hiding, just... contemplating my life choices. You know, the usual."

The corner of my mouth quirks upward, but the smile doesn't reach my eyes. The distance between us stretches like a vast canyon, the chasm filled with unspoken words and unresolved feelings. I take a step closer, trying to bridge that gap, hoping he can feel the warmth radiating from me, urging him to step back into the light.

"Have you talked to Vera yet?" I ask, my curiosity tinged with concern.

His expression darkens, and the flicker of warmth dissipates like morning mist. "Yeah, I did. It was... enlightening." His voice drips with sarcasm, but there's an edge of frustration beneath it that cuts deeper than any sharp comment.

"What does that mean?" I press, unable to let the moment slip away.

"Just the same old critique, you know? I need to 'find my voice' and 'connect with the audience'—the usual literary jargon." He shrugs, but his body language betrays him. Tension ripples through him like a taut wire. "I thought I was getting somewhere, but it seems I'm still just... a nobody."

"You're not a nobody, Marcus." The words spill out before I can stop them, firm and determined. "You have a voice. You have stories to tell. I believe in you."

For a moment, our eyes lock, and I can see the flicker of doubt wrestling with the hope I'm trying to offer. It's the same look he wore when he first shared his writing with me, that blend of vulnerability and desire for validation. But just as quickly as it appears, he looks away, as if he can't bear the weight of my belief.

"Thanks. That means a lot," he mutters, but it's clear he doesn't believe it. The flicker in his eyes dims again, and I can almost hear the gears turning in his mind, the relentless thoughts spiraling into the abyss of his doubts.

"Have you considered taking a break?" I ask, feeling the heaviness of his struggle. "Maybe stepping away from it all would help you gain some perspective."

He laughs, but it's devoid of humor. "Yeah, right. The world doesn't stop just because I need a breather. Besides, I can't afford to be seen as someone who can't handle the pressure."

"Pressure's overrated," I shoot back, attempting to lighten the mood. "You're not in a race. Your journey is yours, not anyone else's."

"Sounds like a nice theory," he replies, his voice dropping into a serious murmur. "But in this industry, it's all about who gets there first. It's dog-eat-dog, and I can't afford to be left behind."

The mention of the industry pulls at my heart, reminding me of the ambition that once united us. I can't shake the feeling that Vera is a specter haunting our relationship, pushing him further away. My fingers itch to reach for him, to pull him back into the warmth of our shared dreams, but the space between us feels like an impenetrable wall.

"Maybe you need to redefine what 'there' means," I suggest, leaning in closer. "What if it's not about the recognition? What if it's about creating something that resonates with you?"

His gaze softens momentarily, and I catch a glimpse of the old Marcus—the one who thrived on creativity and passion. But the moment vanishes as quickly as it appeared, replaced by the walls he's built around himself.

"I wish it were that simple." His voice is barely above a whisper, laced with frustration. "Every day I wake up, and it feels like I'm fighting against a tide that wants to pull me under. I can't just—"

"Fight it," I finish, my heart aching for him. "You don't have to do this alone, you know. I'm here."

He looks at me, and for the briefest moment, I see the flicker of hope I long to nurture. "I don't want to drag you into my chaos," he admits, a note of vulnerability creeping into his tone.

"Too late for that," I say with a wry smile, trying to keep the mood light. "You already have me in the thick of it. Besides, I like chaos. It makes for great stories."

He chuckles, and the sound warms the cool evening air between us. The tension eases, if only for a moment, and I grasp at it like a lifeline.

"What if I take you up on that offer?" he finally asks, his expression shifting into something more hopeful, more honest. "What if I let you help me find my way out of this mess?"

"Consider it a collaboration," I reply, emboldened by his willingness to open up. "We'll tackle this together, like we used to. Just you and me against the world."

"Deal," he says, and for the first time in what feels like an eternity, I see a glimpse of the spark I've been longing for. It flickers back to life, filling the space between us with the possibility of connection.

Just then, a couple walks by, their laughter spilling over us like a refreshing spring breeze. I watch them, feeling the warmth of their connection, a stark contrast to the shadows that have loomed over my own life lately. "It's amazing how love can shift everything," I muse, more to myself than to Marcus.

"Love's overrated," he scoffs playfully, but there's a glimmer of mischief in his eyes. "It's just a distraction."

I raise an eyebrow, unable to suppress a grin. "A distraction? Are you saying you don't believe in love?"

"Not in this chaotic world," he shoots back, but the teasing lilt in his voice betrays his true feelings. "It's messy and complicated—like trying to put together IKEA furniture without the manual."

"Touché," I reply, unable to hold back a laugh. "But it's the messiness that makes it beautiful, isn't it? All those imperfections and the little surprises along the way?"

"Perhaps you're right." He leans against the lamppost, crossing his arms with a thoughtful frown. "Maybe I just haven't found the right chaos yet."

"Or maybe you're just looking in all the wrong places," I suggest, unable to resist the opportunity to nudge him closer to the truth I see lurking beneath the surface.

As we stand there, the world buzzing around us, I feel the distance between us shrinking, the barriers dissolving in the warmth of our renewed connection. Maybe, just maybe, we can find our way back to each other, even amidst the chaos that threatens to pull us apart.

As the evening deepens, we linger on the cusp of an unspoken agreement, an implicit understanding that maybe—just maybe—we can navigate this chaos together. The laughter of passing couples and the clinking of glasses from the nearby bar become the soundtrack to our tentative reconnection. Marcus leans in slightly, his presence warm and familiar, but there's an undercurrent of uncertainty swirling between us, the air thick with questions left unanswered.

"What do you think love is, then?" I venture, emboldened by our earlier banter. "If it's not a distraction, what is it?"

He looks thoughtful, chewing his lip as he processes my question. "I suppose it's... a commitment. A willingness to dive headfirst into the storm, knowing it might rain on your parade. Or, in my case, ruin your carefully crafted narrative."

I can't help but laugh at his unexpected analogy. "So, you're saying love is like a plot twist that leaves the audience gasping?"

"Exactly! Just when you think you've figured it all out, BAM! Something comes out of left field, and you're left wondering if you even know the characters."

"Interesting perspective." I tilt my head, studying him. "But what if the twist makes the story richer? What if it transforms everything into something worth reading?"

"Or," he replies, his eyes glinting with mischief, "it could just leave you with a bunch of unanswered questions and an ending that feels like a giant letdown."

"Ah, the dreaded cliffhanger," I nod knowingly. "You do realize you're living in one right now, right?"

Marcus smirks, and for a moment, it feels like we've slipped back into our old rhythm. But just as quickly, the tension returns, thickening the air around us. "Maybe," he says, his voice lowering, "but at least I know I'm not alone in this mess."

The sincerity of his words sends a shiver down my spine. There's a glimmer of hope in our exchange, but it's wrapped in uncertainty, and I can't shake the feeling that we're standing on a precipice, the ground beneath us soft and treacherous.

"Shall we tackle the chaos together, then?" I ask, my heart racing at the thought of being partners in this unpredictable narrative.

"Why not?" he replies, his expression brightening, and for a heartbeat, the shadows seem to lift. "What's the worst that could happen?"

"Famous last words," I tease, trying to keep the mood light. "You do realize this means we're diving headfirst into the storm, right?"

"Bring it on," he challenges, a daring glint in his eye. "I've faced worse than a little rain. It's all part of the story."

With a shared smile, we stand on the brink of something new. My heart feels buoyant, yet somewhere deep within, a whisper of doubt lingers. As we make our way through the bustling streets, laughter and chatter swirl around us like confetti. It's comforting and exhilarating all at once, a reminder that life, despite its unpredictable nature, can still be beautiful.

Suddenly, I spot a flicker of movement in the corner of my eye. A woman, cloaked in shadows, stands a few feet away, her gaze locked onto us with an intensity that makes the hair on the back of my neck stand on end. Something about her presence sends a jolt of anxiety through me.

"Marcus, do you—" I start, but he's already looking over, his expression shifting from playful to serious.

"Yeah, I see her," he murmurs, his voice low. "We should probably keep moving."

I nod, but the pull of curiosity tugs at me. There's something eerily familiar about the woman, her silhouette echoing the ghosts of past relationships and unresolved tensions. As we walk on, I steal a glance back, only to find she's vanished into the throng of people.

"Who was that?" I ask, my heart racing, a storm of unease gathering in my chest.

"No idea," Marcus replies, but the tightness around his mouth suggests otherwise. "Probably someone from the literary scene. They can be... a little intense."

"Intense? Is that the polite way to say 'crazy'?" I joke, trying to lighten the mood, but the tension lingers.

He chuckles, but it's strained. "Something like that."

The weight of his response sends a chill through me, the earlier warmth of our exchange dissipating like mist in the sunlight. "Are you sure it's nothing?" I press, unable to shake the feeling that there's more to this than he's letting on.

"Honestly, I don't want to think about it," he admits, a flicker of frustration flashing across his features. "We're supposed to be moving forward, right?"

"Right," I agree, but I can't shake the feeling that something is lurking just beyond the horizon, waiting to pounce.

We walk in silence for a few moments, the atmosphere thick with unspoken words and lingering doubts. My mind races, chasing after the implications of that fleeting encounter, the feeling that we're being watched, perhaps even hunted.

As we approach the park, I spot a familiar café with outdoor seating. "How about a little caffeine boost?" I suggest, desperate to ease the tension between us.

"Sure, why not?" he agrees, and relief washes over me.

Inside, the cozy ambiance wraps around us like a warm blanket. The rich aroma of freshly brewed coffee fills the air, mingling with the sweet scent of pastries. I order a cappuccino while Marcus opts for an espresso, his face lighting up at the thought of the concentrated caffeine.

We find a small table outside, the evening sun casting a warm glow over everything. I take a sip of my drink, savoring the velvety foam, but the unease doesn't dissipate. I can't help but steal glances around, scanning for any signs of that shadowy figure.

"Everything okay?" Marcus asks, catching my eye.

"Yeah, just... you know," I reply, forcing a smile. "Paranoia is a delightful friend."

"Paranoia is never a friend," he retorts, his gaze turning serious again. "But if something's bothering you, you can tell me."

"I know," I say, my voice softening. "It's just—"

But before I can finish, a loud crash interrupts us. I turn to see a nearby table overturned, drinks splattering across the pavement. Patrons gasp, startled, and my heart races as I scan the scene.

"Are you okay?" I call to the group, but my attention is suddenly pulled to the figure slipping away into the crowd—someone dressed in a dark hoodie, blending in effortlessly, yet unmistakably familiar.

"Wait!" I shout, instinctively pushing back my chair and rising to my feet.

Marcus grabs my arm, concern etched on his face. "What are you doing? It could be dangerous!"

"I need to know," I insist, adrenaline surging through my veins. "They know something."

Before I can react, the figure disappears down a side alley, and the world around me blurs into a haze. I take off, heart pounding, my senses heightened. The sound of my footsteps echoes in my ears as I chase after a shadow that feels like it holds the key to everything I've been wrestling with—every unanswered question, every doubt lurking in the corners of my mind.

I can feel Marcus close behind me, his breath heavy with urgency, but my focus narrows. I can't let this opportunity slip away, not again. I round the corner, skidding to a halt as I come face-to-face with a dead end, my heart sinking. The figure is nowhere to be seen, the alley stretching ominously in front of me, empty and silent.

"What now?" Marcus asks, his voice filled with equal parts worry and determination.

"I—I don't know," I stammer, glancing back over my shoulder. Just then, a sound catches my attention—soft footsteps, approaching quickly. I turn to see the figure reemerging, but this time they're not alone.

My breath hitches in my throat as the shadows deepen, the scene before me shifting into something that feels far more dangerous than anything I could have anticipated. And then, before I can process what's happening, the figure lifts their hood, revealing a face I never thought I'd see again—a ghost from my past, and a whole new layer of chaos is about to unfold.

Chapter 23: A Chance Encounter

The rain pattered softly against the glass storefront, a gentle percussion that seemed to play a soundtrack for my introspection. The bookstore stood like a warm beacon in the damp chill of the evening, a refuge for weary souls seeking solace among the pages of forgotten tomes. As I crossed the threshold, the comforting smell of aged paper enveloped me, mingling with the distinct scent of leather and a hint of cinnamon wafting from a distant corner where someone was brewing tea. I let out a breath I didn't realize I had been holding, feeling the tension seep from my shoulders as I surrendered to the atmosphere of quiet contemplation.

The shop was narrow but inviting, the walls lined with towering shelves that held treasures in every nook. I felt as though I had stumbled into a different world, one where time slowed and words wove dreams. The glow of soft, yellow lights illuminated the titles, and I wandered deeper, drawn instinctively to the poetry section like a moth to flame. Here, verses danced off the pages, inviting me to get lost in their rhythm and rhymes. I reached for a worn copy of Whitman, my fingers grazing the spine, and for a moment, I was transported to a place where the weight of reality faded, replaced by the power of words.

Just as I was about to lose myself in the musings of great poets, I turned to find Marcus standing there, looking equally surprised and dismayed. The last time we'd seen each other was charged with tension, a lingering argument that felt like a cold gust of wind between us. His dark hair fell just shy of his brows, and his green eyes—those infuriatingly expressive green eyes—seemed to hold a multitude of emotions as they locked onto mine.

"Fancy meeting you here," he said, his voice laced with a wry amusement that caught me off guard.

"Guess we both needed an escape," I replied, attempting to keep my tone light, though the tremor in my voice betrayed me.

He stepped aside, allowing me to maintain my distance, yet the atmosphere felt charged, heavy with everything we hadn't said. The soft rustle of pages turned in the background served as a gentle reminder of our shared history, the unsaid words that danced between us like restless ghosts.

"What brings you to this literary haven?" he asked, tilting his head slightly, a gesture I found endearing despite the gravity of our past.

"Just looking for something to distract me," I admitted, my fingers brushing over the spines of various collections, feeling the embossed titles under my fingertips. "You know how it is—life gets a little too real sometimes."

"Yeah, I get that," he said, his expression softening. "Poetry has a way of making things feel... lighter, doesn't it? Like it carries some of the weight for you."

I nodded, feeling a flicker of connection amid the awkwardness. "Exactly. It's like holding a mirror up to your soul, or maybe even a window. You can see out, but it also reflects what's within."

He chuckled, a genuine sound that resonated in the quiet space. "That's very profound of you. I'm more of a 'read it, feel it' kind of person. But I appreciate your approach."

The tentative exchange began to crack open the barriers we'd erected between us, letting in soft beams of light through the cracks. As we meandered through the shelves, our conversation danced from poet to poet, exploring the lines of Rilke, the passion of Plath, and the haunting melodies of Keats. Every mention of a favorite poem felt like a tiny revelation, a glimpse into each other's souls that we had long buried beneath layers of misunderstandings and unspoken words.

"What about you?" I asked suddenly, curiosity piqued. "What's your go-to poet?"

He paused, glancing down the aisle as if contemplating his response. "I'd have to say Neruda. There's something about the way he writes about love and longing that just resonates with me," he said, his voice low and thoughtful.

I raised an eyebrow, a teasing grin forming on my lips. "You? A romantic?"

"Don't act so surprised," he replied, a playful smirk creeping onto his face. "I'm a man of layers. Just like a poem, I can be complex and deeply misunderstood."

"Layers, huh? I've always thought you were more of an onion. But I guess we all have our moments of poetry," I teased, my heart warming at the lightness creeping back into our interaction.

His laughter echoed softly through the aisle, a sound I had missed more than I realized. "Alright, I'll take that. But you have to admit, there's a certain beauty to being an onion. I mean, I make people cry."

"True, but let's hope that's not the only thing you do," I replied, my tone playfully serious, the tension easing as our laughter mingled with the ambiance of the bookstore.

As the conversation flowed, I could feel the barriers between us starting to dissolve, each shared moment of levity drawing us closer together. It was a precarious dance, one filled with the fear of missteps and the thrill of rediscovery. The bookstore transformed into our private sanctuary, each book an unspoken agreement that perhaps, just perhaps, we could carve out a new path for ourselves, away from the shadows of our past.

But then, just as I began to believe in the possibility of this newfound connection, a familiar figure entered the store, his presence like a thundercloud rolling into an otherwise serene sky. The air grew heavy again, the warmth between us stifled by the sudden chill of uncertainty. I stole a glance at Marcus, who mirrored my apprehension, the easy camaraderie we'd just built now hanging by a thread as we faced the potential disruption of our fragile reconnection.

The air shifted as the familiar figure stepped into the bookstore, his entrance slicing through the warmth of our moment like a winter breeze. The door creaked slightly as he pushed it open, the chime of the bell above signaling his arrival. I felt my heart rate quicken, a jolt of nerves coursing through me as I caught a glimpse of Eric, Marcus's former best friend and my own past entanglement. The spark that had ignited between Marcus and me flickered, and for a moment, it felt like the cozy sanctuary of the bookstore had transformed into a spotlight, illuminating our tangled history.

Eric strolled in, the rain pattering against his navy raincoat, drops cascading off the brim of his dark fedora. He scanned the room, his eyes landing on us with an intensity that sent a shiver down my spine. "Fancy seeing you both here," he said, a lopsided grin spreading across his face, as though he had just walked into a party rather than an awkward reunion.

"Yeah, we're just discussing poetry," I said, attempting to inject some levity into the situation, but my voice wobbled, betraying my unease.

Eric raised an eyebrow, the grin not faltering. "Poetry? You two? Now that's an unexpected collaboration." He stepped closer, feigning interest as he leaned against a nearby shelf. "What's the topic of discussion? Heartbreak? Longing? Or just the usual existential dread?"

"Maybe a little bit of everything," Marcus replied, his tone cooler than the autumn air outside. "What are you doing here, Eric? I thought you'd be drowning in your next big project."

"Projects can wait," Eric replied, a twinkle of mischief in his eyes. "Besides, I heard the rain was a perfect excuse for some literary inspiration."

I shifted slightly, my heart racing as the tension mounted. The warmth of the bookstore began to feel stifling, and I could sense Marcus bracing himself, his body language tightening. I glanced at Marcus, trying to gauge his reaction, but his expression was a careful mask, concealing whatever feelings churned beneath the surface.

"I'd say poetry has its own brand of inspiration," I offered, desperate to steer the conversation back into safer waters. "It has a way of making us confront our inner worlds, don't you think?"

"Ah, the psychological approach," Eric said, his tone teasing, as he folded his arms. "It's like peeling back layers of an onion. All those tears... who wants that?"

"I suppose it depends on what's hiding beneath," Marcus shot back, a subtle edge to his words that hinted at a deeper conversation just beneath the surface.

Eric chuckled, clearly unfazed. "Touché. But maybe not all onions need to be sliced open, you know? Some are just better left whole."

I watched the exchange unfold, caught in a delicate web of camaraderie and rivalry that had developed over years of friendship and competition. While Marcus's retorts were sharp, there was a tension simmering between the two men that felt almost palpable. Their history loomed over us like a shadow, one that I wasn't sure I was prepared to navigate.

"Speaking of peeling layers," I said, trying to defuse the mounting energy, "I just discovered a poet who writes about the complexities of life in such a profound way. Mary Oliver—have you read her?"

Marcus's expression softened at the mention of Oliver's name, as if the poet's words had conjured a safe haven amidst the uncertainty.

"I love her work. It's like a gentle nudge to appreciate the beauty around us. She makes the ordinary feel extraordinary."

"I can see why you'd be drawn to that," Eric remarked, his playful tone returning, though his gaze remained scrutinizing. "You've always been the romantic."

"And you've always preferred the chaos," Marcus replied smoothly, a subtle jab that earned him a smirk from me and a narrowing of Eric's eyes.

The banter continued, each of us skirting the edges of deeper emotions, a dance of wit and underlying tensions. It was as if we were all trapped in a theater, performing for an audience of one—each word carefully chosen, each glance loaded with meaning.

"Anyway," Eric said, changing the subject abruptly, "I have a few new ideas brewing for my next project, and I could use some fresh perspectives." He leaned in, engaging me with a glimmer of interest. "You've always had a knack for finding the silver lining in a storm. Want to join forces? It could be fun."

My heart raced, torn between the thrill of collaboration and the weight of my history with him. "I appreciate the offer, but I'm not sure I'm the right fit for your vision," I replied, my tone hesitant.

"Come on, you know you miss the thrill of working together," he urged, a charming grin returning. "We were a good team once, weren't we?"

Marcus stiffened at my side, the subtle tension between us crackling with unspoken words. "Maybe she's found a different rhythm now," he said, his tone light yet underscored with an edge that made it clear he wasn't entirely comfortable with the direction of the conversation.

Eric held up his hands in mock surrender, a grin spreading across his face. "Fair enough! Just thought I'd throw it out there."

"Appreciated," I said, trying to redirect the conversation back to safer ground. "But I'm really enjoying this whole poetry thing right now."

"Is that code for 'stay away from my territory'?" Eric shot back, laughing lightly.

"Maybe," I said, meeting his playful gaze.

As laughter swirled around us, I felt a strange sense of equilibrium returning, the warmth of friendship pushing against the chill of uncertainty. But even as the air lightened, I could sense that our fragile peace hung by a thread. The past had a way of surfacing, and I knew it wouldn't be long before the inevitable questions about the rift between Marcus and Eric would surface. And as I glanced at Marcus, who was watching the interplay with a mixture of amusement and wariness, I realized that the delicate balance we had built was teetering on the edge of an abyss, one that could plunge us back into the complexities we had only just begun to navigate.

Before I could delve deeper into the moment, the unmistakable scent of coffee wafted through the air, drawing my attention toward the small café nook at the back of the store. It was a haven of warmth and aroma, a place where conversations flowed as freely as the drinks. The thought of a warm cup of coffee offered a comforting distraction, and I seized the moment, gesturing toward the café. "How about we grab some coffee? I think I need a little caffeine to keep this literary conversation going."

"Sounds perfect," Marcus said, relief evident in his voice as he began to move toward the back. Eric followed, and I felt a weight lift as we left the intensity of the poetry section behind. But the uncertainty lingered, a reminder that as we ventured into new territory, the shadows of our past were never far from view.

The café nook was a cozy enclave, a little haven with worn, mismatched chairs and tables that bore the patina of countless conversations. The aroma of freshly brewed coffee enveloped us like a warm hug, stirring the memories of lazy afternoons spent here before life had turned complicated. I made my way to the counter, my fingers brushing against the cool wood as I scanned the menu. The barista, a friendly girl with a bright smile, recognized me instantly, and I returned the gesture, feeling a flutter of nostalgia.

"What can I get for you today?" she asked, her voice cheerful and familiar, pulling me back to a time when my biggest dilemma was whether to try the new caramel macchiato or stick with my beloved chai latte.

"I'll take a chai, please," I replied, grateful for the warmth it promised. I turned to find Marcus and Eric engaged in an animated discussion about their favorite brews, their banter light and easy, the tension from earlier fading like the rain outside.

"Think you can handle my coffee preference?" Eric teased, raising an eyebrow at Marcus as if challenging him. "It's not just about caffeine; it's about the experience."

Marcus crossed his arms, leaning against the counter, the corners of his mouth curling into a smirk. "I'd say your taste is more about style than substance, but sure, enlighten me."

"Look, coffee is an art," Eric insisted, gesturing dramatically. "It's not just a drink; it's an adventure! One that involves the perfect roast, the right temperature, and an artisanal touch."

"Oh please, you just like to sound pretentious," Marcus shot back, his eyes sparkling with mischief.

"I prefer 'cultured,' thank you very much," Eric countered, leaning back in mock arrogance.

I couldn't help but smile at their playful rivalry, the way they danced around each other like two competing musicians trying to find harmony. Their banter was a reminder of the camaraderie they once shared, a stark contrast to the distance that had formed between them over the years.

The barista returned with my steaming cup, and I took a moment to savor the fragrant steam curling up into the air, the warmth seeping into my hands. "Thanks," I said, taking a sip and letting the spicy sweetness envelop me. "Perfect as always."

"Glad to see you haven't lost your touch," Eric said, watching me with that same playful glint in his eye. "You really should come in more often. I could use a good coffee critic."

"Critic? Or taste tester?" I retorted, nudging his shoulder playfully. "There's a fine line, you know."

We settled into a small round table in the corner, the café's soft lighting creating an intimate cocoon around us. The noise of the bookstore faded into the background, and I felt a strange sense of comfort, despite the complexity of our histories.

As we sipped our drinks, Marcus spoke up, his voice low and reflective. "So, Eric, what's this big project you've been working on?"

"Ah, the secret that keeps everyone guessing," Eric replied with a dramatic flair, leaning back in his chair. "Let's just say I'm trying to capture the essence of the human experience... with a little twist."

"Is that code for 'I'm trying to be profound'?" Marcus teased, his smile genuine, though a flicker of challenge lingered in his gaze.

"Something like that," Eric replied, his expression momentarily serious. "But really, it's about exploring the connections we make, the ways we impact each other's lives, both positively and negatively. It's a reflection on choices and their consequences."

"Sounds like a bit of a downer," I interjected, curious about where this conversation was headed.

"Not at all!" Eric defended. "Life is full of highs and lows. It's about finding the beauty in the chaos, the poetry in our struggles."

"Are you sure you're not just trying to woo the barista?" Marcus quipped, nodding toward the girl at the counter, who was now studiously pouring over some papers.

"Hey, I don't need to woo anyone," Eric said, his tone feigning indignation. "I have charm in spades."

"Or a silver tongue," Marcus added, raising an eyebrow.

I laughed, watching them as they slid back into their playful back-and-forth, feeling the comfort of friendship enveloping us like a soft blanket. Yet beneath the banter, a layer of tension simmered, one I could sense lurking just beneath the surface.

As we moved from topic to topic, the conversation drifted toward poetry once more, the verses acting as bridges between us. I found myself slipping into the familiar rhythm, recounting how certain poems had helped me navigate my own emotions. "It's funny," I mused, "how a few carefully chosen words can articulate what we can't even say ourselves."

"Or make us feel things we didn't know we were feeling," Marcus added, his gaze intent as he leaned forward.

"Exactly! It's like they reach into the depths of your soul and pull out the truth," I replied, feeling the heat of the moment between us rise.

"And then you're left wondering why you didn't just say it in the first place," Eric chimed in, his voice teasing yet serious. "You know, poetry can be like a mirror."

A comfortable silence enveloped us, each of us lost in our thoughts, the ambient sounds of the café weaving a backdrop to our unspoken reflections.

Then, without warning, Eric's expression shifted, a sudden seriousness enveloping him. "You know, it's funny how life brings people together in the most unexpected ways," he said, his tone contemplative. "Just like tonight."

I felt a chill run through me, an unsettling awareness that perhaps there was something more beneath our gathering than simple coincidence. The air seemed charged, as if the very universe was holding its breath, waiting for something to unfold.

"Speaking of unexpected," Marcus said, breaking the silence, "do you remember that time we ended up in the middle of that poetry slam? You recited that piece about love lost, and the whole room went silent?"

Eric laughed, but there was a sharpness to it. "Yeah, and then you two decided to join in with your own interpretation of heartbreak."

I shifted in my seat, feeling the weight of shared memories pressing down. "That was a disaster," I said, attempting to chuckle but feeling a twinge of unease.

"Disaster or not, it was memorable," Marcus replied, his gaze lingering on me, a softness creeping back into his expression.

"Memorable is one way to put it," I replied, feeling my pulse quicken under his gaze.

As the conversation ebbed and flowed, I noticed a figure approaching our table from the corner of my eye. The soft footsteps drew closer, and I turned to find the barista standing there, her smile faded, replaced with a look of urgency.

"Excuse me," she interrupted gently, her voice low but insistent. "I need to speak with you. It's important."

A knot formed in my stomach as I exchanged glances with Marcus and Eric, their expressions morphing from casual enjoyment to confusion.

"What's wrong?" I asked, my heart racing as I set my cup down, suddenly feeling the weight of the world descend upon us.

The barista hesitated, glancing over her shoulder as if afraid someone might overhear. "There's something happening in the back room. Something you all need to see," she said, her voice barely above a whisper.

My breath caught in my throat, and the playful atmosphere shifted into a tense uncertainty. The warmth of the café felt suddenly distant, replaced by an unsettling sense of urgency that drew me into its gravity.

"Let's go," Marcus said, the determined edge in his voice cutting through the tension like a knife.

I stood, exchanging a glance with Eric, whose expression mirrored my own confusion and concern. As we followed the barista through the narrow passage toward the back room, the unease curled in my stomach like a coiled spring, ready to unravel. What awaited us on the other side was a mystery that loomed large, a question mark hanging over our heads as we stepped deeper into the unknown, and for the first time, I wondered if this chance encounter would lead to answers—or to new complexities that could change everything we thought we knew.

Chapter 24: The Book Signing

The quaint little bookstore, nestled between a charming café and a vintage record shop, buzzed with an electric energy that thrummed in the air. It was the kind of place that felt like a sanctuary, the walls lined with shelves that housed countless stories waiting to be discovered. The scent of fresh coffee mingled with the faint mustiness of old pages, wrapping around us like a warm embrace. My heart raced as I stood next to Marcus, the man whose presence had once felt so familiar, now tinged with a hint of uncertainty that I couldn't quite place. Yet, there was an undeniable spark, a glimmer of something that ignited when he brushed against me, even in the simplest of gestures.

The crowd was an eclectic mix of fervent fans, each clutching their well-loved copies of the author's latest novel, a tale that had quickly become the talk of the town. As we made our way through the sea of eager faces, the laughter and chatter enveloped us, a comforting backdrop to the whirlwind of emotions swirling within me. I found myself stealing glances at Marcus, his relaxed demeanor a stark contrast to my own nervous energy. It was as if he had slipped effortlessly into the moment, while I struggled to keep pace with the emotions flooding my heart.

"Isn't this place magical?" I mused, trying to ground myself in the present. "It's like stepping into a dream where all the characters are waiting just for us."

He chuckled softly, the sound reverberating through the clamor of voices around us. "You always had a flair for the dramatic. But yes, I can feel it—the anticipation, the possibility of discovering something new. It's intoxicating."

The way he said it, with a hint of admiration and a touch of nostalgia, sent a warmth coursing through me. I missed moments like this—conversations laced with wit, the kind of banter that drew us closer rather than pushed us apart. It was a simple reminder of the friendship we once had, the laughter that had filled the spaces between our words. And just like that, the walls I'd built began to crumble, brick by brick, as we navigated through the crowd.

We settled into the back row, our seats cushioned and worn, surrounded by eager fans whose faces lit up with delight as the author took the stage. A hush fell over the audience, anticipation thick in the air. She was a vibrant woman with an infectious smile, her passion for storytelling spilling forth like a fountain. Her words flowed effortlessly, and as she spoke about the power of narrative to heal and inspire, I felt my heart swell with recognition.

"I believe stories have the ability to change lives," she declared, her eyes sparkling with fervor. "They allow us to escape, to dream, and sometimes to confront our deepest fears. In every page, we find a piece of ourselves."

Marcus leaned in closer, his breath warm against my ear. "She's right, you know. Remember all those times we'd get lost in a book, completely forgetting about the world outside? That was our sanctuary."

I nodded, a smile tugging at my lips. "It was always the best escape. I still think about those late-night conversations we had about our favorite characters—how they made us laugh, cry, or even scream in frustration."

The author's voice wove through the air like a melody, igniting the flames of our shared history. With each anecdote she shared, the distance between Marcus and me shrank. It was as if the universe had conspired to bring us back together, reminding us of the love we had for stories—and for each other.

As the event progressed, she invited questions from the audience. A hand shot up, and a young woman asked about the inspiration behind the author's most beloved character. The author's face lit up, and she spoke passionately about the character's journey—a struggle that mirrored her own. I couldn't help but feel the weight of those words, recognizing the parallels to my life, my struggles, and my own quest for identity.

"Every character is a reflection of the human experience," she concluded, her gaze sweeping over the audience. "In their triumphs and failures, we find our own truths."

I turned to Marcus, the intensity of his gaze capturing my attention. "Do you think we're more than just characters in our own stories? Like, do our choices actually shape who we become?"

His brow furrowed slightly as he contemplated my question. "I think so. Every choice leads us down a different path, just like in a book. But sometimes, we get so caught up in our own narratives that we forget we can edit them, rewrite the chapters we don't like."

His words lingered between us, heavy with unspoken meaning. I wanted to ask him about his story, the chapters he'd written since we'd drifted apart, but the moment felt fragile, like a delicate web that could easily unravel. Instead, I opted for lightheartedness, injecting humor into the air. "So, are you saying I should rewrite my past? Because I could definitely use a do-over on that disastrous haircut from sophomore year."

He burst into laughter, and the sound felt like sunshine breaking through clouds. "That might be a bit ambitious, but who knows? Maybe a little magic from this author could inspire you to do just that."

Our shared laughter floated away, a reminder of the bond we were slowly rebuilding. The atmosphere crackled with an electricity that I hadn't felt in ages, and I savored the feeling, the warmth spreading through me like a cozy blanket. Our fingers brushed again, igniting a spark that reminded me of all the moments we had shared, the unguarded ones that had once made us inseparable.

As the event drew to a close, the author invited us to line up for signings, the crowd buzzing with excitement. I caught sight of

Marcus's anticipation, the way his eyes lit up at the thought of meeting the woman whose words had resonated so deeply with both of us. It was infectious, and my heart swelled with a renewed sense of hope. The world felt vibrant and alive, bursting with possibilities just waiting to be explored. In that moment, standing side by side with Marcus, I could almost believe that our story was only just beginning, each page yet to be filled with laughter, adventure, and perhaps a little love.

The signing table stretched before us, adorned with stacks of books and a radiant bouquet of sunflowers that seemed to bask in the glow of the author's presence. She sat there, a captivating figure, scribbling her signature with a flourish while exchanging pleasantries with the fans who approached her. The air crackled with excitement, and I felt an electric buzz of anticipation coursing through the crowd, amplifying the beat of my heart. Marcus leaned slightly closer, his breath a whisper against my ear, a gentle reminder of his proximity that sent warmth racing through me.

"Are you ready for this?" he asked, his voice low and teasing, as if we were about to embark on a daring adventure.

I glanced at the author, a woman who had woven her words into the very fabric of our lives, and felt a flutter of nerves. "I'm not sure if I'm more excited or terrified. What if I say something completely embarrassing?"

"Welcome to my world," he replied with a smirk. "But seriously, you'll do great. Just be yourself, the one who fell in love with words and their magic. That's who she wants to meet."

His encouragement wrapped around me like a soft blanket, easing the tension in my chest. The queue inched forward, a tapestry of eager faces and well-thumbed paperbacks, each person waiting their turn to share a piece of their journey with the author. I took a moment to observe the exchanges—hushed giggles, wide-eyed admiration, and the spark of connection igniting between fans and the woman who had crafted worlds with her pen.

"What would you say if you had to pick just one thing?" Marcus nudged me lightly, as though drawing me from my reverie. "What's the one question you'd want to ask her?"

I pondered for a moment, my mind racing through a dozen possibilities. "I think I'd want to know how she finds the courage to write her truth. It's such a powerful thing to share your story with the world."

His eyes sparkled with interest. "That's a good one. But what if she answers with something that requires a follow-up question? You'll need a plan B."

"Ah, the art of conversation," I said, rolling my eyes playfully. "Maybe I should have brought flashcards. What's next? A full-blown PowerPoint presentation?"

"Hey, you never know," he quipped. "It might come in handy."

Just then, we shuffled forward in the line, and I could see the author's face more clearly, the kindness in her eyes as she engaged with each fan. My heart raced as we stepped closer, and I caught sight of the title of her latest book resting on the table. A Story Untold glimmered under the soft lighting, a promise of untapped possibilities echoing in its pages. It was a mirror of my own aspirations, an echo of the dreams I'd pushed aside.

When it was finally our turn, I approached the table, my palms slightly clammy as I held my own copy of her book. The author looked up, her smile warm and inviting, and for a moment, all the noise around us faded away.

"Hello!" she said, her voice melodious, laced with enthusiasm. "What's your name?"

"Hi, I'm Ella," I replied, my voice steadier than I expected. "I just wanted to say how much your writing means to me. It's inspired me to explore my own stories."

Her gaze softened, and I felt a thrill of validation wash over me. "Thank you, Ella! That means the world to me. What stories are you working on?"

Before I could answer, Marcus stepped forward, resting his hand on my shoulder possessively. "She's being modest. She's got a talent for weaving words, too. A true storyteller in the making."

The author raised an eyebrow, intrigued. "Really? Tell me more! What do you write about?"

I could feel the heat creeping up my neck as all eyes fell on me. "Well, I dabble in a bit of everything, but I'm particularly drawn to stories about connection and finding one's voice amid the chaos of life." I glanced sideways at Marcus, who wore an encouraging smile, a subtle reminder that I wasn't alone in this moment.

"Those are powerful themes," the author said, nodding thoughtfully. "Remember, your voice is unique, and it deserves to be heard. Don't shy away from it."

The words struck a chord within me, resonating like a note played on a perfect string. I couldn't help but smile, feeling a surge of hope and inspiration that was almost tangible. It was as if, in that moment, she had breathed life into my aspirations.

As we chatted, I felt Marcus's presence like an anchor beside me, grounding me as the conversation flowed. When the author asked me what my favorite scene from her latest book was, I shared a passage that had moved me deeply—one that echoed my own struggles with vulnerability and fear. She nodded in understanding, her expression a blend of compassion and encouragement.

"You see, you're already analyzing my work with such insight! That's the mark of a true writer." She signed my book with a flourish, adding a personal note that made my heart swell.

With a final wave of her hand, she shifted her attention to Marcus, who had been quietly watching with a hint of amusement. "And what about you? Do you write as well?"

"Not unless you count snarky comments and grocery lists," he replied, his playful tone eliciting a chuckle from both the author and me. "I leave the heavy lifting to Ella. I'm just here for moral support and, well, to ensure she doesn't embarrass herself."

"Ah, a guardian of the literary realm!" the author declared, and we all shared a laugh, the atmosphere brightening as we slipped into an easy camaraderie.

As we stepped away from the table, my heart soared, buoyed by the encounter. "That was incredible," I said, turning to Marcus, who had a playful glint in his eye. "You made it feel so effortless."

"Just following your lead, wordsmith," he teased, his tone light but his gaze intent. "I could see the fire in your eyes. It's good to see you this passionate again."

We meandered through the bookshop, the scent of fresh paper and coffee wrapping around us like a cozy shawl. My mind raced with thoughts, the world buzzing around me. Conversations flowed seamlessly, laughter echoing in the corners of the store. The camaraderie we shared felt renewed, and with each passing moment, it became easier to slip back into the rhythm we once had, the rhythm that had defined us before the world had pulled us apart.

In one corner of the store, I spotted a display of book-themed merchandise. "Look at those bookmarks!" I exclaimed, pointing to a collection featuring famous literary quotes. "We need some of those for our next reading marathon."

Marcus grinned, feigning a serious expression. "I refuse to let you buy any more bookmarks. The last time you bought a pack, I think we ended up with more bookmarks than actual books."

"Consider it an investment in our future reading adventures!" I shot back, playfully nudging him.

"Fine," he relented, "but only if I can pick one out too. No more quotes about love, though. I want something that speaks to my soul."

"Your soul, huh? Good luck with that," I laughed. "How about this one? 'The only thing better than reading a good book is talking about it with a friend.'"

"That might be the best idea you've had all day," he replied, his grin infectious.

As we selected our bookmarks, I couldn't shake the feeling that something had shifted between us. The playful banter had taken on a depth I hadn't anticipated, a spark that flickered in the spaces between our laughter. It was an unexpected turn in our reunion, and the possibilities unfurling before us felt tantalizingly close. Each moment we shared felt like a step back toward a connection that was both familiar and excitingly new, igniting hope in the corners of my heart where doubt had once lingered.

The atmosphere shifted as we wandered deeper into the bookstore, a sensory wonderland that enveloped us in its charm. The buzz of conversations swirled around like a warm breeze, punctuated by bursts of laughter and the rustle of pages being turned. I could see new titles lined up on the shelves, waiting to capture the hearts of readers eager for fresh escapes. My fingers trailed along the spines of the books, feeling a tingle of familiarity. Each title whispered secrets, memories of cozy evenings spent lost in stories that made the world outside seem both vast and small.

"Did you see that one?" Marcus pointed toward a display of novels featuring strong female protagonists. "I bet you'd love it. It's about a girl who takes on the world with nothing but her wit and a few sharp knives."

I arched an eyebrow at him, feigning indignation. "You think I need knives? I thought words were my weapons of choice."

"Words can be mighty, but sometimes a girl needs a backup plan," he quipped, his smirk infectious. "You know, just in case the world gets a bit too... literary."

"Or in case a bad plot twist decides to rear its ugly head?" I shot back, laughter bubbling between us, warming the spaces where tension had once resided.

We made our way toward a cozy nook filled with oversized bean bags and scattered cushions, the perfect place to dive into our selections. "Let's sit here and plan our next book heist," I suggested, plopping down onto a plush purple bean bag that swallowed me whole. Marcus settled beside me, the weight of our shared laughter making the moment feel all the more significant.

"I'm in. First, we'll need a list of all the books we've been meaning to read, and then we'll—" he paused, feigning seriousness, "steal away with an armful of treasures."

"You know, they might not appreciate our enthusiasm for literary thievery," I teased, leaning into him playfully. "What if we get caught?"

"Caught? Me? I'm a master of disguise," he proclaimed dramatically, pulling his collar up as if to blend in with the nearby shelves. "They'll never see me coming."

"You mean they'll see your bright red hair shining like a beacon in the night?" I shot back, grinning.

He leaned closer, our shoulders brushing together, the warmth of his presence igniting a familiar thrill. "Alright, so maybe I need a new disguise. But you know, if we get caught, I'll take the blame. I'll even say it was all my idea."

"Such a gallant knight you are," I replied, rolling my eyes affectionately. "But let's save the heist for another day. For now, I think we should just enjoy being here, together. Like old times."

A soft smile danced on his lips, and for a moment, the weight of everything that had transpired between us melted away. The ease of our banter reminded me of late-night talks and shared secrets, a connection I had missed more than I cared to admit.

As we leafed through the pages of our chosen books, I caught snippets of nearby conversations, the excitement in the air palpable. A couple of fans were animatedly discussing their favorite quotes, while another group debated the best plot twists in recent releases. The bookstore thrummed with life, and I couldn't help but feel a swell of joy within me. It was a reminder of the magic that stories brought into our lives, the power of shared experiences to mend hearts and foster connections.

"Okay, let's take a break from our serious planning," Marcus suggested, nudging me playfully. "Tell me, what's the most embarrassing thing that's ever happened to you at a book signing?"

I threw my head back and laughed, the sound echoing through the cozy nook. "Oh, that's easy! It was last year when I accidentally called the author by the wrong name. I was so starstruck that I combined her name with the title of her book. It was something like, 'Thank you, Ms. It's-A-Mystery!'"

He burst into laughter, the sound contagious. "That's brilliant! How did she respond?"

"I think she was more amused than offended," I recalled, my cheeks flushing at the memory. "She gave me a funny look but then said it was a new title she was considering for her next book. We laughed about it, but I could tell I made a lasting impression."

"Looks like you've got a knack for creating unforgettable moments," he remarked, grinning. "Maybe you should take up a career as a professional embarrasser of authors. Sounds lucrative."

"I'd be a legend in my own right," I shot back, my eyes sparkling. "But for now, I'm just happy to enjoy this moment with you."

As we lounged in our little corner, the world outside faded into the background. I could feel a growing sense of connection, each shared laugh a step toward rebuilding what we had lost. The warmth of his presence reminded me of lazy afternoons spent together, the kind of moments that felt eternal.

But just as I began to relax fully into the comfort of our reunion, a familiar voice cut through the haze of contentment like a bolt of lightning. "Ella? Is that you?"

I turned, heart sinking at the sight of Sarah, a friend from my past who had never quite understood the bond between Marcus and me. Her expression was a mix of surprise and skepticism, the corners of her mouth twisting into a smirk that hinted at judgment. I could practically feel Marcus tense beside me, his posture shifting as if bracing for impact.

"Sarah," I greeted, forcing a smile that felt far too tight. "What a surprise!"

She stepped closer, her gaze darting between Marcus and me, her eyes narrowing. "I didn't know you two were back together. I mean, really? After everything that happened?"

"Just enjoying a bit of literature together," I replied, my tone firmer than I intended. "What about you?"

"Oh, you know," she said with a light wave of her hand, her laughter dripping with condescension. "Just here to see if the author has any new secrets to share. You two should be careful. I hear there are rumors about people taking sides in your little... drama."

The tension hung heavy in the air, suffocating the laughter that had just filled our corner. Marcus's fingers brushed against mine in a reassuring gesture, but the warmth that had enveloped us moments ago now felt frigid.

"Rumors? What do you mean by that?" he interjected, his voice steady yet laced with an undercurrent of protectiveness.

"Oh, nothing much," Sarah continued, her tone almost too sweet. "Just that people are starting to talk again. It seems like the past has a funny way of resurfacing when you least expect it."

My heart raced, a storm of emotions swirling inside me. Had we really been so naive to think we could just slip back into the way things once were? Just when I thought we were rekindling something special, a shadow from our past threatened to cast doubt on everything we'd worked toward.

As the laughter from the crowd faded into the background, I caught Marcus's gaze, his expression unreadable. I could feel the weight of Sarah's words settle between us, igniting a spark of uncertainty that threatened to unravel the fragile threads of our renewed connection.

"Anyway, good luck," Sarah chirped, her tone light as she turned to leave, but not before tossing one last glance over her shoulder. "I hope you know what you're getting yourselves into."

The world around us fell silent, the air thick with tension. In that moment, I realized we were standing at a crossroads, the path ahead obscured by doubt and fear. I could feel the ground shifting beneath me, the familiar comfort of Marcus's presence now tinged with uncertainty. Would we truly be able to face the challenges that lay ahead, or would the past continue to haunt us, threatening to tear apart the fragile bond we were trying to rebuild?

Chapter 25: Tides of Change

Every evening, as the golden glow of twilight bathed the city in hues of lavender and amber, Marcus and I found ourselves ensconced in a cozy café that had become our refuge. The faint sound of jazz blended with the comforting clatter of coffee cups, creating a symphony of intimacy that encouraged our whispered exchanges. The world outside faded, and it was just us—two souls dancing through the intricacies of our lives.

The first time Marcus shared the story of his childhood, I could hear the weight of it in his voice, a low rumble that resonated within me. He spoke of his family—his father, a successful but stern figure, and his mother, who seemed to float like a ghost in the periphery, always trying to please but rarely succeeding. "I was the invisible son," he confessed, stirring his coffee with a distracted intensity. "A shadow in the spotlight of expectations." The honesty in his words wrapped around me like a warm embrace, and I couldn't help but lean closer, eager to absorb every detail.

"Marcus, I had no idea," I said softly, my heart swelling with empathy. "That must have been... difficult." I searched his eyes, hoping to find reassurance, but instead, I found a storm brewing just beneath the surface. He nodded, his brow furrowing as he shifted in his seat, revealing a hint of vulnerability.

"It was," he replied, a half-smile playing at the corners of his lips, a fragile mask over his pain. "But it taught me resilience, I suppose. You learn to fight for your place." His gaze met mine, and the unspoken understanding flickered between us, igniting a flame of connection.

In those late-night discussions, we exchanged not just our histories but also our dreams. I shared my aspirations of becoming a recognized author, how I longed to pen stories that resonated with others. My words spilled out, filled with the enthusiasm I had often kept under wraps, a vulnerability that felt exhilarating. "I want to create characters who leap off the page, who make people feel alive," I confessed, my voice gaining strength with each syllable.

His eyes sparkled with encouragement, and I could see the passion for literature igniting within him, a fire that mirrored my own. "You will," he insisted, leaning forward, his confidence contagious. "Your voice is unique. I've seen it firsthand." The sincerity in his tone sent a ripple of warmth through me, and for the first time, I believed him.

Yet, amidst our reconnections, a shadow loomed—Vera. She hovered in the corners of my thoughts like an unwelcome specter, a reminder that our idyllic moments were precarious. Just the mention of her name could send an icy chill down my spine, and I often found myself glancing over my shoulder, half-expecting her to materialize out of thin air.

One night, as we sat beneath the muted glow of the café's vintage lamps, I finally broached the subject that gnawed at my insides. "Marcus, what's going on with Vera?" The question hung in the air, charged with tension.

He hesitated, his fingers drumming against the table, a telltale sign of his unease. "She's... persistent. I thought distancing myself would work, but she has a way of pushing through barriers. It's as if she has a radar for my vulnerabilities." He sighed, running a hand through his hair, a gesture that was becoming all too familiar.

"I just don't want her to disrupt what we have," I admitted, my voice barely above a whisper, afraid that even the air between us could shatter at the mention of her. "I want this—us—to be real."

His gaze met mine, intensity radiating from him. "It is real," he affirmed, his voice steady. "And I'm not going to let her interfere." Yet even as he said it, the unease in his eyes told a different story.

Days passed, and our connection deepened, but the threat of Vera loomed larger with each interaction. Just when I thought we had forged a strong bond, she would creep into our conversations like a dark fog, her name a shadow that dampened the light between us. I couldn't shake the feeling that she was waiting for the opportune moment to pounce, to disrupt our fragile balance.

Then, one evening, everything shifted. The café had closed early, the barista giving us an understanding smile as she locked the door behind us. The streets were quiet, the moon casting a silvery sheen over everything, a deceptive calm that settled around us like a thick fog. We walked side by side, our laughter echoing off the brick buildings, a beautiful contrast to the lingering tension.

Suddenly, I spotted her—Vera, standing just a few feet away, her arms crossed defiantly as she leaned against a lamppost. The sight of her sent a jolt of anxiety through me. "Marcus..." I started, but he had already noticed her, his expression shifting from carefree to guarded in an instant.

"Just... keep walking," he murmured, tension radiating from him.

But Vera had other plans. "Oh, Marcus! Fancy seeing you here," she called out, her voice dripping with feigned sweetness. I could feel the temperature drop as she stepped closer, her gaze locking onto me with an unsettling intensity. "And you must be the famous author I've heard so much about. Quite the captivating presence, aren't you?"

I felt Marcus stiffen beside me, his body a solid wall of defiance. "We're leaving, Vera," he said firmly, but she wasn't having any of it.

"Oh, come now. Why rush away? I'd love to chat." Her eyes glittered with mischief, a predator reveling in the chase. It was clear she thrived on the chaos she could create.

As I felt the energy crackle in the air, I squared my shoulders, unwilling to back down. "I think we're quite fine without your input, Vera," I retorted, injecting as much resolve as I could muster.

Marcus glanced at me, surprise etched across his features. A silent conversation passed between us, a shared acknowledgment that we were standing at a precipice, one that could either bind us together or tear us apart.

With a smirk, she leaned in closer. "Is that so? You must be awfully brave to challenge me, dear. But I assure you, you have no idea what you're up against."

Her words hung in the air, heavy with the threat of her insinuation. A rush of adrenaline surged through me as I realized this confrontation was no longer just about Marcus—it was about me, too. Would I let this woman undermine my resolve? Would I allow her to define my relationship with him?

As we stood there, the tension palpable, I knew the tides of change were upon us. We had traversed a labyrinth of vulnerability and connection, but now, with Vera's presence casting a long shadow over our newfound bond, we faced a choice. Would we stand united against the storm, or would we let it tear us apart?

In that moment, I chose to fight.

The afternoon light filtered through the large windows of my office, casting a golden hue over the cluttered desk. I was buried under a pile of reports, each more tedious than the last, when the door swung open without warning. Vera strode in with an intensity that turned my stomach. Her sharp heels clicked on the wooden floor like a judge's gavel, announcing the gravity of her presence. Dressed in a tailored suit that screamed power, she radiated authority, but the steely glint in her eyes hinted at a storm brewing beneath her composed exterior.

"Can we talk?" she demanded, her voice cool and unyielding, setting the tone for what was about to unfold.

I leaned back in my chair, crossing my arms defensively. "What's on your mind, Vera?"

She wasted no time with pleasantries. "It's about Marcus." The name hung in the air like a weighted promise, conjuring images of late-night discussions and stolen glances across crowded rooms. "You need to step back from him. For his career's sake."

My heart raced, a rapid thumping that echoed the disbelief in my mind. "Step back? Why on earth would I do that?" I shot back, my voice stronger than I felt.

Vera's lips curled into a wry smile that held no warmth. "Because you know how these things work. He's on the brink of a promotion, and your involvement with him could jeopardize everything. You care about him, don't you?"

Her words hung between us like a challenge. "Of course, I care about him," I said, meeting her gaze with equal intensity. "But I'm not going to push him away just because it might ruffle some feathers."

The tension in the room crackled, an invisible thread connecting us, taut with unspoken truths and veiled threats. "You need to think about this carefully," Vera pressed, her tone dropping to a conspiratorial whisper. "This isn't just about you and him. It's about his future."

I squared my shoulders, determination hardening within me. "And who gets to decide what his future looks like? You? The company? No, Vera. Marcus deserves the freedom to make his own choices, to follow his own path, without someone pulling the strings."

Vera's eyes narrowed, a tempest of emotions flickering behind her cool facade. "Don't be naive. In our world, choices come with consequences. You're being reckless."

"Maybe I'm not the one being reckless here," I countered, my voice steady. "Maybe it's you trying to manipulate a situation you have no control over. Marcus isn't a pawn on your chessboard."

Her face darkened, the flicker of admiration I had once seen fading away. "You really think this is just about control?" she asked, her voice rising slightly. "This is about preserving careers, reputations—"

"Or crushing them," I interrupted, the words slipping out before I could second-guess myself.

Vera's silence was heavy, a tangible barrier built from the rift between our intentions. I could see the gears turning in her mind as she calculated her next move, but I wasn't about to back down. "If Marcus wants to be with me, then that's his choice. Not yours, not the company's."

Her nostrils flared in frustration, and for a moment, I feared I'd gone too far. But the fire ignited in my belly pushed me forward, unwilling to cower before her. "He deserves to pursue his happiness, even if it doesn't fit into your neatly crafted plans."

Finally, Vera turned on her heel, storming out of my office with a rustle of fabric that felt like a dismissal. I exhaled, the tension leaving my body in a rush as I processed what had just transpired. Her ultimatum hung in the air, heavy and suffocating, but I felt an unexpected surge of resolve. Whatever consequences lay ahead, I would fight for what we had built, for Marcus and for myself.

As the days passed, the silence between Marcus and me became deafening. We were both navigating a minefield of unspoken words and half-hearted smiles, our connection strained under the weight of unaddressed fears. Each time we met, the glances we exchanged felt laden with meaning, the warmth we once shared now a ghost haunting the corners of our conversations.

"Is everything okay?" I finally blurted out one afternoon, unable to bear the tension any longer.

He glanced up from his phone, surprise flickering in his eyes before they hardened into a thoughtful gaze. "Just busy, you know how it is."

I knew better, but I held back my frustration. "Busy, or avoiding?"

A pause stretched between us, thick with unsaid thoughts. "I've just got a lot on my plate right now," he replied carefully, his words chosen like a tightrope walker inching over an abyss.

"Is it about Vera?"

He flinched at the mention of her name, the shift in his posture telling me everything I needed to know. "She's been... vocal. About us."

"Us?" I echoed, irritation bubbling beneath the surface. "What does she know about us? She doesn't own you, Marcus."

"She might as well," he muttered, frustration spilling into his tone. "I can't afford to lose my chance at this promotion. I need to focus on work."

"So you're just going to let her dictate your life? Your happiness?" I asked, incredulous.

"It's not that simple," he replied, but there was a shadow of doubt in his voice that gave me hope. "It's complicated."

"Maybe you should embrace the complexity, rather than run from it," I countered, my heart racing as I spoke. "What if you choose happiness, Marcus? What if you decide that you deserve to be with someone who makes you feel alive?"

He studied me, his expression softening, but the flicker of uncertainty remained. "What if it costs me everything?"

"What if it doesn't?" I challenged, leaning in closer. "What if it's the best decision you ever make?"

Silence enveloped us, but I could see the wheels turning in his mind. The tension shifted, and suddenly, everything felt charged with possibility. Perhaps I had planted a seed of doubt in his mind about Vera's ultimatum, and I would do whatever it took to nurture it.

"Look," I said softly, "I'm not asking you to choose between us and your career. I'm asking you to fight for both. You deserve that chance."

His gaze locked onto mine, and I held my breath, waiting for him to say something, anything that would bridge the gap between us. In that moment, I understood: love was messy, full of obstacles and unyielding expectations, but it was also worth every struggle.

And as I watched Marcus wrestle with the weight of his decisions, I felt the tides of our fate shifting, ready to carry us toward something unpredictable and beautiful.

The days that followed Vera's visit were like walking through a fog—a thick, heavy mist that blurred the edges of my world. I threw myself into work, desperately trying to focus, but every time I thought of Marcus, the weight of her ultimatum threatened to crush me. He was a whirlwind in my mind, stirring up feelings I couldn't quite categorize: love, fear, hope. Each time we passed in the office, I felt the gravitational pull between us, yet the invisible wall erected by Vera loomed larger.

"Hey, you in there?" Jenna called from across the room, snapping me out of my reverie. Her playful tone was a welcome distraction, cutting through the haze like a ray of sunshine. "You look like you've seen a ghost. Or maybe just Vera."

I managed a weak smile, pushing the papers on my desk aside. "More like a ghost in a power suit."

"Ugh, that woman. What did she want?" Jenna asked, her tone laced with genuine concern.

"Just a little chat about Marcus and his career choices," I replied, trying to sound nonchalant. "You know, the usual threats wrapped in corporate jargon."

"Threats?" She leaned in, eyebrows raised, the wheels of her imagination turning. "Oh, do tell. Is she going to put him in the corner with a 'Time Out' sign? Or maybe send him to the dreaded office of doom?"

I couldn't help but laugh, the tension in my chest easing slightly. "More like an ultimatum. Either I step back, or he risks everything for a relationship with me."

Jenna's expression shifted from amusement to serious concern. "That's a lot to put on someone. Have you talked to him about it?"

"Not really," I admitted, my voice barely above a whisper. "Every time we're together, it's like we're walking on eggshells. I'm terrified that if I bring it up, he'll just... retreat."

Jenna studied me, her gaze piercing as if she could read the tangled threads of my thoughts. "You can't let her dictate your relationship. If he cares about you, he needs to know that you're not a distraction. You're a choice—a good one."

I nodded, her words resonating like a mantra in my mind. Maybe it was time to confront the uncertainty instead of tiptoeing around it. But how? The thought of risking what we had filled me with trepidation.

With renewed resolve, I decided to take a bold step. I texted Marcus, asking him to meet me after work. The seconds dragged into minutes as I paced my office, nerves dancing in my stomach like a thousand butterflies. What if he agreed with Vera? What if he didn't want to fight for us?

At last, the day crept to a close, and I found myself waiting by the front entrance of the building. The air was thick with impending rain, dark clouds swirling above as I scanned the parking lot for his familiar car. When I finally saw him pull in, my heart leaped—only to plummet as I noticed his expression, a mix of determination and worry that sent chills down my spine.

"Hey," he greeted, his voice low as he approached. The way he looked at me made the air crackle between us, both electric and precarious.

"Hey," I replied, attempting a smile that didn't quite reach my eyes. "Thanks for coming."

He gestured toward a nearby café, and we walked in silence, the weight of unspoken words hanging heavily around us. Once seated, he leaned back in his chair, crossing his arms defensively. "So, what's up?"

I took a deep breath, my resolve hardening. "I want to talk about Vera."

His expression hardened slightly, and I braced myself. "Yeah, she made it clear that she doesn't think we should be together."

"It's not just her opinion," he admitted, running a hand through his hair. "She's got a point about the company and my future."

"Marcus," I pressed, leaning forward, my heart racing, "you can't let her dictate your life. You deserve to choose what you want, even if it's messy."

He met my gaze, a flicker of uncertainty crossing his face. "It's not that simple. There's a lot at stake. If I make the wrong move, I could lose everything."

"And what if I'm the right move?" I challenged, my voice steady despite the tremor in my heart. "What if choosing me is what leads to your happiness?"

Silence enveloped us as he wrestled with my words, his gaze dropping to the table. I could see the internal struggle etched across his features, and my heart ached for him. "I want you, but..."

"Then don't let fear dictate your choices!" I interrupted, the urgency of my words echoing in the small space. "You deserve to be with someone who makes you feel alive, not suffocated."

He looked up, our eyes locking in a moment that felt like an eternity. I could sense the shift in his demeanor, a tiny crack in the armor he wore so well. "What if I'm not ready to fight?"

"Then let's fight together," I implored, my voice barely above a whisper. "You're not alone in this, Marcus. I'm here, ready to take on whatever comes our way."

For a moment, hope ignited between us like a flickering candle flame. But just as quickly, shadows crept back in, dimming the light. "What if Vera's threats become real? What if I lose everything, including you?"

The question hung heavily between us, and I fought against the lump in my throat. "You won't lose me," I assured him, reaching across the table to take his hand. "But you have to make the choice."

At that moment, a figure brushed past our table, and I caught a glimpse of familiar dark hair and a tailored suit. Vera stood just inside the café, her eyes sweeping the room until they landed on us. The icy glare she shot my way felt like a winter chill that cut through the warmth of our connection.

Marcus's expression shifted as he realized who had just entered. Panic flared in his eyes, and I squeezed his hand tighter, my heart racing. "Whatever happens now, remember what we talked about," I whispered urgently.

Just as Marcus opened his mouth to speak, Vera approached, her presence an unyielding storm cloud. "Well, well, what do we have here?" she said, her voice dripping with sarcasm. "A little clandestine meeting? I hope you two aren't discussing anything too scandalous."

The tension in the air thickened, suffocating and electric. I held my breath, ready for whatever explosive confrontation was about to unfold. Marcus and I exchanged a glance—one that held all the unspoken promises of our fight for love. But with Vera in the room, the battle was only just beginning.

Chapter 27: A Night of Confessions

The night unfolded like a delicate tapestry, each thread intricately woven with emotions too complex to untangle. I had spent the day preparing for this moment, but now, as I heard the soft knock on my door, my heart thrummed a nervous tattoo against my ribs. Marcus stood there, his silhouette framed by the dim hallway light, a storm brewing behind his eyes that matched the swirling clouds outside. It was as if the universe conspired to echo our tumultuous emotions, each raindrop a whisper of the confessions we both held close.

I opened the door, and as he stepped inside, the warmth of his presence enveloped me, pushing back the lingering chill from my earlier confrontation with Vera. His brow furrowed, and the deep lines etched into his face spoke volumes. I could see the struggle within him, a conflict as palpable as the rain that tapped rhythmically against my window.

"Hey," I murmured, my voice barely above a whisper. I gestured towards the couch, my sanctuary amidst the chaos. "Want to talk?"

He nodded, the tension in his shoulders easing just a fraction as he sank into the cushions, his eyes searching mine for a flicker of understanding. The soft lamplight cast a golden hue across the room, illuminating the small details I'd always cherished—the vibrant paintings on the walls, the eclectic mix of books stacked haphazardly on the coffee table, the lingering scent of vanilla from the candle I had lit earlier.

"Vera... she's not going to let this go," I began, my voice steady, even as my insides quaked with the weight of my earlier confrontation. "I told her that I wouldn't let her manipulate us, that I chose you."

His gaze flickered, a hint of admiration mixed with apprehension. "You stood up to her?" he asked, a smile ghosting across his lips despite the seriousness of the moment. "That's brave."

"Or foolish," I retorted, crossing my arms defensively. "I just— I can't let her have any power over what we have."

He leaned forward, resting his elbows on his knees, his expression shifting into something more contemplative. "I've been torn, you know," he admitted, his voice low and earnest. "Between what she represents and what we have. She's ambitious, driven—everything I thought I wanted."

The admission hung in the air, heavy yet fragile, as if it might shatter with the slightest provocation. I felt a pang of vulnerability stab at my heart. "And what is it that we have, Marcus?" I challenged, the sharpness in my tone surprising even myself.

"Something real," he said, his eyes locking onto mine with an intensity that stole my breath. "Something that's more than ambition or status. With you, I feel... grounded. I can be myself without the weight of expectations."

The tension between us crackled, charged with unspoken words and the shared knowledge of our emotional turmoil. I could sense the flicker of hope igniting within me, a warm ember fighting against the cold reality of the world outside. I took a deep breath, steadying myself against the tide of feelings threatening to overwhelm me.

"I can't pretend that I'm not scared," I confessed, my voice softening. "Scared of losing you to her, scared of how hard it is to fight for what we have."

"Me too," he replied, the sincerity in his tone wrapping around me like a comforting blanket. "But every time I think about it, I realize how much I want to fight. For us."

As the rain pattered against the glass, I felt a swell of emotions building within me, a storm of longing and desire that echoed the tempest outside. The light between us dimmed, the atmosphere thickening with anticipation. I could see the struggle reflected in his eyes, the push and pull of uncertainty woven into the fabric of our reality.

"Marcus," I began, my heart racing as I leaned closer, "I don't want to lose you."

He shifted, closing the distance between us until we were inches apart, the warmth radiating from him a balm against the chilly night. "You won't," he promised, the words laced with a fervor that ignited something deep within me. "Not if we both fight."

And then, as if drawn by an invisible force, he leaned in. Our lips met, tentative at first, exploring the boundaries of what had been unspoken for too long. It was a kiss filled with the weight of confessions, the unburdening of our hearts, the culmination of every moment leading to this.

It was sweet and electric, the taste of longing mingling with the heady rush of possibility. I melted into him, losing myself in the soft cadence of his breath, the warmth radiating from his body seeping into my very core. The world outside faded, the rain a distant echo as we surrendered to the moment, allowing the kiss to tether us in a universe of our own creation.

"Wow," he breathed when we finally broke apart, his forehead resting against mine, both of us panting as if we had just run a marathon. "That was... everything."

I couldn't help but laugh, a sound filled with relief and joy. "Everything, huh? I think I could get used to this 'fighting for us' thing."

"Good," he replied, his eyes sparkling with mischief. "Because I'm not letting you go without a fight."

With that, we settled deeper into the couch, the promise of shared laughter and whispered secrets wrapping around us like the blanket I pulled over our laps. The night stretched on, the rain tapping a gentle lullaby against the windows as we began to peel back the layers of our hearts, exposing the raw truths that lay hidden beneath the surface.

The warmth of the moment lingered in the air, wrapping around us like a well-worn blanket. I could still feel the flutter of our kiss dancing on my lips, and the intimacy we had forged began to feel like a fragile promise held between us. Marcus remained close, his breath mingling with mine as we sank deeper into our conversation, the rain providing a soft backdrop to our confessions.

"What's next for us, then?" I asked, breaking the comfortable silence that had settled. My heart raced at the thought of a future with him, but uncertainty gnawed at the edges of my excitement.

Marcus ran a hand through his tousled hair, a habit I had come to recognize as a signal of his own internal deliberation. "Honestly? I don't know," he admitted, his voice tinged with frustration. "It feels like we're at this crossroads. I want to pursue my career, but I don't want to lose you in the process."

"Career," I echoed, letting the word hang between us like a puzzle piece that didn't quite fit. "Is it really about Vera's ambition, or is it about your own fear of what comes next?"

His gaze shifted, a flicker of realization igniting in his eyes. "I think it's both. I've spent so long chasing success that I've forgotten how to prioritize what really matters."

"And what matters?" I pressed, my curiosity piqued. "Is it the accolades and the promotions, or is it us?"

The honesty of my question hung in the air, a sharp blade poised to cut through the tension. For a moment, he looked pained, caught between the gravitational pull of ambition and the tenderness that existed between us.

"It's definitely us," he finally said, his voice steady. "But the allure of success is hard to ignore. It's a shiny object, and I've always been drawn to it."

"Shiny objects can be distracting," I mused, a playful smile creeping onto my lips. "Especially when they're so much less beautiful than what's right in front of you."

He chuckled, a rich sound that warmed my heart. "That's a very poetic way of putting it."

"Years of reading too many romance novels," I quipped, feigning a dramatic sigh. "I can't help it if I'm a sucker for a happy ending."

Our laughter echoed in the cozy apartment, weaving a tapestry of comfort and warmth. It was a moment I wished could stretch on forever, but reality was a relentless clock, ticking away the minutes we had together.

"What about you?" Marcus asked, turning the tables with a glimmer of mischief in his eyes. "What do you want?"

I hesitated, the question weighing heavier than I expected. I had spent so much time focused on what Marcus needed, on navigating the storm that was Vera, that I hadn't taken a step back to consider my own desires. "I want..." I started, but the words caught in my throat.

"Take your time," he encouraged, his voice low and reassuring, as if he understood the labyrinth of emotions I was traversing.

"I want to be more than just a stepping stone," I finally admitted, the vulnerability of my confession flooding my cheeks with warmth. "I want to carve out my own path, but it's hard when the landscape keeps shifting."

"Are you talking about your writing?" he asked, leaning closer, his eyes searching mine. "You've mentioned it a few times."

"Yes," I breathed, a wave of nostalgia washing over me. "It's always been my dream to write a novel, but I keep pushing it aside like it doesn't matter."

"Why?" His question was direct, cutting through my hesitance. "Why not take that leap? You're clearly passionate about it."

"Because it's risky," I replied, my voice barely above a whisper. "What if I fail? What if no one cares?"

"Or what if you succeed?" he countered, a confident smile spreading across his face. "What if your book becomes the very shiny object that draws people in?"

His faith in me was intoxicating, the kind of encouragement that sparked a flicker of hope within my heart. "Maybe you're right," I said slowly, the idea blooming like a flower against the backdrop of my fears. "But it's hard to prioritize that when I'm so wrapped up in everything else."

"Then let's prioritize it together," he suggested, the earnestness in his voice palpable. "What if we set goals? You know, help each other chase our dreams?"

"Like a buddy system for ambition?" I teased, my lips curving into a smile. "I'm not sure how I feel about having you as my accountability partner. What if I fail?"

He raised an eyebrow, a playful challenge igniting in his gaze. "Then I'll be right there to remind you how brilliant you are, even when you doubt yourself."

The sincerity in his words resonated deep within me, a gentle nudge toward courage I had long neglected. "You make it sound so simple," I said softly, the weight of my dreams resting heavily on my shoulders.

"Because it can be," he replied, his tone serious but tender. "You just have to take that first step."

Before I could respond, a loud crash echoed outside, startling us both. I jumped, instinctively reaching for his hand. "What was that?"

"Let's hope it's not a tree falling on my car," he said, a half-hearted laugh escaping his lips. "But it could be a sign that we need to stay focused."

We both turned our heads toward the window, peering out into the darkness as lightning illuminated the night sky. The world outside was alive with electric energy, each flash revealing fleeting glimpses of our reflections—two souls grappling with their own demons while seeking solace in each other.

The moment was abruptly punctuated by a ringing phone, jolting me back to reality. It was my mom, her name flashing across my screen like a beacon. I hesitated, the tension between us thickening as I weighed the consequences of interrupting this fragile connection.

"Should I answer?" I asked, glancing at Marcus, who nodded encouragingly.

"Definitely. Maybe she has news about that writing contest you entered."

With a mix of anticipation and anxiety, I answered the call. "Hey, Mom! What's up?"

"Sweetheart, I've got news," she said, her voice bubbling with excitement. "You won!"

I blinked, the world around me fading away as her words sunk in. "I won? Are you serious?"

"Absolutely! The judges loved your submission. You're getting published!"

The room erupted in a whirlwind of joy, Marcus's face lighting up with pride as I processed the news. "This is incredible!" I exclaimed, my voice rising with each word. "I can't believe it! When do I find out more?"

As my mom detailed the next steps, I felt Marcus's presence grounding me, a steady force amidst the whirlwind of emotions. I hung up, barely able to contain my elation. "I really did it!" I shouted, throwing my arms around Marcus, who wrapped me in a tight embrace.

"You did it," he said, his voice muffled against my hair. "You're going to be a published author!"

In that moment, I felt like the world had opened up before me, brimming with possibilities. The path ahead might be fraught with challenges, but I was ready to walk it—hand in hand with the man who had become my unexpected partner in this journey of dreams and confessions.

The echoes of laughter still danced in the air, shimmering with the electric thrill of possibility. As I leaned back against the couch, still cradled in the warmth of Marcus's embrace, the enormity of my news settled over me like a gentle blanket. I had won a writing contest, a moment I had dreamed of for as long as I could remember. Yet beneath the excitement lay a flutter of nerves—what came next?

"You realize this means you're officially a published author now, right?" Marcus said, his voice imbued with a mix of pride and disbelief. "Like, you can't just stroll into a coffee shop anymore and order a mocha without someone treating you differently."

"Oh please," I scoffed, rolling my eyes, though I couldn't help the smile that broke across my face. "As if I'd let fame go to my head. I'll still be the same girl awkwardly trying to explain why I'm drinking a chocolate cupcake in liquid form."

He chuckled, the sound resonating deep in my chest. "You know, I'd buy that for you, cupcake and all. Just to keep you grounded."

"Keep me grounded? Or just keep my sugar levels sky-high?"

"Definitely the latter," he teased, leaning in closer, his breath warm against my cheek. "But in all seriousness, you need to start thinking about your next steps. You have a real opportunity here."

The weight of his words pressed against my chest, a reminder that while I was reveling in this moment, the future loomed like a daunting shadow. "You're right," I sighed, the joy momentarily overshadowed by a flicker of anxiety. "I need to figure out how to promote this. How to make sure people actually read it."

"Why not throw a launch party?" he suggested, his enthusiasm palpable. "A celebration! Friends, food, books, maybe even a cake shaped like a typewriter."

"A typewriter? You're such a romantic," I laughed, nudging him playfully. "But it's a cute idea. I can see my friends all gathering, some teary-eyed speeches, and me blushing like a tomato."

"Or you could unleash your inner diva and throw a glitter explosion. You know, keep it classy." His eyes sparkled mischievously, and I swatted at his arm, laughter bubbling up inside me.

"Classy is definitely my middle name," I said, though I couldn't suppress the thrill that came with the idea of a launch party. Perhaps this could be the moment I finally embraced my writing dreams fully, not just as an idea but as a reality.

Before I could delve deeper into that excitement, Marcus's phone buzzed insistently on the coffee table, breaking the moment. He glanced at the screen, and the smile slipped from his face. "It's Vera."

"Take it," I urged, the name sending a prick of unease through my veins. "You should handle it."

He sighed, rubbing the back of his neck, a gesture that betrayed his unease. "What if she tries to twist my words again?"

"Then you stand your ground," I said, my voice firm. "You've come this far. You don't have to play her games anymore."

With a reluctant nod, he answered the call. "Hey, Vera," he said, his tone neutral, though I could sense the tension radiating off him. I leaned back, trying to appear casual, but I couldn't ignore the growing knot of apprehension in my stomach. The rain outside intensified, drumming a chaotic rhythm against the window, mirroring the turmoil brewing inside.

"Why didn't you tell me you were meeting with her?" Vera's voice was sharp, slicing through the air like a knife. "You should have consulted me first."

Marcus's brow furrowed, and I held my breath, waiting for his response. "I don't owe you explanations, Vera. You're not my boss," he said finally, his voice steady but strained.

"Not yet, but I could be," she shot back, a chill lacing her words. "I'm trying to help you, Marcus. This is bigger than you think. We're on the brink of something monumental."

"What, like running over innocent lives in your pursuit of success?" he replied, a hint of anger sparking in his voice.

"Watch your tone," she warned. "This isn't a joke. You're making a mistake if you think you can walk away from this partnership without consequences."

"Consequences?" he echoed, disbelief coloring his voice. "Vera, I'm choosing my life. I won't be part of your game anymore."

As he spoke, I felt the air shift between us, an unseen tension tightening around our hearts. I didn't want to eavesdrop, but every word was a thread pulling me into the storm brewing just outside. I could see his jaw clenching, a struggle raging within him as he wrestled with her manipulation.

"I'm not playing games, Marcus. I'm trying to secure your future," she insisted, her voice laced with urgency. "You're losing focus. Remember what you're capable of."

"Right, and that's why I need to cut ties," he shot back, his resolve shining through the cracks. "You're not going to dictate my choices anymore."

The call ended abruptly, leaving an uncomfortable silence in its wake. Marcus stood there, his expression a mix of frustration and determination. "I'm done with her," he declared, his voice firm.

"Good," I said, stepping closer to him, my heart racing with a mix of pride and apprehension. "You need to believe that."

"I do," he replied, the tension in his shoulders relaxing slightly. "But she's not going to give up easily. She'll find a way to wiggle back in."

"Then we'll just have to keep fighting her off together," I said, my tone resolute. "You have me in your corner."

"I appreciate that," he said, a soft smile breaking through the storm cloud above us. "It helps to know I'm not alone in this."

"Never alone," I whispered, reaching for his hand and squeezing it tightly. "We're a team now, remember?"

But before he could respond, the lights flickered ominously, plunging us into a momentary darkness. The storm raged outside, wind howling like a wounded animal, rattling the windows. I felt my heart race as I turned toward the window, a sense of foreboding settling in my stomach.

"Uh, maybe we should check the circuit breaker?" Marcus suggested, glancing around the dimly lit room, but the uncertainty in his voice mirrored my own.

"Yeah, good idea," I said, trying to keep my voice steady. We moved toward the door, but just as I reached for the knob, the power returned with a flicker, flooding the room with light once more.

Relieved, I turned to Marcus, ready to brush off the moment. But then I saw it—a shadow moving outside the window, just beyond the glass. My breath caught in my throat as I squinted into the rain-soaked darkness, straining to make out the figure.

"Did you see that?" I whispered, dread pooling in my stomach.

"What?" Marcus replied, eyes narrowing as he followed my gaze.

"There was someone there, just for a second," I insisted, heart pounding against my ribcage.

Before he could respond, the doorbell rang, slicing through the tension with an unexpected urgency. We exchanged a look, a silent question hanging in the air: Who could it be at this hour?

I walked slowly to the door, my pulse racing as the doorbell rang again, insistent and harsh. With every step, an unsettling feeling clawed at my gut, the weight of the unknown pressing down on me.

"Maybe it's just the neighbor," Marcus said, trying to ease my anxiety, but his voice held a tremor.

I hesitated, my hand hovering above the doorknob. "What if it's not?"

But before I could voice my fear, I swung the door open, revealing a figure shrouded in shadows, the rain cascading around them like a cloak of mystery. The night had taken a turn, and as I stood there, adrenaline thrumming in my veins, I realized this moment could change everything.

"Surprise," the figure said, their voice dripping with sarcasm as lightning flashed, illuminating their face. And just like that, the safe cocoon we had woven around ourselves unraveled, leaving us exposed to the storm raging both inside and outside.

Chapter 28: The Turning Tide

The morning sun poured through the window, illuminating the classroom with a warm, golden glow. I stood at the front, clutching a stack of papers filled with notes and ideas, the faint smell of fresh coffee mingling with the distinct scent of chalk dust. It was a smell I had come to adore, each whiff reminding me of the magic that unfolded within these four walls. Today felt different; a flutter of excitement coursed through me, igniting a fire I hadn't realized was dimming.

As my students filed in, a mix of yawns and sleepy grins painted their faces. I greeted each one with a genuine smile, their faces becoming more familiar with each passing day. It was in these moments that I realized how much they inspired me. Each question they posed felt like a small victory, a reminder that we were all on this journey together. I had found my rhythm—teaching them felt like dancing, the ebb and flow of ideas creating a beautiful choreography of thoughts and insights.

"Okay, everyone! Let's get this party started!" I announced, my voice breaking through the morning haze. Laughter erupted from the back, and I shot a playful glare in the direction of Jamie, who had just taken a swig of coffee and nearly choked on his laughter. "You know we don't do that here, right?"

"I'm just warming up for the real fun later," he quipped, his eyes sparkling with mischief.

I chuckled, shaking my head. Jamie was a force of nature, with a knack for lightening the mood and coaxing smiles from even the grumpiest souls. I adored my students, each one a vibrant thread woven into the fabric of my classroom, and today, I felt particularly connected to them. I was no longer just their teacher; I was their partner in this intellectual adventure, and together, we would explore the vast expanse of knowledge.

"Alright, let's dive into today's lesson. We're going to explore the concept of narrative perspective, and how it shapes our understanding of a story. Who can tell me the difference between first-person and third-person narratives?"

As hands shot up, the classroom buzzed with energy. I moved around the room, leaning closer to students, engaging them in lively discussions that felt less like lecturing and more like brainstorming sessions. I reveled in their enthusiasm, their faces lighting up with each realization. This was what I had yearned for—an opportunity to foster curiosity and creativity in a world that often stifled it.

Later that afternoon, as the sun dipped below the horizon, painting the sky in hues of pink and orange, I found myself lost in thought. Marcus had been a bright spot in my life, his encouragement and unwavering support providing a sense of stability I hadn't anticipated. Our late-night discussions, filled with laughter and deep reflections, were the highlight of my day. He challenged me, made me question my beliefs, and pushed me to confront my insecurities head-on.

But with every rise, there was a shadow lurking beneath. Vera's disapproval felt like a persistent cloud on an otherwise sunny day. Her scornful remarks and icy demeanor left an indelible mark, and no matter how hard I tried to shake off the unease, it clung to me like a second skin. I couldn't let her negativity overshadow the progress I had made, especially with Marcus at my side.

"Hey, you," a familiar voice pulled me from my reverie. I turned to see Marcus standing at the door, his grin infectious. He looked utterly at ease, casual in his jeans and T-shirt, but there was an intensity in his gaze that always sent a thrill down my spine.

"Hey yourself," I replied, returning his smile. "Just thinking about how we can kick up the energy for tomorrow's lesson."

His brows raised in mock seriousness. "Ah, the pressure is on. I suppose we should brainstorm some ideas together."

"Together? You mean you want to help me plan a lesson?" I feigned shock, clutching my chest dramatically.

He chuckled, stepping further into the room, his presence filling the space. "Of course! I wouldn't dream of leaving you to your own devices. You might turn it into a party without me."

Our banter flowed naturally, each playful jab underscoring the connection we had forged. But beneath the surface, the tension loomed. I wanted to discuss Vera—her presence was a palpable weight that lingered, threatening to overshadow our growing bond.

"Do you have a moment?" I asked, my heart racing slightly as I broached the subject.

Marcus's smile faded, replaced by a look of understanding. "Sure, what's on your mind?"

I took a deep breath, steeling myself. "It's about Vera. I can't shake this feeling that she's... I don't know, watching us?"

"Watching us? Is she some sort of overbearing hawk?" He chuckled lightly, but the concern in his eyes was unmistakable.

"Maybe not in the literal sense, but it feels like she's always lurking," I confessed, my voice trembling slightly. "Her comments during class, the way she looks at me—I can't help but feel judged."

"Vera's just..." he paused, searching for the right words. "She's complicated. But I won't let her get to you. You're doing amazing work, and she's just a distraction."

His reassurance brought a flicker of comfort, but the unease still gnawed at me. "I just wish it didn't feel so personal," I admitted.

"Then let's not give her the power to ruin this for us. We're partners, remember? You and me against the world."

His words wrapped around me like a warm blanket, but the tension remained. I needed to confront Vera, to face the storm head-on rather than hiding behind my fears. It was time to take control—not just of my career but of my life, my relationship, and the insecurities that threatened to hold me back.

As we stood in the dimly lit classroom, the air charged with unspoken promises, I felt a swell of determination rise within me. The tide was turning, and I was ready to ride its waves.

The following day dawned with an unexpected chill in the air, a stark contrast to the warmth that had enveloped me in recent weeks. I wrapped my scarf tighter around my neck, feeling a peculiar unease settle in my stomach as I made my way to the school. The crunch of leaves beneath my boots echoed my growing apprehension; fall had crept in, bringing with it a cascade of vibrant colors that clashed sharply with the gray clouds looming overhead.

Stepping into the building, the familiar sounds of chatter and laughter enveloped me, yet the warmth of my surroundings did little to dispel the knot forming in my gut. I greeted my students as they trickled into the classroom, their energy palpable, and tried to mirror their enthusiasm. But no matter how hard I tried, the specter of Vera's judgment loomed large.

The morning lesson unfolded with the usual cadence, discussions revolving around narrative perspectives. My students were engaged, eyes sparkling with curiosity. I reveled in their eagerness, yet I couldn't shake the thought that, amidst their smiles and laughter, a storm was brewing just beyond the classroom walls.

"Can I ask a question?" Ella, one of my brightest students, raised her hand with a look of determination.

"Absolutely! Lay it on me," I encouraged, hoping to ease the tension swirling in my chest.

"What do you think is more powerful: first-person narrative, where we get the character's direct thoughts, or third-person, where we see everything from a wider view?"

The question hung in the air, igniting a lively discussion. My students debated passionately, their voices intertwining in a delightful symphony of ideas. I listened, nodding and encouraging them, feeling a glimmer of pride for their insights. But Vera's shadow was never far from my mind, lurking like an uninvited guest at a party, waiting for the perfect moment to ruin the fun.

After class, I found myself alone in the teachers' lounge, pouring a cup of lukewarm coffee while listening to the hum of gossip surrounding me. "Did you hear about the new principal? They say she's a real stickler for rules," one teacher remarked, and another nodded knowingly, her eyes narrowed with intrigue.

I leaned against the counter, absorbing their chatter. My thoughts drifted to Vera, the way she had scrutinized my teaching style, how she seemed to relish pointing out my missteps. Perhaps the gossip about the new principal would eventually drift toward her, a flicker of justice in the air.

"Hey, earth to you!" Marcus's voice pulled me from my reverie, a warm smile spreading across his face as he entered the lounge. He wore a soft flannel shirt that clung to his frame just right, the very sight of him sending a rush of warmth through my chilly thoughts.

"Sorry! Just lost in thought," I replied, attempting to hide the tension coiling in my stomach.

He leaned against the counter beside me, filling the space with his easygoing presence. "Thoughts of me, I hope?"

I laughed, shaking my head. "Always. Just trying to figure out how to keep Vera from swallowing my soul."

His laughter echoed, the sound brightening the muted atmosphere. "You know, I think you should turn the tables. Instead of letting her get under your skin, show her what you're made of. Maybe even put her in her place a bit."

I raised an eyebrow, considering his words. "You make it sound so easy. Just whip out a verbal sword and duel her in the hall?"

"Why not? It could be the latest trend in education—combat teaching. I'll be your cheerleader!"

I smirked, envisioning the absurdity of the idea. "Sure, I can see it now: 'Welcome to Combat 101: Surviving the Staff Lounge.'"

"I'd sign up for that class," he said, his eyes twinkling with mischief.

As we continued to banter, I felt a flicker of hope ignite within me. Perhaps confronting Vera didn't have to be a monumental task; maybe it could be as simple as standing my ground and reclaiming my space.

Later, as the sun began its descent, casting long shadows across the school grounds, I gathered my belongings and headed to my car. The crisp air felt invigorating, as if nature itself was urging me to shed my doubts. I glanced at the messages on my phone—Marcus had sent a note suggesting a spontaneous dinner at that little Italian restaurant we both loved. The prospect of escaping the school's tension filled me with anticipation, and a smile crept across my lips.

The restaurant was a cozy haven, twinkling lights strung across the ceiling, casting a soft glow over the mismatched tables. The aroma of garlic and herbs enveloped us as we settled into our corner booth, the outside world fading into a blur. Marcus's presence felt like a warm embrace, and the laughter we shared danced through the air like a melody.

"I can't believe I let you talk me into the spicy meatballs," I said, mock exasperation tinged with affection.

"Come on, they're the best in town! If they don't make you cry, you're not living," he replied, leaning back with an exaggerated swagger.

We exchanged playful jabs as we devoured our food, the evening flowing effortlessly, and for the first time that day, I felt a sense of peace wash over me.

But then, as if the universe had conspired against my bliss, my phone buzzed insistently. I hesitated, my heart sinking as I glanced at the screen. It was a message from one of my students, a picture attached that made my breath hitch in my throat.

"Is that Vera?" Marcus leaned over, his eyes narrowing as he took in the photo. There she was, standing in the school hallway, arms crossed, her expression a perfect blend of disdain and authority. But what caught my attention was the group of students gathered around her, their faces scrunched in disbelief as she pointed at something on her phone, the unmistakable air of gossip swirling around them.

"Is she talking about me?" I murmured, the unease creeping back, threatening to choke the joy from my evening.

Marcus reached across the table, his hand enveloping mine. "You can't let this get to you. She's trying to intimidate you, but you're stronger than that. Just be the amazing teacher you are, and let her eat her heart out."

I nodded, trying to channel his confidence. "You're right. It's just... I hate feeling like a target."

"Targets can be hit, but they can also fight back. Just keep being you, and eventually, they'll see that you're not to be messed with."

His words resonated, a spark of determination igniting within me. I would confront Vera—not with anger, but with the strength of conviction that had blossomed through my teaching.

As the evening unfolded, I could feel the tide turning. My relationship with Marcus had blossomed into something beautiful, a steady anchor in the turbulent waters of my life. Together, we would face whatever challenges lay ahead, including Vera's unwarranted scrutiny. The storm might rage, but I was ready to navigate its choppy seas, one wave at a time.

The following week seemed to stretch out endlessly, each day blurring into the next like watercolors bleeding into one another. My resolve to confront Vera simmered beneath the surface, a quiet storm gathering strength with every passing moment. It was in the wee hours of the night, just after our late conversations fizzled into contented silences, that I found the clarity I needed. With Marcus at my side, our discussions grew deeper, often veering into realms of vulnerability that caught me off guard.

"Have you thought about what you want to achieve?" Marcus asked one evening, his brow furrowed in thought as he absently traced the rim of his coffee mug. "I mean, beyond the classroom."

The question hung in the air, and for a moment, I could feel my heart racing. "I guess I want to empower my students, help them find their voices. But if I'm honest, I'm also trying to find mine," I confessed, the weight of my insecurities spilling out into the warm light of the kitchen.

He leaned forward, his expression earnest. "You've got a voice, and it's a strong one. Vera is just... noise. You know that, right?"

His words wrapped around me, a reassuring embrace that both soothed and challenged me. The notion of using my voice to confront Vera began to take shape, morphing from a timid idea into something much more powerful.

The next day, as I prepared for class, I made sure to dress in my favorite blazer—a crisp navy blue that gave me an air of confidence. The fabric felt like armor against the waves of doubt that threatened to wash over me. My students were vibrant and eager, their enthusiasm bubbling over as they gathered in the classroom. I glanced at the clock, its hands creeping closer to the moment I had dreaded yet longed for.

"Okay, everyone, let's dive into our next project! We're going to write our own narratives, but there's a twist," I announced, a mischievous glint in my eye. "You have to choose a perspective that challenges your comfort zone. It can be first-person, third-person, or even second-person if you're feeling adventurous."

The room erupted with chatter, and I reveled in their excitement. As they paired off to brainstorm, I felt a sense of purpose settle over me. I would channel my energy into this lesson, using my passion for storytelling as a means to inspire my students to take risks, just as I was determined to do.

Halfway through the class, as students passionately shared their ideas, the door creaked open, and there stood Vera, her presence casting an immediate shadow over the room. My heart stuttered; the laughter stilled, eyes darting between me and the unexpected visitor.

"Ms. Thompson," she said, her voice sharp enough to cut through the tension. "I'd like to discuss the recent curriculum changes you've implemented."

I forced myself to stand tall, unwilling to let her discomfort drown out the vibrancy of my classroom. "Of course, Vera. I'm always open to feedback," I replied, my voice steady, though inside I felt a tempest brewing.

Her gaze flickered over my students, her expression unreadable. "I believe you're straying from the approved materials. Perhaps we should have a more formal discussion about your teaching methods."

A low murmur rippled through the room, but I quickly quelled the rising tide of anxiety within me. "If you have concerns, I'd be more than happy to address them," I said, meeting her gaze head-on. "But I assure you, my students are engaged and thriving."

Vera stepped closer, her voice lowering as she leaned in conspiratorially. "Let's not pretend here. You may think you're inspiring them, but I've heard whispers. Not everyone is a fan of your unconventional methods."

"Whispers? Or constructive feedback?" I shot back, a fire igniting within me. "You may not appreciate my approach, but these students are discovering their voices. Isn't that what we want?"

The challenge hung in the air, thick with tension. I felt my pulse quicken, adrenaline coursing through my veins. This was my moment—my chance to assert myself. "If you have actual concerns, let's address them openly. I refuse to have my teaching turned into gossip."

Vera opened her mouth, probably to fire back another cutting remark, but the classroom door swung open again. This time, it was Marcus, his expression a mix of concern and support. "Is everything alright in here?" he asked, his presence instantly lightening the atmosphere.

"Everything's fine," I said, shooting him a grateful glance, but the heat of the confrontation simmered in my core. "Just a friendly discussion about educational methods."

"Friendly?" Marcus raised an eyebrow, stepping fully into the room, the energy shifting as he took a position beside me. "Because it looks a lot like a duel to the death from where I'm standing."

"More like a clash of ideals," I replied, my voice tinged with determination. "Vera is simply concerned about my teaching style."

Vera's expression tightened, her eyes narrowing as she realized she was outnumbered. "Let's take this discussion to my office, shall we?"

As she turned to leave, I couldn't let this moment slip away. "No, Vera. Let's have it here, in front of my students. If you want to discuss my teaching methods, I'd rather do it transparently."

The room fell silent, all eyes on us as the air crackled with anticipation. I felt a surge of adrenaline course through me, and for a moment, I saw the admiration in my students' gazes, a spark of support igniting in the collective breath held in the room.

Vera's jaw tightened, her composure wavering. "Very well, but don't say I didn't warn you."

The tension hung thick, each second dragging like molasses as we faced off in a silent battle of wills. I glanced at Marcus, who gave me a reassuring nod, and in that moment, I felt a sense of camaraderie with my students, a bond forged in the fire of confrontation.

As Vera launched into her critique, the sound of her voice began to fade, replaced by the rhythm of my own heart pounding in my ears. I couldn't focus on the words, only the intent behind them.

With every cutting remark she made about my methods, I could feel the support of my students wrapping around me like a warm blanket, urging me to stand firm.

Suddenly, the classroom door flew open again, this time with a sharpness that sent a chill through the room. I turned, half-expecting another teacher, but instead, a familiar face emerged from the shadows—my mentor, Clara, her expression grim.

"I need to speak with you, now," she said, her tone urgent, eyes darting to Vera before landing on me.

Confusion rippled through me. "What's going on?"

But before she could answer, Vera interjected, "This is not an appropriate time, Clara."

Clara's eyes narrowed, unwavering. "This is exactly the time. You're crossing a line, Vera, and it ends here."

The classroom erupted into chaos as my students began whispering, exchanging glances filled with curiosity and concern. I felt the weight of their gazes, a collective question lingering in the air: What was happening?

"Vera, you're losing control of the narrative," Clara continued, stepping forward.

Panic twisted in my stomach. My heart raced with both fear and anticipation, the sense of impending change buzzing around us. In that moment, I realized we were on the brink of something monumental, a turning point that could shift the very foundation of our roles within this school.

But as the tension reached a fever pitch, a loud bang echoed from the hallway, silencing everyone in an instant. The door swung open forcefully, and the principal stepped inside, her eyes blazing with authority.

"I've had enough of this," she declared, the finality of her words leaving everyone frozen in shock.

The world around me shifted, and as I glanced at Marcus, I saw the same mix of anticipation and dread reflected in his eyes. The tide was turning, but whether it would wash us away or carry us to new shores remained to be seen.

Chapter 29: A Plot Twist

The sun hung low in the sky, casting a golden hue over the small coastal town of Ravenswood, where the salty breeze whispered secrets through the swaying branches of the gnarled oaks lining the narrow streets. I stood on the weathered porch of Marcus's beach house, feeling the warmth of the wooden planks beneath my bare feet as I clutched a steaming mug of chamomile tea. The delicate aroma mingled with the scent of the ocean, creating a symphony of calm that was soon to be shattered.

Marcus was inside, his fingers flying across the keyboard as he poured his soul into the pages of his new novel. I could hear the soft clatter of keys mingling with the distant sound of waves crashing against the shore—a rhythm that had become the soundtrack to our evenings together. Everything felt right in that moment, like the universe was aligning perfectly for us. Or so I thought.

The door swung open, and Marcus stepped out, his tousled hair catching the sunlight like spun gold. He flashed me that crooked smile, the one that made my heart race as if it were the first time I had seen him. "You look like you're contemplating the meaning of life," he teased, his eyes twinkling with mischief.

"Just pondering whether chamomile or a glass of wine would be more fitting for the evening," I replied, attempting to mirror his lightheartedness. But deep down, an unsettling sense of foreboding twisted in my gut.

He joined me on the porch, resting his arm around my shoulders, drawing me close. The warmth of his body felt like a cocoon against the growing chill of the evening air. "You know, I'm starting to think we should celebrate once this draft is done. A little getaway, just you and me."

"Sounds perfect," I said, though my heart wasn't fully in it. Something was brewing beneath the surface, an undercurrent I couldn't shake.

As we watched the sun dip below the horizon, splashing the sky with hues of orange and pink, my thoughts drifted back to Vera. My initial excitement at her role as Marcus's editor had dimmed over the past weeks. Her influence loomed like a storm cloud, darkening our every joyful moment. I had sensed her growing impatience with him, the way she had pushed for changes that felt... off, as if she were trying to mold his voice into something more palatable for the critics she associated with.

"Did you hear from Vera today?" I asked, breaking the comfortable silence that had settled between us.

He sighed, his body tense against mine. "Yeah, she called. She wants me to make some last-minute adjustments. She's anxious to see it hit the right circles."

I frowned. "She's always anxious, isn't she? I wonder if it's the book or something else."

He chuckled softly, but it didn't reach his eyes. "Probably both. You know how it is in this industry. It's all about connections and impressions."

I nodded, but the worry gnawed at me. My instinct told me that there was something sinister about her increasing urgency. Little did I know how quickly my fears would crystallize into a harsh reality.

The next day unfolded with an eerie normalcy. I spent the morning in my own rhythm, filling orders at the local bakery, the sweet scent of vanilla and cinnamon wrapping around me like a comforting shawl. But by the time I returned to the beach house, the atmosphere was electric with tension. Marcus was pacing, his brows knitted tightly together as he ran a hand through his hair.

"Something's wrong," I said, my heart dropping as I took in his ashen face. "What happened?"

"I received an email from one of the critics," he said, his voice strained. "They've been getting pieces of my manuscript—unfinished work. It's all over the internet, and it's being picked apart."

My stomach plummeted. "What do you mean? How could they have access to it?"

"Vera," he spat, the name dripping with venom. "She's been leaking it. I don't even know how long this has been going on."

Shock cascaded over me, the weight of his words crashing down like the waves outside. "Why would she do that? She's supposed to be on your side!"

"She was supposed to be," he muttered, his voice thick with disbelief. "This isn't just a betrayal of trust; it's a direct attack on my work. She's undermining everything I've built. It's like she wants to ruin me."

I could see the storm brewing in his eyes, a mixture of anger and hurt that twisted my heart. "What about our relationship? What about us?"

His expression shifted, panic flickering across his face. "I don't know, Amelia. I thought we were on the same page. But now..." His voice faltered, uncertainty creeping in.

The very ground beneath my feet felt unstable, as if the foundation of our love was crumbling. "We can confront her. We can set this straight."

"Confront her?" He scoffed, raking a hand through his hair again. "What if she doubles down? What if she does more damage?"

The thought sent chills down my spine. "Marcus, we can't just sit back and let her ruin everything. We need to take action."

"Action? What can we even do?" His eyes bore into mine, searching for answers we both knew we didn't have.

In that moment, I realized that this was not just a challenge to his career—it was a test of our bond. The world around us faded into a muted backdrop, our love suspended in a fragile balance.

"Whatever it takes, we will find a way through this," I insisted, determination igniting within me. "I won't let her tear us apart."

He looked at me, uncertainty etched on his face, but there was a flicker of something else—hope? Resolve? "I can't lose you to this, Amelia."

"You won't," I promised, feeling the weight of our love pressing down on us. "We'll fight together."

As the night deepened, we braced ourselves for the storm ahead, knowing that the battle against Vera would not only define Marcus's career but also test the very foundation of our relationship.

The morning light filtered through the sheer curtains, casting soft shadows across the room as I stirred awake, the events of the previous night still clinging to my thoughts like mist. The salty breeze from the ocean wafted through the open window, bringing with it the promise of a new day, yet I felt a heaviness in the air that belied that promise. Marcus was already awake, his silhouette hunched over his laptop at the kitchen table, a sight that tugged at my heartstrings. The sight of him, usually so full of life, was now overshadowed by a cloud of worry.

"Coffee?" I asked, my voice still thick with sleep as I slid out of bed and padded across the cool tile floor.

He glanced up, a tired smile flickering on his lips. "Only if it's strong enough to fuel a small army."

"Strong it is," I replied, already reaching for the coffee grounds, the familiar ritual a comfort in the wake of last night's revelations. As I brewed the coffee, the aroma filled the space, grounding me amidst the chaos of our lives.

"I've been thinking about how to approach Vera," he said, his tone serious as I set a steaming cup in front of him. "She's not going to back down easily."

"Then we need a plan. One that catches her off guard." I took a seat across from him, trying to match his intensity. "If we go in guns blazing, she'll just shut down. We have to be strategic."

Marcus looked at me, a flicker of admiration sparking in his eyes. "What are you suggesting?"

"We start with the critics she's feeding information to. We can gather evidence of her deceit, show them that she's not the reliable editor they think she is. If we expose her for the opportunist she's become, it'll force her hand."

He leaned back, contemplating my words, his brow furrowed in thought. "It's risky. If she finds out..."

"Then we'll make sure she doesn't," I interjected, determination coursing through me. "This is your work, Marcus. You've poured your heart into it, and you deserve to see it succeed without her meddling."

He took a deep breath, his shoulders relaxing just slightly. "You're right. I've been so focused on her betrayal that I forgot to fight for what's mine."

With a newfound sense of purpose, we spent the morning crafting our strategy. We compiled a list of the critics who had received leaked excerpts and strategized ways to reach them. I couldn't help but feel a sense of exhilaration as we mapped out our next steps, the tension of the previous night slowly giving way to a renewed sense of agency.

As the sun climbed higher, casting its warm glow over the beach, Marcus's phone buzzed with a notification. He glanced at the screen and cursed under his breath. "It's Vera."

I raised an eyebrow, curiosity piqued. "Answer it. Let's get this over with."

He hesitated but finally swiped to answer, putting the call on speaker. "What do you want, Vera?"

"Marcus! There you are. I was just thinking about you," she chirped, her voice dripping with false sweetness. "I hope you're not upset about the feedback I shared with the critics. You know how important it is to get exposure!"

"Exposure? You mean leaking my work?" His voice was a low growl, barely containing his fury.

There was a moment of silence before she laughed, an airy sound that grated on my nerves. "Oh, darling, don't be so dramatic. I'm helping you! Everyone knows your name now."

"Not the way you think," I interjected, unable to contain my anger. "You've damaged his reputation, and we're not going to let you twist this into a narrative that suits you."

"Amelia, sweetheart, you really don't understand how this works, do you?" she purred, her tone condescending. "Writers need to create buzz, and sometimes, that means making a few... strategic moves."

"Strategic?" Marcus echoed, incredulous. "You mean deceitful. You're not a collaborator, Vera. You're a parasite."

Her laughter rang out again, this time sharper. "Marcus, you're losing your edge. You should be thanking me. I've just elevated you to the status of 'hot topic.' Don't you want that?"

"You've elevated me to the status of 'cautionary tale,'" he shot back, his frustration palpable. "You've betrayed my trust and used my work as fodder for your games."

"Trust? Oh, sweetie, this is a business. You should know that by now," she replied, the sweetness in her voice replaced by a steely edge. "I have connections, and I'm not afraid to use them."

Before Marcus could respond, she hung up, leaving a heavy silence in the wake of her abrupt departure. He slammed the phone down on the table, his expression a volatile mix of fury and disbelief.

"Can you believe her? She's completely lost it!"

I took a moment, letting the reality of the situation settle in. "She thinks she holds all the cards, but she doesn't know us."

Marcus looked at me, a flicker of hope igniting in his eyes. "You really think we can turn this around?"

"Absolutely. We'll expose her for what she is. But we have to act quickly. If she's already reached out to those critics, we need to get our message to them first."

We spent the rest of the day crafting emails, putting together a narrative that would paint the true picture of Vera's machinations. With every word we typed, the sense of empowerment grew. The stakes felt higher than ever, but so did our determination to reclaim control.

As evening approached, the sun dipped lower, igniting the sky in a riot of color. We stood together on the porch, the sea air filled with the scent of salt and freedom, and I turned to Marcus, feeling a surge of affection. "Whatever happens, we'll face it together."

He pulled me close, his forehead resting against mine. "Together. Always."

In that moment, the world outside felt less daunting. Our resolve had solidified, binding us together against the storm that was brewing on the horizon. As the first stars began to twinkle in the sky, I knew that no matter the outcome, we were ready to fight for our love, our truth, and Marcus's rightful place in the literary world.

The following days unfolded like a slow-moving train wreck. Each moment stretched, heavy with unspoken fears and unrelenting tension. Marcus and I dove into our campaign against Vera with a fervor I hadn't expected, crafting emails that felt more like battle plans than mere correspondence. Every keystroke carried the weight of our hopes, our fears, and a desperate need for justice.

As I sat at the kitchen table, fingers flying across the keyboard, I stole glances at Marcus, who was lost in thought, his brows furrowed in concentration. The soft hum of the coffee maker punctuated the air, a comforting reminder of our routine even amidst the chaos. The sun streamed in through the window, illuminating his handsome features, yet shadows lingered in his eyes—a haunting reminder of the betrayal that threatened to tear us apart.

"Do you really think they'll listen?" he asked suddenly, breaking the silence. His voice was a mix of hope and skepticism, and I could see the flicker of uncertainty in his gaze.

"They will," I replied, my voice steady. "We have the truth on our side. We just need to present it clearly."

He leaned back in his chair, crossing his arms over his chest. "It's just... I never thought Vera would go this far. It's one thing to critique my work; it's another to sabotage it."

"People like her thrive on power. The moment they sense a weakness, they'll exploit it," I said, trying to reinforce his resolve. "But this is your story, Marcus. You wrote it, and you deserve to tell it without her interference."

He nodded, the fire in his eyes reigniting as he leaned forward again, his focus sharpening. "Right. We have to get the truth out before she can spin her version. I'll reach out to a few critics directly. If we can show them the original drafts..."

"Yes! That will help establish your voice and vision before Vera's fingerprints got on it," I encouraged, feeling a surge of optimism.

Just as the atmosphere began to lift, Marcus's phone buzzed again, an insistent vibration that sent a ripple of tension through the room. He glanced at the screen, his expression darkening. "It's Vera again."

"Don't answer it," I urged, sensing the turmoil that swirled beneath his calm exterior. "We don't need her games right now."

But curiosity got the better of him. He answered, putting it on speaker once more. "What is it, Vera?"

"Marcus, darling! We need to talk," she cooed, feigning a charm that made my skin crawl. "I've been hearing some rather unflattering things about you. It seems you've been... ruffling feathers."

"Unflattering? You mean the truth?" he shot back, anger igniting in his voice.

"Oh, please," she said, her tone dripping with condescension. "The truth is subjective. What matters is how it's presented. If I were you, I'd be more concerned about your reputation."

"I'm more concerned about yours," he countered, defiance threading through his words. "You think this is a game? You're playing with people's lives."

"Sweetheart, I'm not playing. I'm simply trying to keep the wheels turning. You want success, don't you? Then you need to learn how to navigate this world." Her voice was smooth as silk, but it carried a warning.

"We'll see about that," Marcus replied, and I could see the resolve building within him, the anger giving way to determination.

Vera laughed lightly, a sound that felt like a dagger to my heart. "You're adorable when you're angry. But be careful, darling. The last thing you want is to become a cautionary tale."

The call ended abruptly, and Marcus slammed the phone down, frustration boiling over. "She's impossible! This isn't just about my work; it's about everything I've built. She wants to destroy it all, and she thinks she can intimidate me into silence."

I reached for his hand, squeezing it tightly. "We won't let her. We're in this together, remember?"

His gaze softened, a flicker of gratitude passing between us. "Together. Always."

But as the evening deepened and the shadows lengthened around us, a gnawing worry took root in my stomach. Vera was dangerous, and I couldn't shake the feeling that she was just getting started. We'd barely begun to push back, and already, she was pulling strings we couldn't see.

The following morning, we drafted our emails, a flurry of words and ideas flowing as we meticulously crafted our narrative. Each sentence became a weapon, each paragraph a shield. I felt a sense of urgency coursing through me; it was as if the clock was ticking down, and we had to act before Vera could twist our truth into her web of lies.

Marcus took a break, stepping outside for fresh air, and I followed him, wanting to keep the momentum going. The beach stretched before us, waves crashing rhythmically against the shore. The salty breeze tangled my hair, and I inhaled deeply, feeling the tension in my muscles ease just a little.

"What if we start a blog?" I suggested, excitement bubbling up. "A space where you can share your journey, your writing process, and your thoughts on the industry. It'll be an avenue to directly connect with your readers, and we can counteract Vera's narrative."

He nodded slowly, considering it. "That's not a bad idea. If I can control my message..."

"Exactly! It'll give you a platform to speak your truth and rally support," I added, my heart racing with possibilities.

Just then, a shadow fell over us, and we turned to see a figure approaching from the path—a man in a dark coat, his expression unreadable. As he got closer, recognition flickered in my mind. It was one of the critics Marcus had been planning to reach out to, someone I had seen at literary events, always scribbling notes and observing from the sidelines.

"Marcus," the man said, his voice low and steady. "I've been looking for you."

"What do you want?" Marcus asked, suspicion lacing his words.

"I need to talk to you about Vera," the critic said, glancing around as if he feared being overheard.

"Is this about the leaks?" I interjected, sensing the weight of this encounter.

The critic nodded gravely. "Yes. We've been hearing some troubling things, and I believe you need to know the full extent of what's happening."

The tension in the air thickened, and I felt my heart race as I exchanged glances with Marcus. "What do you mean?"

"I can't discuss it here," he replied, his voice dropping to a whisper. "Meet me tonight at the café on the corner. I have information that will change everything."

With that, he turned and walked away, leaving us in stunned silence.

"What does that mean?" Marcus asked, his brow furrowed in confusion and worry.

"I don't know," I admitted, but a sense of foreboding settled over me. "But we have to be careful. This could be another game from Vera, or it could be something more."

He took a deep breath, resolve hardening in his eyes. "Then we'll find out together. No more hiding."

As the sun dipped low in the sky, casting long shadows across the sand, I felt a mix of hope and anxiety. We were standing on the precipice of something monumental, but the unknown loomed larger than ever. I had no idea what revelations awaited us at the café, but I could feel the storm gathering, and we were right in its path.

Milton Keynes UK
Ingram Content Group UK Ltd.
UKHW030746221024
449869UK00001B/51